AN AGENT OF DECEIT

CHRIS MORGAN JONES

AN AGENT OF
DECEIT

MANTLE

First published 2011 by Mantle
an imprint of Pan Macmillan, a division of Macmillan Publishers Limited
Pan Macmillan, 20 New Wharf Road, London N1 9RR
Basingstoke and Oxford
Associated companies throughout the world
www.panmacmillan.com

ISBN 978-0-230-75267-2 HB
ISBN 978-0-230-75330-3 TPB

1 3 5 7 9 8 6 4 2

A CIP catalogue record for this book is available from
the British Library.

Printed in the UK by CPI Mackays, Chatham ME5 8TD

For Suzy

1999

High in the air Webster watches the unbroken desert flow past, a deep copper red in the dawn, the sand ridged like waves rolling down towards the south. Next to him Inessa lies curled up, sleeping through the jolts of turbulence and the drunken songs of the Russian engineers across the aisle.

Below, the sand gives way to grass on the vast Kazakh plain and in the distance, if he presses his face to the window, he can see the Altai mountains rising and stretching east into China. He glances across at Inessa; she's small enough to be comfortable in her rigid seat, her knees pulled up against her chest like a child. It's rare to see her be still, rare for her to be silent.

She opens her eyes for a moment, moves a lock of black hair off her forehead and goes back to sleep. Webster tries to rearrange his aching legs against the seat in front. Five hours overnight from Moscow. He wouldn't suffer this for anyone else.

Oskemen is Kazakh now but shows its Russian past: wide highways lined with thickly planted poplars, tall Soviet blocks on scrappy ground, grand imperial buildings and gold-domed churches. The city is hot under the hazy sun and the wind blows powerfully from the plain, bending trees into the road.

The plant is sixty miles away, across a low mountain range. As Webster drives, Inessa rails against its owners, a group of

Russians who pilfer from their workers, steal from the government and seem happy for everything they own to slowly die. He has heard this before, has read her articles, but listens again willingly.

Coming down from the mountains on a twisting road they see a band of heavy grey cloud hanging in the broad valley where the plant stands. The grass at the side of the road is yellow and sparse; young trees, recently planted along the verge, sag limply against their supports; the fields all around lie untilled. The air, fresher in the mountains, has become warm and thick. A mile or two ahead, over the meagre, low town, black smoke leaks from a dozen pairs of chimneys.

The town is a barracks for the plant. Twenty thousand people live in the uniform apartment blocks, buy food at the two supermarkets, learn at the three schools. There is a street of shops, a police station, a dusty park.

At the hospital they talk to doctors who treat brittle bones and pneumonia, to children who never smile and hide their teeth as they talk, to workers in their thirties who have the bodies of old men. No crops grow in the valley. Over decades waste has been dumped in an unlined pit and chemicals have seeped unchecked into the water table. The new owners arrived five years before and nothing has been done.

No one from the company will talk to them and they stand for a while in the heat, arguing to no purpose with a guard sitting in his hut by the gates. Behind him the plant seems to bully the town. Twelve immense, blockish halls hold the furnaces, and from each one chimneys rise a hundred feet in red and white stripes. Webster takes photographs, trying to capture its immensity; it would take a quarter of an hour to walk to the compound's furthest point. Two police officers arrive, sweating in their peaked caps and military uniforms, and move them on. Inessa resists but it's clear they should go. They have enough.

The sun is low in the sky, setting early behind the black ridge of mountains, and it's dark by the time they reach Oskemen. At dinner Inessa is more furious than he has ever seen her. She makes him promise that they will fight this injustice, the betrayal of these people.

Webster sleeps restlessly in the hotel's hard, clean bed. An hour before dawn, half-conscious, he hears a key turning in the lock and as he pulls back his covers the door opens, the fluorescent light flickering on. Two policemen in uniform walk into the room, pushing aside a member of the hotel staff. One stands over Webster so that his cap blocks out the light and tells him in calm, even Russian to stay in bed; the other searches the room, opening drawers, emptying a bag onto the floor. Webster, squinting, tries to stand up, but the first policeman stops him. His colleague tears the film from Webster's camera in three long pulls and starts leafing through his notes.

Webster makes a grab for his book but is pushed backwards onto the bed. As the policemen shut the door behind them they tell him to leave the country on the first flight out.

His camera sits on the chest of drawers, its hinged back open, and scattered over the thin hotel carpet lie yesterday's clothes.

He runs to the floor above, bounding up the tiled steps three at a time in his bare feet. He wants to share his rage. Inessa's door is open, and with a bolt of fear in his chest he looks inside. She's gone.

The night manager is in his office, sitting in an armchair watching television, the sound down low. His forehead is pinched in a frown, and when Webster asks him where the police station is he won't meet his eye.

He runs the whole way, the two bags on his back swinging

wildly, his lungs tight and his breath beginning to rasp. It is six now, and an even grey-blue light is waking the city. Cars pass but he sees no one. At the front desk, out of breath and angry, he tells an officer that he is a journalist and if they don't release his friend now he will call the British embassy and every newspaper editor he knows. The officer looks at him indifferently for a moment, goes to fetch a colleague, and they arrest him.

His cell has grey painted walls, no window, and two bare wooden boards for beds; he's lucky to have it to himself. With his head in his hands he sits under the single, bare bulb, its light finding every stain and crack in the damp concrete floor. This isn't the first time he has been in such a place, and for Inessa this is routine; but a strange fear sits in his chest and he wants to see her, to reassure her that they will soon be released. The silence is broken by occasional noise: a scream, wild singing, a metal door slamming shut. To pass the time he smokes and begins to write his story in his head.

No one comes to question him, and he wonders how long this will take. Towards the middle of the day he hears the cell doors opening in turn and readies himself for something to happen, but it's only a guard bringing food. As he pokes at his tray he hears voices shouting over each other in Kazakh, commands being yelled and heavy boots running past. The commotion doesn't stop. His door opens again and two policemen lead him away, one on each arm, refusing to answer his questions. As they step into the corridor he turns his head and sees three officers standing by the open door of a cell. One of them, his broad chest a patchwork of medals, stands back with his arms folded. There is a stretcher at his feet.

Webster wrenches an arm free and shouts Inessa's name, feeling dread in his throat. As they take hold of him again and march him away he rages and shouts, twisting and straining, but they drag him on, his feet stumbling on the floor. Then a shout like a crack echoes off the walls and the men holding him stop and turn. The officer with the medals beckons once. Slowly they walk Webster back down the corridor until he is level with the cell.

Inside two officers hold a prisoner to the wall, his face pressed against it, his arm twisted up behind his back. He wears a white shirt, filthy and splashed with red. On the floor lies Inessa, on her back, one knee up, gazing at the wall. Her jeans are soaked and dark, her T-shirt crimson. Her neck is taut, and streaked across it, as if drawn with a thick brush, is a single vivid line of blood.

Webster shouts and tries to break free. Strong hands hold him back.

He is handcuffed and locked, still struggling, his head full of noise, in the back of a police van. As the road climbs away from the city all he can see through the barred windows is blank sky.

After two hours they come to a stop. The engine is still running and he can hear shouting in Russian. The doors are opened, the cage unlocked, and at a crouch he shuffles out, his face screwed up against the sudden light. One of the policemen, unable to look him in the eye, unlocks his handcuffs and hands him his bag. The van turns in the dust and drives away.

Soldiers with machine guns stare at him. This is the border. He is back in Russia.

2009

CHAPTER ONE

Lock lay on his back and let the heat scour his body for places to burn. There was no wind, and against his closed eyes the sun blazed red. Now and then some lurking anxiety began to tug at him but he flicked it away: he was not in Moscow, and that was enough. For a while he felt his whole body glow amber and there was a lightness in his chest. How much better he felt here.

Around him people lay prone on loungers. A waitress walked past with soft, brisk steps on the sand. Murmurs of conversation reached him, easing him to sleep; then, loud and insistent, one side of a phone call – in Russian, of course, it would be. He caught only the odd word, but recognized the tone: commanding, expectant. He opened his eyes and wondered whether he should have another drink. For a moment he stared up into the immaculate sky, bathing in the heat, then raised himself up on an elbow and winced at the pain in his back. His wretched back.

Oksana lay next to him, perhaps a yard away, on her front, her tan fresh. Her face was turned to him but her eyes were shut and he couldn't tell if she was sleeping. He looked down at himself. His skin was pale. He had been in the sun for three days but it still looked grey.

That morning his back had woken him early and he had left Oksana sleeping while he went for a run, dressing in the bathroom in order not to wake her, his shirt tight about him and his running shoes strange on his feet. Just before dawn Monte Carlo was cool and calm, framed by a sky lightening at the edges from the darkest blue, and Lock, heavily at first and then with a sort of arduous fluency, had jogged past the marina along a coastal path that headed away from the rising sun into the west. His back stopped hurting and he ran on, breathing ever more deeply, cursing the oily air of Moscow and rejoicing in the world emerging from the twilight. And then abruptly the path had stopped, where Monaco simply stops. His breath harsh in his throat, Lock had pulled up and bent over, his hands on his knees, and felt the weight of his body gently rocking as his heart thumped in his chest.

He would go again tomorrow and pace it better, perhaps find a longer trail. Now, though, he wanted a drink. He gestured to a waitress to bring him the same again and after a minute she arrived with a Scotch and soda. He sat up and drank. His father's drink. How he would have scorned the crushed ice and the long, dainty glass – scorned Monaco, come to that. Holidays for him had meant walking in the Harz mountains or sailing on the Ijsselmeer, Lock and his sister serving as reluctant crew. Activity was one constant, the other a Primus stove that lived neatly in an aluminium case and burned purple meths stored in old water bottles. On it Everhart Lock would cook beans and eggs and bacon with tireless enthusiasm, refusing to let Lock's mother work on her holiday. He was a tall, serious man who was always in motion and whose instinct was to make for wilderness, where people were few, and air was in rich supply. Cities were for work. God, how he would have hated to pay money to sit with the rich in a beach club (where, Lock thought with resentment, he had still needed to slip that ridiculous maître d' two fifty-euro notes to secure a decent spot near the sea), to lie in the sun all day surrounded by yachts and car showrooms and concrete apartment blocks, to eat only at restaurants – to sit like a prisoner in this tiny, moneyed enclave trapped between the mountains and the sea. But Lock felt comfortable here. This was his place, a part of his world. Life was easy, manageable, contained.

He had first come here nearly fifteen years before to meet Maître Cricenti and form a company for Malin, the first of what must now be hundreds. Cricenti was tiny, barely five foot, but like a true Monégasque carried himself with a pride that felt ancient and unassailable. In his office hung nineteenth-century prints of the palace and portraits of Princes Rainier and Albert; flags on poles leant in every corner. He had impressed on Lock, without really saying it, that by choosing Monaco he would be conferring on his company the glory of a seven-hundred-year tradition, a tradition of dignified and bloody-minded independence that would set it apart from the humdrum world of taxes and government interference. This was not some vulgar Caribbean island where the unscrupulous hid their wealth; no, this was a glorious relic of a time, not so distant, when tiny, colourful kingdoms outnumbered nation states and kings could decide how things would be done. Here one's assets and one's conscience could be safe.

Lock had enjoyed the pitch, flattered himself that he bought none of it and signed up. That was the birth of Spirecrest Holdings SA, a ready-made company with a meaningless name that Cricenti had merely brought down from his well-stocked shelf and presented to Lock for signatures, and payment. Lock soon learned that with one's Monégasque société anonyme came such paperwork that the meagre tax benefits were more or less cancelled out, and before long he was going elsewhere for his companies; the long, close relationship he had imagined for himself and Maître Cricenti never came to be. But ever since he had been fond of this place and its neat, heady fiction.

'Richard?'

He looked over at Oksana. Her voice sounded low and full of sleep.

'Ah, there you are,' he said. 'I thought we'd lost you. Would you like a drink?'

'What time is it?'

'Five.'

She breathed in deeply, a half-yawn. 'I didn't want to sleep.' Here they spoke English, in Moscow mostly Russian.

Lock looked at her again. Looking at Oksana was something he found himself doing often. He was astonished by her – not by her being with him, which he understood, but by her flawlessness. Sometimes he was buoyed by it; more often it seemed to mock his own ageing body and the ever-present compromises of his life. She had been born in Almaty, in the crook of the Tien Shan mountains, at the edge of an immense red desert, and Lock wondered whether this was why her beauty seemed always so unexpected. In a normal life, she would have been far beyond his reach.

'What shall we do this evening, Richard?' she said, looking at him now.

'Anything you like. What would you like to do?'

'I like the Sass restaurant. Can we eat there? And then the Casino. I think Jimmy's is boring.'

How right she was. What Lock loved about Oksana – would have loved, if he had let himself – was that she had a clear idea of what she wanted from him and his money, and it did not include dancing with hundreds of leathery men and their beautiful girlfriends in a nightclub that, absurdly – embarrassingly – spelt its name with a Z. Jimmy'z. A few years before Lock might have looked forward to a night in Jimmy'z and the opportunity to ogle and preen, but not now. The place was full of men in their sixties, even their seventies, who plainly never stopped to doubt their standing or prowess

– but they, Lock reflected, were the real rich, and a different breed.

'I'll get the hotel to book. Are you happy here for now? Drink?'

'I will do my front.' Oksana turned herself over with great economy of movement and closed her eyes. Lock picked up his phone, one of three lying by his side, called the hotel, and spoke to the concierge. Then he sat back and drank, watching a Jet Ski whine its way across the bay.

Softly, abruptly, one of his other phones started to vibrate. He looked down at it and recognized the number, a French mobile. He let it buzz away helplessly for a second, closed his eyes briefly in resignation and picked it up.

'Hello,' he said, in Russian. Allo. It sounded strange on the beach, in the sun.

'Hello, Richard.' That hoarse, low voice. 'I need you here this evening. Please come now.'

'Of course.' He hung up, and sighed. He wasn't ready to return to that world.

'Sweetheart?' Lock never knew whether to call her 'sweetheart' or 'darling'. He had called his wife both, over time, but neither seemed right for Oksana who, knowing what he was going to say, didn't respond. 'I have to go for a few hours. I'm sorry.'

'How long?'

'I can never tell. I'll call when I know.'

He gathered up his phones and his wallet, stood up, and bent down towards her. She turned her head away, the smallest fraction, and he kissed her on the side of her mouth. 'Have what you like. I'll pay the bill.' He straightened stiffly, pulled his white linen shirt off the back of his lounger and left.

He could have taken the helicopter to Nice and then a taxi from there – residents of Monaco loved to do this – but he was wary of helicopters. He had never liked them. Planes were fine: planes had wings and resembled birds a little, and birds could fly and land. Planes had a precedent. But nothing in nature was like a helicopter, unless it was a sycamore's winged seed as it slowly, inevitably, dropped to the ground. There was another reason that he avoided them, more superstitious or more practical he couldn't say: his kind seemed to die in helicopter accidents much more often than they should.

So now he was in the back seat of a Mercedes, showered and wearing a tan linen suit, on the fast, sinuous road between Monaco and Nice, travelling through tunnels and between mountains at great speed. He could feel his worries returning. Malin wouldn't have summoned him for something trivial. Lock had spent his working life preparing for the police to come, but the thought of them had always terrified him and terrified him still. His job was to lie, but he did his lying in seclusion, like a writer, not face to face like a salesman. Over the last fifteen years he had wrought an intricate fiction with closed-ended funds and open-ended funds, with limited liability companies and limited liability partnerships, with *sociétés anonymes* and *sociétés anonymes à responsabilité limitée,* with Liechtenstein *anstalts* and Swiss *stiftungs* and Austrian *privatstiftungs*, with every imaginable acronym in every available offshore hideaway. He was proud of his work, if not wholly sure of it. On the wall of his office in Moscow hung a huge white board that showed the ever-changing structure of the network, as he called it. It looked like a technical drawing, unknowably arcane: hubs and spokes and clusters covered the board, changing and proliferating as Malin's operations multiplied. Lock knew it all. He knew each company, each bank account, each company director; he knew the filing requirements territory by territory; he knew when money had to leave one place and be due in another. He also knew that it was well built; it was as solid as it could be. But to justify it to someone, to defend it as fact – that he wasn't sure he would be able to do.

He checked himself. Perhaps this had nothing to do with an investigation. Maybe this was Moscow politics: a tacit edict from the Kremlin, a play for one of Malin's assets by some rival faction. But then, nothing happened in Russia in August. Maybe it was something as benign as a new acquisition, or a request for cash to be freed up from one part of the organization to fund a transaction in another. Maybe Malin was simply lonely. Lock smiled and looked out of the window at the grand sweep of the Côte d'Azur, majestic, hot, overpopulated. Whatever the news was, he would have to seem equal to it.

Past Nice the traffic slowed to a stop. So many Netherlands plates, Lock noticed – did the Dutch never fly?

At Antibes the road cleared a little and they were soon at Cannes, where the car turned south towards Théoule-sur-Mer. Red-brown peaks rose up above the coast road, rough and primitive. Malin, who always seemed to know what was under his feet, had once told him that the Esterel mountains owed their colour to porphyry, a stone loved by the Romans and the Greeks. How ancient they looked, severe, adamantly resisting civilization, at odds with the tidy villas that lined the road.

By the time they reached Malin's compound, they had left Théoule behind and the villas had almost run out. Malin had his own Cap, a small headland bounded on the north by an eight-foot wall that separated it entirely from the mainland. He had taken this house because it was easy to secure: on the remaining three sides terraced gardens ended in red cliffs that dropped sheerly to the sea. To these natural defences he had added guards (Russians, not locals, armed) who patrolled the perimeter day and night. On the western side of the Cap a steep path led down to a small sand beach. When the house had been built, in the 1920s, yachts had no doubt been moored in the small bay and guests would have sailed round from Cannes and La Napoule for dinner. Now two guards were permanently stationed there and guests of any kind were rare.

The car slowed to a stop by a low gatehouse. Lock lowered his window and showed his face; the gates opened.

Another Mercedes was parked in the driveway, its driver asleep in his seat. Lock didn't recognize it. He thanked his own driver, told him in poor French that he might be an hour or more, and walked past the two guards at the front door.

Each time he came here he was struck by the unnecessary elegance of the house. It was of modest size by the standards of the Riviera, low and white, touched here and there with a trace of art deco, and gave the general impression of being ready to set sail at any moment into the sea that it commanded. The back of the house was shaded by live oaks and pines; the front gave out onto simple lawned terraces progressing in steps to the edges of the cliffs, which were fringed with trees; downstairs every room opened through huge French doors onto the garden, where a fountain softly played. Light flowed through the place, but even in high summer it was cool inside. Fifty yards away there was a small chapel, redundant now, that Lock had always felt he should visit but never had.

The dining room was where meetings were held. Malin was sitting at the dining table, leaning back in his chair, his thick arms folded across his chest. He wore a white shirt with short sleeves and a splayed collar, and against the white his skin was sallow. He was big, solid, like a Russian wrestler in retirement. Impermeable, thought Lock: nothing got through, in either direction. His broad face was fleshy and on another man, with its jowls and its baldness and its double chin, could have been jovial, but his eyes overwhelmed the rest. They were dark brown and heavy, neither curious nor passive. Malin never seemed to blink, but nor did he stare. The eyes simply were. Lock still felt uneasy whenever he looked into them. As now.

'Good evening, Richard. I am sorry to interrupt your vacation.' Malin spoke in English with a heavy accent, his voice low and resonant. Lock simply nodded, aware from experience that these would be the only pleasantries. 'Phones, please.' Lock took his three phones from various pockets, removed the back and the battery from each, and put the components on a dresser standing against the wall where two other phones lay, also in pieces.

'You know Mr Kesler.' Malin gestured across the table at the older of the other two men in the room.

'Of course. How are you Skip?'

'Just fine, thank you, Richard. You're looking well. This is Lawrence Griffin, one of our associates.'

Lock shook hands with both men. 'Skip' was in fact Donald, but he preferred to be known as Skip; this suggested a jauntiness at odds with the rest of him. He was a lawyer, a specialist in litigation, and Lock was alarmed to see him here: it meant that what they were about to discuss was serious, as he had feared, since Kesler was not the sort to fly across the Atlantic and spend a client's money without cause. Everything about him suggested discipline. The younger man, Griffin, had taken out a notebook and was already writing. Both were in suits; both looked hot and slightly grimy, as if they had travelled that day and not yet changed their clothes.

Lock sat on his own at the head of the table. Malin turned to look at him.

'Tourna is making noises again. He is still upset.'

'This is about Tourna? Christ, that man makes so much noise. Can't we keep ignoring him?' Tourna, Lock thought, was surely not worth a meeting in August.

'Mr Kesler thinks not. Mr Kesler.'

'Thank you, Konstantin. Richard, Mr Tourna will file against Faringdon in New York on Monday, and is drawing on the relevant clauses in his contract to start arbitration proceedings in Paris. The New York complaint alleges that we reneged on our commitments to Orion Trading over the sale of Marchmont. Specifically, it says that Orion was sold an empty shell and that Faringdon took the assets. Hearings in New York have not yet been scheduled, but we're due in Paris in November.' Kesler always spoke with extraordinary structure and precision, his staccato voice, with a hint of the South in it, beating out all the points. Lock wondered whether he had rehearsed.

'God, he's an idiot,' said Lock. 'What does he stand to gain?' No one spoke. Lock noticed that Kesler's watch was still on Washington time. 'Do we fight it or settle?'

'If all we had to worry about was whether or not we had met our obligations under the contract then, yes, we would either fight it or settle it – a fine judgement and not perhaps worth that much thought.' Kesler's suit was dark blue, a light wool, with a pinstripe, European in its cut. 'This time, however, Mr Tourna has decided to add a little spice. He is alleging that Faringdon – and you – are part of a criminal conspiracy. More particularly, he is claiming that Faringdon is not owned by its immediate shareholders, but by Mr Malin, and that it is the central component of, as he puts it, a global money-laundering operation. He puts the damage to him at a billion dollars.'

'A billion? Where does he get that from?' Now Lock understood why he and Kesler were here. 'Who is he using?'

'Hansons. Lionel Greene. I'm told he's very good.' Kesler looked over the top of his glasses at Lock, waiting for more, but nothing came. 'This creates all manner of problems. We cannot settle, because the complaint is public, and to settle will imply that we acknowledge the charge. And we can be confident that everyone will soon know about this, because Tourna is never discreet, even when it is in his own interests to be so. And that is not the case here.'

Lock felt a weight bearing on his chest, a long-held fear. 'Do we know what he knows?'

'No. The complaint isn't detailed.'

'He's fishing.'

'I don't think so.' Kesler looked from Lock to Malin.

'Then what is he doing?' said Lock. 'It seems crazy. Why allege something you can't prove? And then make sure we can't settle?'

Again Kesler looked between the two. Malin made the smallest movement of his head and Kesler resumed.

'Because he has no intention of settling? I suspect that Mr Tourna is truly vexed, and when Mr Tourna is vexed he doesn't bottle it up. For this Greek, revenge is best served relatively warm.' Kesler paused, clearly pleased with his words. 'I think he is doing this – and we must *assume* he is doing this – because he wants to hurt Mr Malin. By now we can also assume that he's hired investigators and PR and God knows who else to put on an almighty show. When he thinks the time is right.'

Kesler's sidekick was all the while taking notes. Lock glanced at them and wondered how they could possibly be so voluminous already. The sun was lower now and behind Malin, leaving his face in shadow.

'Look,' said Lock, 'if he had proof of something he'd black-mail us with it privately. That's his style. Which means there's no evidence.'

'Maybe not,' said Kesler, 'but it's going to be very uncomfortable demonstrating that. I'm here now because we need to start work immediately. Paris is the priority. I'll be working out of Bryson's London office to save you travelling to DC and me travelling to Moscow . . .'

'Wait, hang on.' Lock looked puzzled. 'Why have an arbitration at all? If he wants to make a noise he can just sue us in New York.'

'That is the most interesting question,' said Kesler. 'I don't know. I simply can't read that part. But I think that New York may be the sideshow. A lawsuit there will make a lot of noise, but . . . My guess is he wants to cause you a lot of pain but still give you a mechanism for settling – perhaps you agree to settle if he completely retracts the complaint. Or perhaps he wants to see you on the stand. We can sidestep that in New York, I think, but not in Paris. You have to attend your own arbitration.'

Lock could feel pain in his lower back. This was the moment at which he should be showing Malin that he was confident and full of fight but his body was registering dismay.

'Can we do him some damage first?'

'Fight fire with fire, you mean? Perhaps. I'm seeing investigators in London next week. It may be that Mr Tourna has something he would rather remain hidden. But it's not as if his reputation has far to fall. Such an asset.' Kesler gave a wry, irritating little chuckle.

Malin stood up, thanked Kesler, and asked Lock to join him outside. As they walked on the lawn in front of the house Lock could feel the spring of the grass under his feet. Through the cypresses he saw headlands and bays linking into the distance, the cliffs deep red in shadow. His fresh shirt was already damp and cool against his back. He and Malin took steps down to a swimming pool whose sky-blue water spilled endlessly over its far lip, the sea beyond a steady, serious cobalt. They sat at a table, out of the setting sun, where Lock, side on to Malin with his elbows on his knees, continued to gaze at the pool and wondered whether anything could make the scene more placid. He was curious to know whether Malin drew pleasure from it.

Malin extracted a packet of cigarettes from his shirt pocket, took one, and lit it. He talked Russian now. 'Richard, I am concerned about this. Tourna is a little crazy. I think Kesler is right – he is not doing this so that we pay him money.'

'Tourna is nuts. We should never have . . .'

'Let me finish.' Malin paused. Lock looked from the water to him, indicating his willingness to listen. 'Kesler called me about this two days ago. This has given me some time to think. I asked him to come out here to discuss it with us in person. I have asked him as I am asking you to take special care of this so that it does not escalate. I want us to find out what Tourna knows. And I want to know everything about Tourna. That is your responsibility. I will not settle this because I do not trust Tourna to keep it settled.' Again he paused, drawing deeply on the cigarette. 'How confident are you that we are protected?'

'Very confident.' Lock's heart stammered. 'There is nothing to link anything to you.'

'Look over your network for weaknesses. They will all be all over it soon. If there are weaknesses, let me know them.'

'I can't think where they could be.'

'Just look. Who do you trust that might talk, knowingly or not? That is what they will be looking for.'

'Understood.'

'It may be that this can still go away. But in the meantime, work with Kesler. Work hard.'

Lock returned Malin's even gaze for as long as he could, then nodded and looked away.

'Richard, I have always paid you well to prepare for this moment. Justify my faith in you.'

As they walked back to the house in the dusk the security

lights clicked on, lighting up the house and the trees and blacking out everything beyond.

Lock arrived back in Monaco a little after ten. Oksana was not in their room at the Metropole. His calls to her went unanswered.

He stood in the shower, turned it up very hot and then very cold, and thought. He thought about why Kesler hadn't spoken to him first but had gone to Malin directly. He thought about Malin's words to him, part pep talk and part threat. And he thought about what he would have to do now, and how little he relished it. The problem, he knew, was not with the nature of the lie, but with the simple fact of it. If anyone looked hard enough (and certainly, they would have to look hard) they would discover that, he, Richard Lock, was the richest foreign investor in Russia, the owner of a huge private energy conglomerate. And he had no plausible account of how he had come by any of it.

CHAPTER TWO

Webster was the first in his house to wake. The night had been close but now a cool breeze was blowing from the window and he pulled the thin sheet around him; by the light along the edges of the blinds he could tell it would be another hot day. Elsa was still asleep, her back to him. There were planes in the sky; it had to be after six.

If he left now perhaps he could fit in a swim before everyone else was up. But as soon as he had the thought he knew he wouldn't go; he wasn't ready to resume the work routine. What did he have today? A mess of things he hadn't thought about since before his holiday: cases, clients, billing. Briefing Hammer on Tourna, and deciding whether to take his money. That alone might take all day.

He heard a floorboard creak in the room above. Nancy was up. Every morning she came downstairs and stood silent by his side of the bed until something in his subconscious told him she was there. It was a slightly disconcerting way to greet the world.

He lay on his side, facing the door, and closed his eyes. She moved so quietly he hardly heard her come in. He let her stand by him for a moment and then shot out a hand from under the sheet and pulled her up onto the bed, twisting onto his back and leaving her sprawled on his chest. Her feet were cold on his legs.

'Daddy!'

'Did you miss me?'

She said nothing but sat up and drummed a rhythm with her hands on his stomach. He picked her up under her arms and held her horizontal at arm's length, her face smiling above his, her cheeks full, her dark hair falling down. She was heavy now, but his thumbs still met on her breastbone.

'Did you miss me?'

'Don't tickle.'

'I'm not going to. Did you miss me?'

Nancy giggled. He gave her the slightest squeeze.

'Don't tickle! Yes! Yes!'

He let her tumble down.

She raised her head. 'Did you get me a present?'

'I was only away for a night.'

'Two nights.'

'I know. Sorry. I had a horrid journey back.'

'Just a little one?'

'Not even a little one. Nothing. Breakfast, if you like.' He pulled himself up onto the pillows and looked at her. 'Is Daniel asleep?' She shook her head.

'What's he doing?'

'Nothing for me?' Elsa was awake. She still had her back to them.

'Morning, baby. No. Not much to buy in Datça.'

She turned onto her other side and raised her head on her elbow. Her eyes were full of sleep. 'Tea, please.'

'In a minute.' Nancy was running her finger down his jaw, feeling the stubble.

'How was it?' said Elsa.

'Beautiful. Hot.'

'Don't. How was your billionaire?'

'Tanned and rich. Though I'm not sure his billions are entirely his.'

'Did you like him?'

'Not much.'

'Hm. Was it worth it?'

'It's the best case I've ever seen.'

'Big?'

'In every way. But we shouldn't take it.'

'Why not?'

'It's a regime-change case. They're trouble.'

'Tea.' Elsa inched closer and ran her hand along Nancy's back.

'Five minutes. When Daniel comes down I'll give them breakfast.' He looked at her. Her eyes were closed. Somebody had once said that Nancy had his looks and Elsa's beauty. It was neat but true. 'How was yesterday? Sorry I was so late.'

'With Thomas? Terrible. His mother doesn't want him to come any more. She thinks talking about it is making him worse.'

'That's sad.'

'It is.' She glanced at Nancy. 'I'll tell you more later.'

For a moment the three of them lay there, Nancy plucking at the hairs at the base of Webster's neck, Elsa watching her.

'Which regime?' she said at last.

Webster turned to her.

'It's not quite a regime. It's a man. Russia's most corrupt, I'd say, at a guess.'

'And what would you be doing?'

'Exposing him.'

'You'd like that.'

'Yes, I would. He deserves it.'

Two days earlier Webster had woken before dawn in the spare bedroom, his alarm set to sound as quietly as possible, his bag packed, his clothes for the day hanging from the back of the door. Elsa and the children lay asleep in the still house. He had queued with the holidaymakers at Gatwick and waited half an hour for a taxi at Dalaman. The pilot had said thirty-three degrees; out of the shade, heat radiating off the concrete and the tarmac, it seemed hotter. The only suit he saw all day was his own. It was wool, grey, the lightest he had – a good, English suit, and the wrong thing to be wearing on the Turkish coast in August.

It took three hours more to reach Datça. Sitting upright on the hard rear seat he watched dusty mountains grow green with thick pine as the road bent towards the sea. Turkish dance music played quietly on the radio. The sun bore down on the side of the car, and he could feel the heat in the metal and the glass.

He had been away when the call came in but Webster thought he knew what Tourna wanted. His reputation needed help. His business was oil, gas, copper, iron, gold, bauxite, coal: anything valuable that could be ripped out of the ground in remote places. He would buy the rights to mine it, convince investors that he'd struck lucky and sell out just as it became clear that there was not so much there after all. What's more, he was a tireless plaintiff who sued anyone who challenged him, usually suckered partners and principled journalists. Webster was sure Tourna would ask him to polish his name; to run the rule over him and find nothing wrong. The one part of the meeting he was looking forward to was explaining that wasn't how he worked.

After two hours the road dropped onto a wide, sloping plain that rose again in the distance into a range of olive-green mountains, guided either side by the solid blue sea. This was the Datça peninsula. They drove through clusters of square, whitewashed houses and past hot almond orchards, the leaves on the trees sandy and brittle. The driver shaded his eyes from the sun, and the road climbed and fell once more before they reached Datça itself.

They stopped on the quayside; Webster paid and tipped

the driver. It was cooler here – later in the day perhaps, and there was a breeze blowing north off the sea. Apartment buildings and stubby palm trees lined the front and in a haze across the water lay the mountains they had just crossed on the mainland. Tourna was on his boat, moored a mile or two out. Webster called the number he had been given and sat down on the edge of the quay to wait, his heavy brown shoes swinging above the water.

The *Belisarius* was long and sleek, a flash of white low in the water. He was greeted by Leon, the ship's steward, who explained with the greatest regret that Mr Tourna had been unexpectedly called away to Athens on business, but would return before nightfall.

Before becoming an investigator, or a spy, or whatever he was, Webster had been a journalist. Fifteen years before, with Yeltsin newly in power and Russia painfully transforming itself, he had gone to Moscow with little more than a degree in Russian to sustain him. Stories were everywhere. He wrote about savings being lost as inflation surged and about coal miners in Siberia unpaid for months; about officials corrupted to demolish fine buildings, tribes threatened by logging in the far east, families from America adopting orphans from Rostov, Samara, Tomsk. At first he wrote the articles and sold them wherever he could, but after six months he was working as a stringer for *The Times*. He travelled across the country, from the forests of Sakhalin to the dockyards of Murmansk, from the Gulag factories in the Arctic north to the Black Sea health spas where the politburo had spent its summers. Sometimes he went beyond, to Kiev and Tbilisi, Ulan Bator and Tashkent. In eight years he saw more ugliness and hope, more dishonesty, dignity and unexpected happiness than he knew he would again. Life was rich in Russia, even while it was cheap.

But slowly, almost without noticing, he came to tire of the endless round of expectation and disappointment. In 1992 he had believed that Russia would be great again; seven years later he worried that it was destined for ever to miss its chance. His editors began to tire, too. And then, three months short of the new century, Inessa had died.

A man called Serik Almaz was charged with her murder, and four weeks after her death he was convicted. He had spent half his life in prison for theft and assault but at his trial, which lasted a morning, he pleaded innocent. Webster couldn't attend because his visa had been revoked.

Novaya Gazeta ran a piece on its front page about her work and her death in the line of duty; *The Times* simply reported that she had died. She was the fourth Russian journalist to be murdered that year. At her funeral in Samara, Webster apologized to her husband, he wasn't sure why, and a month later left Russia for good, his faith undone.

And now he was on a yacht, being kept waiting by the sort of man that Inessa used to write about. It was evening now, and Tourna had still not returned. He pinched a cigarette out of its new pack, and lit it with the cheap lighter he had bought at the airport. Just one was all right; it was hot, after all, and he was abroad. A piece of tobacco clung to his lip and he wiped it off with his thumb. There was no wind now and the smoke drifted off the boat in its own time.

Webster read his book and watched the stars appear in the night. Reaching for his drink he caught sight of himself reflected in the black glass of the cabin. He had swum before dinner and his grey hair was stiff and unruly with salt. He had changed his grubby white shirt for his only clean one and was looking respectable, plausible even – anyone would think he belonged here. But he felt ridiculous, just as he felt trapped on this indecently beautiful boat. This wasn't him. He should have left the moment he found out Tourna wasn't here. He should probably never have come.

The next morning before breakfast, with the sun just up over the peninsula, he swam again, diving off the side of the boat into the blue-green sea. It was almost too warm for his taste; this wasn't Cornwall, where a week before he had swum with the children in water that even in August had shocked the breath from him. And while it was good, it didn't merit the trip. He had decided that whatever Tourna wanted wasn't worth this sustained challenge to his dignity: he would get dressed, eat something and leave for Dalaman before the heat came.

As he climbed the ladder back up to the deck he heard the drone of an engine and looked back to see the launch approaching. Tourna was driving, stooping down to control the outboard motor. There was no doubt this was him. He was short and solid, his thick calves like a rugby player's set firmly apart. He wore baggy navy shorts and a black sports shirt and had tied a white sweater around his neck. His skin was tanned deep and even like cherry wood, his silver hair bright against it.

Webster stood where he was, dripping and holding the towel close across his chest. Tourna sprang up the ladder two rungs at a time and held out his hand. Black sunglasses wrapped around his face.

'Ben. Aristotle Tourna. Delighted you could make it.' His smile revealed two strips of bright white teeth, even and closely packed. His handshake was needlessly strong.

'Likewise.' Webster, taller by a head, gave a half smile. 'I was about to give up on you.'

'Sorry. Unavoidable. You had breakfast?'

'No.'

'Me neither. Get dressed and we'll eat.'

When Webster returned twenty minutes later Tourna was on the phone, talking loudly in Greek and walking back and forth along the side of the boat. Eventually he sat down and started buttering a croissant. His skin sang with health. He had the look of a man who ate well: his jowls were full and his cheekbones fleshy. It was hard to imagine that he denied himself much.

'Better than having breakfast in some hotel on the mainland, no?' he said, beaming at Webster.

'It's beautiful.'

'I love it here. You see that island over there?' Webster turned. 'That's Symi. Greece. And that, the peninsula, that's Turkey. But really, it's all Greece. Always was. One day we'll take it back. Whenever I come here I feel like I'm on a raid.' He laughed. Webster couldn't tell if there was mirth in it.

Tourna began to pile spoonfuls of fruit salad into a bowl. As he ate, his leg jigged up and down.

'So, Ben. What's your background?'

Webster told him about his time in Russia, about finding journalism tame in London after Moscow, about falling into the industry by chance.

'Why did you leave GIC?'

'Too big. Too corporate. A new rule every day. It became hard to get results.'

'And Ikertu's different?'

'I think it has the right balance.'

Tourna nodded, as if to himself.

'OK. OK. That's good.' He put his spoon down. 'Tell me. What happens to what I tell you here?'

'It stays with me. If you want to engage us and we're happy to be engaged then I'll share it with my colleagues.'

'If you're happy?'

'Yes.'

'Why would you not be happy?'

'We might not like the job. We might not like the client.'

Tourna nodded again, and then laughed. 'So I'm on parade here as well?' He took a long drink of orange juice. 'That's OK.' Webster sensed he was being stared at. 'OK. Let's start. You know Russia. Do you know a man called Konstantin Malin?'

'Yes, I do.' He felt his senses jolt awake. Malin. That was unexpected. Malin and his quiet legend.

Tourna nodded and chewed. 'I bought a company from him.'

Webster interrupted. 'Mr Tourna, would you mind taking off your sunglasses? I'd be more comfortable if I could see your eyes.'

Tourna looked up from his bowl and stopped eating. 'You want to look inside, huh?' His forehead creased as he raised his eyebrows. 'You want this work or not?'

Webster smiled. 'We're busy. It's all the same to me.'

'OK,' Tourna said with a dry laugh, and took them off. His eyes were a flat brown, the skin around them slightly lighter than the rest of his face. 'This is more fun than I expected.'

Webster saw something heated, something childish in Tourna's gaze: he gave the impression of being ill-equipped to deal with reverses. He kept his smile but didn't say anything. For a moment the two men looked at each other.

'Tell me about Malin,' said Webster.

Tourna nodded to himself again and took a deep breath.

'He sold me a company. Well, one of his stooges did. It was meant to own a package of exploration licences. Some oil, some gas, all in Yamal-Nenets. We did the due diligence and everything was fine. Then when the deal's done, the licences aren't there. They've been transferred to another company. Incorporated in Cayman two months before. It had some made-up option on them.'

'How much did you pay?'

'Fifty million. Bucks. That was my money, too.'

Webster nodded. 'And you want the licences back.'

'No. I've had it with Russia. Should have known better. I want my money back. But that's not why you're here. I have lawyers for that.'

Webster waited. Tourna looked him in the eye.

'What I want from you,' he went on, 'is the downfall of Konstantin Malin. The man is a crook. He's meant to be the great strategist. The grand vizier, the man who made Russia powerful again. But all he cares about is his empire, and his money. He's a fat crook, and he doesn't deserve any of it. I want him gone.'

Webster said nothing for a moment. He could feel excitement rising in him, in his shoulders and his chest. A chance to take on Malin. This was worth coming here for. This was even worth the waiting.

'What do you mean by gone?'

'Out of the ministry. Humiliated. Under investigation in a dozen countries. I want him strung up from a lamp post.'

'I see. And how would we do that? He's a powerful man.'

'I was hoping to hear your ideas.'

'You must have pictured it.'

'Look, everything he does is bent. But he smells of roses. There must be so much dirt on this guy somewhere. We find it and we use it.' When Tourna talked, his lips, an unexpected pink against the tan, pushed out slightly. They, thought Webster, rather than the eyes, are what tell you not to trust him.

He nodded again. He took a notebook and a pencil from his jacket pocket.

'You mind?'

'No, get it all down. Just don't lose it.'

For an hour Webster questioned Tourna about the story and all the people in it. When had all this happened? How had the deal come about? Had he met Malin? Who else had he dealt with?

By the time he had finished it was ten o'clock and he could feel the sun hot on his shoulders. There was a flight at three. He wanted to leave this place and think about what he had just heard.

'I think that's everything. Thank you.' He looked at his watch. 'I should go.'

'You're not staying? Stay as long as you want. I could drop you in Bodrum tomorrow.'

'Thank you, no.'

Tourna stretched and put his hands behind his head.

'So do I pass?'

Webster smiled. 'I don't know. I'll speak to my boss.'

'You think you can help?' said Tourna, looking up at Webster and shielding his eyes.

Webster thought for a moment.

'You're asking a lot. If we take it on we'll do the same.' It occurred to him as he said it that he would take this on for no money at all. This was the sort of case he had signed up for: the sort that makes a difference.

Tourna laughed. Webster went to collect his things and start the long journey back to London, thinking hard, imagining how this might work.

Malin. Quite a prize.

Tourna had given Webster a thick file before he left. He read it on the plane – a breach of protocol, but the child asleep next to him was hardly likely to be interested.

In it were all manner of documents, carefully organized: news articles, company reports, transcripts of radio programmes, photocopied excerpts from books. Throughout, passages had been marked in fluorescent ink and annotated with exclamation marks and energetic underlinings. Tourna had explained that this was his personal file: he had compiled much of it himself. The most substantial item was a report for a bank that was thinking of lending money to a Viennese company called Langland Resources. It had been written three years earlier by a competitor of Ikertu, but how Tourna had got hold of it wasn't clear.

Webster began with the appendices; they were always more interesting. To his surprise he found two *spravki* there, one on Malin, one on a lawyer called Richard Lock who had sold Tourna the company. He wasn't sure that he would ask for a *spravka* on Malin now, and even three years ago it would have carried some risk – perhaps no one had appreciated how much. No doubt all content had been officially approved.

Spravka simply meant 'certificate'. Every area of Russian life had its *spravki*: you needed one to sell your house, to register with a doctor, to have a telephone installed, to import goods, to export goods, to secure a passport, to takes one's place at university. In Webster's world it meant a summary of a person's life taken from Russian intelligence agencies, so routinely that while the practice was illegal the information itself was now a mere commodity. They were seldom a colourful read. Date of birth, job, immediate family, house, car, education, career. Business interests inside Russia, business interests outside Russia. Observations concerning career and character. Evidence of or speculation concerning wrongdoing. Speculation about sexuality (half the reports he had ever read concluded that, in a favourite, equivocal construction of Russian bureaucracy, 'it was not excluded' that the subject was homosexual). A life narrowed to its basic coordinates and its susceptibility to blackmail or corruption. He was always impressed by the discipline required to be so reductive.

As a rule the more significant you were – the more wealthy, the more politically lively, the more troublesome – the longer and fuller your *spravka*. Every person living in Russia had a file, of course, but most contained little beyond mundane details gathered from other government departments. Anything richer or deeper suggested that at some point you had been the subject of attention from the intelligence authorities themselves, and through the blankness of the language it was sometimes possible to see the phone calls overheard, the neighbours quietly consulted, the bank accounts inspected, the lives slowly but inevitably opened up to view. Russia might feel itself diminished but in this easy power over its people it seemed hardly to have changed at all.

The rule broke down, though, on the largest scales: no oligarch or government minister would be so careless as to leave his file intact. Through money or influence his *spravka* would be edited and cleaned until it said little at all, the information it had once contained now so far inside the deep dark vault of the Russian state that only those equivalently powerful could ever get it out.

The first *spravka* he had ever seen, so many years before, was about Inessa; she had shown it to him herself. It began with bare paragraphs about her upbringing, her family, her education, but what she was proud of was the four or five pages describing her writing and the threat she posed to the Russian state. Someone, she had explained, was keeping an active watch on her: she was being taken seriously. All her articles were attached. Corruption in Togliatti, pollution in Norilsk, smuggling in Vladivostok, aluminium murders in Krasnoyarsk, workers striking in Rostov, Tyumen, Yekaterinburg, Tomsk: a sampler for Russia's first free decade. Next to her Webster had felt like a dabbler.

Inessa Kirova, the file had said, was a 'politically committed journalist with a tendency to address sensitive subjects', a freelancer who wrote about crime and corruption and sold most of her articles to the campaigning newspaper *Novaya Gazeta*. She had connections with 'difficult . . . independent'

foreign journalists – 'that's you!' she had told Webster, glee-
fully – and a special interest in the relationship between 'big
business' and politics: in other words, who was bribing whom.
He wondered whether her file was still there, on a numbered
shelf in some dank basement, and whether anyone still had
reason to refer to it.

The two *spravki* in front of Webster now suggested less
interesting, less productive lives. They had been faxed in a
poor translation, gave no clue to their origin and conformed
wholly to type. Lock's was the file of an unremarkable expat,
Malin's of a career bureaucrat. His father was an administrator at a mining equipment company in Novosibirsk and had
had two children: Konstantin in 1948, and Natalya in 1952.
Malin had married Katerina Karelov in 1971, and they had
had two children. They lived, officially, in an apartment of
thirty square metres near Leningradsky station in Moscow,
but it was highly unlikely they were ever there; the Malins' real
apartment would almost certainly be a rather grander affair.

He had been educated at the Tyumen Industrial Institute,
and later at the Gubkin Russian State University of Oil and
Gas in Moscow. Since 1971 he had worked at what was now
the Ministry of Natural Resources, in what positions it did
not say. He was a very old hand.

It went on. Malin was a man of 'high inner discipline' who
had through 'loyalty and clear purpose' risen to a position of
'total trust and positive influence' within the ministry. His
contribution was valued 'at highest levels' and had resulted
in his being awarded an Order of Merit for the Fatherland in
2003. He was a man of 'true principle' and this had allowed
him a career 'free of the fighting of political factions'.

This was instructive – such a clean file told him that Malin
was well protected – but useless nevertheless; even a little
discouraging. Webster's brief from Tourna had a crazed
simplicity about it, and was probably impossible, not to say

dangerous. He would need something rather stronger than an intelligence file that Malin had probably approved himself.

He turned from the source material to the summary of the whole report. Langland Resources, it seemed, was Malin's oil trading company and was based in Vienna. It had been run by a Dmitry Gerstman, but he had left three years before and another Russian, Nikolai Grachev, had taken his place. There were profiles of each, and a description of Langland, which employed twenty people, or thereabouts, and sold Russian oil into markets around the world.

Webster skipped a long paragraph on Malin's background, taken not quite verbatim from the *spravka*. The next section was more interesting.

> Langland's profit margin is believed to be artificially high because it engages in transfer pricing with its suppliers in Russia. Producers sell oil to Langland at reduced prices and Langland sells at normal prices to its customers, taking the difference. Any losses are borne by the state-owned suppliers affected and ultimately by the state itself.
>
> Sources close to Russian intelligence have indicated that Langland's profits are channelled back into Russia through a series of offshore companies and funds and ultimately through another Malin-controlled entity, Faringdon Holdings Ltd. Faringdon is an Irish offshore company . . . that owns majority stakes in a number of oil and gas exploration and production companies in Russia and Kazakhstan. Media reports state that Faringdon was set up and is managed by Richard Lock, a lawyer of Dutch descent qualified in England. Lock has lived in Moscow since 1993 and is understood to work full-time for Malin.

Not too bad, thought Webster, for what it was. A useful start.

At the very back of the file was a cutting from a magazine, neatly folded and kept in a plastic wallet. It showed a group of Russian dignitaries, perhaps a dozen, posing for a photograph. Malin was in the front row, third from the left. Webster peered at the likeness; he had never seen a picture of him before. With his eyes half closed, in black and white, his jaw set, unsmiling, he could have been a Soviet functionary from any decade of Communism. But there was a difference. Malin was rich – had grown rich stealing from the state; his money was Russia's money. Webster dared to imagine for a moment Malin paraded through the streets of Moscow as a traitor to the people, his image on every newspaper front page below fat black headlines proclaiming his demise.

Until two months earlier, Ikertu Consulting Limited had occupied three floors of a Georgian building on Marylebone Lane. Webster had loved it there, and so had everyone else. Next door on one side was a tiny Japanese restaurant; on the other a haberdasher's; and opposite in a row a delicatessen, a pub and a launderette. Snaking through a grid of sober streets Marylebone Lane was insistently London: various, high and low, apparently unplanned.

The company had grown too big for such levity, however, and had moved two miles east to a modern building on Cursitor Street, just off Chancery Lane. Hammer liked being in amongst the lawyers; Webster did not. He preferred being near the crooked square mile of Mayfair, with its front companies and its brass plates and the strong smell of unexplained wealth, because that, in a city that invited them, was where intrigues tended to begin and end. Here in Holborn lawyers earned their money in transparent six-minute units and worked hard to extinguish intrigue wherever they saw it.

Webster was back in the office. He stared at his email, thought in a disconnected way about the cases he had left behind while on holiday, and waited for Hammer, who came to work late and left late and was no doubt still running in. Hammer lived in Hampstead so that he could run on the Heath. He ran to work, and he often ran home from work. He was fifty-seven and must have run fifty miles a week, unmistakably a New Yorker in his short shorts and his baseball cap. His small frame carried no weight, and he had the clipped, straight-legged style, neck forward, almost a speed-walk, of a man who had been running all his life. When he got to the office he would shower straight away and dress in clothes that were too big for him and unconsciously American (pleated trousers, tasselled loafers, boxed jackets with boxy shoulders and wide lapels) before wandering round greeting his staff, still aglow, his yellow shirt newly spotted with sweat.

Ikertu was everything to Hammer. He lived alone, with a housekeeper, ate badly, read books about military campaigns and game theory, and worked for his clients, who adored him. What Hammer and Ikertu did best, and liked to do to the exclusion of all else when times were good, was contentious work, in the jargon of their legal neighbours. They fought for their clients. They fought to recover money, to redeem reputations and dismantle them, to expose corruption, to overtake the competition, to right wrongs and sometimes to cover them up. Most of the time they worked for the right side.

On the wall of Webster's office hung a political map of Europe and Asia, and into it he had stuck coloured pins to mark the heart of each project. He looked at it now and wondered where this case would take him. There were tight clusters over Kiev and Almaty, Warsaw and Vienna; looser groups across the Urals, the Caucasus and southern Siberia; four or five apiece in Prague, Budapest, and Sofia; and solitary outliers in Tallinn, Ashgabat, Yerevan, Minsk. It was a heat map of money and trouble. He had stopped sticking pins in Moscow, a thick dark mass in the middle.

His phone rang.

'Hi,' he said. 'Where are you?'

'Downstairs. Come for a coffee.'

'There's nowhere to go for a coffee.'

Hammer laughed. 'Meet me in Starbucks.'

Webster started to say that he didn't think Starbucks was a good place to discuss anything, let alone what they had to discuss, but the line had gone dead.

Hammer had bought him a coffee, which he didn't really want. He drank it anyway, absent-mindedly. He noticed that behind his bird-like keenness and thick-rimmed black spectacles Hammer was beginning to look old. But there was still something daunting there, and Webster as always felt the need to perform well for him.

'Jesus, you were less grumpy before your holiday,' said Hammer, emptying a sachet of sugar into his coffee. 'How was it?'

'Wet and short. But lovely, thank you. Spent most of it pottering about in a bass boat in the drizzle trying to catch mackerel.'

'Any luck?'

'Elsa caught six on our first outing. Then nothing. Nancy ate it raw off my penknife. I was amazed.'

'And how was Turkey?'

'Hot. Tourna's a piece of work.'

'What does he want?'

They were sitting at a counter in the window. Before he began, Webster instinctively looked round behind him to make sure no one could hear. He leaned in to Hammer a little and spoke softly.

'Do you know who Konstantin Malin is?'

'I know he's come up before. Oil?'

'Oil. He's the power behind the throne at the energy ministry. He advises the Kremlin on energy policy – some say he

42

pretty much sets it. And he enforces it. He's also extremely rich – one of the new breed. A silent oligarch.'

'What does the minister think about that?' Hammer was a fiddler, a tapper, a chewer of pens. He found it difficult to sit altogether still. Now he was blowing on his coffee to cool it, letting his glasses mist up and then clear, not looking at Webster.

'I suspect he gets his share, but a fraction of what Malin is taking. He's been there for decades. He must have served under dozens of ministers.'

Hammer drank some coffee and watched people pass by on the street, then turned to Webster with a look of fresh concentration.

'How powerful is he?'

'A government intimate. For ten years or more, as far as I know, which is very rare. He may be unique. Every case we do in energy he's there, somewhere. He's the grey cardinal of the Kremlin.'

'Who looks after his affairs?'

'In Russia, I don't know. A guy called Lock has been his lawyer for fifteen years or so. He manages an Irish company that seems to own most of the assets. And there's a Russian called Grachev who runs a trading operation in Vienna.'

Hammer thought for a moment, tapping out a precise rhythm with his thumb and forefinger on the counter. His shirt collar, far too big, hung round his neck like a noose.

Webster continued. 'I know Lock. Or know of him. There's a joke in Moscow: why did Malin lose all his money? Because it was Locked up.'

'Hilarious.'

'It's a pun. Lock means sucker.'

After a pause, Hammer said, 'Who's he fallen out with?'

'Malin? Besides Tourna? There's an ex-employee who looks interesting. No obvious animus. There must be a few

Russians who don't like him, inside the Kremlin and out. Otherwise I don't know. As far as I can see there's no litigation we might follow.'

'That's interesting.'

'It is?'

'And what does Tourna want?'

Webster told him. The fall of Malin.

'Is that all?' Hammer sat back and thought, tapping on the rim of his cup with his thumbs. 'Did you discuss fees?'

'No. I told him I'd need to speak to you first about whether we do the work.'

Hammer frowned. 'Why wouldn't we?'

'Because being seen to work for Tourna is grubby. I don't mind that but you might. But the main thing is, Malin's a real player. He'll have his own security people, good ones, and he has a lot to lose.'

'What's the worst he might do?'

'Set his people on us, rake muck, make life difficult, especially in Russia. Revoke my visa, which would be a pain.'

'Will he shoot you?'

Webster laughed. 'No, I shouldn't think so. They tend not to kill Westerners. But thanks.'

'What about our sources in Russia?'

'I think the same applies. If Malin gets wind of us, and he will, he'll disrupt life for them, maybe put them out of business. But we may not need to do that much in Russia. If Malin's vulnerable it'll be offshore somewhere. Perhaps in his past, but I doubt it.'

Hammer folded his arms and beamed at Webster. 'This is juicy, isn't it? Have you had any thoughts?'

'God yes. My head's spinning with ideas. For once I need you to keep me in check.'

'That'll be novel.'

Webster paused. Outside two men were getting out of a

taxi, struggling with boxes of legal papers. He turned to Hammer. 'Look. I need to be straight with you. I've been waiting for this case. Or one like it. I may not be the best judge.'

'You want to afflict the corrupt?'

'Something like that.'

Neither said anything for a moment.

'Maybe we shouldn't take it,' said Webster at last.

'Can we do what he wants?'

'We'd have to be very lucky and very clever.'

Hammer leaned in confidentially, lowering his voice. 'I think this has the makings of a landmark project.'

'I thought you might say that.' Webster felt a flutter in his chest.

'Tell Tourna we want two million US up front. We'll keep that on account and bill him a million a month until the end of the project. If we help him get his fifty back we want five per cent. If we finish off Malin, we want another ten million.'

'You're serious.'

'I am. You said it. If we can crack this without doing much in Russia, fantastic. If we can't, we haven't lost anything and we'll probably help Tourna get his money back at least. If Malin kicks up a fuss it'll die down and in the meantime you can do a few Kazakh cases. It's not like we've got an office in Moscow to raid or employees to imprison.' He paused. 'Where does Lock live?'

'Moscow.'

'That's a shame.'

'Why?'

'Because he started to work for Malin before either of them knew what they were doing. That means he knows where the mistakes are. And if you're right, he's not exactly battle-hardened. Get him out of Moscow. He's protected there.'

'With pleasure.'

'He's worth a lot to us. Go after him.'

CHAPTER THREE

London was a gateway for Lock; he passed through it often on the way to his island world, where the sun shone and he was in charge. But in a broader sense it led to a life that was closed to him in Moscow. He would buy his suits there, from Henry Poole – the oldest tailors on Savile Row, he had once discovered with satisfaction – and the shirts and ties, shoes and socks that set him apart, he liked to think, from his Russian colleagues. There he would boss his lawyers, have his hair cut, dine well with the very few friends he still had, and feel briefly his old self, part of a confident, distinguished fraternity, the equal of his peers. In London, too, he would occasionally see his family.

But he hadn't seen Marina or Vika on his recent visits. He told himself that there were good reasons for this: he was usually passing through and was seldom in town for long; the greater the size of Malin's secret empire the more meetings he was forced to have; Vika was in bed by eight, just as his working day tended to finish. Today, however, on his way to Holland Park to see them, scenes from the Riviera playing in his mind, he found guilt mixed in with the usual apprehension.

He had discharged his driver, and to stretch his back after the morning's flight was walking across Hyde Park, happy that August and Monaco were behind him. His last four days there had been uncomfortable: he had been tetchy, Oksana sullen. He wanted to tell her what was troubling him but knew he couldn't; she had taken his nervousness to mean that he didn't trust her. Monaco, hot and threatening thunder, had tightened around him, and trips to Cannes and up into the hills around Grasse had failed to give release. The storms never came. He had felt relief when Oksana had boarded her flight, and no doubt she had too. Ten days were simply too many to spend in Monaco – perhaps too many, he thought, to spend with me.

The park was green, vivid, old, full of tourists. It was five o'clock but the sun was still high and Lock, in his shirtsleeves, his jacket over his shoulder, walked at an idling pace past the Reformers Tree and the Old Police House, across the Serpentine Bridge and towards Kensington Palace. He was aware of loving London for reasons that he imperfectly understood, something to do with its confidence: London never pretended to be something it was not.

He had never walked to her flat before. He continued to go slowly, eager and hesitant at once. He wondered which Marina would be there to greet him: the romantic whose broken hopes she still struggled to conceal or the cool rationalist who had understood long before him that they needed to be broken. It was this crisis in her that he loved, and it was this that made him dread seeing her: in her company he felt like either a heel or a quisling.

They had met in Moscow, early in Lock's time there. She was a lawyer – she worked in Moscow City Hall, selling off state property to private developers – and Malin's goddaughter. It was he that introduced them, inviting them to a small dinner at his dacha, where he made a big show of playing matchmaker, embarrassing them both. There were moments later when Lock would wonder if this had all been part of his grand plan.

For over six months Lock had been living the expatriate life in a city that absorbed him completely, and now he found himself in the Russian countryside for the first time. It was spring, and the low sun picked out the bright new leaves of the alders and silver birch. He first saw Marina as she walked with Yekaterina Malin in a grove of apple trees, and he thought immediately that even in this place she seemed to glow more intensely than the world around her. She was slight and fair-haired, with clear, white skin and a small nose, a little upturned. Her eyes were green, even and light, like peridots.

That night they talked about Russia. Lock had never been invited to a Russian's home before, and it was made clear to him that this was an honour only granted to a few. Russians, he was told, were by nature an open and friendly people but their recent history – perhaps all their history – had caused them to reserve friendship for longer than they might like. Lock had suggested that perhaps now, for the first time truly democratic, Russia could look forward to a warming of its relationships, at a diplomatic and a personal level. One of the other guests, a doctor and an old friend of Yekaterina, thanked Lock for his eloquent words but feared that it would take more to repair this broken nation, ravaged for centuries by the cruelty of the leaders it craved and probably deserved. Marina bridled at this: she objected to the notion that Russians loved to suffer; and she saw now the opportunity for a real people's revolution that would allow Russia to achieve at last the greatness that had always been its destiny. As she talked, her cheeks flushed red. Marina in argument captivated Lock, and he watched rapt as she made her case with passion, not caring, it seemed, that she was in the company of her elders. Malin, less forbidding then, had seemed to enjoy every moment, cheerfully goading on both sides.

Still dwelling on the past he arrived at her flat. It was on Holland Park, the road, and looked out onto the park itself. Lock remembered Vika telling him delightedly that she lived on Holland Park, in Holland Park, next to Holland Park. That too was London, ignoring any obligation to make sense. He stood outside the gate for a moment and looked up at the building: white stucco, double-fronted, huge but discreet about it. He breathed deeply, walked up the path and rang the bell.

He saw from the name card next to it that she was still Marina Lock. She had kept his name when she left him, and he still, despite attempts to be disciplined, found in this some small, unrealistic hope of reconciliation. In the rare moments when he honestly reviewed his life he knew, with a certainty he was generally denied, that Marina was too good for him – not perhaps for the man he had once been but certainly for the one he had become. This knowledge pained him, partly for her sake but mainly because it shook the delicate fiction on which his remaining self-esteem rested. He might sometimes succeed in forgetting who he had once been but Marina was always there to help him remember.

Her voice came over the intercom. 'Hello?' Each time he heard it now it was a little less Russian.

'It's Richard.'

'Come up.'

The two long flights of stairs left him out of breath. Vika was waiting for him on the landing, and ran to him as he climbed the last steps.

'Papa!'

He stooped to hug her but felt a short stabbing in his back and knelt down instead. His head rested on her shoulder. It was a long time, he realized, since he had hugged anyone.

Marina was in the door, smiling, less guarded than she would once have been. He stood up and gave her a kiss on each cheek.

'Come in,' she said. 'You look well. Where have you been?'

'Monaco, for a week or so. It was hot.' A pause. He

wouldn't mention Oksana and Marina wouldn't ask. And he wasn't at all sure that he did look well.

'Come into the kitchen. I'm making Vika her tea.'

Lock ruffled the girl's hair. She was fair, like her mother, but had his straight nose and his blue eyes. 'And what are you having for tea, rabbit?'

'Daddy, I'm not a rabbit. I'm eight years old. And I'm having fish fingers.'

'Such an English girl these days.' Vika walked into the flat and he followed.

For an hour Lock sat at the kitchen table and talked with his wife and his daughter. Vika was shy with him, but relaxed as he quizzed her about school and England and her holidays. She and Marina looked deeply healthy. They had been to Cape Kolka in Latvia with Marina's parents for three weeks. They had walked, and swum, and gathered berries. Vika had seen a buzzard. Marina had claimed to have seen an eagle, but Vika didn't believe her. Lock remembered sitting in hides with his father-in-law; it had never really suited him.

'Daddy, when can you come on holiday with us?'

'Well,' said Lock, 'perhaps you and I could go to Holland and see Opa. We could go at half-term.'

'Can you come too, Mummy?'

'We'll see.'

They discussed Vika's friends, and Marina's parents, and Christmas arrangements. Lock would be in London for Christmas, he hoped. Marina cooked and tidied; Lock and Vika sat at the table. After her tea, Vika went to get ready for bed.

'Might you come again?' said Marina.

'I could. I have endless meetings with the lawyers. I may be here at the weekend as well. One night later in the week?'

'Don't disappoint her, Richard. It's getting harder to explain why you never see us.'

'I won't.'

'Let's set a day.'

'I can't until I've seen the lawyer. I'll know tomorrow.'

'All right. You'll call?'

'I'll call.'

Marina looked at him steadily and said, 'How are you?'

'I'm fine. Things are good.'

'So no change?'

'Marina, come on.'

'Why don't you move to London? I don't miss Moscow. I'm ashamed to say it but I don't. Not at all. You could be freer here.'

'It won't work. You know that. He needs me where he can see me.'

'You know, I used to think Konstantin was the most wonderful man in the world. Like my father but more serious. Committed. I don't understand what he's become.'

Lock did not reply.

'What if you find a replacement?' said Marina. 'For yourself?'

'What, put an ad in *Kommersant*? Monkey wanted for oligarch? Must be quiet and domesticated?'

'Please, Richard, don't.'

Lock sighed and rested his head in his hands, rubbing his temples. 'I'm sorry. I'm sorry. I've sometimes thought the same myself. It won't work.'

'But Dmitry managed it. Nina sent me an email in the spring. They're in Berlin and they're happy. It's like a new life.'

'Dmitry was different.' Lock shook his head. 'He'd only been there for what – four years? Five? And Konstantin always preferred Grachev in any case. Part of the problem is he still likes me. But in the end we've been together too long. The balloon's too high.'

Marina looked at him closely. Her silence meant that she

didn't concede that he was right but wouldn't press her point. He was grateful to her for it.

Before he left, Lock read to Vika, lying next to her on her pink bed. He wondered whether he was making a good job of it: he wasn't sure he was expressive enough. He was no actor. The book was about a Palestinian girl who longed to play football for her country; it seemed very grown up. It was cool in Vika's room, and safe, and he wanted to fall asleep next to her and never leave.

By the time he said goodbye to Marina it was almost night outside; from the landing he could see the oaks in the park full and black against the dark blue of the sky.

'Look,' he said. 'You're right. Sod the lawyers. Let's go away at the weekend. We could go to that place in Bath. The three of us.'

Marina crossed her arms. 'No, Richard. That's too much.'

'Vika would love it.'

'Until she came home.' She shook her head. 'It isn't right. And anyway she has dance on Saturdays.'

Lock's smile was disappointed. He put his hands in his pockets and looked down, turning slightly as if to leave.

'You should come,' said Marina. 'To watch her dance. She loves it.'

'When is it?'

'It's at ten. Near the school.'

'On Saturday?'

'Saturday. It would mean more to her. Really.'

Lock nodded. He kissed Marina on the cheek, just once, and left.

The next day Kesler, in grey pinstripe, sat at the table, looking grave. Lock was eating a Bryson Joyce biscuit, sitting back in his chair, his right ankle resting on his left leg, his foot tapping impatiently in space.

He had spent the morning instructing a firm of investigators to take Tourna's affairs apart. Kesler had decided that he should maintain a distance, and Lock had gone alone. He had used the firm before and was reassured by its air of secrecy and menace; rather Muscovite, he thought. It even had a portmanteau name that had a Russian ring: InvestSol Ltd – Investigative Solutions. There were three partners: one had worked for MI5, one for Special Branch, and the other came with no obvious pedigree. Their office, in a large seventies block somewhere in Victoria, had the air of a slightly under-funded government department. All three partners had been present this morning, no doubt sensing a big assignment. Lock had told them what he wanted and they hadn't told him much at all, but he knew that soon Tourna's bank accounts, phone records, credit card statements, dustbins and medical history would be sifted through for signs of anything that looked like ammunition. When he got back to Moscow he would ask the Russians to look into Tourna's Russian profile, perhaps see what they could get from Greek intelligence. He wasn't sure the Londoners were up to that.

And now he was in an office on the twenty-first floor of a building near Moorgate, answering the many questions that Kesler was reading from a prepared list. There seemed to be several sheets and they were still on the first.

'So who ultimately owns Faringdon? Ultimately?' Kesler was looking down at his notes, searching them as if for an answer he knew was not there. Griffin, the associate, was to Kesler's left, and another junior lawyer sat beyond him; Lock hadn't caught his name. They were all taking notes.

'We've been through this,' said Lock.

'We have, and I apologize, but if I don't understand it I can't defend you, and at the moment I don't.'

Lock breathed in deeply and let it out again, almost a sigh. As a lawyer himself he had always enjoyed telling other lawyers what to do, and over the years he had got used to it. He didn't like this reversal, but more particularly he didn't like to imagine the reasons for it. He wondered where Emily was. Was it Emily? Emma? On his previous visits, Kesler had always been accompanied by a pretty junior lawyer. Her absence no doubt indicated a shift in his status.

'I don't really feel like the client here, Skip.'

'With respect, Richard, you're not my client.'

'Faringdon's your client. Whose signature's on the engagement letter?'

'Yes. And my duty is to Faringdon, not necessarily to you – to the board and not the shareholder, to be precise.' Kesler held Lock's eye for a moment. He looked over at his colleagues. 'Lawrence, David, can you give us a moment?' Griffin hesitated. 'Leave your things. Thank you.'

Griffin and the junior left the room with the air of schoolboys who aren't sure what they have done wrong.

'Look,' Kesler said, staring hard at Lock, his palms open on the table, 'leaving aside legal niceties, can we agree that our interests are aligned? What works for you works for Faringdon and that works for Konstantin. For now. We both know that you don't own Faringdon and we both know who does. The world knows it. Tourna definitely knows it. But I have to know what lies between, because I have to know how likely Tourna is to prove that.'

'I've told you everything to a certain point. If it becomes necessary I can tell you more.'

Kesler looked at his watch. Now he was emphatic. 'Richard, we've been talking for barely an hour. In Paris you're likely to be on the stand for a day or two at least. Do you think their QC will get bored and just stop? Thank you very much, Mr Lock, I think that will do? He will be much less nice than me. Much less. Now, we'll be coaching you for that, but in the meantime,' slowly now, each word stressed, 'you need to open up.'

'Konstantin has nothing to worry about,' said Lock airily, with a small wave of his hand. He wasn't sure whether this communicated the right air of unconcern. He didn't trust Kesler; or, more precisely, he didn't trust what Kesler had been asked to do.

'I know, Richard. OK, I see. Christ.' Kesler looked down at his notes, resting his forehead on his hand, then slowly back to Lock. 'Let me reassure you. I'm not here to conduct an audit. I'm not here to inspect the quality of your work and tell him to get a new man to plug the holes. You've had a big job to do for Malin but you are not the boss, and you don't get to decide what to tell me. It's already been decided.'

So he was no longer the client. Malin and Kesler were talking directly. That wasn't surprising – he knew that much from the meeting in Théoule – but he had still expected to play a role.

There was a time, Lock thought, when I wasn't this constricted, when my first response wouldn't have been coloured by fear. He asked himself what his old self would do now. Leave with a humiliating put-down to Kesler? Hire new lawyers? His old self would have had choices. But now, as Kesler had correctly identified, he was as frightened of Malin as he was of the law, and not to cooperate with Kesler was to invite the fury of both.

He leaned forward and took another biscuit, still trying to project confidence.

'All right. But you know how delicate this is.'

'I do.'

'Do you trust him?' Lock, delaying, nodded to the empty space where Griffin had sat.

'Completely. He's worked with me for five years.'

'Why haven't I seen him before?'

'Because it hasn't been a criminal defence matter before. Which is what this is.'

'It's an arbitration, for God's sake. An arbitration. We've sat through or settled a dozen of them.' Lock was becoming a little louder and sarcastic now, beginning to gesticulate.

'This is different, Richard. Because of where it may end up. Because they're accusing you of being a criminal. Even if Tourna isn't shit-stirring, and he will be, if that tribunal thinks you're a money-launderer – even hints at it – you can guarantee that the Swiss will be all over it, the Americans – God knows who else.'

The Swiss. The Americans. The unnamed others. With unassailable authority, indefatigable, righteous, rooting out the wrongdoers and sending them to jail. But if Lock went down, so would Malin, and Malin, therefore, wouldn't let him. Therefore he was safe. There was logic to this. For a brief time he even welcomed the idea of relinquishing control of this mess to Kesler.

Over the course of the next six days Lock tried to tell Kesler everything. Six days and five evenings with Kesler, Griffin and the junior, describing a professional lifetime of routine, dishonest transactions. Almost a whole week in Bryson's offices. Bored but nervous, he insisted on sitting opposite the large window that looked east towards Liverpool Street, so that while he talked he could watch London become lower and sparser as it faded into the east, finally giving hints of the countryside beyond. It was hot out there, clearly, but in their conference room (still quite a sizeable one, Lock noted – he might no longer be a client, he might even be a criminal, but at least his boss was important enough to run up impressive fees) the temperature was steadily just above chilly.

Lock didn't have access to his files, but this hardly mattered because he knew it all. He explained to Kesler that his first piece of work for Malin had been in 1993, when Malin was head of the Ministry of Industry and Energy's Transportation department. He had told Lock that he wanted to take advantage of some opportunities in the private sector, and for this would need an offshore company capable of making investments in Russia. It would also need an offshore bank account, into which payments could be made. This first company was Spirecrest Holdings, now defunct, and it had been a minor mistake. It had soon been replaced by a Cyprus company, Arctec Holdings, which for a while had done exactly what Malin had wanted. Money from Russia flowed into it and was then funnelled back into Russia, to be invested in small independent gas producers and oil equipment manufacturers.

Kesler wanted to know where the money had come from. Lock explained that at the beginning he didn't really know. He only saw payments coming in. His job wasn't to worry about where the money was made but simply to process it and make sure it didn't attract the attention of the taxman – or anyone else. He knew that payments were sometimes made in cash (in the days when cash wasn't a problem), sometimes from other offshore companies, sometimes from more established Western companies, but in every case its precise origin he could only guess.

Arctec had had the most simple of structures. It had few assets – cash, mainly, safely stowed in a Swiss account – and was owned by a Liechtenstein *anstalt*, a particularly impenetrable form of company which was in turn owned by a Liechtenstein trust: Longway Trust, the beneficiary of which was not named. Any taxman or investigator trying to find out who owned Arctec would be lucky to get as far as Liechtenstein, but there would meet a thick wall of impenetrable Mitteleuropean discretion.

Arctec would have taken a morning, at most, to discuss.

Now, though, the whole affair was very much more complex. It was its own world. Faringdon Holdings, right in the middle, held assets in over forty different companies in Russia and its neighbours. Up above it was a consortium of nine shareholders, each of which owned a roughly equal share. These shareholders were companies registered in the British Virgin Islands, in Cayman, in Malta, in Gibraltar, all over. Lock had set up each of these and each one had its own shareholders in many different places. And above these was another layer still, every company lovingly incorporated by Lock. Draw the whole thing, and it would look like an hourglass, if you stood far enough back. Finally, when it seemed like there was no end to it, everything came together in the airless heights of the scheme in the only constant, Longway, the same unbreakable trust that Lock had set up almost fifteen years earlier. A finial, of sorts.

Kesler and Lock went over every company in the scheme. Griffin had eventually counted and announced that there were eighty-three of them. (These were just the live ones – they ignored for now the dozens that had done their job and been discarded.) Each had a bank account, which Lock, with help, had set up. Each had its directors, whom Lock had had to find. Each required that its fees be paid every year to the local company register; Lock estimated that the annual expense was well over a million dollars. Most had a story that Kesler was determined to know.

On it went. When they had systematically worked their way from the middle of the hourglass to the top and then back to the bottom, Kesler again relieved his colleagues and came to settle on the three questions that seemed to exercise him most of all.

'So, Richard, where does Malin get his money?' he asked when Griffin and the junior had left the room.

'What do you mean?'

'Well, in the ministry he earns what, a thousand dollars a month? But that's not how he lives. How does he get cash?'

Lock looked down at his hands and then back at Kesler. 'There are two Russian consulting companies that provide services to companies in the group. They lend money to him sometimes.'

'Is that all?'

'The companies I look after don't pay for anything. He's very careful about that. If money is made in Russia and comes to him in Russia, I wouldn't know about it. I don't see it. I only know about everything outside Russia. That's my job.'

Then Kesler wanted to know who owned Longway. Lock told him that he, Lock, owned it.

'You mean that you own Faringdon?'

'All of it,' said Lock.

'You're rich.'

'I am. I sometimes wonder why I don't feel better about it.'

'Why?'

'Well, it's not always the most comfortable place to sit.'

'No. No. Why do it that way?'

'Why did we do it that way? We changed it three years ago. Think about it. If anyone ever sees the deeds of that trust and Malin's name is on them he has nowhere to fall back to. Every-thing is clearly his. There's nothing left to deny. My name on it creates an extra layer. And you have to prove a negative – that I don't own it. That's not easy.'

'He must trust you.'

Lock laughed grimly. 'It's not like I can run off with it all.' More to the point, he thought, Malin knows that I'm a coward. The whole scheme depends on it.

But for the rest of that day, most of an afternoon and into the evening, Kesler grilled Lock on what he called 'the real crux': how the money was made. Where did it come from? What of value was exchanged for it? Could it be shown that it was made honestly? More to the point, could it be shown that it wasn't? Over and over, Lock said that he really didn't know.

'I'm not holding out on you, Skip. Really. I take the money offshore, bring it back again, and then make sure it's invested where Konstantin wants it. That's it. I may have been in Moscow for fifteen years but I'm not an honorary Russian. There's a lot they don't tell me.'

'OK.' Kesler thought for a moment. 'Tell me this. If you wanted to prove that Malin was defrauding the Russian state, where would you look?'

'I wouldn't begin to.'

'Of course not.' Kesler betrayed a touch of impatience, then collected himself. 'Let me tell you why this is important. Tourna says that Faringdon exists only to process money. That you are a money-launderer. Now, to prove that, he needs to show – with evidence – that the money flowing through Faringdon is dirty. And there has to be a crime that creates the money in the first place – in the jargon, a predicate crime. Without it, all you have is something that *looks* like a money-laundering scheme, and that's not enough. So if anyone is going to destroy Malin – or you for that matter – they have to show an offence. No way round it. So my question is: where is it? Where's the crime?'

Lock felt his shoulders relax, and felt the urge to stretch. This was heartening. The crimes were deep in Russia, buried under layers of permafrost. If he didn't know about them – and he really didn't, not in any detail – then even the Americans would struggle to get close. How often had Moscow fallen to invading powers? Never, he was fairly sure. Not since the Mongols anyway. Russia was impregnable. The Ministry of Internal Affairs would never cooperate with the FBI, and no private investigation would get close. No crime was ever discovered in Russia unless someone more powerful than you wanted to hurt you, and Malin would have to fall badly out of favour to begin to be vulnerable.

'I don't know,' he said, smiling at Kesler for the first time that week. 'I think Tourna's got his work cut out. He really has.'

For two hours on Saturday morning Lock was released to watch his daughter dance. He arrived early and waited outside in the cool morning light, ill at ease in the only casual clothes he had brought with him on this trip: tan corduroys, a pale-blue work shirt, heavy brown shoes. The church hall was some way north of Marina's apartment in an area less refined, less pristine: it was a box of stained yellow brick set amongst older houses, its uniform walls segmented with long, narrow windows of frosted glass. Lock watched the mothers and fathers arriving with their children and wondered how many lived alone.

'Daddy!' Vika's voice cut through the noise of traffic passing and he turned to see her running to him from the corner. As she reached him, he crouched a little to receive her hug and in one movement picked her up, his back stiff and weak. She was so much heavier than he expected, and the plumpness he remembered had given way to ribs and muscle. She was strong.

'Hello, rabbit.' He put her down and smiled at Marina as she walked towards them. 'Morning.'

'Morning. How are you?'

'Daddy, are you going to stay and watch?'

'Of course. If I'm allowed.'

Vika pushed him playfully, as if he must be joking.

'Mummy, he can, can't he?'

'I didn't mean . . .' said Lock.

'It's fine,' said Marina, smiling. 'I know. We'll watch from upstairs.'

Vika took Lock's hand and led him into the hall. 'Come on, Daddy.' Inside, parents were saying goodbye to their children or taking stairs up to a gallery that ran the length of the building. The walls were bare brick, the floor a scuffed parquet.

'Don't you have to get changed?' said Lock.

'Into what?' said Vika.

'I don't know. Dancing clothes.'

'These are my dancing clothes.' She was wearing trainers, grey leggings and a grass-green T-shirt with a stylized oak tree on the front, its roots reaching down to the word 'growth' printed in bold white letters.

'Come on,' said Marina, and with her hand on his arm guided Lock towards the stairs. 'Have fun, darling.'

Vika ran into the hall, turning halfway to wave. Her hair was tied back in a ponytail, and Lock thought how much older she looked, how like her mother – her nose straight, her neck slight but strong. She was less like him now.

He and Marina sat on a bench in the gallery. He rested his forearms on the railing in front of him and looked down at Vika, who was in a cluster of children talking excitedly about their holidays and practising moves: squatting on their haunches, striking poses. She was on the edge of the group, listening to the others interrupt each other in their need to get their stories out and waiting for her moment.

Marina put her hand on his forearm. 'Thank you for coming. It's nice to see you.'

'I should have been before.'

Marina didn't reply; she was watching Vika below. After a moment she said, 'She's so pleased to see you.'

'I know. It's a relief.'

'I've been careful not to blame you.'

Lock wanted to thank her but it didn't feel appropriate. They were quiet for a while.

'What happened to ballet?' he asked.

'She does that on Wednesdays. But she loves this now. She practises all the time.'

'I bet she's good.'

Marina smiled and looked down at the dancers. They had lined up, in two rows of ten, and were listening to their teacher, a woman of twenty or so who wore a baggy grey T-shirt and held herself in a way that was somehow set and sprung at the same time. The chattering had stopped and the children watched her closely as she walked back and forth. Vika's face was grave with concentration.

'Good morning, everybody.' She had a teacher's voice, ringing and clear. 'Lovely to see you all looking so well. Let's hope you're feeling fit.' One or two of the children grinned, but Vika's expression didn't change. 'I see we've got quite a few new faces, which is lovely. Welcome to St Luke's Dance. I'm Jennifer. What I think we'll do is let the new dancers see what they're going to be able to do. So everyone who was here last year, let's have a go at our routine from the show. Let's see what you can remember. We'll be missing some dancers but just do your part and don't worry too much.'

Lock watched Vika walk to the left of the group, bend fluidly down on one knee and crouch in a ball, her hands clasped over her head. Beside her, the other children shaped themselves carefully into their starting positions, some curled up like Vika, some in stars, some arching backwards, their arms stretched to the corners of the room. At a nod from the teacher the hall filled with the thump of bass-heavy music. For four bars the dancers were still, almost uncannily so, until with great precision they broke into a syncopated rush of movement, spinning, leaping, kicking, arms and legs making intricate patterns in the air, some keeping better time than others. Each dancer had a style. Vika's was serious but light, the intent in her eyes at odds with the easy grace of her steps, resembling her mother even in this. She was an inch taller than the others and despite her naturalness more stately, as if something from all those ballet lessons, something of Russia perhaps, would never leave her.

Lock felt tears starting to rise from his chest; he didn't know why. He was not a sentimental man. When he was on his own in Moscow he missed Vika, but what he missed most plainly was practical: being with her, talking to her, teaching her things, hearing her laugh. What he realized now was that he had fallen behind in his idea of her. She was a different person now, different for being in London, different for being eight years old, different for dancing in this way that was so new and yet so fully her. Watching her move with the music, at once free and in command, he felt some small hint of terror at the thought that he might never really know her again. But the tears that he held in check were not for himself, and had nothing to do with sadness, or fear.

He swallowed, consciously, smiled at Marina and looked away. Down below the dance came to an end, Vika sliding to a stop on her knees with her arms and head thrown back. He clapped, and the handful of parents in the gallery followed. Vika got to her feet and smiled up at him.

'Are you OK?' Marina said.

He turned to her and smiled again, not wholly convincing himself. 'It's just lovely to see her.'

'We're very lucky.'

'We are.'

Lock paused. He was faintly aware of needing to air a question he couldn't frame. 'Is she happy? Here in London.'

'I think so. She loves London.' Marina looked at him closely, a slight frown across her brow. 'Is that what you mean?'

'I don't know.' He looked down. The teacher was telling the children to form a circle. 'I worry about what I've done to her.'

'She doesn't see it as your fault.'

'That doesn't mean it isn't. She'll know one day.'

Marina crossed her arms and watched the dancers. 'Is this leading somewhere?'

'I . . . I suppose I'd like to say I'm sorry.'

'She wouldn't understand.'

'I don't mean actually say it.'

'What, then?' Marina glanced at him and then turned back to the lesson.

Lock thought. He couldn't find the words, because he didn't yet know what he wanted to say. Marina always knew what was in her heart, and the more complicated the situation – where he would grope around amongst desires and fears that sat for ever in shadow, reticent, unassuming – the more clearly she knew it. This was what he remembered of their arguments. What he had since come to realize was that there can have been no sense of triumph for Marina in these easy victories, that they must have been at best an additional disappointment, and he was conscious now, at least, of wanting to show her that he had changed.

So: what did he want? Some knowledge must have been distilled from the slow, dripping process of the last four years. In his mind a pair of images sat juxtaposed: his flat in Moscow, hard and bright, its marble floors polished to a shine, the leather furniture unworn, the kitchen redundant, the whole thing empty now and always empty; and his daughter in her T-shirt dancing and spinning below him.

He wanted to be away from money. That he did know. In his world every act was a transaction, every relationship a wary contract. He had always thought himself a shrewd if minor player of the game, but since Monaco he had become aware for the first time of the price of competing, of the steep and perhaps unavoidable cost.

He looked at Marina. How often had he sat like this,

watching her in profile and failing to find the words that would turn her to him? He felt a flush of guilt and then of failure at the thought.

'I'd . . . I'd like to see more of you,' he said. 'Of both of you.'

'You've said that before.'

'I haven't. I've said I'd visit more often. This is different.' Marina closed her eyes and pinched the bridge of her nose. He went on. 'I want to see more of you. Not just visit but spend time together. Do things.' Marina didn't reply. 'Normal things.'

She turned to look at him and he felt the coolness that was sometimes in her eyes.

'You have work to do, Richard. You know that.' She paused. 'Leave Moscow. Find a way. I don't want that in our family any more.'

Lock nodded gently, his eyes down. 'And if I do?'

Her eyes softened. At times like this they seemed to suggest that there were greater sorrows than her own. 'The worst part of this was seeing you lost. I still hate it.'

He nodded again. Below him the dance teacher was counting out a four-four rhythm and Vika, watching her intently, was trying to follow a new move. Lost. It was a good word for him. He had drifted way off course; perhaps too far.

CHAPTER FOUR

Sometimes when a job began you surveyed the ground, found it undisturbed, and simply had to start digging to see what was there; sometimes you arrived to find it churned up by others before you, and set to it with enthusiasm in the loose earth they had left behind. But this was new to Webster. He could guess what was buried and where, almost see it, but he couldn't get near enough to dig.

Now he sat with his hands clasped behind his head, slouching almost off his chair, looking at the wall and wondering what he would do when he ran out of space. He had his own chart. It was made up of eight sheets of flip-chart paper and took up one wall of his office. On it he was writing in soft dark pencil everything of note about Project Snowdrop (Ikertu, ever hungry for project names, was working its way through flowers). He had a box for Malin at the top left; at the bottom left, one for Faringdon; top right, Lock; bottom right, Grachev. In each, in slanting capitals, were growing lists of ideas, attributes, facts. In the middle of the chart and expanding outwards was what looked like a complex molecule, circles of different sizes connected by arrowed lines, and within the circles names of people, companies, organizations, places: Lock, Malin, Faringdon, Langland, Uralsknefteprom, Rosenergo, the Ministry of Industry and Energy, the Kremlin, Berlin, Cayman, Ireland. At least a dozen circles had been ringed in red: Dominic

Swift, Ken McGee, Savas Onder, Mikkel Friis, Marina Lock, Dmitry Gerstman and others.

His researchers thought his pencil and paper approach primitive and even ridiculous; they had database programs that would map this information in moments and never miss anything. Webster would patiently explain to them that this wall of notes wasn't a calculation but an inching towards the truth, something requiring experience and intuition, patience and a soft eye. This was at once grander and murkier than an investigation of anything as mundane as a crime: it was a battle, silently fought, where victory would come to the man who could best understand his enemy's weakness. Laid out here was Malin's world, and until you really saw it – knew how it looked to him – you couldn't hope to unpick it.

But after four weeks he had only a faint and frustrated sense of it. He had had four researchers reading every news-paper article they could find in Russian and English. Two had taken Malin and the ministry; one had taken Faringdon, Langland and all the companies connected to them; and one had focused entirely on Lock and Grachev. A further two had been deep in company registries, reconstructing the network that Lock had created and trying to work out from the scant information available what the companies within it actually did.

They had started with Faringdon. The corporate registry in Dublin gave them the names of its directors (Lock and a Swiss national called Ulrich Rast), an address, and its shareholders: nine further offshore companies, each several degrees more obscure than their Irish offspring. There was little else. The address belonged to a company that existed solely to set up and administer other companies and was therefore of no consequence; the company secretary worked for the same firm; Herr Rast, too, was merely a professional administrator, if of a rather exalted Swiss variety. The only point of interest was the nine shareholders; to have so many was unusual, and the purpose of the structure wasn't clear. It suggested the work of someone clever or someone cautious. At least Faringdon itself was active; at least it did something. It bought companies, or stakes in them. From scouring the press – in Russia, in Azerbaijan, in Bulgaria, Kazakhstan, Ukraine – Webster's researchers found eighteen deals that Faringdon had made, and carefully noted the timing and circumstances of each. Then they researched every counterparty, every co-shareholder, and recorded all their findings on an ever-growing plan in the hope of finding patterns, coincidences, meaning of any kind.

Its lesson was not immediately clear. Looking down from Faringdon, you saw eighteen investments with no obvious commercial theme or logic to link them, lumped together rather than arranged. Looking up, you saw little at all. Between them, the nine shareholders were based in five tiny islands that had their own sovereignty and similarly stubborn ideas about the availability of information. For each, all Webster's people had been able to find was an address and some directors (Lock again amongst them, the rest mere cutouts). There was no straightforward way of knowing who owned these companies, how much money passed through them, where it came from and where it went. Every project hit this wall, and Webster was used to it. There were ways of getting round it, but they were underhand and difficult, and the information they produced was seldom as useful as you wanted it to be. What was he expecting to find there, after all, except another layer of the same?

In Russia itself he was inclined to be cautious for a while. He and Hammer had discussed this at length. Hammer wanted him to let Lock, in particular, know that people were asking questions about him, but Webster wanted to wait until he knew his subject better. For now, then, all he had done was to ask Alan Knight, the oddest Englishman in the Urals, to do a little work for him.

So this was what was on the wall. First, he knew that few people knew anything about Malin. In Russia you had to look hard to find him at all, and in the West, nothing. His name was on a list of attendees at a Kremlin meeting in 2000 that had brought together managers of energy companies with academics and policy-makers. In 2002, he had attended talks in Budapest as part of an official Russian delegation that had included the then Minister of Industry and Energy; the following year he had been in Almaty as part of a similar group. He had been mentioned on a Ukrainian blog as one of a number of Kremlin insiders influencing the Russians' decision to block gas supplies to Ukraine in 2006, and later that year he had been awarded The Order of Honour by the state, for 'high achievements in economic production and for promoting the true value of Russia's economic resources'. Real Five Year Plan stuff, Webster had thought, but the Russian press had barely shown any interest.

Webster had expected to find dirt on Malin, because there was dirt on everyone of note. If you were powerful you had enemies and your enemies wrote bad things about you – made them up if that was easier. This, in Russian, was *kompromat*, or compromising material. There was no *kompromat* on Malin – it was difficult to believe that someone quite so corrupt could appear quite so polished – and without it it was difficult to know where to start.

Nor was there much of interest on Lock. His name was on a thousand corporate documents and countless press articles but none was instructive. Whenever Faringdon bought something, or sold something, or formed a partnership, he was there as a spokesman for the company, providing a quote – always bland, always taken from the approved press release. Webster's researcher had found two photographs in *Profil*, the gossip magazine of Moscow, that showed Lock at gaudy parties with improbably glossy young women. Webster was pleased to know what he looked like, at least: ash-blond, broad-faced, his thin lips, almost entirely disappeared, suggesting someone who had said 'no' too often to the world. His skin was lightly pockmarked around the cheekbones but his eyes were blue and clear. Less worn, his face would have been handsome. In both pictures he was smiling and looking studiedly carefree, and in both was wearing well-cut suits that somehow contradicted his casual expression and seemed out of place amid the Moscow glitz.

This was all that Webster knew about Lock's life now. He knew a little about his life before he went to Russia as well, but the two ends hardly matched. He was born in 1960 in Den Haag. His parents were Dutch, but had moved to London in the late 1960s when his father was transferred there by Royal Dutch Shell. In Britain Lock had had a good, regular, middle-class education – boarding school, history at Nottingham University, law conversion at Keele – and on leaving had joined a decent second division London law firm called Witney & Parks, which specialized in shipping and commodities work. He had a sister but Webster hadn't found her yet. In his last year at school his parents had moved back to Holland but he had stayed on in England. In 2002 his mother had died in the same hospital where Lock had been born; his father now lived in the seaside town of Noordwijk.

Otherwise there was nothing: no profiles in the newspapers, no public spats with competitors, no scandals of any kind. No one had stopped to find this man interesting before – or no one had seen the use in doing so. Grachev was worse, a complete nonentity; and while the companies were busier, there was nothing that caused Webster's instincts to spark. His researchers had given him histories of Faringdon and Langland but each was merely a list of transactions, on the surface irredeemably dry and impenetrable underneath. He imagined reporting so little to Tourna and realized just how much they had taken on.

There was no story here, and he knew the story was essential. What he was hoping to find was a route, the first few feet of a path: it might be a hint of a character, a glimpse of some hidden incident. He didn't have it yet. Hammer was fond of saying that if what you needed wasn't within reach on a piece of paper it would be in someone's head. So perhaps he would simply have to talk to people sooner than he would have liked. The names circled on the wall knew Lock or Malin and had done business with them. Some would be loyal to them, and some would not, and he would have greatly preferred to leave them until he was sure of his plan and their allegiances. So be it. And in the meantime there was always Alan Knight.

The only signs that Alan Knight was English were his name, his briefcase and his accent, a soft Derbyshire burr that when nervous lowered to a mumble. Otherwise, he was Russian; he had steadily become so over the last twenty years. Even now, in a barely autumnal London, he wore heavy rubber-soled black shoes and a thick quilted coat that ended well below his knees. Underneath that, Webster knew, would be a blazer, and his shirt would be shortsleeved. His trousers were half an inch too short, mid-grey, and pressed to a military finish. He had metal-framed glasses with light brown lenses, and the only colour in his face was in his ruddy nose and, just detectable, in his grey-blue eyes. He was fifty, or thereabouts, and walked with a stoop, bowed by the weight of what he knew.

Knight lived in Tyumen, in the eastern Urals, the capital of Russia's oil industry, a thousand miles from Moscow on the edge of the rich, bleak flatlands of western Siberia. There were many Westerners in Tyumen, but they all lived in expatriate compounds, sent their children to the American school, and left as soon as they could. Knight was a local. He had met his future wife there in the last days of the Soviet Union and when it became possible had married her and stayed. He had three children, all of whom were in the local Russian school. He supported his family by writing about oil for the Western press, and by working for companies like Ikertu.

Webster had no idea whether this had made him wealthy or poor, but he was valuable, without doubt. Knight knew oil and gas better than anyone but the Russians themselves. How he was suffered to know so much was a question that had always intrigued Webster: either he was in the pay of someone, or he was merely too lowly to be noticed. But Webster had known him for fifteen years, since his own days in Russia, and had never detected any bias in his information. In any case it hardly mattered here: if Knight failed to tell him anything interesting no damage would be done, and if he knew that Ikertu was investigating Malin and told people, that would merely accelerate things.

Knight resembled his adopted countrymen in one other respect: he was authentically scared of power. Giving him instructions was complicated and expensive. Email correspondence to his Russian account about anything of substance was forbidden. He came to London regularly; Webster knew his schedule, but if he had an urgent task he had to send him an email enquiring when he would next be in England. Knight would then leave Tyumen and fly to Istanbul, where he would retrieve from a Turkish email account the real brief that Webster had also sent him. Until Knight flew out of Russia to report, any further correspondence about the case was impossible unless Webster was prepared to bring him to London for the purpose. Clients who breached these rules were struck off. Webster and others put up with this degree of caution because Knight was good and because he had no competitors. If Russian business was famously opaque, energy was its dark centre, and Knight was one of the few peering in from the very rim.

This time they met in the Chancery Court Hotel in Holborn. Webster had chosen it because it was anonymous and quiet and because no Russians ever stayed there. Knight wouldn't go to the Ikertu offices. It was mid-morning and the lobby was more or less empty. Webster was early; he took a chair and started playing idly with his BlackBerry. This was an important moment. Knight had better know something useful.

After five minutes he arrived, looking agitated and hot in his coat. As Webster greeted him and shook his hand he remembered his sour, soft smell of tobacco and must.

'Good to see you, Alan,' said Webster. 'You look well.'

'Hi, hi,' said Knight, looking round at the three or four guests checking out or sitting waiting themselves. 'Can we go somewhere else? Let's go somewhere else.'

'Why? We're fine. There's no one here.'

'That's not it. Who knows we're meeting?'

'One or two people at Ikertu. Alan, what's wrong?'

'Nothing, nothing. No, nothing. I just need to be sure.'

'Really?' said Webster, the subtlest shade of exasperation in his voice. 'All right. Let's go.'

They left the hotel and Webster hailed a taxi. 'Ludgate Circus please.' He turned to Knight. 'I know a cafe about ten minutes from here,' he said. 'There's never anyone there between breakfast and lunch, and if there is it's big enough for no one to overhear us. If you think we're being followed let me know.' He sat back and watched the world through the window, wondering what on earth went on in Alan's mind. Knight shifted in his seat from time to time to look at the cars behind.

In the cafe, which was indeed empty but for them, they ordered teas and took a table in the furthest corner, away from the window. Knight took his coat off and sat with his back to the wall, monitoring the door.

'Is this better?' said Webster.

'I'm sorry. Yes. Yes, this is better.'

'Did you get my email?'

'I did. I should have deleted it. Actually, what I should have done is just tell you no.'

Webster looked at him, not understanding.

'Have you got your phone on you?' said Knight.

'Yes.'

'We should take the batteries out.' Knight took a phone from an inside pocket and after a struggle with the case removed its battery. Webster did the same and waited for Knight to speak.

'Your Russian friend – the big one. Christ, Ben. He's the real deal. I'm not kidding.'

'You mean Malin?'

'Are you working for Tourna?' Knight was talking down into the table and so quietly now that Webster could hardly make out what he was saying.

'Do you want to know?'

'Christ. No. I don't, no.' Knight played with his spoon in both hands, staring hard at it and occasionally glancing up.

'Alan, I know you think I'm a greenhorn who plays with things he doesn't understand but you can be too sensitive. No one's here. No one can hear us. If anyone knows we're together they don't know what we're talking about. You clearly know something about all this. Knowing you it's a lot. And so far I haven't found a sodding thing. What can you tell me?'

Knight looked up and at Webster, as if trying to gauge his honesty once and for all. After a moment he said, 'I don't want a fee, no contract, nothing. What I tell you here is just what I know now. I'm not doing any work on this. And no notes.'

'All right. That's disappointing but I understand. Just tell me what you can.'

'OK. OK.' Knight was still fiddling with the spoon. 'OK.' He leant forward again, as if there were people at the next table intent on every word. The cafe was still empty. 'First of all, he's powerful. In his own right. He's been in the ministry for longer than anyone else. He runs it. Has done for the last seven or eight years.'

'How did he manage that?'

'New minister, new administration. He saw his chance and took it. He knew more than anyone else. Controlled it all already, really. And he sold the Kremlin an idea of what Russia could be.' Knight looked up at the door and back to Webster, who drank his tea and waited for Knight to go on.

'Mighty once more. Not a second-class world citizen. Do you know how much gas Russia's got? A fifth of the lot. Some days it produces more oil than Saudi. You look at how output's gone up since Yeltsin went. That's not private sector dynamism, that's Kremlin pressure. And your friend is at the heart of it. He's in the Kremlin directing policy and in the ministry enforcing it.'

Knight put his spoon down and looked at Webster steadily for the first time.

'So why is he so frightening?' said Webster, returning his gaze.

'Because of what he wants to do.'

'Which is?'

'Every winter Russia switches off the pipelines to Ukraine, right? The press goes nuts, the Ukrainians make a lot of noise, not much happens in the negotiations and then the tap's on again. That's not about how much Ukraine pays for its gas. That's Russia reminding the world that it's there, and that it can't be trusted. Anything might happen. Maybe they'll stop supply to Europe altogether. Last winter the Romanians were freezing, next time it might be the Germans.'

'OK. So what does Malin have in mind?'

'Are you sure you want to know?'

'I am.'

'It's not going to help your case.'

'Alan, just tell me. I need something. If I can't use it you have nothing to worry about.'

'OK,' said Knight and looked set to begin when he called the waitress over and ordered more tea. 'Do you want anything?'

'No, thank you.'

When the waitress was the other end of the room he resumed. 'OK. This is the thing. He wants to make Russia more powerful still. That's what Faringdon's for. Your friend was right.'

'Which friend?'

'The girl. The journalist. In her article.'

'Inessa?'

'Yes.'

'What article? She never wrote about it.' He was thrown, and annoyed to think that Knight knew something about Inessa that he did not. Even now any mention of her gave him a sharp jolt of parallel emotions: an urge to protect her memory; a need, still raw, to know who had killed her; a terrible lingering fear, almost an assumption now, that he would never be sure; and behind it all a thread of shame that he hadn't done enough to find out. He hadn't felt it in a long time, but here it was, familiar and fresh.

'She was the only one who did. Years ago.' He looked at Webster for a moment, genuinely puzzled. 'You haven't read it?'

Webster shook his head. He knew all Inessa's work. In the months after her death he had read every article, taking them apart, organizing them into themes, searching behind every word for some sort of certainty. Had he forgotten something? Or was Alan confused, finally addled by twenty years immersed in oil and conspiracy theories?

'In *Energy East Europe*. Must have been summer '99,' said Knight.

'No.' Come to that, how had his researchers missed it?

'Well read it. There wasn't much of it but it caused a stir in my world.'

Webster nodded. He hated to feel foolish; particularly, he hated to be unprepared. 'I will.'

'I don't mean to open old wounds.'

'It's fine.' He unclasped his watch, took it off his wrist and began to wind it. 'I will.' He looked up at Knight. 'Tell me about Faringdon.'

The look of incredulity hadn't wholly left Knight's face but he consciously changed mode and began. 'It's a vehicle. It buys things. Look at everything it owns. What we know it owns. Refineries in Bulgaria and Poland, new fields in Uzbekistan, producing fields in the Caspian and the Black Sea – Christ, PVC manufacturers in Turkey for God's sake.' Knight was excited now, talking faster but no louder than before. 'Upstream, downstream, midstream. It's huge. It must be the biggest private energy consortium in the world, and I probably don't know half of it. You definitely don't. Your friend caught it when it was newborn, more or less. It's been growing ever since. Now, what do you think it's for?'

'A nest egg for Malin? Somewhere to put all that money he's skimming.'

'That's part of it, but no. It's for winning back what Russia lost in 1989. It's part of the new economic empire. Put Faringdon together with everything that the oil majors own, and Gazprom, and everything else, and you get Russia controlling half its neighbours' energy industry – more even.'

'Frightening thought.'

'Isn't it? It means they know everything that's going on. And if the shit hits they own half the companies that matter.'

Webster sat and thought about it. He wasn't sure any of this made sense.

'I can see some logic in it. What I don't understand,' he said, 'is why they'd bother. If there's a real crisis they won't be able to control what they own. And if they're hiding the fact that they own it, it won't make anyone more afraid of them.'

'It's about influence, Ben. And having options. And they know they own it, which makes them feel clever. Which they are, of course.'

'And making money.'

'And making money.'

'What about Lock? Why involve him?'

'The dummy oligarch? Because someone has to own everything. Or be seen to.'

'But why him?'

'Why any of those people? There's always one. I don't think it matters who it is.'

Knight was right, thought Webster: this is less than useful to me, no matter how much of it is true. I need to expose Malin for corruption, not megalomania. Knight's tea arrived. The first two fingers on his left hand were orange with nicotine. Usually by now, thought Webster, he'd have had at least one cigarette. He remembered him ranting inconsolably after Aeroflot finally banned smoking on all its flights.

'Do you know Grachev?' said Webster.

'Nikolai? Yes. He's a stooge. And a spook. He's an old FSB man. Not a trader at all. Unlike his predecessor.'

'Yes, what was that about? If what you say is right why would they let Gerstman leave?'

'That,' said Knight, 'is an excellent question. I tried to interview him once, about a year before he went. Not very cooperative. Only a nipper, mind. He was different, more of a technocrat. Different breed, that – no oilman. He'd not have been out of place in a bank. A Western one at that.'

'Have you spoken to him since?'

'Since he left? No, no reason to. Too delicate. I hear he really did leave, though, didn't just pretend. He's in Berlin now, I think. God knows what he's doing but word was he and Malin fell out.'

'Over what?'

'I've got no idea, Ben. None at all. Could be anything.'

That was better, at least.

Webster ran through in this head all the questions he might ask Knight and discarded most of them, partly because he didn't want to reveal too much and partly because he could predict the answers. There was one, though.

'How secure is Malin? Politically?'

'That's another good one.' Knight drank some tea. 'As far as I know, rock solid. Well, solid as someone like him can be in Russia. I dare say Trotsky felt pretty comfortable at one point. Put it this way, I can't imagine what would do for him.'

'Then why are you so nervous?' This was a more intimate question than Webster had ever asked him before, and he watched carefully for Knight's reaction.

'That's the bit I'd rather not discuss, if you don't mind.'

'You can't leave it at that.'

'I can, Ben, I can. Christ. You've got no idea, have you? None at all.' He took a last gulp of tea. 'That's all. That's your lot.'

'Alan. Tell me this at least. Is it something that could hurt him?'

Knight sighed in frustration. 'Christ, Ben.' A pause. 'No, it isn't. Quite the bloody reverse. Now that's enough.'

Webster looked at him for a moment and saw that he

meant it. 'OK, Alan. Sorry. Thanks for saying as much as you have. I appreciate it.'

'Just promise me you won't send me any more emails.'

'Promise. Are you sure you don't want any money?'

'Quite sure, my lad. Quite sure. You can pay for my tea.'

Webster did, and they parted outside the cafe, Webster to walk back to Ikertu, Knight off in the sunshine to see his next client, stooped in his coat.

On his return, checking the urge to shout at his team, Webster shut himself away in his office and began to look for the article. He set about searching every database he knew, vast repositories of articles taken from the newspapers, magazines and unimaginably obscure trade journals of every country in the world. Most of Inessa's writing was there – the straightforward early work, growing in commitment over time; the longer investigations for *Novaya Gazeta*; the handful of pieces in English – but he darted past it in fruitless pursuit of this one piece he half suspected did not exist, except, perhaps, in the increasingly fantastic mind of Alan Knight. He looked for Inessa's name, for Faringdon, for Lock, for Malin. He tried every possible transliteration of her name and several outright misspellings. He searched in Roman text and Cyrillic. It simply wasn't there.

Finally, desperate to find it and desperate not to, he researched *Energy East Europe* itself, a journal he only dimly knew. Its articles first appeared in March 2001 but stopped in April three years later, suggesting that it no longer existed. Some of its reporting had found its way on to the Internet, referenced or stolen by other sites, and there Webster found enough to explain why he hadn't been able to find what he was looking for. The earliest pieces he saw had been published in 1998, which meant that for its first three years its output hadn't found its way into any electronic file; quite simply, the databases had taken a while to pick it up.

EEE seemed to have been largely the work of one man. Half the articles had been written by Steve Elder, an American who now worked for a lobbying company in Washington. Webster thought he remembered him as one of the many journalists who had come to Moscow for a season or two and then left before it took full hold of them. His or not, the magazine had been published in London, and that, at least, was good news.

He found it after twenty minutes at the microfiche readers in Westminster Reference Library. He went himself because he wanted to be the one who read it first.

'Irish Company Buys Assets On Behalf of Russian State' was the title, halfway through the August edition. It was four pages, probably two thousand words, and there was the byline: 'Inessa Kirova, Russia Correspondent'. Webster read it through three times, forcing himself to concentrate on the text and ignoring the voice that kept asking why he hadn't known about this before.

The Irish company was Faringdon, which in recent months had been busy buying assets across what the article called 'Russia's near-abroad': a Romanian refinery on the Black Sea, a petrochemical plant in Belarus and a gas storage facility in Azerbaijan. Inessa had found Faringdon as anonymous then as he found it now – more so, perhaps, because back then it had done less. She gave its address, its date of incorporation, its directors (Lock was dismissed in a sentence as a 'lawyer of little reputation') but went no further, content, perhaps, to leave it mysterious.

The second half of the article was fascinating, not for what it said (Knight had intimated as much, and more) but for what it left out. Faringdon, she wrote, was a vehicle directed by factions within the Ministry of Industry and Energy to channel Russian influence over its neighbours' energy industries. Where companies had once been used for espionage, to provide cover or logistics, the newly open arms of capitalism now allowed the Russians to own what they had once only thought to observe. The plan had taken on fresh urgency when the financial crisis of 1998 left assets cheap and Russia looking weak and foolish in the eyes of the world. The article finished with some well-reasoned speculation about what Faringdon would turn its attention to next.

Malin wasn't mentioned. It seemed odd that Inessa should have learned so much from such a good source and not know the name of the person within the ministry pulling the strings. But then the whole article rang false. Unusually for Inessa's work it made no mention of its sources, not even to say that they couldn't be revealed, and the story read as if it had been brought to her already half-formed by someone who had an interest in seeing it in print. But if that was the case, why publish it in an obscure London trade magazine with a tiny and specialist audience? Why fail to name Malin? Why write it without any form of substantiation? Why, for heaven's sake, give it to Inessa, of all people?

That was the strangest thing of all. It didn't read like Inessa's work. It was unbalanced; it failed to convince; it wasn't good enough. It was no wonder that no one else had thought to take up the story.

Webster spent another half-hour checking earlier and later editions for any further mention of Inessa's name, found none, and left less wise and more preoccupied than after his conversation with Alan Knight.

Almost ten years earlier, in the days after Inessa's funeral, he had made a list of the stories that might have killed her. Eventually he had trimmed it, according to wherewithal and motive, from a dozen to three: a story about a corrupt Duma member and the head of organized crime in Sverdlovsk, the killing of a chemicals executive in Moscow, and the series about the owners of the Kazakh aluminium factory. But the same problem undermined each. It made no sense for a Russian to kill a journalist on foreign soil, even just across the border in Kazakhstan, because to do so was to complicate what had become almost routine. In Russia journalists seemed to die in two places – in Chechnya, where law did not exist and violence came to everyone; and in their homes, mugged on the landings of their apartments, robbed, dashed to their deaths by their own hand – and convictions followed either too quickly or not at all. During his time in Russia three or four journalists a year had died this way, and for every murder that was filed neatly away as an opportunist crime by vagrants or drunken neo-Nazis there were half a dozen that would simply never be solved. Whoever had felt threatened by Inessa would have been wise to finish her at home, because that's where she was least safe and they most protected.

But this story was different. There was enough at stake here, and enough that was already strange, for its ending to be an anomaly. Webster imagined Malin at the beginning of his great project, the patient loyalist, national glory and untold profit ahead of him, threatened by a young woman who knew so much more than she should. For him it might make sense. Webster could feel unseen components of the puzzle rearranging themselves in his subconscious, moving into place, tempting him to believe that this, at last, was the knowledge he had been missing for ten years.

To have a theory, though, was not unusual. He had had theories before and nothing had come of them. The important thing with a theory was to let it settle, resist its charms, interrogate it quietly and see if it held up.

But before being disciplined about it he called Steve Elder at his new job and found him happy to talk. Elder had indeed been in Moscow: stringer for the *New York Times* from 1993 to 1994; they had met once, at a British embassy reception. He could remember the article, and Inessa, even though they had never met. She had sent him the piece, half-finished, as the first instalment of a series about the new politics of Russia's reviving energy industry. She wasn't an energy specialist but he knew her work and liked this story; oil prices were beginning to rise after the crisis the year before and everyone was looking to see what Russia would do in its energy policy – and besides, it was 'juicy'. He had paid the usual rate for the first article only, but had promised to look at the others when she knew exactly what they were going to be about; at the time she hadn't been wholly clear.

It was late summer when he published. When he read of her death, perhaps two months later, he had written a note to *Novaya Gazeta*. His wife had commented that it was strange, almost, that she was the first Russian journalist he knew to die, there were so many.

No, he hadn't thought it odd that she should send him the article. Even then, in the early days of the magazine, he had had all manner of people sending him ideas and stories. Had anyone suggested a connection between the article and her death? No, they had not. Elder had always assumed that it was one of the many minor oligarchs she had done so much to annoy. And no, it hadn't occurred to him that it was inadequately sourced. In fact he remembered it quite differently.

The conversation had ended there, more or less, with Elder a little prickly and Webster satisfied that this was all he was going to learn.

The theory would just have to settle. In the meantime he had his case, and there Alan Knight and Inessa had left him with the sense that he knew at once much more and no more than he had before; as if he'd asked for directions and been given only a full history of his destination. The one thing that he could act on was what Knight had said about Dmitry Gerstman. Every investigator loved a disgruntled ex-employee, and Gerstman was mysterious to boot. People didn't simply leave organizations like Malin's without fuss. They stayed, or they were thrown out, or there was a fight.

The only thing that gave Webster pause was that he knew nothing about the man. There was a little in the report that Tourna had given him but, he discovered, it had all been taken from the website of Gerstman's new company. Also there, at least, was a photograph of him, a good one, as these things go, in black and white. In it he looked neat, disciplined, a little severe; but not, thought Webster, haunted. Probably in his mid-thirties. One of the young Russian technocrats, raised on margins and business models rather than rigorous central planning. His new company, Finist Advisory Services PartG, offered strategy consulting to energy and petrochemical companies. It wasn't really clear what that meant, but whatever it was it seemed to be focused on central Europe. Gerstman had a partner called Prock, and elegant offices just off Kurfürstendamm in west Berlin.

Webster's preference was to steer a friendly journalist towards him to tease out some clue that might magically unlock his motivation. Gerstman was so precious – their only real source – that they might have only one chance to win him over. Hammer had thought this a waste of time and an insult to Gerstman. 'He deserves you, not some stringer. What are we going to find out? We know he doesn't like Malin. We know he's not going to tell you anything straight away. But he might over time, and he might talk to Lock. And it's something to tell Tourna. You need a relationship with him. Better to start one now.'

Berlin was warm for October but Webster, misled by the forecast, had brought a coat, which was now annoying him. The more one carried the more irritating travel became. For a single night away he would take his briefcase, and in it a fresh shirt and fresh underwear, a razor and a toothbrush, a notebook, a pen and something not too heavy to read; never, if he could help it, a laptop. Gliding through the airport with no bag to wheel round like a helpless dependant made him feel light and purposeful, somehow more agile. Today the coat was weighing him down.

No matter. He would go straight to the hotel. Unusually, he only had one meeting in Berlin, and that he had not yet arranged. Through some mild subterfuge he had learnt from Gerstman's secretary that he would be in Berlin until Friday, after which he would be travelling for several weeks. Today was Tuesday. He had spent some time trying to find or engineer an introduction to him through some shared acquaintance, but without success. So now he had arrived with no plan, his only thought being that to be in Berlin would make it more difficult for Gerstman to decline a meeting.

Webster didn't know the city – he had been here only once before, and that for a meeting at the airport with a client from Ecuador – and now he wasn't really taking it in. He was pre-occupied by what he wanted from Gerstman. To see Malin's weaknesses; to understand Lock; to verify Knight's theory. Ideally, to find a lead that would support Tourna's allegations of massive corruption. As the thought came to him he knew it was ridiculous to expect so much. Perhaps the true value of talking to Knight had been to show him this was hopeless. He chided himself for failing to recognize early enough the one objection to the case that really mattered: that it was impossible. It was laughable to think that he and Hammer and a ragbag of failed spies and conflicted journalists posed any threat to a man like Malin. They were an instrument of Tourna's vanity, and vain enough themselves.

But he would still try. You never knew. If Gerstman was

nursing a grudge that hadn't yet played out, if he saw the opportunity to take revenge, well, you never knew. It happened. What one man knows can bring down an organization. Every so often.

It was noon as they approached the western centre of the city. He decided to have a look at his target first and check in to the hotel later, so he asked the driver to take him to the western end of Kurfürstendamm where Gerstman had his offices, on a side street just round the corner from the theatre. Webster paid his fare and sat on a bench opposite the nineteenth-century building. With luck Gerstman would go out for his lunch; Europeans, sensibly, usually did.

With an eye on the door he went through his messages. Tourna had called when he was on the plane. He was going to be in London in a fortnight's time and wanted to discuss progress. If there wasn't any movement by then, thought Webster, that might be the time to stop. The very thought made his spirits sink.

At quarter past, people began leaving the building in ones and twos. Webster hoped that he would recognize Gerstman from his picture; he had no idea of his height or colouring. A little after half past, a tall, rather sleek man appeared, dressed in a black suit, white shirt, and dark-blue tie; this was Gerstman. Walking with him was someone shorter and broader whom Webster recognized as Gerstman's partner, Prock. Webster followed them at a distance of perhaps twenty yards. The two men were walking briskly enough, and talked all the while. After five minutes they went into an Italian restaurant, not particularly smart, and there Webster left them, returning to his bench.

Exactly an hour later Gerstman and Prock returned. Webster waited five minutes and then called the main Finist office number. He spoke to the receptionist, then to Gerstman's secretary; he explained that his name was Benedict Webster, that he was calling from a company called Ikertu Consulting, and that he would like to speak to Mr Gerstman about a subject of shared interest. There, he thought, now we're out in the open. She told him that she was very sorry but Mr Gerstman was not available. Had he gone out? Yes he had. When would he return? She couldn't say. Webster thanked her and hung up.

Finist's number was Berlin 6974 5600. Webster dialled 6974 5601 and reached a fax machine. 5602 rang for a while and diverted to Prock's secretary. He hung up and dialled 5603.

'Gerstman.'

'Herr Gerstman, this is Benedict Webster. I work for a company called Ikertu Consulting. I was wondering whether . . .'

'How do you have my direct line?'

'I was wondering whether I might talk to you for half an hour.'

'I don't talk to people I don't know,' said Gerstman, and hung up.

Webster dialled the number again. Gerstman picked up the phone on the first ring and immediately put it down again.

Webster looked at his phone, raised an eyebrow, and stood up. It was a short walk to his hotel. He left his briefcase and coat there and wandered out to find lunch.

At four o'clock he took up his station on the bench, now in sun, and watched the Berliners going about their business. He found them difficult to place: in London and in Moscow he could read fluently the signs that suggested what a person might do, where he might live, what he might hold important – the cut of a suit, the quality of a shoe, the newspaper carried, the accent spoken, the unconscious gait – but here the language was different and the people, he began to suspect, less easy to classify. These observations kept Webster occupied for a while but by five the offices were beginning to empty and his thoughts to stray, despite himself, to Inessa.

He had met her first in Rostov, in the south of Russia, where they were both reporting on strikes that had spread over the summer from the far east. They had talked on the plane from Moscow and driven together to the mining town of Shakhty, Inessa railing with indignation against the treatment of the miners, some of whom hadn't been paid for six months. Her round face was cropped with thick hair cut short, as black as her eyes, and she walked everywhere at speed, almost at a march.

After Rostov they saw each other often in Moscow, found themselves from time to time in the same remote hotspot, helped each other with sources and ideas. Inessa would feed him stories in the hope they would find their way into *The Times*, and sometimes they did. She talked about founding her own magazine, and told him that he must find her some wealthy foreign patrons so that together they would transform Russian journalism. He met her friends and three months before her death had gone to her wedding in Samara, where she had grown up.

Inessa, he came to realize, was what he had gone to Russia to find: in amongst all that furious and chaotic change she had been a constant of anger, courage and hope. So long as it had people like her, he had thought, Russia might be all right.

She was the reverse of Malin, as if they had been created as opposites, and to bring him into her narrative made such tempting sense. Instinct insisted that he belonged there, and logic agreed. Amongst all the candidates for her murder he was the only one with no reputation. He was already more powerful than the others, destined for greater things, but his name was not known and his project still the greatest of secrets. None of Inessa's enemies would fear being caught; Malin was the only one who would fear being suspected. And so he broke with tradition. Kill a journalist in Russia and it will be clear to all that she died for her work; kill her in

Kazakhstan and it will fade away as a freak event. It was a blind, and Webster himself, he had always suspected, the means by which the trick had been validated: why have him present at her death unless to have him write and talk about it afterwards?

His job then was to justify this certainty until all arguments dropped away, and for a while he let his mind play on how he might prove his case. If this were a project, what would he do? Interview the Kazakh convicted of her murder; go over the court documents; identify Malin's security team; dig up immigration and flight details for Kazakhstan in the days leading up to her death; hope in vain to find a conscientious source. On his bench in Berlin Webster gave a cynical snort and shook his head slowly in frustration. None of this would work. None of it would be allowed to work. Some things in Russia were simply never meant to be known.

At six he called home and spoke to the children. Elsa was still at work and the nanny was cooking them tea. He wished he'd bought himself a bottle of water. It was almost eight when Prock left number 20, and a little after eight when Gerstman himself appeared. He turned right out of the door and walked purposefully towards Kurfürstendamm. Webster followed him, this time at a slow run, and caught up with him as he reached the main street.

'Herr Gerstman?'

'Yes?'

'My name's Benedict Webster. I called earlier.'

'I have nothing to say to you,' said Gerstman and walked on, crossing the street through slow traffic. Webster was impressed by his coolness. He decided to take a risk.

'It's about Richard Lock. I think he might be in danger.'

Gerstman stopped and looked at Webster properly for the first time.

'What sort of danger?'

'The sort where you go to prison. Or where you never get the chance.'

Gerstman continued to stare at Webster, judging his face, his expression blank.

'All right. I cannot see you now. Meet me in the bar of the Adlon at eleven. The lobby bar.'

Webster went back to the hotel, showered, and put on his fresh shirt. He had dinner where Gerstman and Prock had had lunch, and got to the Adlon at ten. What a grand hotel this was; how much grander the original must have been before it was torn down. The lobby bar, all deep chairs and soft lamp-light and gentle piano music piped from the ceiling, was not busy. He took a seat at the bar, ordered a whisky with ice and a little water and phoned Elsa. They were odd, these conversations: the further away from London he was the better they tended to be. This one was fine, but Webster, half watching for Gerstman's arrival over his shoulder, was distracted. They talked for ten minutes at most.

Gerstman was on time. Webster watched him walk across the lobby and noted his long, elegant stride. His face was tanned and fit to the point of being gaunt, and a raised vein snaked across his left temple. Hammer had such a vein, and Webster wondered what it signified.

Webster got down off his stool – upholstered in leather, of course, with a low back – and held out his hand to Gerstman, who ignored it and sat down on the next stool, shifting it so that he almost faced Webster.

'What do you have to say?' said Gerstman, his eyes impatient and cold. His accent was clipped and heavily Russian.

'Well – first, thank you for coming. Can I get you a drink?'

'No drink, thank you. Just tell me why you bother me here.'

Webster took a sip of whisky and tried to work out what was behind this hostility, which was starker than he had expected. There must be a way round it. Gerstman had known Malin: worked for him day in, day out; sat with him in meetings; listened to his confidences. He knew how his business was organized, who sat where, where the money came from. He was about as good a source as you could hope for, and Webster could feel him slipping away.

'I work for a company called Ikertu Consulting,' Webster said, looking Gerstman in the eye and hoping to appear frank, straightforward.

'I know it.'

'Good. That helps. We've been hired to do some work relating to Konstantin Malin. As part of that work we have become aware that Richard Lock's position is highly compromised.'

'I don't know what that means.'

Webster took another drink. 'Well, briefly, that agencies all over the world would like to investigate him. When they do they'll think he's a money-launderer. Which he probably is.'

'You mean you would like them to investigate him.'

'No, we wouldn't. That doesn't suit us. I'd like to give him the chance to avoid that.' Gerstman didn't respond. 'Can I ask you some questions about Malin?'

'No, you cannot. You do not tell me who you are working for and I do not know how you will help Richard. But I do not talk about my past career to anyone, so it does not matter. I do not talk about it under any circumstances. I met with you so that you could know that. Beyond doubt.'

Webster did his best to look unconcerned. 'I understand. Not even to help Lock?'

'Please, do not be silly.' Gerstman stood up. 'You do not care for Lock. You pretend this for reasons I do not understand. Now, do not trouble me again. And tell your client that I do not talk. Clear? I do not talk.'

Webster watched as he walked away across the lobby, his

heels clicking on the marble floor. With his long stride and bowed head he seemed propelled, forced onwards by something that might have been pride but to Webster looked like fear.

CHAPTER FIVE

Lock stood in the almost empty ballroom and wondered what Maria Sergeevna Galinin would be getting for her birthday. The children of the Moscow rich could expect good presents: he had seen a six-year-old boy presented with a Ferrari, and a nine-year-old girl with a dacha outside the city, an immense Wendy house fitted out for children with its own servants and a maze planted in yew.

For his own sixth birthday Lock's father had given him a wooden boat. It was modelled on a Dutch clipper, with three masts, each with sails of undyed canvas, and but for a metal keel was made of cedar and therefore, his father had said, strong enough to be sailed. On windy days they would take it to the boating lake in Den Haag park and Lock's father would teach his son about rigging and tacking, how one could sail a real boat into the wind. 'One day we will do this for real and you can take the tiller,' he would say. Lock had loved the boat. When not on the water it had sat on a shelf in his room rousing his imagination to great maritime feats. But when the time had come he had never taken to the sea itself. Where he had expected adventure there were long afternoons clumsily following his father's commands; where he had expected loneliness and calm there were the battering roar of the wind and the angry snapping of the sails. The sea frightened him, he had discovered, and under his father's impatient instruction he became still more nervous around it. In time they barely went out any more, and what Everhart Lock never understood was that his own disappointment was no greater than his son's.

Now Lock saw his father only rarely – perhaps once a year, since the death of his mother. He would visit in the summer with Vika, and the three of them would go to the beach, Vika playing in the dunes, the two men talking about her and little else. Often they sat in silence, having tacitly agreed long ago not to discuss work or Russia or family. Any mention of Lock's life would instantly spark Everhart's disapproval, at once fiery and stern, like a rock glowing with heat. Side by side on the sand they would sit, quietly watching the sea that had for so long lain between them.

The invitation had said to come to the Hyatt Ararat at six o'clock on Friday evening for a tea party. Lock and Oksana had arrived at twenty past to find only eight other guests there, all couples, all, Lock saw with a glance, professionals and their wives. He had assumed that because this was a child's party they should be more punctual than usual but had clearly miscalculated. Perhaps they could leave and come back in an hour. A waitress in a pink pinafore and matching maid's cap approached with a tray full of delicate glass teacups, frosted with cold.

'Tea cocktail,' she said, offering the tray.

'Thank you,' said Lock, taking two and passing one to Oksana, who was wearing a sheer silver dress and towering silver shoes. She took it and drank, unimpressed, looking coolly around the room.

'The place looks amazing,' he said to her, taking a large sip of his drink and feeling grateful for it. It was good: vodka, he thought, and bergamot, and something else he couldn't quite make out. Oksana didn't reply.

Usually one vast room, the ballroom had become a forest of silvered birch branches, arranged in translucent screens to create airy spaces. In the first, the largest, were ornate samovars on tables and around them divans draped in pink and silver fabric. On each samovar was a label, in silver lettering, describing its contents: black tea, iced tea, apple juice, chocolate milk, strawberry milk, kvass. Human statues in elaborate silver and pink regency dress stood against the walls, already motionless. The ceiling had been lowered and was now dusky pink fabric, lit up by the dozens of chandeliers hanging from it. In a space to the left Lock could see through the branches pyramids of fairy cakes of every colour; ahead of him two chocolate fountains, one brown, one somehow pink, gurgled thickly. In the far corner of the ballroom he could make out what looked like a teacup merry-go-round, and beside it a band in silver suits playing surreptitious jazz. He thought simultaneously that as a child his own birthday parties had been rather different, and that nowhere else on earth might one see one quite like this.

They should disappear to the hotel bar for an hour. People were arriving steadily but slowly, and Lock didn't want to make small talk with Oksana in this sort of mood. He was about to suggest this when he felt a firm hold on his elbow.

'Richard! How good to see you.'

He turned to see a squat, wide man with thick black hair and thick tortoiseshell glasses. At first he couldn't place him. He was English, and almost certainly a lawyer; or was he PwC? He was grinning; accountants tended not to grin. Then it came to him.

'Andrew. Good evening. Nice to see you too.' Andrew Beresford. Yes, he was a lawyer. For some colossal American firm that Lock for the moment had forgotten. They shook hands.

'Good, good, good. How's tricks, then?' Beresford continued to pump Lock's hand for several moments after Lock had loosened his grip, his other hand on Lock's forearm.

'Fine, thank you, fine. Pretty good.' Lock would have given a large sum to be spirited away.

'This is Katerina,' said Beresford, letting go of Lock and indicating a well-built blonde woman in a peach suit. Lock shook her hand and introduced Oksana, who to his surprise was tolerably gracious.

'Some tea party, no?' said Beresford, grinning and looking round at the room. 'Not like the parties I had as a child! Christ, no.'

'No,' said Lock, smiling fixedly, 'quite.'

'We were lucky if we got a magician!' Beresford grinned at each of his audience in turn. 'Actually, Richard, I'm glad I caught you. Can I have a quick word – *entre nous*, as it were? I'm sure the ladies won't mind. Won't take a moment. Excuse us.' His hand returned to Lock's elbow and he steered him a few feet away. Glancing over his shoulder Lock saw Katerina opening a conversation with Oksana and wondered how long it would last.

'Sorry to tear you away, Richard, but I just wanted a quick word. Hope you don't mind. It's just that I couldn't help noticing the other day that you're in a spot of bother.'

'I am?'

'Well, you're not quite the talk of the town yet, but if I know about it, ten to one so does everyone else.' Beresford laughed and touched Lock's shoulder as if to reassure him. 'No, I saw the complaint and it looked quite nasty. Seen worse, but these things are never fun. All I wondered was – well, who's representing you?'

'Andrew, if it's all the same to you I'd rather not discuss it.'

'Is it Kesler? I know he does a lot for you. He's very good but I wonder if he – if he fully understands the Russian component.'

'Andrew, really, we'll be fine.'

'Oh, I'm sure you will, quite sure. You'll be fine. It's just that – I've seen how these things can go. Look, Richard, don't take this the wrong way but – all I'm saying is that if you ever find that you need independent legal advice – for you – I'd be happy to be considered. That's all.'

Lock felt himself flushing, whether from fear or anger he wasn't sure.

'Thank you, Andrew. I'll bear that in mind.'

'Look, Richard – these things often come to nothing. But I've seen – being brutally honest about it – I've seen people in your position get hurt. You can get – what's the best word? – squeezed.'

'Andrew, I think I should get back to the party,' Lock said, looking over at Oksana. His throat was dry and sore, and his glass empty.

'Sure, sure, sure. Not much of a party yet though, is it? Apparently the big cheeses have been stuffing themselves all afternoon and are coming on here to lord it over the little people. Anyway, Richard, just bear it in mind. You know where I am.' Still grinning, he gave Lock his card. Lowe & Procter of New York City, London, Hong Kong and just about everywhere else. That was it. Lock found himself putting the card in his wallet.

Oksana had found herself another cocktail and was standing defiantly on her own, watching Katerina and Beresford as they wandered around the room inspecting the samovars.

'Richard, how long do we need to stay? I feel silly here.' As ever Oksana sounded wholly reasonable; Lock doubted he would have been so measured in her place.

'So do I,' he said, giving his empty cup to a waitress and passing up the offer of another. 'Let's go upstairs for an hour and come back. We don't even need to stay for long. I just need to see Sergei, that's all. And make sure he sees me. Come on.'

He took Oksana's teacup, put it down on the nearest table and together they made for the door. The party was a little busier now. People were standing in clusters and the noise of conversation was beginning to dull the sound of the band. A security guard held the door of the ballroom open for them and they walked into the hotel's lobby towards the lifts.

'Is this them?' said Oksana. Through the lobby's glass facade Lock could see a black Mercedes pulling up in front of the hotel. Four men in black suits and black shirts got out simultaneously. A moment later a silver BMW pulled up behind the first car and was followed by a cavalcade of discreet German saloons. Three of the men in black opened the doors of the BMW and a man, a woman and a young girl got out. The girl was wearing a tiara and a dress of raspberry and lilac taffeta.

'Shit. Yes, that's them.'

'She looks sweet,' said Oksana, staring at the group as they came into the hotel. Maria Sergeevna was now flanked by her parents, a pretty, round woman and a strikingly ugly man: his mouth, always open, looked as if it had sheered a little across his face, and behind it small, sharp teeth peeped out. Sergei Galinin was known behind his back as Baba Yaga, the hideous crone of Russian fairy tales. His hair was dark grey with large, stark patches of silver-grey and white, like a lynx. He owned a company that made equipment for the oil industry and was famous for his whoring.

'Without the tiara she probably is,' said Lock in English, hastily steering Oksana back towards the party.

Maria and her parents hung back in the lobby while their lunch guests made their way into the ballroom. Galinin was not in the first league of Russian business but his company supplied all the large oil producers and had made him rich, and for these two reasons most of Moscow's oil aristocracy were present, many of them with their children, the girls in party frocks, the boys in suits, some with brocade waistcoats and bow ties. It took fifteen minutes for them all to amble slowly in, and then, finally, as the band struck up Happy Birthday, Maria made her grand entrance. By this time there were three or four hundred people in the room and they all cheered and clapped as the little girl walked shyly through the party, still holding her parents' hands and looking timidly back and forth from the smiling faces to the ballroom floor.

Against the far wall of the ballroom, looking out onto the main room in its own screened space, was a small stage or dais on which stood a microphone. The family walked up onto it and Galinin addressed the crowd.

'Ladies and gentlemen, welcome. I would like to thank you all for being here. Today we celebrate the birthday of a very special young lady,' much applause and cheering, 'who is now six years old. I can hardly believe it. Maria Sergeevna, as beautiful as a princess in her birthday dress, is six years old today.' Galinin waited for a second burst of applause. 'On her behalf I would like to invite you to enjoy our party here. I think maybe it is the best tea party ever thrown in Moscow!' Another pause, and much clapping. 'We have tea – of different strengths! – we have cakes, we have music and entertainment. In a moment I shall leave you to enjoy yourselves but first of all I have one very important duty to perform: to give Maria Sergeevna her birthday present.' At this he ruffled his daughter's hair, slightly dislodging her tiara. People at the back of the crowd craned for a look at her expectant face.

In the wall behind the stage, a door opened, and through it stepped a man wearing the costume of a circus ringmaster. He held a thick rope in his right hand and at the other end of it, slowly emerging in the doorway, was a crocodile, perhaps seven feet long, lumbering forward deliberately on its angular legs. A gasp went up in the front rows and several people took an unconscious step backwards. Lock watched as the ringmaster and the crocodile mounted the stage and the ringmaster passed the rope to Galinin.

'From Asia, a beast for my beautiful girl!' shouted Galinin to the crowd, eschewing the microphone. 'His name is Gena! What do you think of him, my darling?' Maria looked at the animal with something between fear and delight. 'Do not worry. He will not hurt you. He is only young.' He offered Maria the rope but she hesitated, looking up into his eyes for reassurance; then she turned abruptly away and pressed her face into her mother's skirt. Guests laughed, and so did Galinin, who took up the microphone again. 'It is right for the princess to be afraid of her beast. Do not worry, my dear – he will live with us and you will come to know him. Now, is there any man here brave enough to wrestle Gena?' He laughed, and his guests nervously followed. 'Sorry, Gena, no takers today. Thank you anyway. Say goodbye to your friends.' To new applause the ringmaster took the crocodile down the steps and away.

'Now!' said Galinin, clapping his hands together, 'let the party begin! Enjoy yourselves, please!' As the applause rose once more he knelt by Maria, took her by the arms and gave her an emphatic kiss on each cheek. As the audience dispersed Lock saw the little girl, her eyes red but not crying, hugging her father and being coaxed into a laugh.

'Thirty minutes,' he said to Oksana, 'at most. Just let me congratulate Sergei.'

'Is she their only child?' said Oksana, still watching the stage.

'I think so, yes. Why?'

'I wonder what they will give her next year. I'm going to find some food.'

Lock watched her go. There was now a press of people round Galinin. He found a drink and stood on the edge of the group, as if waiting in line.

One day he would give a speech for Vika, at her eighteenth birthday, perhaps her wedding: a short, perfect speech that would let her know how proud he was and how much he loved her. At her last birthday party – no, the one before: the last one he had managed to attend – he had stood in a room full of screaming girls in party dresses and felt stiff and remote, making stilted conversation with other parents while Vika, alight with excitement, watched a magician conjure doves from a velvet bag. She was seven that day, and Lock had brought her a beautiful winter coat that Marina had said she would adore. In the end it was spring before he was in London again, and he never saw her wear it.

Someone touched his arm and asked him whether Konstantin was at the party. No, said Lock; urgent business at the ministry. The truth was that Malin didn't like parties, still less the parties of not wholly important people, and preferred to keep his distance from his commercial partners in public. This was why Lock was here, to pay respect on his behalf. He and this man, an oil company executive, a Russian, talked for some time about the industry, Lock keeping a distracted eye on his target. But no matter how swift Galinin was with each guest, the queue never seemed to shorten as important Russians, and brazen ones, simply went straight up to him and shook his hand. Lock's acquaintance left to talk to someone else and Lock was left alone, not for the first time regretting his reserve. He could see Oksana halfway across the room talking to Galinin's right-hand man, who was improbably young and clean-cut.

He felt his phone vibrate in his pocket. He took it out and saw that it was a London number calling.

'Hello?' he said, moving away from Galinin's little congregation. 'Hold on, it's very loud in here. Let me step out. Hold on.' He walked quickly across the room and out into the lobby.

'OK. Sorry about that. Go ahead.'

'Richard Lock?'

'Yes, speaking.'

'This is Gavin Hewson of *The Times* in London, Mr Lock. I was wondering whether you'd like to make a comment on the lawsuit that's been brought against you in New York. Do you mind if I ask you a few questions?'

Lock hesitated. He was terrified of talking to the press. Journalists, he believed, had only one intention, to expose him to public shame and humiliation. His PR people had given him some advice about how to deal with them: be relaxed, be polite, and give them something that they want, not everything but something. Polite perhaps he could manage.

'To be honest this isn't a very good time. I'm at a social gathering.' A social gathering? Lock wondered as he said it whether he could sound less relaxed. 'And it's getting late in Moscow. Could I call you after the weekend?'

'I'd rather speak now if we could,' said Hewson. 'We have a piece appearing in tomorrow's paper and I was hoping for a comment.'

'Tomorrow?' Fuck, thought Lock. Fuck. Malin hated surprises like this. 'In London?' Christ. Where else would it be published?

'Yes.'

'Look, is there any chance you could set it back a day or two? I'd love to make a comment but I should speak to my PR people first. You understand.'

'I'm afraid not. It's all blocked out. Can you tell me for a start what you make of Mr Tourna's allegation that Faringdon Holdings is a money-laundering operation?'

Lock had been pacing the hotel lobby but at this question he made his way to the entrance and went out into the cold. What do I make of the allegation? he thought. Well, it's completely true, of course. How could it be anything but? I'm amazed no one has ever challenged it before.

'You're going to have to speak to my PR people. I'll have them call you.'

'So you're not prepared to make a comment yourself?'

'No, sorry.'

'So just no comment?'

'Yes.'

'Who does your PR?'

'Aylward Associates.'

'Who? Martin Cassidy?'

'Yes.'

'Thanks. I'll give him a call.' Hewson hung up.

Lock put his phone back in his pocket and sat down on the steps of an old office building opposite the hotel. He was going to have to get much better at answering these questions. On an impulse he stood up, walked back into the hotel, went to the concierge's desk and asked him where he could buy cigarettes. At the bar on the top floor he bought twenty Marlboro Reds and some matches, stepped out onto the hotel's roof terrace, tapped a cigarette from its soft pack and lit it, leaning on a railing and looking out over Moscow.

This was his first cigarette in eight years – since Vika was born. In a moment, after one more, he would go and find Oksana, and a little after that, but as late as he could leave it, he would call Malin about *The Times*. The smoke was heavy in his lungs.

He felt ill. Whenever he was in Moscow now he felt ill. Almost immediately on his return his breathing would become tight and his throat sore, his bones would ache, and his back could leave him shuffling like an old man. He wondered sometimes whether this was divine redress for the time he spent avoiding responsibility and tax in the paradises of the world: St Nevis, Vanuatu, Grand Cayman, Mauritius – the scattered archipelago of his evasive half-life. Or perhaps it was just contrast. Even now on a brisk October evening Moscow seemed cold, its air somehow thin and thick at once, lit through the cloud with a yellow grey light that looked to

Lock like the colour of contagion. Drizzle fell, and it occurred to him at last that this was how Moscow should feel – uncomfortable, oppressive. This was how most people experienced it. The scene in the ballroom below, he would do well to remember, was not typical, and did not include him. Squeezed. Beresford was right. He was beginning to feel it.

The weekend was bright and warm, a throwback to September, but Lock spent much of it in his apartment. The article appeared in *The Times* on Saturday, as Hewson had said it would. Lock and Oksana had left the Galinins' party and gone on for dinner, during which Lock was preoccupied, despite his best efforts to be light, and Oksana had told him at length why smoking was foul and wouldn't endear him to her at all. They had gone back to his apartment a little before midnight, and on the way Lock had called Malin and told him to expect an article the next day. Malin had merely thanked him, reminded him that it would be useful to have something from the investigators soon, and hung up. Oksana had gone silently to bed; Lock had stayed up in his study with his laptop and stared for hours at *The Times* website waiting for his story to appear. Marina would see it, for sure. He wondered who else. His father perhaps, though only if the Dutch papers picked it up.

At about three in the morning he refreshed the page again and there it was: 'Russian Energy Tsar Accused of Corruption', prominently displayed in the business section. It concerned itself almost entirely with the lawsuit, reporting Tourna's complaint in some detail, but also gave sketches of the principal characters. Malin was a 'shadowy but powerful presence in the Ministry of Industry and Energy' amongst other things; Lock was 'an Anglo-Dutch lawyer who has worked in Moscow since the early 1990s and . . . is connected with Faringdon Holdings Ltd, an Irish company that owns sizeable shareholdings in energy companies in Russia.' Malin, it reported, had not been available for comment, while Lock had 'declined to comment last night'. Tourna, unsurprisingly, had been loquacious. For an instant, before he began to imagine what it would entail, Lock wondered whether they might have a libel case against him.

He read it through three times. There was no original reporting here: Hewson had described the New York complaint and allowed Tourna some ripe remarks. He hadn't even mentioned the Paris arbitration, and there was no analysis of Faringdon's various assets – no indication at all, in fact, of whether Tourna had a case. But what worried Lock was precisely that it seemed to say so little. Why print it if there wasn't more to come? The PR people, Lock supposed, would no doubt tell him that the trick now was to ensure that Hewson got bored and didn't try to write any more stories – a highly desirable trick, if they could pull it off. It was possible there would be no more – after all, this wasn't the first time that stories of Russian corruption had broken in the UK press only to die quietly away. Corruption in Russia was hardly news. He went to bed, not wholly reassured.

When he woke in the late morning Oksana had gone, leaving him a note that simply read: 'Please stop worrying. It's not good for you and I like you more when you don't.' He smiled as he read it. He made coffee, and toast from a square, dry loaf and went back to his computer. The article was still there. He read it again a few times, found that it caused him no fresh alarm, and searched *The Times* website to make sure that there was nothing else there about him. He found an article from two years earlier, all of a hundred and fifty words, reporting that Faringdon had increased its stake in the Romanian company Romgaz and would soon force a takeover offer to all shareholders. Otherwise nothing.

The next thing to do was call Colonel Bazhaev, but Lock

was nervous of the colonel and preferred to keep their encounters to a minimum. On his return from London they had met and Bazhaev had said that he would need fifty thousand dollars to find everything there was to be found on Tourna. Lock had meekly agreed and left the colonel's sinister, fluorescent-lit office as quickly as he could.

Years ago he had been given Bazhaev's name by Malin, who didn't trouble his own security team, large and powerful though it was, with matters concerning his private business outside Russia. Lock had never fully understood this. Malin's security people sat outside the ministry – its head, another former FSB colonel called Horkov, was not a state employee – but appeared to have authority equivalent to a state organization. They could put people under surveillance, listen to their telephone calls, follow their movements in and out of Moscow, and gain access to the files of the security services and the police. Lock had seen them collaborate with the FSB when recalcitrant management refused to vacate a company that Malin had taken over. They worked on all manner of problems for Malin, some relating to his business, some to his role in the ministry. Lock used to wonder who paid for them, but had come to realize that the question wasn't important.

Horkov, Lock thought, was probably marginally more frightening than Bazhaev, but there wasn't much in it. Physically they didn't resemble each other – Bazhaev was solid and grey, Horkov tall, angular and quick – but they were of the same generation that had become senior in the KGB just as it had ceased to exist, and time in their company felt much the same. These were men who were practised in making decisions about people's lives without recourse to conscience; they were not necessarily cruel, but they had no need for delicacy, and they had never known regret. Lock was always conscious that under other circumstances they, and many like them, could have made his life painful and difficult. He was lucky, he now thought, to have them on his side.

He put off calling Bazhaev and instead called Paul Scott at InvestSol in London. He sounded a little surprised to be called on a Saturday. He told Lock that they were making good progress, finding some interesting stuff, very interesting lines of enquiry emerging, but that he couldn't discuss specific findings over the telephone because of who might be listening. Was there anything Scott was prepared to say that might be useful to his client now? No, sadly it was all too delicate. Lock, cursing investigators everywhere, told him that he would see him in London in two weeks' time, and that he was expecting great things.

At last, having made himself more coffee and smoked a cigarette, noting with something like shame how immediately and precisely this made his apartment smell like all his old apartments had smelt, he phoned Bazhaev, who answered before a single ring and without allowing Lock to speak told him that he would visit his offices on Wednesday at eleven in the morning – and hung up. This meant that Lock had nothing to tell Malin when they met for their regular Tuesday evening meeting. He hated having nothing to tell Malin.

His chores done, Lock sat with his coffee and wondered what to do with his day. Oksana was busy this evening, she had told him; she needed to work on her thesis. This, Lock reflected, was probably true, but even if it wasn't, it didn't matter. He wasn't jealous of her, mainly, he supposed, because he had only ever had her on loan. When she finished her PhD she would no longer need his support, and she would go. It was a civilized arrangement, and he had never felt the need to make it uncivilized by claiming more than they had tacitly agreed.

So he wouldn't see her now for two or three days, and weekends in Moscow without Oksana were difficult. He could go to Izmailovsky for a walk, or to the baths, or to Starlite for a long lunch with other lonely Englishmen and Americans, stretching into dinner and a drunken, staggering visit to whichever nightclub had been decreed shinier than its peers this week.

In the end he sat in his apartment and read every mention of himself he could find on the Internet, nervous that he would find something he didn't know was there. Twelve thousand hits. He was surprised to see so many. Some were about him, repetitive mentions of deals, acquisitions, transactions. Some were about Richard Lock the social entrepreneur, some about Richard Lock the singer-songwriter from Montana. Even when he was fairly certain that he had seen every pertinent, original mention of his name he carried on looking, morbidly expecting that he would finally find the article that showed him to be a fraud, a stooge, a money-launderer. When he finished, it was dark outside and he felt relieved but still anxious, as if he had been given a health check that addressed only symptoms and not causes.

That evening he sent out for pizza and drank Scotch in front of the television, finishing his last cigarette around eleven.

On Sunday morning he checked the newspapers. Reuters had taken the story up, and he found small pieces in the *Globe* and *Mail*, the *Observer* and, bizarrely, the *Hong Kong Standard*. There was nothing new in any of them. He should let his various colleagues around the world know, he thought, so that they hear it from me and not somebody else. Later. He could do that tomorrow.

He went to the gym, cursed the tightness in his lungs, and managed a short, stiff run and twenty minutes on an exercise bike before capitulating and making his way to the sauna. Afterwards he went to the Radisson on Tverskaya for lunch, where expats tended to congregate, breaking away from the group at around four and making his way home, wondering when it was that his appetite for days like this had died.

At one on Monday Lock had an appointment with Mikkel Friis, his partner in the restaurant project. Lock had long wanted to have a restaurant in Moscow. He thought that it would confer on him a visible glory that his everyday role could not. It was his idea, inspired by a trip to Istanbul with Oksana, and was set to be the city's finest Turkish restaurant, rich and dark and exclusive, sumptuously Ottoman. The refurbishment had begun, they had their chef, they had sourced rugs and furniture from Turkey itself, and they had a name, Dolmabahce, that Lock liked. Today he and Friis, a young Dane who had made a premature fortune in private equity, were eating at the current holder of the zeitgeist crown, a supremely sleek modern place with a menu 'fused' from the cuisines of a dozen countries, to see what they could learn.

Lock had spent the morning sending calming messages to all his contacts in the offshore world and was late. He apologized as he sat down, slightly out of breath.

'That's quite all right,' said Friis. 'I should think you have a lot on.'

'What do you mean?'

'Your supporting role in *The Times*.'

'Oh God, did you see it? Yes, I've had better weekends.'

'Someone sent it to me. It didn't look too bad. Everyone has lawsuits, don't they?'

'Exactly. They do. Yes, they do. Have you ordered a drink?' Lock looked around for a waiter, his hand in the air. 'Yes, it could have been worse. The *FT* had an inch on it this morning and I expect *Vedomosti* will wake up to it sometime this week. Look, Mikkel, I . . . well, look, I wouldn't want you to think that this was a problem.'

'Not at all, not at all,' said Friis, looking at Lock unwaveringly. Next to Lock he looked the model of health and potential. 'If you are forced to drop out I will just finish everything myself.'

Friis held Lock's eye and then laughed, and Lock laughed with him, not really knowing whether he was joking or not. A waiter arrived. Lock ordered a gin and tonic, Friis a sparkling water.

Their conversation from that point was about restaurants. Where to find their maître d'. Whether he should be Turkish. What music to play in the bar. The problems of sourcing good aubergines in Moscow. How to manage their chef's inability to speak much English or any Russian. And, critically, how to ensure that this would be a mistresses' restaurant and not a wives' restaurant. In a practical and apparently organic scheme the good restaurants in Moscow, or at least the expensive ones, were all designated as one or the other, and the average bill would vary greatly between the two. The history of Moscow nightlife was dotted with extravagantly chic restaurants that had failed because rich, middle-aged Russians didn't splash out on their middle-aged wives. The incentive for the restaurateur to create a mistresses' restaurant was therefore great, but neither Lock nor Friis would have any say in the classification; all they could hope to do was influence the process. 'The thing is,' said Lock, letting a piece of raw wagyū beef slip from his chopsticks, 'if you make it sexy enough, people won't want to bring their wives. It just doesn't feel right. Well, some might, but they're the ones who don't have mistresses.'

'Hm,' said Friis. 'I don't know. I think you're half right. I think it's about price. Look at this: two thousand roubles for that. And that's your starter. How much was your fish? Another two thousand? Three? No one wants to spend this on their wife. It's simple. For this much you're expecting to get laid. With some degree of certainty. You look at Cinquecento, that Italian place on Petrovka. It's beautiful. It's not even like Moscow in there. It's like a day trip to Sardinia or something. The food is amazing. But it's full of fifty-five-year-old Russian women in navy suits with their fat husbands. No one talks. It's like a state archive. I bet you they don't last another year. And why? Because they're too cheap. You spend half what you spend here. It's a fantastic deal, and no one wants to look cheap in front of his latest dim blonde. Or smart brunette, in your case.' Friis smiled and forked the last of his starter into his mouth. 'Which is why', he concluded, pushing away his plate, his mouth full, 'we are going to be very expensive.'

'I don't know,' said Lock. 'There are a lot of very expensive restaurants in Moscow.'

'Yes, and a lot of not so expensive ones too. And the expensive ones are always full. Trust me on this. I'm the businessman. You worry about getting the permissions from City Hall. A nudge from friend Konstantin will be very useful.'

Lock nodded and finished his drink.

'What about Oksana to be front of house?' said Friis. 'She'd be amazing.'

'Christ, really?' Lock laughed. 'People would come for a look, I suppose, but she doesn't suffer fools. You've never seen her on form. Quite frightening. She might teach the punters some manners but they wouldn't come back.'

Friis laughed and wiped his mouth neatly with his napkin. 'So how much does Tourna want?'

Lock looked over Friis's shoulder for the waitress.

'I don't know. We'll find out. A little more than the others probably. That's usually how it works.'

'Is Malin worried?'

That was good, thought Lock – Malin worried. In his experience, when things went wrong Malin could rage silently but he doubted that he ever worried.

'It's got nothing to do with him,' he said. 'It's a Faringdon matter.'

Friis smiled. Lock raised his hand to attract their waitress and as he did so one of his phones rang. The dedicated phone.

'Excuse me Mikkel, I have to take this,' he said, sliding out from his bench seat and silently asking the waitress to bring him the same again. What was Malin going to say about the article? He had to have expected one sooner or later, and this hadn't been too bad. He walked between tables towards the door.

'Konstantin, hello. How are you?'

'I am fine, Richard.'

'Did you see the piece?'

'I am not calling about the article. I have news that I thought you should hear. Dmitry Gerstman is dead.'

Lock didn't react. A hundred thoughts struggled to form. He was outside now.

'He died in Budapest. He fell from a roof.' Malin said. 'I know no more. Perhaps you could try to find out.'

'When?' said Lock, looking across the river at the Cathedral of Christ the Saviour, an unearthly block of white in the stark sunlight.

'Yesterday. It is sad news. Please send flowers to his wife. Not from me, from you.'

'I will. Of course.'

'I will see you later, Richard.'

'Yes, I'll see you tomorrow.'

Lock crossed the road, not quite heedless of the cars, and stood by the railings above the river. The wind was stronger than it had been in the morning. He had liked Gerstman; he had felt kinship with him. They had occupied the same world, and when Gerstman had left he had given hope to Lock that one day, if he could find his courage, he might do the same. It was childish, he thought, the stuff of boys' adventure books, but he felt like a prisoner of war who learns that his fellow officer has been shot while trying to escape. And he knew, without having to learn more, that that was why Gerstman had died.

CHAPTER SIX

Webster was pleased to see the name of Savas Onder appear in the file; it was like finding an old friend at rather a stiff party. Onder, he hoped, might actually speak to him.

He was beginning to feel unpopular. Since Dmitry Gerstman had shown such aversion to him in Berlin, he had been calling and visiting anyone he could find who knew Malin or Lock. He had spoken to friends in the oil industry who had known little, and to friends of Lock who had said less. In Baku he had tracked down a Scot who had set up a business with Lock in 1993; he had talked more than most Scots but told him only that Lock was no businessman: 'there's a man who buggers the notion that lawyers know how to make money'. He had found two people who remembered Lock from university – one, in fact, still saw him on his trips to London – but neither thought it seemly to talk and Webster couldn't fault their loyalty. And he had called eleven directors and company agents associated with the ever more complicated corporate knot that Lock had tied; none had said anything of substance, but it would have been strange if they had. Nervous though he was of wives (former or not), he was even preparing to see Mrs Lock, who seemed to have left her husband and moved to London.

So to see Onder's name felt like luck. One of Webster's better researchers had been working her way through a list of companies that had traded with Faringdon or Langland, and after some determined work had found that the mysterious-sounding Katon Services LS was a part of Onder's oil-trading empire. Webster wasn't surprised to see him there: it was on a Russian matter that Onder had first engaged him years before and it would have been strange if he and Malin had never crossed paths.

It was Friday, the first day that felt like autumn, and they were to meet that morning at Onder's London office; to Webster's regret Onder was not in Istanbul, one of the few places that he was always happy to travel to. He and Elsa had spent half of an unorthodox honeymoon there one December (the other on the coast by North Berwick, so cold that thick frost lay on the dune grass) and he hoped one day to take her there again.

Instead of the Pera Palace Hotel, then, Webster was in his kitchen that morning doing his best to leave the house. He had woken early and cycled to the Heath for a swim in the mixed pond, where the water was turning from cool to cold. When he got back he made porridge for himself and the children, took Elsa tea, showered, shaved, and dressed in the same suit as the day before, deciding that Onder probably didn't expect a tie, even though he might merit one. Webster's taste was for the serious and unadorned: dark suits, single-breasted, either navy or charcoal grey, with white shirts and dark ties, never patterned. Everything was well made and well worn. Elsa told him that he looked for ever on the verge of delivering bad news, a death or a sacking, and he told her that nobody wanted their investigator to dress like a fop.

On his walk to the Tube across a newly frosty Queen's Park he thought about Lock. He found himself thinking about him more and more. He should be feeling uncomfortable by now. He would have seen the article – articles, as a few other papers had taken up the story. Webster was pleased with Hewson's piece in *The Times*, but surprised that it hadn't gone further; he would have expected a second article to follow swiftly on the first. He should give Gavin another call. Perhaps it didn't matter: he had also spoken to the *FT*, to the *Journal*, to *Forbes*, and felt sure that there was more to come. He wanted Lock to feel that a process had started that no one could stop.

What would have him really unsettled, though, were the calls from his friends. No one liked to learn that someone was asking questions about them. Even if you had nothing to hide it made you wonder whether in fact you did; and if, like Lock, you had made a career of hiding things it tended to make you decidedly nervous. For Webster, though, this was a strange way of operating: he spent so much of his life asking questions in the dark that to be out in the light made him feel a little uncomfortable himself.

So Gerstman would probably have mentioned it to Lock, unless he was keen to stay out of Russia altogether, and all those offshore directors would certainly have reported to their client. Webster wondered how much of this Lock would share with Malin. From the outside there was no way of telling how close they were, and accounts differed. The Scot had described the two as 'friendly, but not intimate', while those who knew Russia's oil industry simply saw Lock, as Tourna did, as a stooge.

Webster thought about the type, these men – always men – who sold their identity to protect that of another. In every big project they appeared, the first line of defence, often shabbily prepared for battle. They were professionals, lawyers and accountants to a man, and of the second rank, their early careers suggesting that they had never been bound for the top. Some started young, others in middle age. In Webster's world there were legions of them, of every nationality, operating out of unreal little offices in London, Dubai, Geneva, New York, setting up companies, dissolving them, tinkering endlessly with money. What did they get out if it, this unnatural, unbreakable arrangement? In Webster's experience there were three motives, usually entwined. There was money – and easy money it was. Judging from his properties and his lifestyle, Lock must be worth ten million, perhaps twenty, and for this what did he do, really? Administer companies. There was security of income, since this was always a job for life: your client couldn't walk away and neither could you. And there was power. Or rather, proximity to power. They had in common the mistaken belief that in serving a big man some of his stature would rub off.

Onder's offices were in Mayfair, in the narrow streets by Shepherd Market. Odd shops inexplicably survived there: Italian outfitters selling pale-blue shoes and mustard leather jackets, to whom Webster couldn't imagine; tiny beauty salons offering French pedicure and electrolysis; a toy shop that stocked only toy soldiers, each one historically accurate in its uniform. Webster found Onder's battered red door next to a florist, rang the buzzer, and was let in.

He climbed a flight of stairs and Onder himself came to greet him on the first landing. Hammer had once said of Onder that his size, 'in every respect', was his best quality. He was a tall man, perhaps three inches over six feet, his chest inflated, his hand enclosing Webster's entirely as they shook. What Hammer had meant, though, was that Onder's actions and his character were grand: his voice was loud, his generosity instant and complete, his transgressions wholehearted. He was wearing a light grey suit that verged on the silvery and a bright pink tie. Webster was pleased to see him. In his company he remembered vividly what a rare combination Onder was: a trader, a man used to making dozens of subtle calculations every moment, who could nevertheless really think, and plan ahead, and exercise great wisdom when called upon.

'Benedict!' Onder said, with almost actorly diction, smiling broadly. 'How nice to see you. Please, please. Come in.' One of the stranger facts about this unusual man was that at sixteen he had moved to England with his family and had spent the last two years of school at Eton. This had given him a certain stateliness that forty years later seemed old-fashioned, even imperial.

He ushered Webster through a faded reception area to his office at the back of the building. They saw no one else on the way. Onder's office was large, and light enough, but drab. It had too much furniture in it: three wooden-topped desks, their varnish dry and worn; four dull grey filing cabinets; chairs everywhere, some stacked against the wall. Only the phones and the computers suggested that any time had passed since 1970. A bay window, its lower panes frosted, gave out onto a channel of grey house-backs.

'I apologize for our surroundings, Benedict. Please, sit down. As you know I don't go in for fancy offices.'

Webster sat on one of the chairs lined up in front of Onder's desk, the biggest of the three. 'Istanbul is a little smarter than this.'

'True. More by accident than by design.' Onder smiled. 'I would offer you coffee but I would have to make it myself and it would be awful. There's never anyone else here.'

'That's fine. I'm trying to stop drinking it.'

They sat for a moment looking at each other. Onder's eyes were a dark, almost Prussian blue. He had a friendly but distinctly firm gaze. Webster wasn't sure how long he should hold it – was never sure, in fact, what these little sizing-up exercises, so favoured by certain clients, really meant. He decided to start.

'Thank you for seeing me at such short notice.'

'Not at all, not at all. I'm always happy to help.' Onder didn't only trade oil: amongst other things he also traded cartridges of printer ink, and three years earlier Webster had retrieved a large consignment from a Russian distributor who had forgotten to pay. Onder had liked Ikertu ever since.

'I didn't want to talk about this on the phone, for reasons you'll understand, I hope. It's about Konstantin Malin.'

Onder looked closely at him again, a slight frown in his eyes.

'Malin.' He raised his eyebrows a quarter of an inch. 'You deal with some charming people.'

'I know. He's universally liked. I was hoping you could tell me something about him. Of course, if he's a partner and you'd rather not we can end it here.'

Onder continued to look at him. Then he laughed and broke the gaze.

'No, Konstantin and I will not be doing business again. There is a kind of Russian who thinks it all right – no, *clever* – to cheat whenever there is an opportunity. Whenever they can make money. They calculate that there will be another fool along in a minute, and that the world is full of fools. One day they will find out they are wrong.'

'I hope so,' said Webster. 'How much does he owe you?'

'Actually, he did not take money from me. He just reneged on an agreement. I have to go elsewhere for oil from Russia now. That is all. It has cost me a lot of money but I cannot say that he stole from me.'

'Is there oil elsewhere?'

'Yes, there is. He doesn't control everything. Not yet.'

'Did you meet him?'

'Oh yes. Once or twice.' He smiled at Webster. 'Perhaps you should tell me why you are interested?'

Webster told Onder the story. When he mentioned Tourna, Onder let out a snort. 'That crook! My God, this is fighting amongst thieves. I thought you would be more choosy about your clients.' He smiled at Webster, who smiled back and carried on. He explained what Tourna wanted, and what his own priority was now: Lock.

'You want to bring down Malin? Good luck. A noble undertaking.'

'I know. We don't get many shots at nobility.'

Onder smiled. 'I know Richard,' he said. 'Quite well. I used to deal with Dmitry Gerstman but when he left I refused to have anything to do with the thug they put in his place. I didn't trust him – one of the new breed, who look a lot like the old, old breed. It was easy to imagine him arresting people at five in the morning. So they sent Lock. I liked him. Not an oil man but useful enough. Quite a simple character. I do not think he really belonged there.'

They talked for a while about Lock and Malin, Malin and Lock, and Webster felt that he was coming to understand them. The moment you met Malin, Onder told him, it was clear that he was 'a creature of the Soviet'. He had been born when Stalin was in power, became an adult under Brezhnev, and worked for twenty-five years before Gorbachev departed, his job too well done, and Yeltsin finally appeared. If you were to give him the choice, he would reinstate Communist rule tomorrow, not because he despised capitalism, not because he didn't enjoy its spoils, but because Communism had made Russia strong and, more important, feared. To sit opposite Malin and negotiate with him was to understand something about a totalitarian state: they shared the same refusal to communicate, and both equated that refusal with strength.

Onder had met Malin three times, it turned out, once socially, and on each occasion had been impressed by his reluctance to engage with the world; the world, it seemed, was obliged to engage with him. He was therefore a difficult man to read – Onder had seldom met anyone so difficult. But from his behaviour he had eventually deduced certain things. He was obstinate; he cared little for his reputation in the West, whose opinion was nothing to him; but for all his apparent immobility he made decisions quickly and shrewdly, and was probably a more subtle and delicate thinker than his rather brutish persona would suggest. What drove him, though, was unknowable. 'My guess', said Onder, 'is that he does every- thing for Russia, and for himself. Which is more dear to him I cannot say.'

Lock, meanwhile, was an unlikely associate. Onder thought him competent, but not talented; vain; both flattered and cowed by the company he kept.

'What you must understand,' said Onder, leaning forward and tapping out the important words with a finger on his desk, 'is that Malin never expected to be so big. Every Russian is corrupt according to his station in life. If you are a school- teacher, you sell grades. If you are a fishmonger, you give the best fish to those who can do something for you in return. Malin expected to be a mid-level technocrat taking a few mil- lion a year from the odd opportunity here and there. But he has managed to make himself a player and now it's hundreds of millions, maybe billions. And for this he has Lock.' He gave a short laugh. 'Lock is a great man for millions, but for billions he's out of his depth. But he's convinced himself somehow he belongs. It's almost funny. And Malin's not stupid, not at all – but he can't change Lock. They cannot rewrite that story. They cannot divorce. It's worse than a bad marriage.' Onder laughed at his own joke.

'So what's wrong with Lock? Why can't he cut it?'

'Listen, I may be wrong about him. He is smart enough, a decent lawyer, but he just doesn't look the part.' Onder thought for a moment, all the while looking hard at Webster. 'Do you know what it is? He's not a shit. He's too nice. He is deluded, yes, petty probably, limited, but not a shit. To survive in that world you have to be really hard or really stupid. Lock is pretty clever and soft. Much too soft. He would like to be a part of that world but deep down he doesn't believe it. Maybe not even that deep.'

Webster nodded; this rang true. Experience told him that few of the Locks of this world had complete faith in their own myth. Another question sat waiting to be aired, and for a moment he considered whether he should ask it. Perhaps it simply wasn't relevant.

'How nasty is Malin?'

'What do you mean?'

'How ruthless?'

'You mean, does he hurt people?'

'Yes.'

Onder smiled and thought. 'To protect himself, maybe. To get ahead, I doubt he has needed to. He's of the old school. I shouldn't think he fears justice.'

A sensible, balanced answer. In truth it was no more than Webster knew already.

They talked a little more, but he had enough. He knew now that this case would come down not to a story, a lead, a document, but to a man. It all came down to Lock. He was Malin's great weakness. Turn him, and you would not only have the perfect witness but leave Malin unmanned and exposed.

'Would you be prepared to be a witness?' Webster asked Onder when they were done.

Onder looked at him and thought for a moment. 'Against Malin, yes. For Tourna, I am not sure. Maybe. Let me think.'

'And how about doing a little work for me?'

Onder gave another smile, and held it for a moment. 'Have you ever investigated me?'

'Remarkably, no. Why?'

'I was thinking that then I could be subject, client and

source. A true honour that would be. What did you have in mind?'

'I might like you to have a word with Richard Lock.'

One of the things that Webster enjoyed about no longer being a journalist, and not being a proper spy, was that he spent time with his family. He guarded that time diligently. Hammer was always on call; his phone was never switched off. He liked nothing better than to be called in the middle of the night because that meant something interesting was happening. But Webster would happily turn his phone off at six o'clock every evening and leave it in some dark drawer all weekend. Eventually Hammer had forced him to have it switched on every day until nine, Webster reluctantly conceding that if a client was good enough to give you money he had a right to talk to you when he wanted. But he still resented having to answer the thing, as he resented client dinners or breakfast meetings or trips that ate into weekends. He had an old-fashioned, sometimes indignant sense of the distinction between work and rest.

When his phone rang that Sunday, then, he was inclined not to answer it. The clear, cold weather of the previous two days had given way to low, dark cloud and a closeness that Webster found enervating. He, Elsa and the children were in the playground. Daniel was taking handfuls of wood-chippings from under the climbing frame and putting them in three neat piles by a bench. He had shed his coat and was going about his work with concentration, squatting on his thick toddler's legs, standing, walking, squatting again. Webster watched him, fascinated by his determination. That was proper work. Elsa was on the see-saw, forcing her seat abruptly into the ground so that Nancy lifted clear off hers into the air. Nancy laughed each time, a conspiratorial chuckle.

His phone buzzed in his pocket. The caller came up as unknown and in that moment he imagined half a dozen conversations he didn't want to have. Apologizing to Elsa he walked a few feet away and answered.

'Ben Webster.'

'Mr Webster, hello, this is Philip on security. We've had a call to the main Ikertu number asking for you. We didn't give your number out, sir, obviously, but perhaps you'd like to return it.'

'Thank you, Philip. What was the name?'

'A Mr Prock, sir. P-R-O-C-K. He left a number. German, I think.'

'Thanks. I'll take it.' Philip gave him the number, twice, slowly. Webster keyed it into his phone.

Prock. Why would Prock call? If he had Webster's name then Gerstman must have given it to him: if he was calling Ikertu about anything else he wouldn't have known to ask for him by name. Perhaps he knew something that Gerstman wasn't prepared to disclose; perhaps he was going to warn him off. Perhaps he had a job for him. That wouldn't have been unusual.

Webster gestured to Elsa that he had to make a call and left the playground. The line rang several times before Prock picked up.

'Grüss Gott. Prock.'

'Mr Prock this is Ben Webster. You've been trying to reach me.'

'Wait a moment.'

Webster could hear Prock's hand over the receiver and the muffled noise of a door closing.

'Mr Webster.' Prock had a tenor voice with a thin, constricted tone, as if he was forcing out the words. His accent was demonstrative, even a little theatrical: Austrian, Webster

126

thought. 'I am with Nina Gerstman at the moment, Mr Webster. Does that suggest anything to you?'

Webster answered honestly that it did not.

'I have been with Nina Gerstman from this morning, Mr Webster. She is trying to understand who is responsible for the death of her husband.' Prock paused. Webster, off balance, said nothing, his mind empty of everything but a distant, closing fear. 'Because somebody is, and I think it is you. I think it is you, Mr Webster. I have not told her, because I do not want her to know that something so *trivial*,' Prock, quiet before, almost shouted the word, 'so *pointless*, could have made her husband to die. What do you think, Mr Webster?' Quietly again now. 'What do you think?'

Webster felt a sharp pain in his right temple. He had been pacing but now he stopped and looked down at the ground. Pinching his eyes closed with his hand he saw Gerstman on his back, immaculate in a suit, his white shirt-collar red with blood.

'I don't understand you. What happened?'

'You don't know what happened? I thought you knew everything that happened. I thought that was your job.' The line was quiet for a moment. 'You don't know? Let me tell you then. Two weeks ago, you threatened Dmitry Gerstman to meet with you. This morning, in Budapest, he was killed. The rest you will run off and discover, no doubt. You see, Mr Webster? You don't know everything. Not at all. You know nothing. And what you didn't know about Dmitry Gerstman has killed him. It was you who did this. It was you who pushed him. I wanted you to know.'

Webster opened his eyes. A group of runners in training, each with a laden backpack, sprinted up the steepest part of Primrose Hill, their feet slipping in the mud. Tarmac paths divided the grass, and where they crossed wrought-iron lamp posts stood, black and upright. His thoughts were thick but the world around unnervingly crisp. He could feel dread and guilt in his throat. But even as he feared, somehow, that Prock was right, he could feel a fragile sense of injustice asserting itself.

'I'm sorry. We barely spoke.'

'That was all it took.'

There was silence between them.

'Now,' said Prock. 'I cannot prosecute you. I cannot sue you. But I can make sure you understand. I will let your conscience do the work. Goodbye.' The line went dead.

Webster felt hollow. He looked back at the playground, now a few hundred yards away, and began to walk towards it, unsurely, like a man who has just been knocked down.

As he walked through the gate he saw Elsa crouching down by Daniel, who was in tears, Elsa holding a handkerchief to his nose.

'There you are,' said Elsa. 'Can you take over? Nancy wants me to push her.' She stood up with Daniel's hand in hers. 'What's wrong? You look white.'

'I'm sorry, I . . . Christ, I . . .'

'What is it?' She looked at him, worried.

'The man I went to Berlin to see . . .' He hesitated, not knowing how to say it.

'The one who wouldn't talk?'

Webster nodded. 'He's dead. That was his partner. He wanted to tell me.'

'Jesus. How?'

'He didn't say.'

'Come here.' She took his hand and pulled him to her; he rested his head against hers for a moment. Daniel gave a little whimpering noise. 'That's quite a shock. Look, let's go home. You need a cup of tea.'

He pulled back a little and looked at her. 'Thanks, baby, but . . . I should see Ike. He was saying that it's my fault.'

'Ike?'

'No, Christ no. The call. I'm sorry. It's just . . . He seemed to think that if I hadn't been to see him he'd still be alive.'

'Daniel, shush – just a minute. But that's nonsense. You don't even know how he died.'

'I don't. I don't know. I need to see Ike. I'm sorry. I . . . Can you manage here?'

'Of course. Why don't we drive?'

'It's OK. I think I'll walk. Will you be OK?'

She took his hand again. 'What if he's not there?'

'He'll be there.'

'All right. Be careful. And don't walk under a truck, for God's sake.' She looked at him, gripped his hand and then let go.

It takes half an hour, more or less, to walk from Primrose Hill to Well Walk in Hampstead. For all his urgent need to understand what had happened, Webster walked slowly, and it took him forty minutes. He wanted to recover himself before he got to Hammer's house, and to make some calls. First, as he walked along, he used his phone to search the Internet for any reporting of Gerstman's death. Nothing. He thought the newswires might have had it by now. Then he called Istvan in Budapest, and asked him to find out what he could from his former colleagues in the police. He called people in Germany to see whether news had reached there. Then he searched his mind for others to phone, as if by casting as many lines as possible he could improve the chances of discovering that he wasn't to blame. But there was no one else. He would simply have to wait.

Prock's theory wasn't logical, of course. If Gerstman had actually revealed something, if their meeting had been clandestine, if it had been significant in any way, then perhaps it would have made sense. Gerstman must have known things – after all, that was why Webster had wanted to talk to him – but enough to make him dangerous? It seemed so unlikely. This rising anxiety wasn't logical either, but rise it did. He imagined Gerstman being tailed by sinister men in silhouette and then shot, strangled, poisoned, his tanned skin growing pale and rigid. How slow he had been, how stupid not to realize that violence was lurking so close. That, of course, is what Inessa's article should have told him. It was a sign that he had almost wilfully ignored.

Slowly he climbed towards Hampstead through ever older, ever greener streets, the world around him still vivid in the coming dusk, the colours richer in the half dark. In the absence of facts, ideas and images churned inside him. Inessa pulled from her hotel room by uniformed men, Gerstman dragged from his by dark, shapeless forms. They fitted together, these stories; they were of a piece.

Hammer's house seemed to glow beside its neighbours. It was a brick building of four storeys, not counting the attic floor where his housekeeper lived; three centuries old, narrow, its bright mortar and clean red bricks gave it an almost colonial look. Most of its windows were Georgian sashes but a large wooden oriel, painted white with three pointed ogee windows, hung over the street from the second floor. The place was much too big for Hammer, thought Webster, who coveted its position and its splendidly entitled views across London to the City. Down in the lowlands of Kensal Green this would be seen as grandeur indeed. He had often wondered whether the whole house was used; he suspected that room after room simply stored old newspapers and books of military campaigns. Did Hammer entertain? Did he have house guests? Surely not.

Webster gave a brisk rap on the knocker. Hammer answered the door. This was strange because Mary, his housekeeper, usually had Mondays off. Webster, noticing this, wondered irritably what it would take for his habit of trivial observation to switch off.

'Ben. Come in.' Hammer betrayed the faintest surprise, the merest crease of a frown. Webster was grateful for the plain greeting. He didn't need to be told that he looked terrible or asked what was the matter. Hammer was wearing a thick cardigan of muddy beige with a shawl collar, his glasses propped on his forehead. He led Webster into his study. Either side of the fireplace was an armchair, and by the further one, on a low table by a cheap spotlight, lay a thick hardback, open and face down. Books lined the walls on old oak shelves and occupied much of the floor in ambitious columns. In between them sat lower piles of newspapers, journals and magazines. There was a fire laid in the hearth but it hadn't yet been lit and the room was cold. Hammer sat down in his chair and Webster sat opposite, keeping his coat on.

'Where would you like to start?' asked Hammer, as ever asking the pertinent question. Webster told Hammer about the call, and Gerstman; about the content of their meeting in Berlin, again, as near verbatim as he could, and Prock's accusation; about Prock's fury and his own attempts to understand whether there could be anything in it; about the calls he had made to Berlin and Budapest. The ordering of his thoughts made him calmer.

When he was done Hammer sat for a moment. He took off his glasses and cleaned them with a cloth.

'Mary's gone to the store,' he said, putting them back on. 'We're out of milk. When she's back she can make us tea.' He looked at Webster for a while, then said, 'Let's talk about you first. Then the case.' He took his glasses off and put them on the table by his chair. 'We'll find out soon how he died. It may not be murder. But if it is, the method should suggest the motive. If he was shot by a woman, that's one thing; if he was poisoned with an umbrella, that's another. Assuming it's the latter, where does that leave you? Prock's theory seems to be that Gerstman knew something dangerous, and that he was killed by someone who feared that he was about to reveal it. To you. Or would in time. Let's say that's the case. You hardly spoke to the guy, so the people who had him killed were already nervous. The safety was already off. So your role is minimal, almost accidental. It could have been a journalist, it could have been some other investigator – or some chance meeting that got interpreted the wrong way. As yours might have been, incidentally.' He was leaning back in his chair, his legs crossed, playing with a pencil. 'They could have been going to kill him anyway, regardless. So you're the catalyst, at worst, but you're not the cause, and the whole thing was so delicate you couldn't possibly know what you were setting off. Like a landmine with a faulty mechanism – you just happened to get too close. Assuming, of course, that you set anything off.'

He paused, looking at Webster with his plainest expression. 'So you didn't kill him. That's really important, Ben. I'm not just saying that someone else stabbed him or shot him. What killed him was in his life for years before today.'

'I got over-excited and blundered around. For my own benefit. I set it off.'

'Listen, I told you to go. Right? Sooner rather than later. And I won't feel guilty if Prock turns out to be right. Which, by the way, we'll probably never know for sure, the way these things go. And you know why? I didn't introduce Dmitry Gerstman to Konstantin Malin. I didn't bully him into taking a job that compromised him the moment he took it. I didn't encourage him to think he could leave that behind. That's what killed him.' Hammer smiled. 'If, of course, that's what killed him.'

Webster heard keys turning in the front door lock and at the same time his phone rang. Number unknown. He looked at Hammer and answered it.

'Hello,' said the voice on the other end. 'This is Istvan.'

Webster put his hand over the phone, told Hammer who was calling, and left the room. He managed to smile at Mary as he passed her in the hall, and took himself into the dining room. Ten minutes later he returned to Hammer's study and reported.

At 2.37 a.m. Dmitry Gerstman had fallen from the roof of the Hotel Gellért in Budapest and died instantly. Cause of death had not been formally established but superficial examination suggested he had been killed by the fall. He had not been staying at the Gellért but at the Four Seasons. He had checked in there on Friday morning, and was due to check out on Tuesday – he had a flight booked back to Berlin at 6.55 p.m. on that day. He appeared to have fallen from the roof itself rather than from one of the rooms, although tests to determine how far he had fallen would confirm that. Police had found no sign of any struggle at any of the points from which he could have fallen. None of the hotel staff on duty remembered seeing him enter the hotel; in fact, no one remembered seeing him in the hotel at all. Guests had not been systematically interviewed. He had left no note, but had emailed his wife from his BlackBerry half an hour before he died. The message had simply read, 'Goodbye. I'm sorry. Dmitry.' When the German police had informed Mrs Gerstman of her husband's death at around 8.30 a.m. Berlin time, she had already received the message and had been trying to call him on his phone and at the Four Seasons. She had notified the German police. The BlackBerry itself had been found smashed in his inside jacket pocket. He had been wearing a suit but no coat, even though it had been a cold night.

'Why was he there?' said Hammer.

'In Budapest? That's a little garbled. The Germans have been speaking to his wife and to Prock but I think something's being lost in translation. He had two clients in Hungary, one in Budapest, the other in Miskolc. He had dinner with one of them on Friday but it's not clear which one. He had meetings in his diary for Monday and Tuesday but that's all I know.'

'And what was he doing that night?'

'They don't know yet. They're trying to put his movements together now. I've asked Istvan to keep an eye on it.'

They sat for a few moments in silence. Webster realized that, ridiculous though it was, Hammer's conclusion was important to him. It held the promise of absolution.

'Does that sound like suicide to you?' asked Hammer.

Webster sighed. 'No. No, it doesn't. Might you email your suicide note? I suppose so. The coat seems strange but if you're going out to kill yourself maybe you don't think about coats. I don't know. A hotel just seems an odd place to choose. Particularly when you're staying in another hotel. Why not just throw yourself out of your own window?'

'Maybe he'd had a bad experience at the Gellért.'

'Thanks.'

'Sorry. What about him? Was he the type?'

'He wasn't exactly cheerful but . . . I don't know. He was fit. Obviously fit. Like a serious runner or a rower or something. But more than that he seemed driven. Purposeful.'

'Depressed?'

'Not at all. He was scared about something, clearly, looking back, but not depressed. No, I'm fairly sure.'

Hammer chewed on his pencil. Then he got up, rooted around on the mantelpiece, found some matches and crouched to light the fire. It took a single match to get the rolls of newspaper burning. He stood up and watched the kindling begin to crackle and take.

'Should have done that when you arrived. Sorry. Do you want to take your coat off? No?' Sitting back in his chair he looked at the ceiling for a moment and closed his eyes. He sat like that for perhaps a minute, then looked at Webster.

'Why was it for your benefit?'

'What?'

'You said you got overexcited. What about?'

Webster looked away and watched the fire for a moment, taking off his watch and rubbing his wrist. This wasn't something he had wanted to discuss with Ike, but he hadn't stopped to consider why. Now he knew: it was foolish, and he felt faintly ashamed.

'It doesn't matter.'

'Is it that article?'

Webster nodded. 'It's been hard to leave it alone.'

Hammer waited for Webster to look up. 'You're not thinking straight. You'll never know who killed her, unless someone tells you. Was it Malin? He's a candidate, sure. But it's gone. It's too long ago. You'll never know. But on this case – you'd have seen Gerstman anyway. The job is to finish Malin, whatever he might have done ten years ago. That's the best justice you're ever likely to get.'

Webster held his watch in his hands and studied the second hand ticking round before putting it back on his wrist, squeezing the clasp shut and sitting back in the chair. Hammer went on.

'For what it's worth, I'd be amazed if he killed himself. Either way you shouldn't blame yourself, but you will, for a bit. But that's not important. What's important is what happens to Lock. If you put Gerstman at risk then presumably Lock is in danger too. And he'll know that. He'll be scared. That may be why Gerstman died. So we have a choice. Do we keep pushing Lock? Or do we leave him, even though we may be the best hope he has of a future?'

Until that moment, Webster hadn't realized that this, of course, was where the conversation would end: with him agreeing to go on with the case or walking away from it for good. He had come here wanting to hear that Gerstman's death was not his fault. He hadn't even thought about his responsibility to Lock.

Hammer waited patiently for his response. I know what he wants me to say, thought Webster. Never back away. Finish what you start.

'I think we should stop work,' he said at last. Hammer, his face lit by the fire, said nothing. 'I don't want to set off any more mines. No more meddling. I think we should have known how big this was. I'm sorry.'

Webster stood up, apologized again, and left the room and Hammer's house. Outside it was dark. He set off on the walk home, down the hill and west for two or three miles. No more meddling. This reckless campaign was over, its casualties already too great.

That night Webster dreamed short, stark dreams that never resolved. In one, he sat with Lock in a rowing boat on a narrow river heavily shaded by trees. He had the oars and was rowing with a slow, regular stroke while Lock, opposite him, in a black suit and a floppy red bow tie, talked happily about his life in the South Seas, as if he were Stevenson or Gauguin. Then Lock's face tensed and he gripped the sides of the boat; Webster felt himself tipping backwards as the river fell sharply downwards behind him. When he woke the back of his head was wet with sweat.

CHAPTER SEVEN

After Gerstman's death Lock's imagination began to work again. It had never been energetic but at some point, in Russia, without his noticing, it had simply switched off. He had never really needed it, nor missed it, but when he found out what had happened to Dmitry Gerstman it came irresistibly back to life, resist though he might.

The scene always played backwards, in stages. He heard screams from a guest. He saw the doormen stop with bags in their hands. He saw the broken body flat on the flagstones outside the hotel, the dark suit covering it still strangely pristine. He heard the short heavy slam as it hit. But most vivid was Gerstman in the air, falling, not far, about fifty feet, perhaps for only a second or two. The image sat squarely in his mind, and he wondered whether his friend knew as he fell, as any sane man had to suspect, that his death was no accident.

As he set off to his regular meeting with Malin the day after the news this was all that was in his head, vivid and continuous. He had very little to report: from reading newspapers online he had discovered only that Dmitry had fallen to his death, and that alcohol was suspected to have played a part. The police were treating his death as suicide. Lock was not.

Lock's office was on Kozhevnichesky pereulok, two miles down the Moscow River from the Kremlin and the Ministry of Industry and Energy. Every Tuesday he would go downstairs at 7.15 p.m. and his driver would take him to the ministry. There at eight he would brief Malin on the events of the week, always following the same agenda: Events, Opportunities, Threats. The meeting would last half an hour, sometimes forty-five minutes. There had been a time, before Malin had become the man he had become, when they would have dinner afterwards, but for many years now Lock had simply had his driver take him home.

This evening, though, he felt like walking. This was unusual. He was no walker, and Moscow didn't encourage a casual stroll. But after a day of sitting and worrying his back ached and his head ached and he longed for air and movement. And he had a call to make.

He set off for the river, joining it at Novospassky Bridge, and walked north along its west bank. A frost was beginning to set in, and in his thin raincoat he felt underdressed; he quickened his step to compensate. Beside him queues of cars breathed grey fumes into the air and across the water the low, white, martial walls of the Novospassky Monastery, sparsely floodlit, shone amber in the dark through bare, scrubby trees. But the cold was exhilarating and Lock was reminded that on nights like these, when real cold first steeped the city after its airless summer, even he could find it beautiful.

He took one of his phones from his coat pocket and found the number for his father. It was his birthday today. Lock should have called him that morning but hadn't. Somehow speaking to his father from the office was too jarring, like calling home from the bed of your mistress.

He pressed the key and after a long pause the line began to ring.

'*Hallo, met Everhart.*'

'Happy birthday, father. It's Richard.' Lock spoke English to his father; his Dutch hadn't been strong since he was young.

'*Dank u*, Richard. It's good of you to call.'

'Not at all. How are you?'

'I'm well, thank you.' Everhart tended to terseness on the phone. He saw it as a device to exchange information, no more.

'Did you get my card?'

'I did. Thank you.'

There had been a time when Lock, newly rich, would buy his father expensive presents: a watch, a fountain pen. After the third year his father had told him that he didn't need anything and had asked him to stop.

'Have you had a good day?' Lock's hand, exposed to the northerly wind that whipped down the river, was already stiff with cold.

'Yes. I walked to Zandvoort.'

'Not there and back?' Zandvoort was at least a dozen miles from Noordwijk.

'I took the bus back. It was a beautiful day.'

'Good, I'm glad. What about this evening? Are you doing anything?'

'Maartje is coming to cook for me.' Maartje lived in Noordwijk. Lock got the impression that she and his father saw a lot of each other.

'Good. Well, happy birthday.'

'Thank you for calling, Richard. Goodbye.'

'Goodbye.'

For a moment Lock felt that faint, residual sadness he felt whenever they spoke. He had no idea whether the call he had just made would please his father or sadden him too. It was this unknowability that was so wearing.

It wasn't enough to distract him, though, from what had occupied him all day: Gerstman and Malin. Questions pressed against him, but one kept returning. Why would he want Gerstman dead? Why would Malin, so powerful, so safe in Russia, want his former underling dead? Dmitry had left years before, and had never done anything to suggest he was a threat. He was too clever for that.

After twenty minutes, as he crossed the river, his face now stinging with cold, the immense, impassable red wall of the Kremlin came into view. So much of Moscow felt fortified. The whole city could seem like a castle, the Kremlin the keep, the rest a vast bailey of peasants paying homage. Perhaps, he thought, despite that precise sense of dread in my stomach, Malin had nothing to do with this. After all, no one really knew what Dmitry had been doing in Berlin; he had had time enough to make enemies there. By the time Lock arrived at the ministry, an entirely nondescript building behind the gaping space that had once been the Rossiya Hotel, he had convinced himself that it made no sense for Malin to have killed Gerstman. It wasn't logical, and Malin was always logical.

In the lobby he stated his business to a security guard behind a glass screen and surrendered his passport. He walked through a metal detector and was accompanied by another guard to Malin's office, up two flights of stairs and along a broad, bare corridor. He knew the guard, and all the guards knew him.

He was a little early. He sat in his usual seat in the anteroom to the office and waited, making halting small talk with Malin's secretary. At twenty-five past eight Malin's door opened and a slight, canny-looking man came out carrying a briefcase. He had a mild stoop and his neck looked unnaturally taut from the effort of looking up.

'Alexei.'

'Richard.' They shook hands. This was Alexei Chekhanov, Lock's opposite number. If Lock was offshore, Chekhanov was Russia. He ran Malin's business there; he had no title, but his job, in effect, was chief executive of Malin Enterprises ZAO. As Lock had come to understand it through observation over the years – it had never been explained to him –

Chekhanov made money for Malin in Russia and oversaw how that money was invested. When a foreign oil company paid over the odds for an exploration licence, Chekhanov set the price and handled the arrangements. When the resulting profit needed investing, Chekhanov saw that it was wisely spent. When that investment threatened to go awry, it was he who made sure that it did not. He was the more important man by far but had the decency to treat Lock as an equal.

'That was a long one,' said Lock. 'How is he?'

'We had a lot to discuss. This is a busy time.'

'You too? All good, I hope?'

'Yes, everything is good. I need to see you soon. There are things we need to discuss.'

'Anything interesting?'

'It is always interesting. A company in Bulgaria. Maybe something to sell in Kazakhstan. We will see.'

'Fine. Call me.'

'Very good. You should go.'

'I should. Good to see you, Alexei.'

Lock held his hand out, a little awkwardly, and they shook again. He knocked lightly on Malin's door and went in. It was not a large or opulent office. Malin was reading some papers laid out on his desk, which was otherwise bare: a glass of water, a row of pens, no computer. On the wall behind the desk were two photographs: in one he was shaking hands with Yeltsin, in the other with President Putin. A third frame held his Order of Merit for the Fatherland, an eight-pointed star with a double-headed eagle in gold at its centre.

'Good evening, Richard.' Malin did not look up. 'Please, sit.'

Lock watched him read. Was this an evil man? Behind those blank eyes what was there? Blackness? A cold hatred? Efficiency, thought Lock. A single-minded commitment to an end. What end, he had never known.

Malin finished reading and put the document lightly to one side.

'How are you, Richard?'

'I'm fine, thank you. A little shaken. You know. But fine.'

'It was a great shock. He was young and it was not his time. It is never pleasant when this happens.' Malin paused and looked at Lock, who despite himself looked down at his lap. 'I have heard no more since yesterday.'

'I haven't found out a great deal, I'm afraid. He fell from the roof of the Hotel Gellért in Budapest, apparently. The police think it was suicide. I don't know much more than that to be honest. I'm waiting for a call from Colonel Bashaev.'

Malin considered the information for a moment.

'If Dmitry had a failing,' he said at last, 'it was that he was emotional about business. He was emotional about all things.'

Lock didn't know what to say. This seemed unfair to Gerstman, who had always seemed, if anything, a zealous rationalist.

'Did you send flowers?' Malin asked.

'Yes,' said Lock. 'To his office.'

'Good. Good. I was sorry to lose Dmitry. He was an effective worker. But in business it is important to keep one's head, and he did not, I think. He did not.' Malin shook his head slightly, a gesture of considered regret. 'This you must remember, Richard, especially now.'

Malin's gaze seemed to deepen. Lock, lost in it for a moment, managed to respond only with a weak, 'Yes.'

'Do you understand?'

'I understand. You know I do.'

'I know you do.' Malin let Lock shift in his stare for a further second or two, then asked, 'When is Paris?'

Paris. God, he had forgotten about Paris. A day or two of lying under oath. With an audience.

'It's next week. I go to London tomorrow to have a final run-through with Kesler.'

'How is Mr Kesler?'

'Good, I think.' He had spoken to Kesler three times in the previous week, each time to talk through some new materials that had to be absorbed before he gave testimony. In fact, Kesler, for the first time since Lock had known him, was beginning to sound exasperated; his last words had been that they had a great deal of work to do in London. Had he told Malin this directly? 'He seems to think we can convince the tribunal that Tourna's claim is vexatious. Let's hope so.'

'But he is expecting that you will be questioned about the facts?'

'Almost certainly, yes.'

'And your position will be that I do not exist?'

'Our position – my position will be that I own Faringdon.'

Malin made a soft, low noise, something between a snort and a grunt.

'How did you come by it?'

'Faringdon? Well, you can trace the history back through the companies, all the way back to Arctec. My name is on everything. Ostensibly I own the lot anyway, always have done.'

Malin propped his elbows on his desk, clasped his hands together and rested his chin on them. He thought for a moment.

'This makes you a big man in Russia.'

'They can't prove that I'm not.' Lock knew what he meant. Who would believe such a thing? 'That's the point.'

'All right. All right. Any more on Tourna?'

'Nothing interesting. I'm going to see the London guys this week. Bashaev is promising me good stuff for when I get back.'

'It would have been good to have something before Paris.'

Malin pinched the skin on his chin with his thumbs. Then he sat back and looked hard at Lock. 'You have worked hard for this, Richard, for a long time, but in one moment so much can be undone. A whole life can be undone. For you and for me.'

Lock didn't respond.

'I think that's all now, Richard. Concentrate on Paris. Do not let Dmitry's death distract you.'

Lock said that he would not, got up from his seat, agreed to see Malin in a fortnight and left. As he walked out of the office he could feel Malin's eyes on his back and a chill ran across it. A life undone.

Bashaev called Lock in his office the next morning. He confirmed what Lock already knew and added some new, jarring details. A post-mortem had revealed that Gerstman had had a blood alcohol level of 0.4 per cent, enough to render him more or less senseless. At midnight, about two hours before he died, he had been seen in the Black Cat, a gay bar ten minutes from the Gellért. He had seemed crazed: according to one witness, 'beside himself'. No one was with him. The police hadn't been able to establish when he had left the club, or what he had done between there and the Gellért. He had emailed his wife a suicide note five minutes before he jumped. The police were now convinced that he had died as a result of suicide or misadventure and were not expecting to investigate further.

For Lock, who had spent a dark night dwelling on Malin's words and convincing himself again that now more than ever he was indispensable, this news was disabling. Dmitry didn't drink. He never had. Lock had never seen him drink so much as a single beer. He was famous for it throughout Malin's team. Could he have been gay? He had never been at home in

Moscow, that was true: whenever Lock had seen him there people had ribbed him about his running, about his sharp suits, about not drinking vodka. Lock imagined that others who had known Gerstman would nod their heads when they heard the news and congratulate themselves on knowing all along. But he and Nina had always seemed real. They were close, natural – Lock had seen it. Could you fake that?

In the end, thought Lock, I'm not subtle enough to think this through. What I do know is that in Russia there are few accidents. I'm wise enough to know that. And I can't simply wait for one to happen to me.

That evening, before leaving for London and Paris, Lock took Oksana to dinner at Café Pushkin. On his way to meet her he thought about something Kesler had asked him: if you wanted to prove Malin was corrupt, where would you look? That, surely, was what the whole thing was about. If Malin had ordered Gerstman dead, it wasn't because he objected to his drinking habits or his sexual preference. Gerstman must have known something. That much was clear.

What was less clear was how much Lock himself really knew; murkier still, what Malin thought he knew. Less than Gerstman, surely? Maybe not. Perhaps he knew all manner of things but didn't understand their significance. If that was true, he risked meeting with an accident for no reason at all. After all these years being governed by others he had no desire to end his days so powerless. So he had a choice: he could show Malin that he was no threat, or he could become a threat after all.

His car sat in lanes of traffic on Tverskaya. He looked out of the window at the boxy Ladas and bulky ZiLs around him; even in his own BMW the petrol fumes were thick. What would a Russian do? A Russian never did anything for a single reason. That was one important principle. And he never revealed his true position. He was two-faced: he showed one to the world and the other he hid. Lock had never learned this trick. If his Russian colleagues had laughed at Gerstman's softness they undoubtedly laughed still at Lock's naivety. But here, surely, was an easy opportunity to exploit that. If he could convince Malin that he was harmless while building up what he knew, that must be sensible. A dossier. That was what he needed. That's what people in his position did, drew up a secret file, to be deployed when necessary – with luck, perhaps never. And after all, what else did he have, except what he knew?

Lock felt a new energy inside him. He had had an idea: for the first time in years, a positive idea about his own fate. Now all he had to do was find the courage to act on it.

Café Pushkin was a recreation of a rich Russian's town-house from the first twenty years of the nineteenth century. It was pedantically, absurdly authentic: huge, worn flagstones covered the ground floor and wood panelling the walls throughout. The cloakroom, in the cellar, was appropriately dank. In the library, on the first floor, where Lock had booked his table, and where real oak bookshelves held real Russian books, a brass telescope and a Victorian globe sat by huge sash windows, as if the owner of the house, an amateur scientist perhaps, had merely stepped outside for a moment and invited you to improve yourself while he was gone. From the cream-white walls brass sconces gave out fake candlelight. Lock liked it here because in amongst the fashionable Russians, who more than a decade on still came here, were tourists and even middle-class Muscovites celebrating. It felt democratic in a way that much of Moscow did not.

It took them a while to find his reservation but then it always did. He waited patiently while his waitress, dressed in a burgundy waistcoat and apron, slowly extracted it from the computer, an ugly anachronism in the warm light. Finally he sat, and ordered a gin and tonic. Oksana would of course be late. He read the menu: Russian food: blinis, pelmeni, solyanka, borscht, caviar, sturgeon, stroganoff. He would have the solyanka as he always did, and then maybe some duck. His drink came, and he poured a small amount of tonic into the glass: like the water and the wine, he told himself.

If he moved his flight to the evening he could make a start on his file tomorrow morning. All he needed to do was download everything on the network. It would probably fit on a single memory stick – two at the most. That would leave a record, of course, but he was the administrator of the system and in all his time working for Malin no one had ever inspected it. And he could always say that he'd needed to take it all to London and Paris. He should make a copy or two, and leave them somewhere secret but accessible. One in Moscow, one in London perhaps. Marina could look after one. If this was one of those thrillers I half-heartedly read, he thought, I would entrust one to my lawyer and have him publish it should anything terrible happen to me, but I don't have a lawyer and even if I did no one would publish the little I know. We could always vanity-publish. He smiled at the thought, wondered whether Oksana would be much longer and ordered another drink.

That is the problem with this scheme, he thought. My value to Malin relies solely on my not being him. I don't actually know very much. I'm not important enough to know things. The one devastating thing that I know is that I'm a fraud, but that in itself is not enough to finish Malin. And the hard irony is that Malin probably doesn't know that – or can't afford to believe it. He thinks I'm more dangerous than I am.

His second drink arrived. He looked at his watch. Twenty past. Oksana could be another twenty minutes. He sipped his gin and tried to remember what she had been doing that day; there was something at the university. He couldn't, and returned to his new project. How to find out how Malin stole? For a long time he considered this without a single thought occurring to him. God, he thought: I am no spy.

As he tilted his head back to finish the last of his drink he saw Oksana arrive, stately in black, a head taller than the waitress who led her to the table. For a moment it occurred to him that she would make a perfect accomplice. She had poise and coolness enough for the both of them. He stood to greet her and they kissed. On his empty stomach the gin was making him feel warm and slightly giddy. He ordered another and a vodka for Oksana. She looked around the room and took a long time to settle herself on her chair; she seemed exercised about something. Her long nails, painted a deep red, rapped on the tabletop.

'You look amazing.'

'Thank you, Richard. This is a good table.'

'Of course. How was your day?'

'Hm. Not so good. Unbelievable in fact. I need that drink.' She looked round for the waitress.

'She'll be here soon. What's wrong?'

'Nothing.' She met his eye but couldn't hold it. 'Just a bad day.'

'Tell me.'

She sighed. 'All right. Christ. It's that little fucker Kovalchik. I had a review with him today, you remember?' Lock gave a grave little nod. 'I hadn't seen him since the summer, not since I decided to include those chapters on the Gulag. So we go over the new plan, and he tells me that the Gulag is not a "profitable" area of research. Too many people have already written about it, apparently. Academic exhaustion. But you can't write about . . . ah, at last. Bring me another, please.' She took her shotglass, held it up to Lock, and knocked it back. 'You cannot write about displacement without mentioning the Gulag. Hundreds of thousands of people began life – if you can call it that – began life in Kazakhstan because they were sent to the gulags. Idiot.' She played with her empty glass. 'Idiot.'

Lock waited for a moment to see whether she had finished. Could he not discuss his plan with her? She was from Almaty. She was a foreigner, more or less. 'So what does that mean?'

'That means I have to go back to the original plan and scrap everything I've done for the last three months. Or I carry on and risk being failed.'

'Would he do that?' He should talk to her. She might be the difference between doing it and just thinking about it for ever. When they had finished discussing Kozlovsky or whatever his name was he would test the ground.

'Oh yes. Yes, he would. He's a nasty little shit.'

'Who does he report to?'

Oksana gave a hard, short laugh. 'Maybe I could have him sacked?'

'No, that's not what I mean. Do you have any right of appeal? Can someone have a word with him?'

'He's my professor. If I piss him off I won't get another one.' She had stopped fidgeting now and looked at him with a coldness he didn't enjoy. 'Not every problem can be solved by finding a bigger bully, Richard. Even in Russia. You should understand that.'

'What do you mean?'

'I know who you are, Richard. You have a pretty unpleasant boss of your own.'

'I don't follow you.'

'Never mind. Never mind. Let's just have a nice dinner like we always do. You can pretend to be interested in my thesis.'

'I am interested in your thesis.'

She laughed again. 'You know, when I first met you I liked you. We have an arrangement, I know that, but I liked you.

Here's a man, I thought, who knows things, who doesn't care only for money. Here's a man with self-respect. And then I see the papers and I see what you do. For that slug. It saddens me, Richard. I can't tell you how much. You should have been more than this.'

She held his eye for a moment and then stood up.

'I'm sorry, Richard. I didn't want to be disappointed by you. Let me know if I owe you anything.'

Lock watched her as she walked away, betraying no emotion in her even stride. The waitress came and put new drinks on the table. Lock drained Oksana's vodka and sat for some time watching the space she had left.

'My name is Richard Lock.'

'Thank you, Mr Lock. And can you tell us in what capacity you are here today?'

'I am here as a representative of Faringdon Holdings, one of the companies named in Mr Tourna's complaint.'

'Very good. Let me start with some establishing questions. What is Faringdon's business, Mr Lock?'

'Faringdon is a private energy business that invests in oil and gas in the former Soviet Union. We own stakes in companies in Russia and Kazakhstan, mainly.'

'And what is the turnover of the group?'

'That's commercially confidential. I would prefer not to answer that.'

From the end of the table Kesler gave a small nod of approval.

Across from Lock, Griffin resumed. 'And what is your role in the company, Mr Lock?'

'I am a shareholder.'

'The sole shareholder?'

'I would prefer not to answer that. I own a majority holding in the company. That shareholding is structured through various offshore companies in order to minimize my tax obligations.'

'Legitimately minimize,' said Kesler.

'Sorry, legitimately minimize my tax obligations. I don't see that the exact shareholding structure is relevant to Mr Tourna's claim. I own a majority position and am authorized to speak on behalf of all shareholders.'

'Good,' said Kesler. 'OK. That's how it's likely to start. If I was Greene I'd want to look at your career, the founding of Faringdon, how it's grown. I'd leave the charges until last. That's probably how he'll play it. Now the main thing to remember is not to be drawn on ownership, not to be drawn on financing. Stick to the version we've established. Let's deal with the background now. We can go through the charges tomorrow. Lawrence, please continue.'

It was Friday, and Lock was back in the offices of Bryson Joyce drinking his second cup of stale coffee. He, Kesler and Griffin were sat around a table in a small, hot meeting room. Thursday had been final coaching; today and tomorrow, mock questioning; Monday, Paris. He would have preferred to have been anywhere else. Kesler was annoying him. His manner was now openly critical. He, thought Lock, is the despairing impresario to my talentless gangster's moll. Every mistake Lock made he felt less like the client and more like a liability. If this exercise was meant to give him confidence it seemed set to fail.

At least this was work, and at least this was London, and the two together helped to distract him from Oksana. He was surprised by how keenly he felt the loss of her; he had expected that arrangement to be easier to break. But what hurt more, of course, was that she was right, as Marina had been, and blunt, as Marina had not.

'So, Mr Lock. Can you help us all, please, by giving an account of your career to date? It would be useful to know how you came to Russia and what business you have had there.'

The problem is, thought Lock, that Griffin is being much too polite. Will it be this genteel on Monday? Presumably Lionel Greene didn't get to be the man he is by talking to his witness like the local parson. Nevertheless, as Lock went through his answers he didn't mind. Overall he would rather be roughed up only once.

And so the day went on, Griffin asking neat questions and Lock delivering neat answers. After an hour or so Lock's mouth was dry and he had become conscious of the flat monotone of his voice. Two days of this.

'And how would you describe yourself, Mr Lock? In business terms.' Griffin seemed to be enjoying calling him Mr Lock.

'What do you mean?'

'I mean, what sort of a businessman are you?'

'I'm a private equity investor. I invest in private companies at any stage of their history. Usually I take a majority stake. While I hold my investments I work with the management of the company to optimize value.' All carefully scripted, to within an inch of being meaningless.

At lunch, Lock left Bryson's office and walked towards the Barbican, which rose boldly above the City like the relic of some strange and ancient civilization. He lit a cigarette, regretted it instantly and stubbed it out. The day was grey and warm. He called Marina – he should have called her yesterday but he hadn't felt like talking to anyone. A piercing, scrambled digital squall began the call and then the line went dead. He tried again and reached her voicemail straight away.

'Hi, it's me. I got in late last night. Call me. I . . . I'd like to take you to dinner. Tomorrow? I've been thinking about what you said when I was here last. Love to Vika.' It felt strange to be talking about normal things after so long with Kesler. Reluctantly he took himself back to the office, and the barrage continued.

'Can you please describe your relationship with Konstantin Malin?'

'I know him. Anyone who has worked in Russian energy knows him.'

'Would you say that he was a friend of yours?'

'A strong acquaintance, I would say.' Kesler's phrase.

'I see. So you have met Mr Malin?'

'Of course, a number of times.'

'Have you ever done business together?'

'Not personally, no. Faringdon has many dealings with the Ministry of Industry and Energy where Mr Malin works.'

'So Faringdon has never profited from a close relationship with Mr Malin?'

'Certainly not.'

'Really? Your paths certainly seem to cross often enough. Let's take Sibirskenergo ZAO. This is a Faringdon company, yes?'

'We own sixty-eight per cent.'

'We?' Kesler interjected.

'Sorry.' Lock took a breath. 'Faringdon owns sixty-eight per cent.'

Griffin resumed. 'What does it do? Sibirskenergo.'

'It explores inaccessible oil properties in the far north of Siberia. Skip, why are we doing this? We didn't prepare for this.'

'You won't be prepared for everything. That's the point. Carry on, Lawrence.'

'And in 2006 Sibirskenergo won how many exploration licences in that territory?'

'Skip, I don't see the relevance of this.'

'You will. You do. Carry on.'

'How many licences?'

'Four.'

'Who had previously owned the licences?'

'A state-run company called Neftenergo.'

'And how many companies competed for the licences when Neftenergo decided to sell them?'

'None. Well, one.'

'Only Sibirskenergo?'

'Yes.'

'For state-owned assets.'

'Yes.'

'How much was paid? For all four.'

'I'm not at liberty to say. I don't recall.'

'Which? You can't say or you don't know?'

'I can't say.' Lock looked over at Kesler, but Kesler merely nodded at Griffin to continue.

'Does it strike you as unusual, Mr Lock, that four highly valuable licences should be sold to your company without competition?'

'No. I think that's quite normal in Russia.'

'Indeed? Even though it contravenes all guidelines for the sale of state assets?'

Lock had no answer.

'Mr Lock, can you tell me which ministry oversaw the sale of the licences?'

'The Ministry of Industry and Energy.'

'Where Mr Malin works?'

'Yes.'

'Thank you Mr Lock.' Griffin looked at Kesler.

'You see, Richard?' Kesler was somewhere between exasperated and triumphant. 'You never told us about those licences. Can you tell me why?'

'I'd forgotten all about it. It didn't seem relevant.'

'Now Richard, right there is something you're going to

have to stop, by the way. Either you forgot or it wasn't relevant. Either you can't say or you don't know. It can't be both. Say one thing, then stop. Be clear. Understand?'

Lock sighed. He was tired of being scolded. 'Yes. I understand.'

'Now what you say, in this situation, is that you can't recall exactly how much the company paid for the licences – you're too important to know such details – but it was a market rate and you believe that the Russian Audit Chamber approved it. If the tribunal requires exact figures you will get back to them.'

'OK.'

'Don't be afraid to give them less than they want. You're an important man. You can't be expected to know all the details.'

Lock felt the USB memory stick in his trouser pocket: a little over a gigabyte of records, transactions, statements, spreadsheets, memoranda. No, he thought, I know lots of details. But always the wrong ones.

As the tribunal approached, Lock greeted with childish relief any respite from Kesler and the unbroken sequence of questions and commands. He wasn't even safe in his hotel: the Connaught was full and Kesler was staying at Claridge's. So he had to cherish moments of freedom – breakfast in his room, cigarettes outside, phone calls to Moscow (some real, some invented) – and Sunday morning was luxurious: nothing to do until noon, when he would take a cab to St Pancras for the train to Paris.

He had spent the evening before with Marina and Vika. His first idea had been to visit their apartment and take Marina for dinner once Vika had gone to bed, but Marina had suggested they all three go to eat, and that had felt right. He had finished at Bryson Joyce's eerily empty office around six and had met them at Vika's favourite restaurant in

Kensington. The London of neighbourhoods was new to him – he was used to the centre, to Mayfair, to the City, and to seeing what lay between from the windows of taxis – and he felt privileged to be inducted into its quiet, almost secret pleasures. They had eaten burgers, and teased each other, and watched Vika scooping ice cream from a tall glass with a long spoon. The place was full of families doing the same thing, and for an hour or two Lock had forgotten that the evening would end with him returning to his hotel room.

That was always a wrench. He supposed it was the same for Vika, momentarily, and wondered whether Marina suffered too. He had wanted to talk to her after dinner, about Dmitry, about them, but somehow the chance hadn't arisen. Marina had said that it was late, Vika should get to bed, and that had been that. He didn't know which subject she was more keen to avoid. For Lock this was a reverse, but not a serious one. For years he had done his best not to hear Marina when she told him how she felt and now, more and more keenly, if he was being honest, he wanted to know. So he could wait a little longer; he would be here again soon.

But for all that, he would rather have been in Holland Park than packing his bag in preparation for two and a half hours on a train with Kesler. They wouldn't be able to discuss business, that was something, but what would take its place? What did Kesler talk about when he wasn't talking about work? It took a moment for Lock to acknowledge that Kesler might be wondering the same about him.

Kesler was there at reception as he came down to check out.

'Good morning, Richard. Or is it afternoon? Sleep well?'

Lock said that he had, and asked for his bill. With it came a letter, delivered by hand that morning. His name was written in Marina's hand on the envelope.

'A billet-doux?' said Kesler.

Lock felt himself redden. 'No, no. Just some personal busi-ness.' He tucked the envelope inside his jacket and handed his credit card to the receptionist.

On the way to the station, waiting in the business lounge for Griffin to join them (Griffin didn't get to stay at Claridge's at Malin's expense, Lock noted with approval), boarding the train, he could feel the letter against his heart; it seemed to be radiating heat. Only when they had settled in their carriage and the train was well on its way through east London did he feel comfortable enough to excuse himself. He walked through two carriages towards the buffet, sat in an empty seat and opened the letter. It was written in black ink on heavy ivory paper with a distinct grain, the hand delicate but precise, the lines level and evenly spaced. As soon as he saw it he could see all the letters Marina had ever sent him: serious and impassioned before they married; chatty when he was away on some pointless trip; pained and resolute at the end. She had written to him far more often than he had to her; his own letters were inelegant next to hers, and he had always found them hard to write. He wondered whether she had kept them nevertheless, as he had kept hers.

There were three pages, with writing on each side. It was no mere note.

Holland Park
Saturday evening

Dearest Richard

Thank you so much for a lovely evening. I hope you didn't mind changing your plans. It's important to me that the three of us can still have fun together. Vika enjoyed herself, but she is always sad to leave you. In a sense, that's what this letter is about.

When we got home she asked me whether you were happy. I said that yes, you were, but your job was very hard

*and perhaps you had too much to worry about. I tell you this
because knowing Vika she will ask you questions about that,
but also because I found myself thinking how much truth
there was in my words. The difference between you now and
when we saw you in the summer is so marked. There is
something new in your face.*

*I apologize for not talking to you about Dmitry
properly. It's very hard for me. If what you fear is true I have
to accept that a man I once respected – the man who brought
us together – has become something bad. I do not say that it
isn't true – I have a painful feeling that you are right – but
you must understand that it hurts me to believe it.*

*Whether it is true or not I think it tells you something.
The fact that it could be is enough. You are right to be scared.
You may not want to hear this again but now you might truly
hear it: you work for a corrupt man in a corrupt business in
a corrupt country, and it has corrupted you. I do not want
it to finish you.*

Lock stopped here and for a moment watched the city
slowly thinning into countryside. She was right – always,
unerringly – and for once he was in the mood to embrace it.

*You were once a man of curiosity and everything seemed
like a possibility to you. I loved you for this. I loved you for
wanting Russia to change. I loved you for not being scared.
And I loved you for being funny about it all. All our passions
dim, our energy always fades, but your job has done more
than that. It has taken most of you, Richard, and it pains me
so much.*

*I fear two things. I fear that one day I will get a call to
tell me that something terrible has happened to you, and
that I will then have to tell Vika. Since before Dmitry this
has scared me.*

But more than this I fear that before long it will be too

late for you anyway. That everything you once were will be gone. The worst thing they have done to you is convince you that the world is about money and power and oil. That is not you. When I see you make Vika laugh I still know that. This time I thought I saw that you know it too.

When I see that in you, I dare to hope. What a dangerous thing that is. When I imagine the three of us together, I say to myself that I want it because I want Vika to be happy. But it's because I want to be happy, too. It would be easier if you were beyond saving, but you're not.

There is a point to this letter – a practical point. You have to leave Russia. I know this is difficult but it cannot be impossible. I will do whatever I can to help. The plan has to be yours: make it, and let's talk about it. When you're next here. Perhaps I can talk to Konstantin. The spirit of my father is still important to him, I think.

Dmitry's death is a sign, or a signal. There has to be a way. Please find it. I want my fears to be needless.

With all my love still

M.

He held the letter in his hands for a long time, his eyes wandering over the familiar script, and let her thoughts come together in his mind and settle. Without having to think, he knew that she had captured it, as she always did. It was clear, and simple, and complicated beyond words.

CHAPTER EIGHT

It was Wednesday and Gerstman had been dead for three days. Webster had gone to the office but had done little work, and nothing at all on Project Snowdrop. There were a few small cases that needed his attention: a client was buying a ball-bearing manufacturer in the Czech Republic and wanted to know what he was getting; another was wondering why the manager of its Kiev business was losing so much money (because he had been stealing it himself, was the eventual answer). Webster checked on their progress, thanked providence that his team was so good, and spent the rest of the time in his office, thinking formless thoughts about his responsibilities to others and the risks of trying to improve the world. He felt betrayed by his suspicions, by his enthusiasm, but still his theory sat by him, stronger for Gerstman's death, at once goading his powerlessness and tempting him to resume work. Hammer took him for lunch and tried to persuade him to turn his mind back to the case. His colleagues kept a distance.

That evening Webster went to the cinema with Elsa: *Tokyo Story* at The Tricycle. Afterwards they ate at a Japanese restaurant in Hampstead, a tiny place where he and Elsa would sit at the counter to watch the chef at the hibachi. His hands, calloused and red with heat, moved with endless fluency, placing skewers of pork and chicken skin and quails' eggs on the blackened grill, salting and turning them, knowing precisely when they were done. Webster looked at Elsa as she read the menu on the counter. In profile, her head bowed, she looked girlish. Her hair, so dark a brown that it was taken for black, not curled and not straight, hung about her face.

They ordered: some skewers, some sushi, sea bream and mackerel with salt. Sake came in square wooden cups with more salt. They touched them together and drank.

'How was lunch?' said Elsa.

'Good. We went to that dreadful Indian he likes.'

She laughed. 'Empty?'

'One other table. I don't know how they survived before he found it.'

She turned on her chair so she was almost facing him. He continued to look down at his sake. 'And what did he say?'

'You can probably guess.'

'Anything new?'

'Not really.'

'He wants you to go on?'

Webster nodded. 'If I don't, he will.' He turned to look at her. 'There's a lot at stake.'

'I thought you'd made up your mind.'

'I had.' Elsa didn't respond. 'He was very persuasive.'

'As always.'

He paused. 'This isn't like you.'

'What?'

'To be down on Ike.'

'I'm not down on Ike. You know I love Ike. But he wants different things from life.' She paused while a waitress brought two bowls of soup and set them down on the counter. 'He doesn't have children, for a start.'

Webster gave his soup a stir with his chopsticks. Bright little cubes of tofu swam about in the broth. He frowned, not understanding her. 'Where does that come in?'

'I don't want anyone throwing you off a roof.'

'That's silly.'

'Two of you had a conversation in Berlin. A few weeks later one of you is dead. Why aren't you a loose end?'

He laughed. 'They don't kill advisers. They never have. It's too much trouble. And someone else would just pop up in my place.'

Elsa didn't say anything. She looked down at the counter, played with her chopsticks.

He put his hand on her back. 'Are you worried?'

'I don't like it. I know you when you get like this. It's better when you have a case you don't like.'

'If I thought I was in danger I'd stop. But I'm not. Really. After what happened in Budapest there's no way they'll do anything to me. How would it look?'

'Would they care?'

'Perhaps not. But killing an Englishman's a pain in the arse. The police actually investigate. They're not used to it.'

More food came. Elsa took a skewer and began to push the meat onto her plate with her chopsticks.

Without looking at him she said, 'Don't you think you should stop?'

'Yes and no.'

'For decency's sake.'

He hesitated. 'I found an article that Inessa wrote about him. Two months before she died. I never knew about it.'

'So?'

'With him it all makes sense. He had enough to lose. And friends all over government. He could have done it.'

'You think he killed Inessa?'

'He's a candidate.'

Elsa shook her head and sighed. 'This is new. But familiar.'

'It's not important, in a way.' He watched her raise her eyebrows in response. 'I know I'm never going to know. It's not a crusade.'

'No. It's a quest. For some sort of absolution.'

'I shouldn't have just left. You know I regret that.'

'They threw you out.'

'I mean Russia.'

Elsa nodded. 'So this is about justice.'

Webster could feel his ground crumbling. 'I don't know.'

'You attack the big Russian and hope he was responsible.'

'He deserves it anyway. And what if he was? It looks like he's capable of it.'

'What if he wasn't? What do you have? An article and a hunch?'

'If he goes down, things will come out,' he said. 'He won't be protected any more. It could all come out.'

'And how likely is that?'

Webster was quiet. One of the things he loved about Elsa, but didn't always enjoy, was that she allowed him no space to deceive himself. Only in this respect did her work spill over into their lives. She was a psychologist who worked with families, and her commitment to honesty never waned.

A waitress came to clear their bowls and asked if they would like more sake. Elsa smiled distractedly and politely told her no.

'Sweetheart,' she said, leaning in to him and resting her hand on his arm, 'you don't owe him anything. Gerstman. Just like Inessa. Ike's right about that.'

'I think I do.' He picked up his cup, saw it was empty and set it down again. 'It would be nice if someone was held to account. Just once. If not for Inessa then for everyone else.'

Elsa said nothing. He went on. 'Look, I'm going to go to Berlin and see his widow. I have to. And then I see the client next week. He may put a stop to it in any case. We haven't got very far.'

Elsa nodded slowly. 'OK. OK.' She looked him in the eye. 'But you have to promise me that if it gets worse, you stop.

If you think even for a second that you're in danger, you tell me, and you stop.'

He smiled. 'Of course.'

'I'm serious, Ben.'

'I know. I love you for it.'

She laughed, relenting, shook her head, and looked round for the waitress. 'We need another drink.' She turned back to him. 'Wouldn't it be nice to be a baker, or a gardener, or a bank manager? Don't you think? Something simple?'

'I've been thinking just that. All week.'

Nina's street was narrow for Berlin, the buildings tall, and dotted along it were a handful of discreetly expensive shops. You had to look carefully, thought Webster, to realize just how exclusive a neighbourhood this was; not showy, but solid, and moneyed. Webster paid his driver, found number 23 and posted the letter through Nina's letterbox. He had little to do now except wait. He decided to walk back to the hotel. In a few minutes the arbitration hearing will begin in Paris, he thought, and wondered whether he should be there.

This time he took in the city. The day was cold and icy grey and cast a dull, even light over the wide streets. He walked from Charlottenburg, where the wealthy lived in their town-houses, through the old western centre, shabby now, a mess of trams and cars and roadworks, and up to the Tiergarten, where the silver birches had lost all their leaves and reminded him of Russia, of walking in Izmailovsky Park with Inessa and her friends. She would have come here, he thought; she would have seen Nina. Inessa had never knowingly left a story unfinished.

By five he was beginning to think that he wouldn't hear from Nina that day. Perhaps she had left early that morning for the university and hadn't seen his note. He had made no clear agreement with himself about how long to stay in Berlin.

He was due to fly to Paris to see Onder the following evening but he might well change it; the arbitration would go on all week and Onder would be there for much of it. If Nina didn't respond should he see Prock? Against every instinct he probably should. He decided that he would write another note, and deliver it to Prock's office so that he would have it the following morning. He delivered it that evening on his way to dinner.

A little before nine his phone gave a short chime to tell him that he had a text message. *Mr Webster. Please come to my apartment at 9 a.m. tomorrow morning. Thank you. Nina Gerstman.* So she was there. He realized at that moment that he would find it far easier to talk to Prock.

He woke early. By eight he had showered, shaved and dressed in a dark navy suit, white shirt and dark blue tie. Today was a day to look as grave as possible. As he left the room he looked at himself in the mirror. Was that the face he deserved? It looked honest enough to him, but he could hardly judge. His eyes were brown and candid, with specks of green and black; his hair, silver for years now and cropped short, suggested serious, responsible. There were enough flaws in his face to make it somehow convincing: a short scar on his chin where his beard didn't grow, the nose not quite straight. He was plausible, certainly. But it was one thing to convince people that you were trustworthy, and quite another to deserve their trust.

At nine he stood outside Nina's building and rang the doorbell for Flat 12. The sky was still dull. While he waited he looked through the glass doors into the entrance hall, cupping his hands round his eyes to keep out the light. Stone stairs, an art nouveau balustrade, an intricate tiled floor, marble lining the walls up to shoulder height. A woman's voice asked him who he was and buzzed him in. An old lift in its iron cage took him up to the fourth floor and as he pulled the concertina gate back Nina was waiting for him.

She wasn't what he had expected. His research had discovered that she was an academic, a physicist who lectured at Humboldt University, and he had pictured her as small and somehow scientific – glasses perhaps, mousy hair and practical clothes. In fact she was tall, almost his height, and dark, her eyes black and childishly full in a narrow face. She stood with her legs slightly apart, her calves full, her feet turned out like a dancer, and she wore black: a black skirt, black stockings and shoes, a black cardigan over a grey blouse. Webster realized that he hadn't been with someone in mourning since his grandfather had died ten years earlier.

'Frau Gerstman.' He found himself giving a slight bow of the head.

'Mr Webster.'

'Thank you for seeing me. I hope I'm not intruding.'

Nina said nothing but gestured for him to follow her into the apartment. They walked down a long corridor with doors either side, all closed. The floor was golden parquetry, and on the walls hung a series of colour photographs of the modern buildings of Berlin: the Neue Nationalgalerie, the revived Reichstag, several buildings that Webster didn't recognize. They were good, and he wondered whether Nina had taken them. Or Gerstman.

The corridor opened into a bright sitting-room at the far end of the apartment with large windows on two sides. Here there were no photographs but many paintings, abstracts and portraits, hung in clusters.

'Would you like something to drink, Mr Webster?' asked Nina. Her voice was low and dry. Webster thanked her, but no, he was fine. She sat down, quite upright at the front of a deep sofa, and Webster sat opposite in an armchair. On the glass table between them were sales catalogues for auctions of modern art in London and Paris. His chair was low and he struggled to find an attitude that seemed appropriate.

Nina looked at Webster. I wonder what she sees, he thought. In the light her face was pale but for the skin under her eyes, which was a deep purple-grey.

'Thank you for seeing me. I'm grateful,' he said.

'I wanted to see you.'

'I wanted to say first how . . . how sorry I was to hear your news.' The words sounded thin and brittle as he said them.

'Thank you.'

'I heard it from your husband's partner. He called me. He told me that . . .' He hesitated. 'He suggested that my meeting with Dmitry might have brought about his death.'

Nina said nothing.

'It wasn't my intention to cause anybody harm.'

Again, Nina didn't reply, but looked at him steadily all the while. She was composed; Webster felt wholly uncomfortable. He couldn't tell whether she was resigned or calmly furious. Eventually she said, 'I don't know why he died, Mr Webster. I would like the Hungarians to tell me but I think they will not.' She paused. 'Why do you think he died?'

'In a sense I barely knew him. I'm probably the last person who should say.' Webster shifted his position.

'But what do you think?'

'I have a sense that he was murdered.'

'Why do you say that?'

'Because of what I hear from Hungary. Because it was a very strange way to . . . to end it. Because the Hungarians seem to have been quick to make up their minds.'

'I have the same sense. But I would like to know.'

'So would I.'

Nina had her hands clasped in her lap. She loosened them and scratched her forearm lightly.

'That is what I want to know from you, Mr Webster. Why

you want to know. In a way this is not your business. You met Dmitry once. You did not know him.'

Webster had anticipated this. He had an answer prepared, but now it hardly seemed adequate. As he began, a mobile phone began to buzz across a table in the corner of the room.

'Excuse me.' Nina stood and went to pick it up. 'Gerstman.' She walked into the corridor, speaking softly. Webster could still make out what she was saying. The person on the other end of the call talked more than she did. '*Ja,*' he heard her say. '*Nein, nicht jetzt. Ich bin nicht allein. Ja.*' A long pause. '*Das geht Sie nichts an. Ich wollte ihn sehen.*' Webster's German was still good enough to make some of this out. *That's not for you to say. I wanted to see him.* '*Ja, mir geht es gut. Morgen vielleicht. Oder Mittwoch. Ja. Auf Wiedersehen. Auf Wiedersehen.*'

Nina came back into the room and sat down, putting the phone on the glass table in front of her.

'I'm sorry,' she said. 'Just a friend.'

'You must tell me if you'd like me to go.'

'No, it's OK.'

'Thank you.' Webster chanced what he hoped was a sympathetic smile; Nina did not return it. Her face was hard to read. It was stony, set, but not in anger; there was something else there. He tried again. 'You asked me why I'm still interested. I'd like to stop the man responsible.'

Nina nodded. 'And why are you here?'

He had anticipated this, too. 'I'm here because . . . I'm here to say sorry, for anything I might have done.'

'In my work, Mr Webster, it is understood that you cannot see a thing without changing it. It is impossible to simply be an observer. So you have played a part, whatever it might be.'

'That's true.'

'I will be open with you. I am not interested in what you did. Dmitry was never free of Russia. It followed him here. I do not think you brought it. He tried to stop it. He took out insurance. He was very careful. My only interest, all I want to do . . .' For the first time she looked down at her hands. 'All I want is to know how he died.' Tears formed in her eyes. She wiped them away with the back of her hand and sat for a moment looking away from Webster, out of the window to the rooftops beyond. She took a deep breath and went on. 'I do not know whether they are paid to stop investigating, or whether they do not care to. It must be a . . . how do you say it . . . it must be annoying to have a dead Russian from Berlin in your city.' She paused for a moment and looked at him. 'But it is not logical. I know he did not send me that email. I know it.' She leaned forward, rested her forehead in her hands and sat gently shaking her head.

Webster watched her. After some time she looked up at him.

'Frau Gerstman,' he said, 'I have friends in Budapest who tell me what is happening with the investigation. I'm happy to share that information with you.' She looked up, and for the first time her eyes, red with tears, looked curious. 'Very happy.'

'Thank you.'

With a small nod he indicated that he would keep his word. They sat in silence.

'What did you mean by insurance?' said Webster at last.

'I'm sorry?'

'You mentioned insurance earlier. That Dmitry had taken out insurance.'

'I did not know I said that.'

Webster decided not to push it. Instead he asked her whether she knew Richard Lock.

'Richard? Yes, of course. He sent me some flowers. Why?'

'He still works with Konstantin Malin. I worry that if Dmitry was in danger he may be too.' He had tried this line with Nina's husband, and as he said it he felt a pang of conscience; back then he hadn't wholly meant it.

'If he still works for Malin he will be fine.'

'What sort of a man is Lock?'

'A normal man. Dmitry liked him. Mr Webster, I prefer not to . . .' The doorbell rang. Nina looked puzzled for a moment and then she seemed to gather herself, as if preparing for an encounter she didn't relish. 'Excuse me.'

Webster stood as she left the room to open the front door. He heard muffled, urgent exchanges in German, followed by a man's footsteps, heavy and stark on the wood. The man kept talking in a high voice. Webster caught a few words: '. . . *zuerst die Russen und jetzt die Engländer. Zumindest ist er nicht einge-brochen.*' *First the Russians, now the English. At least he didn't break in.* He was still standing when a short, florid man, with a twisted moustache and all but bald, stomped into the room muttering, '*Wo ist er? Wo ist er?*' Seeing Webster he stopped, fixed him with a stare and told him to leave. 'Get out. Go on. Leave.'

Nina, right behind him, took his arm and tried to usher him back out of the room, saying something in German that Webster couldn't make out. The man replied in firm, slightly patronizing tones – '*Hat er Dich auch bedroht? Dann ist es nur eine Frage der Zeit*' – and she let go of his arm. *Has he threat-ened you as well? Then it's only a matter of time.*

'Do you know who I am?' he said to Webster.

'I think so, yes.' Webster had seen him with Gerstman on his first visit to Berlin. He was wearing a tweed suit. His accent was almost grotesquely rich.

'I am Heinrich Prock, Herr Webster. Partner of Herr Gerstman, who is now dead. Perhaps, Herr Webster, when I called you I did not make myself clear. Hm? We want this *out* of our lives. *Out.*' Prock was still emphatic, but in person there was something ineffectual about him, something ridiculous, like a well-groomed little dog with a substantial bark. It occurred to Webster that had he spoken to Prock in person that Sunday in the park he might not have taken him so seriously. '. . . *for ever.*' He went on. 'I do not know who you are working for, or what you want. I do not care. What I care about, Herr Webster, is that this woman is left alone. She has been bothered enough. But you come here, to the flat of a widow, not a week after her husband died, to search for answers of your own. You are no different from the others. Now I would like you to leave before I call the police. Go now, please.' He pointed to the door, an unnecessary gesture.

Nina turned to him and said something in a low voice. Prock responded in an urgent hiss. '*Wann kamen die Anrufe? Vor zehn Tagen? Und dann taucht er auf? Woher weißt Du, dass er nicht für sie arbeitet?*' When were the calls? Ten days ago? And then he shows up. How do you know he isn't working for them?

Webster looked at Nina, who stood with her arms crossed beside Prock. She gave a regretful nod, which seemed to say that she would rather this had ended differently, but that he should go.

Walking past Prock he stopped in front of Nina and said, 'Thank you. If I hear anything from Budapest I'll let you know.' She nodded again and he left. As he walked away he could feel Prock's indignation behind him bursting to be given vent.

After Berlin Webster spent a day in Paris with a hearty Onder, who had seen Lock and had plenty to report, and then flew back to London for a meeting with Tourna the next day, Friday. Despite himself he could feel the case beginning to pull at him again, teasing ideas out of him, leading him on from one place to the next. Firing his imagination. The good ones did this; they wouldn't leave you alone. Nina knew something, he was sure of it – sure, too, that she would part with it if she thought it would truly hurt Malin. He wondered how much of him wanted to find justice for Nina, and how much of him simply had to know.

When he got off the plane from Paris he found a voicemail message waiting for him from Alan Knight. He had called from his Russian phone, which was unusual.

'Ben, this is Alan. It's Thursday. Someone's probably listening but I'm past caring. If they hear this maybe they'll believe me.' He was quiet and hoarse, as if he was losing his voice. 'Just to say we won't be working together again, Ben. Sorry about that. But life here's got a bit difficult. Seems I can't get into the country without spending half a day being asked questions about my clients. Twice it's happened now. I've been advised not to work for Westerners any more, so that's that. Not much I can do about it. I wish there was. Wish I could do something about the tax police raiding my office as well, but no doubt that'll be cleared up soon, eh? These things usually are.' There was a long pause. He thought the message had come to an end. 'So if you're in Tyumen don't look me up, Ben, all right? If it's all the same to you. Best leave me alone for a bit. Best leave well alone.'

He had never heard Knight sound like that. He had complained before about the attention he was given by the security services, about his calls being overheard, but Webster had always assumed that whatever arrangement he had made for himself in Russia was stable. He'd been doing it for so long. He was one of them.

That evening Webster tried to write a progress report for Tourna, and rather to his surprise there was a lot to say. He left out all mention of Inessa. But Knight continued to prey on his mind. He told himself that any one of Alan's jobs could be behind this, that there was no reason to think that his problems had anything to do with Malin, but every instinct in him cried otherwise.

At ten on Friday morning Hammer and Webster sat in the boardroom at Ikertu. Hammer had not run in. This was unusual and Webster wondered what it meant.

'Is he the sort to be late?' said Hammer.

'He was a day late last time.'

'I read the report. You've been busier than you think.'

'Yes, that occurred to me, too.'

'How was Onder?'

'Enjoying himself.'

'You going to tell me about Berlin?'

'It was good. You were right.'

'I didn't want you to go.'

'No, I mean about the whole thing. I feel better. I met my accuser, which helped. He burst in and rescued Mrs Gerstman from me. He was a bit of a buffoon.'

'Good for him.'

'He still doesn't like me very much, but he said something interesting.'

Hammer waited for him to go on.

'How's your German?' said Webster.

'Minimal.'

'Mine isn't what it was, but he said something which caught my ear and clearly wasn't meant to. I think he said, "First the Russians, now the English. At least he didn't break in." And then "Has he threatened you as well? It's only a matter of time."'

'Which means?'

'Someone thinks she knows something. It sounds as if her flat was broken into and they think it was Russians. Or perhaps Gerstman's office. Then as he was ordering me out he said something about calls she'd had in the last ten days.

I didn't get a chance to ask her. I was more or less marched off the premises.'

'Could you call her?'

'Perhaps. I've promised her news from Hungary, if I get any. I don't think she likes me either, but she doesn't seem to hate me.'

The phone on the boardroom table rang. Mr Tourna was in reception. Webster collected him and introduced him to Hammer, who looked skinny and pale beside him. Tourna, pristine in a light tweed jacket, baby-blue cashmere jumper and white shirt, looked as ostentatiously healthy as he had on his yacht.

Hammer was always delighted to meet a rogue and took on most of the small talk; Tourna, like most clients, was charmed. Hammer had a conman's talent for finding a person's passion and appearing to know all about it, and for five minutes he quizzed Tourna about boats, and sailing, and the relative merits of marinas throughout the Mediterranean and beyond.

'No, only sail, Mr Hammer, only sail. I may look vulgar but I despise those floating brothels with their helicopter pads and their swimming pools. You can swim in the sea, no, if you want to swim? Ridiculous. Let me tell you, Mr Hammer, I met a man once in Shanghai. We had been discussing some business. He asked me to come aboard his yacht. You have a yacht in Shanghai I ask, and yes, he says, in the harbour. The most beautiful yacht you will see. Well, there are many ships in Shanghai harbour but not so many yachts, I think. So I go. And there in the harbour is this monstrous big shining cream office block – with a helicopter on it, naturally. And we go on board and there are gold taps and beds in the shape of sea shells. All very tasteful. And I ask my friend, where do you go? And he doesn't understand. I say, where do you take her – because, for the life of me, I cannot think where I would want to sail near Shanghai. And he looks at me for a moment, still not understanding, and then he laughs, and he says, oh no, there's no engine. You can't go anywhere in it. The engine room is empty.' Tourna bellowed out a laugh. 'It's probably still there now!' Hammer laughed too, and Webster gave what he hoped was an enthusiastic smile. 'So, gentlemen,' said Tourna, his face taking on the look of urgency that Webster had seen in Datça, 'how are you getting on?'

They sat at the table. Webster handed out copies of the agenda and his report. Tourna took a minute to scan each document, then set them carefully to one side and looked Webster square in the eye.

'OK. This is interesting. This is nice. But this is not progress. Your fees are killing me. There is more in your invoices than in these reports, that's for sure. You seem to have forgotten what I want.'

'I understand. There have been times in the last few weeks when I've thought we simply couldn't do it.'

'If you can't do it then we stop today. This is not a fishing expedition.'

'I think we can. Let me tell you what I think we've learned. You're right about Malin. He's creaming off more from the Russian state than all his peers. But that's not enough. To prove that you'd need to go deep into Russia, so deep you'd probably never come back. And there's nothing in his past to convict him. No one talks. He owns everyone who might know something.'

'So,' said Tourna, with a glance at Hammer, 'how is that not hopeless?'

'You stop looking at him and look at his organization.' Webster was animated now, leaning forward and tapping his points home on the table. He took a copy of the report, turned it over and with a pencil drew on it a figure of eight on its side – an infinity sign. 'In Russia, he has this big operation, beautifully organized and black as pitch.' He started shading in the right-hand side of the eight. 'You can't see in. It's in there that he steals the money, and it's in there that he runs his investments. But the money has to come out before it can go back in. So in the West, in a hundred offshore companies, is the other big operation.' With his pencil he pointed to the other side. 'More beautiful still, if anything. Layer upon layer. You can get a glimpse of it but you can't get past the front door. And here, where the two sides meet, here sits Richard Lock, looking both ways.'

'So he knows everything?' said Tourna.

'So he knows everything. But better, if anything, without him none of this works. Everything has to go through him.' Webster paused for a second. 'Have you read the updates I've been sending you?'

'I have.'

'Then you know about Dmitry Gerstman?'

'Yes, I do. Nasty business. Around Malin it does not surprise me.'

'It surprised me.' Webster and Tourna shared a look. 'We don't know who killed Gerstman, or if anyone did. But one thing I do know is that Lock is very scared.'

'This is a hypothesis?'

'No, this is fact. We had someone talk to him after he had given evidence in Paris.'

'My God, he was horrible in Paris.' Tourna gave a short bark of a laugh. 'I've never seen anything like it. He started OK, he'd been prepared, but Christ, when our QC got his claws out? It was bloody. Bloody. If I were Malin I'd have called me after an hour and begged to settle. Who spoke to Lock?'

'I can't tell you that.'

'OK. What did he say?'

'He's scared. He knows he did badly this week and he's

scared to go back to Moscow. At least he was; he might be back there by now. I should imagine he's terrified that he's going to be next.'

'He's scared. Good. He should be. So what?'

Webster hesitated for a moment. It crossed his mind that this was an ugly business, trading in a scared man's fear. He went on. 'Malin can't live without Lock. Without Lock the fiction collapses. It's a big lie, and he's the man paid to do the lying. If we persuade him to tell the truth, then it will almost certainly win your lawsuits. Malin has to explain himself to everyone, and his business will be crippled at the same time. All his financing will dry up. Bryson Joyce may have to resign.'

'I don't get it. If Lock gives evidence for us, he's out of a job and he's just made a big fucking enemy. Why would he do it?'

'Because,' Hammer said, 'we're at the stage now where the FBI and a number of others are taking an active interest in Mr Lock's case. I had a conversation with a friend of mine at the Bureau this week and they see great potential in him. In pure dollar terms, he's one of the biggest money-launderers they've ever seen. And I hear from them that the Swiss are having a good look, too.'

Tourna sat back, pushed his chair a foot or two away from the table, and pulled at his bottom lip while he thought. Like Hammer, he was a fidget, but where Hammer tapped and chewed he used his whole body. His leg jigged, he sat forward. As he watched him, Webster wondered whether Hammer had indeed made that call, and if so what had been said. He thought they were holding off until after this meeting.

'Mr Hammer,' Tourna said at last. 'What do you think?'

Hammer put down his pen. 'It's a big opportunity. Like all big opportunities, it comes with risks. The risks here are not really to us. They're to Mr Lock. You risk some fees, we risk reputation, but Lock could be in real trouble. Ben has had a difficult couple of weeks. It's not usual for the people we interview to wind up dead. It's not usual for us to be accused of causing it, either. But I think I've persuaded him that the best way to protect Lock, long term, is to help him out of this mess. He's in way over his head. I can tell. I've seen so many of these guys. Some are tough enough, but he isn't. So one day, something's going to happen to bring Malin's castle tumbling down, and Lock? He's going to wind up dead or in jail. If he's lucky, under house arrest in Moscow. The one way he can avoid that is by seeing the light. I suggest we show it to him.'

For perhaps a full minute Tourna sat pulling at his lip.

'What happens to your fees?'

Webster fielded it. 'We've spent a lot of money so far because we had to have a lot of people doing a lot of work. Where this case is now, the only person billing hours to it is me. We'll probably need some surveillance as well. We're going to need to know where Lock is and what he's doing. When he comes west. But we can scale back the monthly payment quite hard. The success arrangement remains the same.'

'How long do you think you need?'

'I'd say two months,' said Webster, 'perhaps one.'

'What if Lock doesn't go for it?'

'No harm done,' said Webster. Hammer nodded.

Tourna thought for a moment longer, pulling at his lip again.

'This is the only way,' said Webster.

Tourna nodded. 'OK. Let's do it. I want a cap on surveillance, though. I know what that shit can cost. If I need to follow my second wife I'll just give her the money in alimony. It's about the same.' He gave another short laugh and stood up to leave. 'Mr Webster. Mr Hammer, nice to meet you. Do this for me, gentlemen. At any time this looks like not working, stop the clock, yes? I know you're having fun but not at my expense, OK?' Hammer smiled.

Webster saw Tourna out and then returned to the board-room. Hammer was still there, still smiling.

'What was that about the Bureau?' said Webster, half enjoying one of Ike's occasional surprises, half irritated by it.

'Sorry. I meant to tell you before he arrived. I called when you were in Berlin.'

'Are they interested?'

'Oh yes,' said Hammer. 'They are.'

CHAPTER NINE

No one could get you in the air, thought Lock. No one could point out your mistakes. No one could politely criticize your performance. Best of all, no one could treat you with that embarrassed delicacy that suggested you were already incurable.

It was only a brief recess. Four hours from Paris to Moscow in the sun above the clouds. Then at Sheremetyevo airport he would switch his BlackBerry back on and it would all start again. The calls from Cayman, from Cyprus, from Gibraltar, everyone nervous about those people from Ikertu; emails from Kesler and Griffin about the horrors of Paris and what on earth we do next; maybe for good measure a call or two from a journalist late to the party. He wondered which had been the worst moment of this relentlessly grim week: being unpicked piece by piece by the acid Mr Lionel Greene, QC; learning from his secretary that Malin had asked to see him immediately on his return; or being told by the dependable and normally untroubled Herr Rast, the oldest and calmest of Lock's cohorts in Switzerland, that the Zurich prosecutor had been asking him questions about Faringdon and Langland. Probably the call from Rast, by a shade. Greene had done his worst, and at least Malin was the devil he knew; Swiss prosecutors, however, were a new and frightening apparition.

God, these Queen's Counsels were good. As he looked at

the virgin world of sunshine and deep blue and pure white outside his window it occurred to him that he had been in awe of Greene, and that even while he was being savaged a small part of him had been held rapt by his agility, his utter sureness. Lock wondered whether, in another life, he could ever have been that good. He wasn't sure he had the appetite to scoop all the meat from a man's bones as Greene had done to him, like a surgeon eating a crab.

There were faint reasons for hope; Kesler, at least, was forcing himself to be optimistic. Lock may have failed to convince anyone that he was an oil tycoon but Tourna had failed to demonstrate that he had been defrauded. Paris was unlikely to be the end of it by any means. Kesler had also reminded Lock that it was not his plausibility that was on trial, which was just as well, and that none of it would be reported in the press. And that was the greatest relief.

But Malin. Christ. Lock wondered how much he would know. Presumably Kesler would report how the hearing had gone, and it was in his interests to spare the direst details. But that wouldn't be like Kesler. He could feel the shame of it all rising from his chest into his throat.

Still, at least it was done, and he wouldn't have to do it again. Malin would be angry, that was certain, but there was little he could do. Little he could say, perhaps, since hadn't he, after all, hired Lock in the first place for this ridiculous job? Ultimately Malin was responsible, in every sense. Lock smiled, without enthusiasm.

He looked at his watch. Half past ten by French time, half past one in Russia. A respectable time for another drink. He finished the one in front of him.

To distract himself, he took a notebook from his briefcase, cleared pretzel wrappers from the flimsy drop-down table, passed all the rubbish across the empty seat beside him to a stewardess and asked her for more gin. He opened the book at a fresh page and took a pen from his pocket. He started with the date, and was about to write 'Dossier' before he decided that was imprudent and changed it to 'Ideas'. Then he sat for a while, looking at the words, waiting for inspiration to come, doodling on the opposite page. Under his original heading he drew three boxes and annotated each: *What Malin Knows*, *What I Know* and *What I Need to Know*. Concentrating now, he wrote in each box. The last slowly began to fill up.

What he needed to know was where the money came from. This was difficult. What he saw was only the first layer. His offshore companies received transfers from a dozen companies incorporated all over Russia, and it was only beyond these that real businesses generated the money itself. From sitting in a thousand meetings Lock knew roughly what these did: they overcharged their captive, state-owned clients for goods and services; they bought product cheap and sold it on at market rates; they secured licences that they never intended to use and could sell on at vast profit. But that was all. He had never been shown the workings.

Finally he drew a fourth box: *Where That Information Exists*. He thought for a while. Malin's head; it existed there. He wrote it down. Government files. Probably, somewhere, deep inside some unimaginable part of the Kremlin, there was a file that he and many others would dearly love to see. Where else? Malin's office at the ministry. Malin's home? Possibly. He wrote that down. Chekhanov's office. What about the Russian lawyers? Yes, there might be something there.

Chekhanov's office. Everything must be in that office, surely? If you were going to pick someone to testify against Malin, it would be Chekhanov. He knew everything. Every corrupt payment, every shaky transaction, every fraud Malin had ever committed.

That was the place. Could he break in? A crazy idea. But he could have others do it for him. Any one of those former government security companies that advertised in the Moscow papers would do it. They would have to do it discreetly, of course; any indication that the office had been breached might lead back to him. Was there some way of making it look like Ikertu? Leave a trace back to London. He could ask those half-soaked London investigators to engage the Russians on his behalf.

Lock sat back in his seat, wondering dizzily about the plan. It wasn't bad. In fact it was good. This, after all, was the sort of thing that happened in Moscow every day. He was beginning to think like a Russian.

But then he began to think like a lawyer. The loyalty of Lock's investigators, of InvestSol, could that be relied upon? All it would take was for one of them to realize what was going on and he could end up being blackmailed. Or, more likely and far more dangerous, someone would mess up the job and the fearsome Horkov, or some even more frightening creature from Malin's crack regiment of brutal old spooks, would track it all back to him.

He was not a master criminal. After three large gin and tonics on a morning flight it was important to remember that.

He circled round the problem for a while, discounting ideas as too timid or too reckless. Chekhanov, though, wouldn't go away. He was the weak spot. Well, the only spot that felt weak at all. There had been a time, years before, when he and Lock had had offices next to each other in a building just off Novy Arbat until Malin had decided that this gave the wrong impression and separated them. But even now he was in Alexei's office regularly. If he could only have twenty minutes in there alone. There were what, five or six filing cabinets in there?

Every Tuesday at seven, an hour before Lock, Chekhanov met with Malin, and every two or three weeks he and Lock would see each other beforehand to prepare for their respective sessions. Invariably Chekhanov ran out of these meetings in a rush, apologizing to Lock and leaving him to see himself out. All Lock had to do was arrange their meeting for next Tuesday and arrive a little late with a full agenda. Better still, what if his phone rang as Chekhanov was leaving? He could take it, make some grave noises, and ask Alexei whether he could stay to finish it. The scene played out neatly in his mind.

Lock slept for the last part of the flight, a heavy sleep that left him feeling slow and thick; he woke as the plane bounced gently off the runway at Sheremetyevo. Moscow looked flat and grey, beset by low cloud, already almost dark. Aching across his shoulders and down his back, Lock unclicked his seatbelt, stood up to retrieve his suitcase and stretched in the aisle. It was a quiet flight. At least that was something; no London flight was ever like this. With luck he would be near the front of the passport queue and be through the airport without that awful shuffling wait.

An hour and fifteen minutes, in the end: two planes' worth of Koreans and Bulgarians had arrived just before him. He had had worse. Wheeling his bag behind him he strolled through Customs, handing his declaration to an officer, and then out into Russia proper to search for Andrei and his car. Usually he waited by the Hertz desk, but today he wasn't there. Lock stopped and looked down the length of the hall in each direction. No sign. He set his bag straight and took out his Russian phone. As he was finding the number he felt a hand on his upper arm.

'Mr Lock.' A deep, flat voice, Russian. Lock looked round to his right and then up. The man talking to him was tall, perhaps six three, and broad. He had fine, fair hair cropped so short that Lock could see the white scalp beneath.

'Yes.'

'Can you come with us please? We will take you into the city.'

Lock turned to his left. Another man, similar in build, a little shorter, with grey hair and a broken nose stood there with his hands clasped respectfully in front of him. Both were wearing impenetrable black winter jackets and jeans.

'Where's Andrei?'

'We are standing in for Andrei today.'

Lock was awake now. He had no idea what this meant. Fear flickered through him.

'Who sent you?'

'We're from the ministry.'

The grey-haired man took Lock's bag and started wheeling it across the concourse. His colleague let go of Lock's arm.

'Come. Please.'

Lock followed. He became conscious of his briefcase. Why had he written those stupid notes? He should tell them that he needed to go to the bathroom, then tear out the page and flush it away. What if they took the briefcase off him while he went? God, he was hopeless at this. They hadn't taken it, he reasoned; if they had wanted to, they would have.

Down below in the mess of smoking cars parking and waiting a black BMW flashed its lights and the three of them got in, Lock in the back, his reception party bulky in the front. It was dark now, and the grey-haired man drove at speed through the lumbering traffic like someone used to immunity. Lock didn't talk. He knew that he wouldn't get answers from these two. They looked like special forces. Not that he really knew about such things, but they were clearly a different breed from Andrei.

Slowly the tower blocks and the billboards became denser and from the dark Moscow began to coalesce into a city. They passed Dynamo Stadium and carried on down Leningradsky

Prospect towards the ministry. But at Mayakovskaya they turned east onto the Garden Ring. That didn't make sense. Lock felt, like a shock, a new fear: what if these men had nothing to do with Malin at all? What if they were FSB? Or worse, someone else's people, which would mean – what? That Malin had fallen from grace?

They were off the Ring now and into the messy heart of the city. The BMW swept through a tangle of small streets, the stuccoed buildings low around them and a dull orange in the street light. Lock knew this route. It would take him close to his flat. The car turned left into Maly Zlatoustinsky pereulok, his street, and pulled up outside his building. The blond man got out of the car and opened Lock's door for him. Lock, wary, lifted himself slowly out of the car while the blond man fetched his suitcase.

'What are we doing?' Lock asked.

'We're taking you home. That is all.'

Lock walked up to the building, found his keys and opened the front door. In the lobby he called the lift. The blond man stood next to him as they waited, looking straight ahead at the lift door.

Lock's apartment was on the fifth floor. He took his keys, opened the three deadlocks, and went in. The blond man followed, setting the case down in the hall.

'Thank you,' said Lock.

The blond man said nothing and left.

Lock took off his coat, threw it over a chair and went into the kitchen. He had gin, but no tonic. There was vodka in the freezer and he poured himself two inches into a water glass and drank it in one slack swallow. It felt like light, cool and warm in his throat.

He closed his eyes for a moment and gave a small shudder. He had no idea what was going on. Was Andrei simply sick? Of all the outlandish possibilities flying round his head this, absurdly, was one of the more plausible. He walked into his sitting room, which ran the length of the apartment at the front, and looked out of the window. The BMW was still there, parked right outside. Presumably it would wait to take him to the ministry in an hour or so. As far as Lock could tell only the driver's seat was occupied. He watched for a while. The army veteran in winter camouflage who looked after parking for this building left the car alone. Two or three minutes passed.

Then an icy thought took Lock. He went to his front door and looked through the spyhole. It was clear. He opened the door to scan the corridor, and there, standing to the right with his arms crossed and his back straight against the wall, was the blond man. Now Lock understood.

'What are you doing?' he asked.

'Waiting for you.'

He didn't need to ask anything more. He closed the door, went to pour himself another drink, and sat at the kitchen table. He was under house arrest.

That was the logical assumption. If they had wanted to shoot him they would have done it by now.

There were different kinds of house arrest. Sometimes you were allowed out under close watch; sometimes you weren't allowed out at all. Sometimes it ran and ran; sometimes it came to a most definite end. How long had the Romanovs had? A year? A little more?

For twenty minutes he sat and thought and drank. Then his doorbell rang. Again he walked to the spyhole. A large man in a suit was there, rounder than usual in the distorting lens. Malin had never been to his apartment before. Lock opened the door.

'Richard.'

'Konstantin.'

'May I come in?'

'Of course, of course.'

Malin followed Lock into the sitting room.

'Can I get you a drink?' said Lock.

'No, thank you.'

'Please, have a seat.'

Malin sat in the one armchair, where Lock usually sat when he was watching television. The room was sparsely decorated; this was not a home. Lock sat on the sofa and tried to appear relaxed.

For a second or two Malin simply looked at Lock, and Lock as ever was at a loss to read his face. It held no expression. The eyes were blank and sharp at once. Had they always been like that? Were these the eyes that slowly seduced me so long ago?

'How was Paris?' Malin said at last.

'Not as good as it could have been. No doubt you've heard.'

Malin nodded. A slow nod, three times, looking at Lock all the while. Then he took a long deliberate breath, let it out through his nose, and reached into his jacket pocket for his cigarettes, a Russian brand. He took one from its soft pack and lit it with a plastic lighter, letting all the smoke leave his lungs before talking.

'I thought Kesler coached you.'

'He did.'

'Then it was your fault?'

Lock didn't reply. He tried to hold Malin's look. Malin watched him and smoked. He tapped his ash, curling it into the ashtray, and spoke again.

'Do you think it likely, Richard, that the largest foreign investor in Russia's oil industry would not know the difference between kerosene and gasoline?'

'I didn't . . . I'm just the shareholder.'

'Or the standard terms of an oil exploration licence?'

Lock looked down at his shoes. Malin went on.

'Or the combined revenue of the group over the last ten years?'

Lock could feel a sharp, constricting pain in his breastbone. There was a stagnant smell about him. He wanted to have a shower.

Malin was still looking at him.

'I'm sorry.' It was all he could find to say.

Malin stubbed out his cigarette, separating the burning ember from the filter, his eyes held on Lock.

'You have had too much international exposure, I think.' Malin sat hunched forward like a frog, his thick shoulders sloping. 'Things are difficult. There are stories in the newspaper and the lawsuit goes on. Tourna's people are more and more aggressive. They will put pressure on you, and I do not want any harm to come to you.' He paused. 'You are too important to me.' This seemed to demand a response but Lock waited. 'This is why I have arranged for new bodyguards for you. These men are good. They will make sure that you are looked after. They will make sure that no one gets to you.'

Lock tried to think of something to say. 'What about Andrei?' was all that he could manage.

'He has been reassigned.' Malin shifted forward in the chair. 'Is there anything else you need to ask me?'

'Will I . . . Can I come and go as I please?'

'Of course. It is exactly as before.'

'How long will this last?'

'Not long. It is a temporary measure. When things have died down we can go back to normal.' Lock felt himself being scanned and at the same time being told something: don't underestimate how serious this is.

Malin stood up and held out his hand. Lock took it.

'Goodbye, Richard. I will see you at the ministry on Monday.'

'Yes. Good night.'

Malin let himself out. Lock was left in his sitting room, wondering. He wondered about many things, but what troubled him the most was what hadn't been said. No mention of the investigation into Tourna. No steely pep talk. Almost as if he didn't matter any more.

Malin was right: it was exactly as it was before. Lock was surprised by how little difference it made to his life to have an armed guard watching over him. He went to the office, he had dinner, he came home, he had a solitary and dreary weekend. Liberty would have been wasted on him.

His guard changed at nine each night. He knew that every movement he made was noted and reported, and he knew, though it was unspoken, that he couldn't leave the country, or flit to St Petersburg for the weekend. But that wasn't so different either. For years now he had lived at the permission of someone else. Now he knew it. That was all.

What was different was Oksana's absence. For a week after his return from Paris he had tried to live a simple life and ignore the weight he felt on him every morning when he woke, but any setback, any reminder of his plight and he found himself wanting to see her. More than anything else he wanted to talk to someone who didn't occupy his world. He chided himself for his weakness but it made him no stronger.

And then there was Marina, and the letter. He had taken to carrying it with him in his inside pocket, where it felt at once like a comfort and a risk: after all, if anyone were to read it they would surely conclude that he was now on the verge of defecting, or of simply breaking down. He didn't know why he kept it with him. He told himself that she was right in her analysis but wrong, or unrealistic, in her prescription, and so her words didn't serve as inspiration, or guide, or spur (there ought to be spur enough in finding a guard outside his apartment door each morning, as certain as the sun). But they stayed with him nevertheless, on his person and circling in his head, perhaps because what they said most clearly was that she still cared for him, that in some other universe where his confinement was not as close or as total there might yet be hope.

The papers were alive again. The *Wall Street Journal* had published a profile of Malin which, while it mentioned his official achievements, was not flattering. 'Russia's Secret Oligarch' was the headline, and it went much further than the story in *The Times* in setting out his connections to Langland, Faringdon and Lock. The *FT* had followed it up with an article about Faringdon, its extraordinary string of assets and its shadowy proprietor, one Richard Lock.

The one thing that gave him some hope was his plan, now more critical than ever. And more dangerous. Every evening after dinner he worked on it. He had burned his original notes, and was now storing all the details in his head; it wasn't complicated in any case. He had two problems to work on: how to get his phone to ring as Chekhanov was due to leave, and how to pick the lock on a filing cabinet. He had been practising the latter on one of his own at home. He began with a straightened paperclip, but that was too flimsy and he moved on to a hairclip that Oksana had left in his bathroom. With some practice he could feel the pins moving up and down inside the lock, but he couldn't get the mechanism to turn.

That Saturday he woke early after an unsettled sleep and took himself to the *banya* to be steamed and scrubbed. His escort waited outside. When he left he felt lighter and the fug in his head had cleared. Moscow was still cold but there was no cloud and the air for once felt good to breathe. He told his guards that he was going to walk for a while. The driver stayed with the car; the blond man followed five yards behind him.

Lock walked briskly down to Red Square, charging his lungs, determined to fill his day so that he could convince himself and Malin that his spirit wasn't lost.

He would do something he had never done: he would visit the Kremlin. It might do him good to see behind those immense red walls. The Kremlin was still the dark, unknowable centre of things, a silent threat to every Russian. If it chose it could exile you, jail you, take everything you had. It owned you. Even Malin was wary of it, as if it were some arbitrary and alien power. In that mysterious citadel by the river people worked, and talked to each other, and made decisions. Malin knew most of them. And yet he still talked of the Kremlin not as a collection of politicians and administrators but as a fearsome creature that might savage you for the merest slight or simply on a whim. Lock, for his part, was awed by it, and a little scared. He prayed that he would never give it cause to notice him.

From the kiosk on the far side of Red Square he bought two tickets, one for himself and one for his blond companion, who took it with some awkwardness. In amongst bands of tourists he passed through the broad wooden gate in the outer wall and into a long avenue of trees. As he walked he was amazed by how fine the buildings were, and how immaculately everything was kept – the paths clean, the verges trimmed, the grass a deep green even now, in winter. Russian government buildings weren't like this. They were grubby and practical. This was luminous and serene, and rich with the spirit of the country it governed. The offices, vast and painted a deep yellow, had a rationalist air at odds with the pure white and onion domes of the churches and cathedrals; the one looked north and west, the other south and east. Together they suggested to him the sentimental greatness of Russia. Against every expectation, he was moved. There was such beauty here. How easy, he thought, to rule without fear of redress from a place such as this.

He spent a little over an hour there, then tired. He would have liked to discuss some of what he was thinking with his chaperone but didn't feel that he could. He was hungry, but didn't want to eat alone. He wanted to see Oksana. In fact, he needed to: he needed someone to call him at Chekhanov's office, and she was the only person he knew in Moscow he might trust. As he walked back into Red Square he took his phone and called her, for the first time since she had left him in Café Pushkin. As he dialled, the same electronic squeal that he had heard in London the week before played in his ear, and he realized with a new sting of anxiety that someone was probably listening to his calls. Of course they were. Only dimly hearing Oksana's voicemail message, he hung up.

His spirits, so carefully buoyed, collapsed. Who was listening to his calls? Probably Malin. Possibly Ikertu. Both? Could two lots of people tap the same phone? He had no idea. It hardly mattered. He had no one to talk to anyway. Putting the phone back in his pocket he turned to his bodyguard and told him that he wanted to go home.

On Tuesday morning he was in the office early, around eight. There was an email waiting for him from Kesler, sent a little after ten, his time, the evening before. Lock expected it to be about New York, the next item on the legal agenda. Instead it told him that the Financial Crimes Unit of the Royal Cayman Islands Police Service wanted to interview him about 'irregu-larities of ownership' in certain companies under his control. If he could attend a meeting the following week that would suit them. Kesler explained that if he did go it would only be with a guarantee from the island of temporary immunity.

This was the first official investigation. Newspapers and lawsuits and hints from Swiss prosecutors were one thing, this was another. Kesler was in the United States this week. Lock couldn't call him until the afternoon. He wanted to know whether this was serious. He also wanted to know whether he would be allowed to go. His guess was that if he knew about it, he would be going. He would find out this evening when he saw Malin.

In the meantime, he had some last minute planning to do. Even if he couldn't be arrested in Cayman he wanted to be prepared to negotiate. He wanted something to offer them, and this meant that he had to go through with his plan that evening. He might not get another chance.

He had made some progress with the lock. He had realized finally that he needed two pins, not one, and fashioned something near the thickness of the hairclip, the only one he could find, from tightly twisting two paperclips together. It now took him about thirty seconds to open his own filing cabinet. He could only hope that Chekhanov's locks were the same.

Oksana would not be helping him. He had called her once more, on Sunday morning, but again she hadn't answered. He suspected she wasn't talking to him for his own good. In any case, he had thought of a way round the practical problem. There was a stopwatch on one of his phones that had a countdown function. By changing the sounds you could make it ring as if for a new call when the count reached zero. Before his meeting, he would set it to count down from fifteen seconds, and then activate it from his pocket. He had practised, and it worked: down button twice, right once, down once, centre button.

His day was not productive, nor quick. Normal life continued in the network of companies, and he should have been signing documents and transferring money and opening bank accounts and making sure that everybody else was doing what they should be doing. But he couldn't concentrate. Two scenes occupied his mind. In one, he was being led away from Chekhanov's office by two enormous henchmen as Chekhanov himself looked coldly on; in the other, he was in a fluorescent-lit office in Cayman, bargaining feverishly with a pair of stony-eyed policemen.

Time dragged. He skipped lunch, and then regretted doing so. He smoked half-heartedly. By the time he came to leave for the meeting he was feeling light-headed and oddly detached.

Chekhanov's office was in a low building above a row of shops: a cafe, a shoe shop, an electrical repair shop. It gave no hint of how much money and influence lay within. Wooden doors in the middle of the row opened onto a wooden stair-case, its grey paint chipped away, lit by a single fluorescent bulb on the wall. Lock walked up two flights. Two doors opened off the landing at the top. He turned to the right and pressed the bell. A dull brass sign by the door read 'Industrial and Economic Holdings Z.A.O.' As he waited Lock checked his equipment: one hairclip, the paperclips wound together, his countdown phone, his normal phone, his BlackBerry with its camera. All present, and none of it incriminating. His hand felt clammy in his pocket and he tried to dry it on the lining.

A key turned in the lock on the other side and the door opened. Chekhanov's secretary showed Lock in, without pleasantries, and for a minute or two he stood in the reception area, unable to decide whether to sit down. Not many people were received here, he thought. Throughout the offices the walls were lined with wood, vertical strips of pine varnished a deep red-brown, and the only decoration was a single frame displaying an incorporation document for Industrial and Economic Holdings. Two low steel chairs, their upholstery worn, were set against the wall facing the receptionist's desk, between them a chipboard coffee table with nothing on it. The room smelled dusty, as if someone had just vacuumed.

The receptionist's phone rang. 'Mr Chekhanov is ready now.'

Lock walked past her desk and down a corridor, taking the second door on the right. In here were the same pine walls, the same institutional hard grey carpet. Hanging behind Chekhanov's desk was a Russian coat of arms, a gold double-headed eagle against a field of bright red.

Chekhanov rose, leaned forward across the desk and shook hands. His hand felt small and dry. His skin looked stretched across his face and the sharp ridge of his nose. Lock had noticed long ago that he never seemed to blink.

'Richard. It is good to see you.'

'Alexei. I hope you're well.'

'Yes. Busy. I was in Tyumen last week. I have returned to a mess.'

Lock smiled what he hoped was an easy smile. 'I know the feeling.'

'Hm?'

'I've been away since I saw you last. I'm only just recovering.'

'Good. Good.' Chekhanov was looking at his computer, distracted. At least he made no comment about Paris. 'Has Konstantin mentioned this company in Burgas? Refining. I need to talk to you about it.'

'No. No, he hasn't.'

Chekhanov sat down. On his desk were three mobile phones. Two were dismantled, their batteries out; one was not. He picked it up and slid the battery casing off.

'Shall we?'

Lock hesitated for a moment. 'Yes, of course.' Fuck. How could he have been so stupid? Fuck. Would Alexei remember how many phones he usually had? If he took two out, and Alexei commented, then he could produce the other one and claim absent-mindedness. It was the best he could do. He removed his BlackBerry and a regular phone, took their batteries out and left them on the desk. He smiled again. 'So? Where do you want to start?'

Chekhanov was still checking his email. He glanced at his desk and then looked back at Lock, his eyebrows raised. His eyes were grey and quick. 'You ready?'

'Yes.' Lock waited for the question. It didn't come.

'Let us start with Kazakhstan. It isn't making us any money and the manager's defrauding us. I think I found a purchaser last week. If we sell it there will be about a hundred and eighty million coming in. Be ready to put it somewhere.'

Chekhanov talked and Lock took sketchy notes. The refinery in Romania was close to breaching its debt covenants and needed money; there were bribes to be paid in Bulgaria, decent ones, if they were going to buy this refinery in Burgas; the group's financing company needed funds to buy equipment before leasing it on into Russia. And on and on. All the while Lock could feel the phone in his trouser pocket pressing against the top of his thigh.

He looked at his watch. It was 6.35. Surely Alexei had to leave soon? He was talking about some problem with Langland, some customer who hadn't paid, and checking his email for the details.

'This is no good. I have to go. This one can wait.' He looked up at Lock. 'Did you get all that?'

'Yes. I think so.'

'Good. Let's go.'

Chekhanov put his phones back together and stood up, dropping them in his briefcase. Lock stood too and put the batteries back in his dismantled phones. He put one in his trouser pocket and as he did so keyed in the sequence on the other: down down right down centre. As Chekhanov bent over his desk to shut down his computer, the phone rang. Lock took it out, looked at it, pressed a key as if to answer it and then covered the microphone.

'Sorry,' he said to Chekhanov in a half whisper. 'Do you mind?'

Chekhanov, gathering up papers now, waved him on.

'Philip, hi. How are you?' Lock answered in English, then paused. 'Sorry, I've been in a meeting. Yes, I can. Shit, really? That's not good. Well, I have to leave for another meeting shortly but yes, I've got twenty minutes or so. Hold on.' Another short pause. 'Hold on a second.' He covered the phone again. Chekhanov was ready to go, briefcase in hand, a quilted coat over his arm. 'Alexei, do you mind if I finish this call? It's important.'

Chekhanov looked at Lock. He seemed to have hardened somehow in the last minute. 'Come with me. I'll drive you to the ministry. Finish your call on the way.'

'It could go on a bit,' said Lock. 'I don't want to bore you.'

'No.' Chekhanov was firm now. 'Come with me in the car. Otherwise call this person back.'

'Well, I don't need to be in the ministry for . . . Yes, OK. Yes. I'll come with you.' Lock felt himself flush around his neck. Chekhanov had been briefed about him. He was no longer trusted. 'Right, Philip. Sorry about that. How can I help?' This is ridiculous, he thought, as he went down the stairs after Chekhanov, saying the occasional yes or no to keep the fiction up. Chekhanov left the building and walked to his car, which was directly outside. Lock followed, wondering how on earth he was going to finish this. 'Quite. Hm. OK, I see.' He got into the back seat, next to Chekhanov, and shut the door. It was suddenly so quiet that his phone felt glaringly dead and silent in his hand. 'Philip, listen. I don't think that sounds so bad. I think the thing to do is to talk to the accountants this afternoon and see if they can do a full, do a full audit on everything. Do you have a sense of how much we're talking about? Hm. OK. That could be worse.' He gave a sigh in the hope that it would seem authentic. 'Listen, let's talk tomorrow when you know more. Yes. Yes. OK then. Bye. Goodbye.' He sat back in his seat and let the phone fall by his side.

Chekhanov looked down at the phone and then at Lock. 'Everything all right?'

'Yes, fine. Fine.'

'What was that?'

'Oh nothing. Some money gone missing in the BVI. Probably an oversight.'

'Not such a long call.'

'No, it was nothing really. In the end. Nothing.'

CHAPTER TEN

For a week London had been dark and cold. A fine, dense rain fell like sea mist and the city felt empty, like a resort town off season; as he walked to the Tube in the mornings Webster half expected to turn a corner and find the wind blowing at him on a broad promenade beaten by waves. From time to time the sky lightened from lead to limestone and his spirit dared to lift a little, but this was an oppressive time.

London had felt like this when he moved back from Moscow; an unfamiliar, insidious cold across the shoulders, endless rain that had left him yearning for snow. In those first weeks home he had found his home city more impenetrable than the one he had left behind, and for a while he had regretted trading Moscow's movement and wild spontaneity for all this admirable solidity. Even now, sometimes, he felt a pang of regret at having left Russia, a sort of homesickness that he could never quite explain. But more than anything this weather brought to mind his long-dead plans – undoubtedly good, never robust – to stop writing stories that never seemed to have any effect, to get out of journalism altogether and do some good; reminded him, too, of the day he got the call from Global Investigations Corporation and signed up instead for this strange career that ever since he had relished and distrusted in equal measure.

What good did he do? What was his tally? Webster was by instinct an agnostic, but he couldn't rid himself of the idea that somewhere one's deeds were being reckoned and that his own score was in the balance. GIC had been convinced of its own worthiness; Ike was more circumspect but believed ultimately that Ikertu was a positive force in the world. Webster even now simply wasn't sure. What did he accomplish, exactly? How was the world different for what he did? He helped his clients not to lose money or reputation. That was all. If his client was upright, he told himself, this was good work, if hardly saintly; when, as now, his client was at best a rogue, how did he help anyone at all?

Snowdrop was unsettling him. It was the case he had always wanted, his chance finally to afflict those who tended to do the afflicting. But Elsa's words wouldn't leave him. This had become a quest – a twin quest, Tourna's and his own – and his sense of proportion was unbalanced. He was no longer sure why he was pursuing Malin. Was it to restore to Tourna what was rightfully his? To show the corruption that still ravaged Russia, and by doing so accelerate its end? Or simply to destroy a life in compensation for the life he had seen destroyed?

Hammer's advice, as ever, was simple and good. Do what it says on the engagement letter; remember the commitment you made. And while Webster's motive might have troubled him, at least his next step was clear.

He had to get a message to Lock, and in such a way that no one else would know of it. The message itself was simple: you have options; do not assume that there isn't a way out of this; you will need expert help, and I am the expert. Webster had taken down and folded away the hand-drawn map of Malin's world that he had stared at for so long, and in its place was now a single sheet of poster-sized paper. On it was a circle drawn in thick black ink, and inside the word 'Lock'. One other smaller circle marked 'Onder' sat to one side. That was as far as he had got.

Lock was in Moscow. He had flown back immediately after Paris and hadn't been anywhere else since. Webster knew this because he had primed his source at the travel agency to check three times a day for bookings in the name of Richard Lock. So far there was nothing.

The plan, not yet fully formed, was that Onder would find an excuse to see Lock and gauge his mood. If he was feeling trapped, as Webster had to believe he would be, Onder would offer to make the introduction. The problem was that this couldn't happen in Moscow, because it was too dangerous, and in any case Onder was not the sort of person one could send off on missions; everything had to fit with his schedule.

Hammer's advice was clear and constant: just wait. We're not in any hurry; our client wants us to stop spending money, and this way we don't spend any until we have an opportunity that justifies it. But Webster lacked Hammer's restraint, partly because he was consumed by the case, and partly because Hammer enjoyed waiting as part of the game. For all that Hammer was constantly in motion Webster admired his ability to sit still.

So as the rain fell in the gloom Webster struggled with the obvious truth that there wasn't anything to do and tried to occupy himself with other projects. But two things happened that week nevertheless, and neither served to make him any calmer.

The Wednesday after his meeting with Tourna he received a call from Elsa at work.

'Have you seen this email?'

'What email?'

'You clearly haven't.' Her voice was anxious, tight.

'I'm not in my office. What is it?'

'I don't know. It's in Russian. But it has our address on it.'

'Hold on. I'm nearly there. Let me see.' He sat at his desk

and clicked on his screen. There was one new email, from a Nicholas Stokes, the subject blank.

'I was at school with Nicholas Stokes.' He opened it.

'Then he has a strange sense of humour.'

The email was addressed to Elsa, and he had been copied. It was laid out like a letter; in the top left hand corner was Webster's home address in Queen's Park, complete with post-code. The body of the message was the full, Russian text of an article from *Kommersant* reporting the death of Inessa. Webster had read it at the time; it was notable for being one of the few to print details of her writing. Otherwise the email was empty: no introduction, no Dear Ben, nothing. He looked at it for a moment blankly, conscious that his heart was beat-ing faster.

'What does it say?' said Elsa.

'It's an article about Inessa. From just after she died.'

'What the hell for? Why is our address there?'

'I don't know. I don't know. It's OK. Let me look at it.' He began to inspect it more closely. The name that had shown up in his inbox was Nicholas Stokes, but the email address itself was borisstrokov5789@googlemail.com. The name meant nothing to him. He opened up the detailed information that showed the electronic path the email had taken, but that, too, was meaningless.

'I don't know what it is,' he said. 'A message to me.'

'To us.'

'Hold on.' He searched for Boris Strokov on the Internet. Only a handful of results came back. 'OK. Well, whoever sent it wants me to know that they know all about me. I haven't seen Nick Stokes since I was seventeen. And they know our address.'

'And my email.'

'And your email. They've been busy.'

'Who is Boris Strokov?'

'I don't know. Hardly any seem to exist.' By now he had discovered that Boris Strokov was a character dreamt up by Tom Clancy to inject Georgi Markov full of ricin on Waterloo Bridge. Russians, this meant, have a proud history of getting to people outside Russia. He kept the thought to himself.

'Ben, I hate this. I hate it. It's your case, isn't it?'

'Probably.'

'Probably? If it isn't that what on earth is it?'

'It's the case.'

'Right. And now they know where our children live. And they're telling me, their mother, in an email.' She paused. It occurred to Webster that that was the cleverest aspect of it. 'Tell me this doesn't scare you.'

'It doesn't. I've had these things before. They're unnerving.'

'Unnerving? That's good. Well listen. I am unnerved. Distinctly unnerved. I don't let my work intrude on our lives and I don't think you should either.'

'Baby, look. You really shouldn't worry. It's a warning to the curious. They want me to stop work.'

'Then maybe you should.'

In his office Webster looked at the email and shook his head. Instinctively he thought it through. If Malin was doing this it meant that he was rattled, and that could only be good.

'No. Not now. This doesn't mean anything. It's nothing.'

Elsa was silent on the other end of the line.

'Listen. If someone wants to hurt you they don't tell you they're going to do it.'

'But there's no rule against it, is there?'

No. There was no rule.

Over the next few days the email hovered on the edge of Webster's thoughts, tugging insistently, the abuse of Inessa's memory a constant barb. Elsa was tense. He tried to reassure her but his arguments, at once perfectly logical and somehow irrelevant, sounded hollow in his ear. The simple truth was that his pride wouldn't allow such an ugly and simple device to have its effect. It was too base, too easy. If anything he felt newly galvanized.

That weekend the Websters left London for the south coast. They stayed in a cottage in Winchelsea, on a cliff a mile from the sea. They walked on the great beach at Camber Sands in the rain, with not a soul in sight; ate fish and chips in Rye; were chased by a herd of friendly bullocks on a farm. London and Moscow began to feel far away.

On the Saturday evening, Webster was reading to Daniel when his phone started buzzing in his pocket. He ignored it, finished the story, kissed him goodnight and went downstairs to the kitchen.

There was no message, and the call was from a Russian number he didn't recognize. He dialled it, cradling the phone against his neck and taking a glass down from a shelf.

'Hello, this is Ben Webster. You just called me.'

'Ben. This is Leonard. Cahill. In Moscow.'

'Leonard. Good to hear from you. How are you?' He reached for a bottle of whisky and poured himself an inch, then a dash of water from the jug. He could hear Elsa walking around upstairs.

'Ben, have you heard from Alan? In the last few days.'

'He left me a voicemail last week.'

'When was that?'

'I was at Heathrow, so Thursday. Late afternoon.'

'Nothing since?'

'Nothing. Why?'

'He's gone missing.'

Webster took a drink and put his glass down. 'What sort of missing?'

'He was in Tyumen at the weekend. Then he had a story for

us in Sakhalin. He never showed up. His wife saw him off on Monday morning and hasn't heard from him since.'

'What was he working on?' Elsa came into the kitchen. She took a bottle of wine from the fridge and poured herself a glass. He mouthed 'sorry' to her and stepped out into the hall.

'A piece about Sakhalin II. A puff piece. Nothing exciting. I was going to ask you the same thing.'

'He hasn't done any work for me for six months.' This, of course, was strictly true.

'You don't know what he was working on?'

'No. We talked about something but it never happened.'

'Fuck. His wife's beside herself. Says he's never done this before. Had he told you about his problems?'

'He mentioned something about the tax police.'

'I hope he hasn't done anything stupid.'

'I can't see it. Not Alan.' Christ. I hope no one has done it for him. 'Have you told the police?'

'The Tyumen police aren't big on missing persons.'

'But you've told them.'

'I've notified them.'

'And you don't know whether he took a flight?'

'No. We know nothing. He left his house at eight on Monday and that's it. He booked the flights. Hasn't phoned anyone. His phone's off, needless to say. Car's still at home.'

'Have you tried his Turkish phone?'

'I didn't know he had a Turkish phone.'

Webster sat down on the stairs. The different possibilities cycled through his mind. 'Look, Leonard. Maybe I can do something. I'll have a look at his flights and see if anyone's been using his phone. Get Irina to send me his credit card details, all his cards. Any phone numbers I might not have. I'll have a look.'

'Thanks Ben. This isn't like him.'

'Tell me if anything happens.'

'I will.'

Webster hung up. He found the Turkish number for Knight and dialled it. It went straight to voicemail. Where was he? Perhaps he had bolted; gone to Turkey while things calmed down. Perhaps his home life wasn't as solid as it seemed. Perhaps he was in debt.

In the kitchen he picked up his glass and took a good swallow. None of these was convincing.

'What was that?' Elsa was chopping an onion, her face half turned away from the fumes.

'Nothing. A case.'

'You look worried.'

'It's nothing. Just a wayward source.'

Webster did what he could to track down Knight. His travel-agent source found out that he had been booked on the 10.35 from Tyumen to Vladivostok; he never checked in, not to that flight or to any other that had left Tyumen that week – or any Russian airport, for that matter. With Mrs Knight's permission Webster spoke to the phone company as Knight and reported his phone missing; no calls had been made since Monday morning when he had rung for a taxi to take him to the airport. His wife had seen him leave in the car, and the taxi controller told Webster that they had dropped him off at around eight in the morning. He had paid the driver in cash, but in the airport made one purchase on his credit card, for three hundred rubles, from a cafe. That was the last trace he had left. It would take about a week to discover whether he had taken any money from his offshore account, but somehow it seemed unlikely; he had withdrawn no money from the joint account he held with his wife.

Alan Knight was definitely gone. If he had decided to make himself disappear he had done a very good job of it. He was clever enough for that. And the alternative, while it seemed so much more likely, simply didn't make sense. Why abduct him? Why not have him die in a car crash or a hit and run? Why not arrest him on some absurd charge and ship him off to a distant prison? He was a Russian citizen. They could do what they liked to him. But what Webster really couldn't accept was that whatever was happening to Alan had anything to do with a conversation they had had two months ago about not very much. It seemed so disproportionate. And if they were sending him messages, surely Alan's disappearance would come with some sort of message attached; if this was meant to frighten off Ikertu, why leave it ambiguous?

It was while he was dwelling on these questions, wondering whether he should wait for answers before finally conceding that this case was no longer worth the prize, that he received a call from his friend at the travel agency. The news was not about Knight but about Lock: he was booked on flights to Cayman through London, leaving Moscow on Wednesday and stopping in London for two nights on his way back.

Surveillance consumed everything: time, money, attention. Webster never relished it. While he had an operation running it was impossible for him to concentrate on anything else, and the returns were often meagre: it never told you quite as much as you wanted.

Today, for now, everything was running smoothly enough. The team had picked up Lock at Heathrow. He had flown in from Cayman with two bodyguards and what looked like a lawyer, probably a Bryson Joyce man, who had said goodbye after Customs and taken the train into town. One of Lock's men had hired a car; there was some argument with the hire company, and Lock had become agitated by the delay, but eventually a silver Volvo saloon had arrived outside Arrivals and taken him and the remaining bodyguard into London.

One of the first text messages Webster received from his team that morning read, in a familiar, flat tone, 'Enquiries with the Hertz desk established that the gentleman was disappointed not to receive the Mercedes that he believed he had booked.'

George Black, purveyor of first-rate surveillance and counter-surveillance, had listened to what Webster needed and arranged a team of six: four in a car and two on a motor-bike. One woman in the car, one on the back of the bike – a good woman, George had told Webster many times, being an essential part of any successful operation. Black himself was in the car, managing the operation and sending text message after text message to Webster. He was a soldier, or had been, with a career that had straddled special forces and military intelligence. He said little about his past, but what he did say you knew was true, and he had followed many people trickier and nastier than Lock. He was direct, efficient, wholly com-mitted to the job, and better than anyone else Webster had ever tried. But even he lost people now and then.

Today that didn't matter, not terribly. Later on Lock would be having dinner with Onder (the hardest part of the opera-tion to set up – Webster had eventually had to blackmail Onder with visions of Lock's imminent demise to persuade him to come to London) and through him they knew where he would be staying – Claridge's, in Mayfair. There was no crit-ical meeting that they had to catch, and that made the whole operation less nervy than it might have been.

Webster's brief to George was unusual: report how Lock behaves. Is he relaxed or busy? Is he smiling, rushing, hiding? Is he doing Malin's business or his own?

The text messages came every ten to fifteen minutes. 'Sub-ject proceeding east on M4.' . . . 'Subject proceeding east on A4.' . . . 'Subject approaching Claridge's along Upper Brook Street.' Black never abbreviated. Webster tried to deal with his email but was getting little done. In the end he left his office and went for a walk.

It was the middle of the morning, raining still, and the people of Chancery Lane, having picked up their breakfasts and not yet gone for lunch, were working. Webster could sense the industry around him, in new glass buildings and older concrete blocks, in the offices where the lawyers opined and the accountants added up. No one made anything here. No one sold anything either, except for sandwiches and ties and birthday cards. They calculated, they assessed risk, they checked, they analysed; they disputed, and resolved, and testified; they reported, and then they invoiced. They helped their clients to make money, to avoid losing it, to sidestep drudgery. They did what Webster did, in short. And Lock, he thought. We help others do.

What was it to be Lock at the moment? Until the summer he must have felt so comfortable. Hammer was right: as Malin's shield, if that's what he was, he had had no real shielding to do until now. His path had been easy. He was used to the Russians, knew the companies and the tax treaties by heart, had his regiment of advisers out there to do his bidding. Hammer's man in the FBI had hinted that Lock had been answering formal questions in Cayman; if that was true, then for him to be sitting across from a policeman – there of all places, where he must have felt most safe, a sanctuary made for him and his type – that must have felt like the end of his world. He must be ready. Surely.

Webster wandered west into Covent Garden through the insistent rain, his trousers left damp by the short coat he kept hunched about him. His phone buzzed: Lock had checked in to the hotel. He bought a paper and sat in a cafe with a cup of tea waiting for new alerts. For an hour or so, there was no movement. One of George's team discovered through some sleight of hand that Lock was staying in room 324, a junior suite. Then shortly after noon, a message: 'Subject leaving in silver Volvo, east on Brook Street.' Immediately after it came another: 'Have reason to believe others interested in subject. Please call.'

Black had been thorough. His people had checked the area around Claridge's before Lock's arrival and had noticed an anonymous dark grey Ford with three men in it parked in a mews behind the hotel. The same car was now following Lock east across the city. Black asked Webster whether he wanted to switch to counter-surveillance, which, in the jargon, meant to start following the car following Lock. Webster thought about it. Stick with Lock, he decided, and Black did just that.

Webster sat with his tea for a long time, then bought another. People began to come in to order their lunch. Lock entered Bryson's offices in the City at 12.32. The team settled down to wait for him to reappear, but Webster was sure that Lock would be in with the lawyers for at least a couple of hours and would then go back to his hotel.

That was what happened. Lock returned to Claridge's in the middle of the afternoon, and didn't emerge again until the evening, when he left for his dinner with Onder. Webster spent the afternoon writing a report he had been delaying, picking up the odd message from Black and waiting for news of Alan Knight. He would stay in the office for this evening's programme because he wanted to be close.

Onder had picked the place, an Italian restaurant near Sloane Square where the waiters knew half the customers by name. He had wanted to know if he should wear a wire and Webster told him it wasn't that sort of a meeting. Lock was there early, a little before eight, with his unseen caravan close behind him. His bodyguards waited outside in the car.

Onder was there shortly afterwards. Webster found it impossible to concentrate: if Lock was going to leave it would be in the first half an hour. When it became clear that they were going to finish dinner he began to relax, and after a further hour was rather wishing that the two of them would hurry up. He heard nothing until a little after ten, when George let him know that both individuals had left the premises. Onder called two minutes after that, a little breathless on the line, evidently walking back to his Mayfair house. Webster had been in his office for hours now and his eyes were dry from the blueish fluorescent light. Still no news of Knight. Pizza crusts sat in a box on the floor beside his desk.

'I think I did well,' said Onder. 'I like this spying game.'

Webster laughed but was too tense to be amused. 'How did it go?'

'Well, I think. Not for him, but for you? Very well. He is a scared man.'

'What's he scared of?'

'You. Malin. The FBI.'

'The FBI?' That seemed premature. Unless Hammer had been nudging things along again.

'He said that Cayman was OK, not too serious, but they mentioned the FBI.'

'OK. We're in good company. What did they say?'

'All he said was, now I've got to deal with the fucking FBI. I'm quoting.'

'What did he say about Malin?'

'That they do not see eye to eye. He wants Malin to settle but Malin will not. He feels that all Malin wants him for these days is his name. The rest of him is a liability. He did not open up, though. He cannot quite bring himself to say that Malin has him by the balls.'

'What about Gerstman?'

'I mentioned Gerstman. He went quiet. Said he had been a dear friend.'

'And did you talk about us?'

'He did. He said you have been calling everyone he knows and then they call him. He blames you for the press.'

'That's good. Probably.'

'I said I knew you. Not you by name, but Ikertu. I said you were good guys, that I had used you.'

'Did you talk about an introduction?'

'No. I didn't. He's still proud. He wants me to think that he's a big man. Big men don't run to people like you.'

'So what did he say?'

'About you? Nothing. He just sat. I left a silence. He was thinking about it. Thinking hard I would say.'

Webster, too, was quiet for a moment. He knew what he needed to know.

'How did you leave it with him?'

'I told him to come to Istanbul and I would take his mind off it. Have some fun. He said he would need an excuse. He looked like he didn't want fun. He was drinking a lot.'

'Thank you, Savas. That's good. Thank you. Send me your expenses.'

Onder laughed, a jolly laugh. 'That's all right, Ben. Let us keep it clean between us. I enjoyed it. When Konstantin is begging on the street, send me a picture.' He hung up.

Webster had another text from George: Lock was on his way back to the hotel. He looked at his watch. He could be at Claridge's by half past ten. Why leave it until tomorrow? Lock was tired. He would be dwelling on his conversation at dinner. Probably he was not looking forward to whatever he had to do tomorrow. This was the moment.

Webster looked out of the window, saw that it was still raining, and took his coat off the back of his chair. He left his office, skipped down the stairs and walked briskly from the building, looking behind him from time to time for a taxi. He found one on Chancery Lane, and it took him through Lincoln's Inn and along New Oxford Street, the pavements shining yellow in the rain. London was quiet. People walked in twos and threes, heads down. A girl ran across the road with her coat pulled up over her head, her heels skittering in the wet. Webster watched and shivered. Now was the time for him to perform. It was cold but he kept the window open an inch.

At Claridge's a doorman in a top hat opened the taxi door for him. Past the black revolving doors the hotel was alight with yellows and pale greens, reflected and absorbed by the white and black check of the marble floor. A fire burned in a grand hearth by empty leather chairs and in the room beyond white roses and lilies in giant vases bloomed. In this impeccable world Webster felt conspicuous, and his mission shabby. He took off his coat, still cold and heavy with rain, and went downstairs to wash his hands. As he did so he looked up at himself in the mirror. That same deceptively honest face. Had Gerstman seen in it any hint of his undoing? More troubling, should Lock?

He walked back up to the lobby, and then took the grand staircase up through the hotel. At the third floor he turned right and then right again. 316, 318. At the end of this corridor another ran across it. 324 was to the right. As Webster turned the corner he saw a large man with short grey hair standing outside one of the rooms. He was wearing a dark suit with a grey polo neck and stood with his hands clasped in front of him. He looked up at Webster as he passed. Webster gave him a casual glance and walked on, turning into another corridor that opened off this and led back to the stairs.

A bodyguard outside the room. That meant that Lock was either very important or under guard. It also meant that Lock was inside.

Webster went to the lobby and asked at reception how he could make an internal call. A bellboy showed him to a bank of phones in a quiet passage. Webster dialled and the phone rang, four times. It had a long ring, like an American line.

'Yes.' A short yes. Lock sounded irritable. Webster was surprised by his voice. It was rich and full.

'Mr Lock?'

'Yes.'

'Excuse my calling so late, Mr Lock. This is Benedict Webster. From Ikertu.' He paused. 'I was hoping we could talk.'

Webster heard only silence. He couldn't even hear breathing. He wondered whether Lock still had the phone by his ear or had let it drop to his side.

Eventually Lock spoke, not whispering but quietly. 'How do you know where I am?'

'I'm an investigator. I called the big hotels.'

'How do you know I'm in London?'

'I guessed you'd be here after Cayman.'

Silence again. 'Does Tourna know you're talking to me?'

'No one does. Just my boss.'

'What do you want? It's late.'

'I think our interests might be more aligned than you think.' A couple passed Webster and he glanced at them, the man slightly ahead, neither talking. Lock took his time. Onder was right, he was in thinking mode. Before he could think too much Webster said, 'I'm downstairs. We could meet now.' Again a pause. 'If your bodyguard is a problem I could tell you how to lose him.'

That was too much. 'We have nothing to discuss,' said Lock, louder now and stiffer than before. 'Unless it's a settlement.'

'Please understand, Mr Lock. Our interest is in Konstantin Malin, not in you.'

'I have nothing to say. Mr Malin is a friend. You have harassed my associates all round the world and dredged up muck where there is none. Now you are harassing me. Goodnight. If you call again I'll call the police.' He put down the phone.

Webster put the receiver back in its cradle and thought for a moment. This was promising. He found the nearest lift and took it to the fourth floor. He walked down one broad corridor, then another, then a third. Outside a room that must have been directly above Lock's there was a large trolley laden with towels, toilet rolls, notepaper, soaps, bottles of shampoo. The door to the room was open and Webster waited a few yards away for the maid to come out. She was young and thickset, with fair hair tied back in a bun. She closed the door behind her.

'Evening,' Webster said, walking up to her. The maid turned round. 'I was wondering whether I could ask a favour?'

From an inside pocket he brought out a pen and one of his cards and wrote something on its blank side. Then he took an envelope from the trolley, put the card inside and gave the maid two twenty-pound notes.

'Here. Would you give this to the man inside room 324? It's very important the man outside doesn't see it. Take it in some towels or something.'

The maid looked at him doubtfully.

'It's OK. There's nothing else in there. Could you do it now?'

She moved the trolley away from the door of the room and parked it carefully against a wall. Then she walked towards the back stairs. Webster followed her, along the corridor, across the landing and down one flight of stairs. He watched her turn a corner towards Lock's room and then carried on down to the lobby, out of the hotel and home to wait.

CHAPTER ELEVEN

Now they were phoning him. Ikertu knew where he was, they knew where he'd been, and now they were calling him. Perhaps they could tell him what was going to happen to him. He wanted badly to know. What a strange business Webster's was. The Cayman police he could understand. They had a purpose. But what sort of a person did the bidding of a man like Tourna?

Lock was half undressed. On his return from dinner with Onder he had taken off his jacket, shoes and trousers and poured himself a Scotch; the gin wasn't quite working this evening. When Webster had phoned he was sitting on his bed, trying to find a film to watch on television. His body was confused: half of him was four hours east of here, the other half ten hours west, and he had no idea whether he was tired or not. He didn't want to sleep, though. He needed something to occupy his mind.

He flicked through the hotel's on-demand service. No heist films, he thought; no romances, comic or otherwise; no drama either. Mindless action was all he could take.

Lock looked at the phone in its cradle. What had Webster wanted, really? To confirm he was in his room? To make him nervous probably. How funny that Ikertu now felt like an irritant; how funny that just a day ago he had still been in Cayman and daring to think that life was not all bad. He would have stayed there, given any chance. Of all the islands in his offshore world Lock had always liked Cayman. It was tiny, a small town; nothing happened there; the weather was always the same. It had a beach that was seven miles long.

Many years before, Lock had taken Marina to Grand Cayman. He wanted her to see what he saw when he went away, to know how generous the world could be. They stayed at the Ritz-Carlton, a newly built palace by the sea, in a vast suite that overlooked the seven-mile beach. It had two bathrooms and a kitchen that they never used. The walls were a tasteful yellow that sometimes looked like cream, and the French windows, all three of them, had pelmets pleated from some deep red, faintly rustic fabric. On their first morning, awake early with jet lag, they went down to the sea to swim before dawn. As they stepped onto the sand an old man in shorts and a baseball cap ran past; otherwise they saw no one. By the sea's quiet edge they kicked off their plastic hotel slippers and let their white gowns drop to the sand and ran in together, Lock diving as the water reached his knees, Marina screaming with surprise at its warmth. On the eastern horizon the dawn was a slim line of bronze behind black cloud.

They spent a week in Cayman, and most of it in the hotel. Every morning they ate breakfast on the terrace – papayas and mangoes, eggs with broiled ham, a basket of bread and cakes that they always left – and then lay on the beach, read, swam in the luminous sea. Marina kept to the shade. She was reading *Middlemarch*, he remembered, a book he had never finished. He ran in the evenings along the beach, the fine sand making heavy work for his bare feet. At night he could feel the charge between his tanned, dry skin and her cool, pale body, untouched by the sun.

After three days Marina wanted to get out of the hotel and explore. They hired mopeds and rode along the coast road around three-quarters of the island; on their left in amongst the scrub and the thickets of red birch were hotels and golf courses, on their right only the sea. At Rum Point they stopped at a bar and had sandwiches and cold beer in a low cabin on the white sand. Marina had wanted to carry on and Lock had had to explain to her that the road went no further. That was it. That was the island.

That afternoon he went snorkelling with a guide and Marina stayed at the hotel. She was bored. It took him a while to realize it, but she was. At the time he told himself that this was because he worked hard in a stressful job and needed to switch off, completely – had earned the right to, in fact – whereas she had space left in her head. Marina seemed to think the same. For the rest of their stay they were happy with each other but somehow this was his holiday now, not hers.

And ten years later here he was, back at the Ritz-Carlton, in a smaller room, preparing for his interview with the Cayman police. This time, instead of his beautiful wife, he had with him Lawrence Griffin and two immense Russian men. Still, he was happy to arrive. After checking in he stood by the window in his room, unable to concentrate; he was meant to be going through long lists of companies and transactions that he had drawn up for the following day. Looking down on the beach he could only think of Marina. The reason she didn't like it here, he finally understood, was that she needed to remain engaged with the world. Always. Escape made no sense to her because she had nothing to escape from.

It still made sense to him, though, a little to his surprise. He might be about to be questioned by a policeman for the first time in his life, he might be silently terrified, but he was pleased to be here. He liked his room, with its high bed, its radio alarm clock, the top layers of bedding that were magically removed every night before he went to sleep. He liked going down to breakfast and filling his bowl with yoghurt and orange segments before going to the chef for fried eggs. He liked changing the settings on the showerhead so that the water in a hard jet buffeted the back of his neck. He liked hanging up his suits and his shirts, rolling his ties, arranging his razor and his toothbrush in the bathroom and making a compact, temporary world for himself where Russians, even the one stationed outside his door, didn't exist. He liked the heat, and the calmness of the sea. Most of all, though, he liked remembering Marina, and a time when he was still fresh enough to want to impress her.

The police were not terrifying, in the end. They were both Englishmen, in their fifties, polite but firm. They asked him many of the same questions that Greene had asked two weeks earlier in Paris, but fewer of them, and without the same sneer. And Griffin was there to prevent him from digging any holes. It wasn't comfortable, but nor was it bloody. Lock got the impression that they were being as thorough as their resources allowed. He attended two sessions, one the afternoon he arrived and one the following morning, and towards the end, when it was clear that loose ends were now being tied up, he began to think about what he would do with his day of freedom in paradise. Later he would see that as the moment he must have irritated fate.

One of the detectives, until now the quieter of the two, began to ask Lock detailed questions about the banks that his Cayman companies used. Lock named them: two in Cayman, one in the BVI, one in Bermuda. Then the detective began to concentrate on which international banks those banks used to hold and transfer money for them. This was new to Lock, and to Griffin; in fact, neither knew. The final question was whether Lock knew if any of his banks had correspondent relationships with US banks. Again, Lock said he didn't know. After some final formalities, Lock and Griffin left.

Outside the police station, Lock breezily suggested that he and Griffin go to get lunch and a beer. He couldn't remember the last time he had felt relieved about anything. He might even buy a drink for his bodyguards, if they'd take it. But Griffin was preoccupied.

'Why do you think they asked you about the banks?'

'I have no idea,' said Lock, squinting at Griffin in the sun. 'Maybe they always ask about the banks. They are the financial crimes unit. Maybe they can't help themselves.'

Griffin didn't say anything. Lock started to steer him up the street towards a bar he knew. God, it was a beautiful day, hot, enough breeze.

'Wait,' said Griffin. 'I think it meant something. That thing about the US? My guess is that either they're hoping to get the Bureau involved because they know they can't crack this, or the Bureau's already expressed an interest. That would explain why we had it so easy in there.'

Lock looked down at the ground and shook his head. 'Fuck, Lawrence. You are a tonic. You could at least have let me have my beer. What do you mean? Why the fuck would the FBI – you mean the FBI, yes? Why would the FBI be interested, all of a sudden, in Cayman companies and Russian oil? For crying out loud. I thought that went well, for once.'

'Because the money flows through the States. All money flows through the States, just about. Let me tell you something. In Manhattan, southern district, on an ugly stretch of wall in the Assistant US Attorney's office, there's a big poster showing the Milky Way. And underneath, it reads "Jurisdiction of the Southern District of Manhattan".' Griffin looked at Lock, who was staring up the street and out to sea. 'They can go anywhere. They'd love this.'

FBI. Those three letters followed Lock all the way back to London. They wouldn't leave his head. He saw men in dark suits and white shirts coming for him in the night, locking him in a dark room under a bright light and refusing to believe that he didn't know enough to convict Malin. He needed a lawyer. How on earth was he going to find a lawyer with his constant escort?

A prisoner in Claridge's. At least that was funny. Quite funny. He was tired of the constant attention. How could the politicians and the oligarchs stand it? Apart from anything else they were so big, his two henchmen; at every moment they seemed to occupy most of the space around him. He felt small and airless in between. And still he didn't know whether they were there to stop him running, or to keep him out of trouble.

Someone knocked on the door. 'Housekeeping.'

'Wait a moment. Hang on.' Lock went to the bathroom for a dressing gown. Wrapping it round him he went and opened the door.

'Housekeeping. Turn-down service. May I come in?' A maid in a white pinafore and pale-blue housecoat was standing there, a pile of fresh white towels in her arms.

'Yes. Yes, come in,' said Lock automatically, standing out of the maid's way. She closed the door. 'But the bed's already turned down.'

The maid adjusted her grip on the towels and pulled an envelope from in amongst them. 'A gentleman asked me to give you this,' she said, handing it to Lock and taking the towels into the bathroom. He looked at it for a moment, front and back, and then opened it. The maid came back into the room, said goodnight and left. Inside the envelope was a card: Benedict Webster, Principal, Ikertu Consulting Ltd. Nothing else. He threw it into a waste-paper basket and then thought better of it. He didn't want someone finding it there. As he retrieved it he saw that there was writing on the back: *I meant what I said.*

Taking his whisky from his bedside table Lock sat down on the bed and flicked the card in his fingers. He found his phone, keyed in Webster's number and added it to the memory under his father's name. Then he took the card and inserted it in between a chest of drawers and the wall, letting it drop down out of sight.

For a moment he stood and thought. Then he put his trousers on, his socks and shoes, grabbed his coat and a sweater from his suitcase and left the room.

'I'm going to see my wife,' he said to the bodyguard. This one was called Ivan. Lock had tried talking to him on the flight back from Cayman but conversation hadn't flowed. 'Are you coming?'

He set off towards the stairs. Ivan, taken aback for a second, followed him at a run, reaching into his pocket for his phone and snapping Russian into it as they waited for the lift. Downstairs they walked together through the lobby, Lock a few paces ahead and walking quickly.

'Arkady is bringing the car,' said Ivan, as Lock slipped through the revolving doors.

Arkady was clearly annoyed at being disturbed, perhaps at being woken, and he drove fast through the wet streets, Lock giving him directions. At Holland Park Lock told them that he didn't know how long he would be and that they could go back to bed if they liked. Neither said anything. Lock walked up the broad white steps to Marina's porch and rang the buzzer. He looked at his watch; it was nearly eleven. It was possible she was in bed. He waited for a full minute, conscious of Arkady watching him from the car. Then the intercom clicked.

'Hello.'

'Hi. It's me.'

'Richard? Richard, why . . .' She let the sentence die away and buzzed him in.

Halfway up the stairs Lock heard Marina's door open on the landing above. When he reached it she wasn't there – he gave a delicate double knock and went in. She was in the kitchen, wearing a pale-green cotton dressing gown printed with lilies. As Lock entered, she was at the sink pouring herself a glass of water, half turned away from him. A large pine table was between them, and on it a small crystal vase full of blue and purple anemones. Lock could smell onions and coffee.

'I'm sorry,' he said. 'I had to talk to someone.'

She put the glass down on the draining board and turned to him. 'You woke Vika.'

'I'm sorry. Is she still awake?'

'I told her to go back to sleep.' Marina moved past him and shut the kitchen door. 'What are you doing here?' She went back to the sink and stood against it, her arms crossed.

'I wanted to see you.'

'Richard, I didn't even know you were in London. Why didn't you call?'

'It's not been an easy time.' He moved towards the table, rested his hands on the back of a chair and dipped his head so that his chin almost touched his chest. 'I'm sorry.' When he looked up again there were tears starting in his eyes. Marina watched him, worried. 'I wanted to see someone who didn't want anything from me. That's all.'

Neither said anything for a moment. Lock looked down at the table. 'Can I have a drink?'

'I don't have much. There's some vodka. How much have you had?'

'Not a lot.' He looked up and smiled, his charming smile. 'I managed the stairs.'

Marina went to the freezer, produced a frosted bottle and poured the thick liquid, like syrup, into a tumbler.

'We don't have proper glasses.' She handed it to him and he sat down at the table.

'Will you join me?'

'It's late, Richard. I was in bed.'

'Please.'

'No. Thank you.'

'Well, sit, at least.'

Marina pulled out a chair and sat across the table from him. She rested her chin on her thumbs and watched him take a sip of the vodka. The bags under his eyes were heavy and grey.

'What is it? Has something happened?'

He took a moment to respond, as if trying to frame everything right.

'Outside,' he said, gesturing to the window with his glass, 'are two ugly Russians in a Volvo. They go everywhere with me. I've just been to Cayman with them, and they'll be going back to Moscow with me tomorrow. They're a new feature. They daren't leave me alone. I should be flattered.'

Marina looked at him with serious eyes. 'I don't understand.'

'They're here to stop me making good my escape. They're Malin's. When I went back to Moscow after Paris they were waiting for me. I think they're here to make sure I don't fall off a hotel roof. Or that I do. I can't work it out.'

'You look terrible.'

'I'm tired. Some of it's jet lag. Some of it's thinking about Dmitry.' He drank again, a gulp this time. 'And I'm sure that . . . when we went for dinner – with Vika, before Paris. God, Paris. That's another story. But that night, when I walked you back here I'm sure I was being followed. Sure of it. There was a car outside the restaurant and as we turned into your road it pulled past us and into the next street.' He put his glass down and ran his hand through his hair. 'My phone squawks all the time. I think they're listening to it. And Ivan and bloody Igor at my side all day. I can't stand it. It's driving me nuts. And meanwhile, Christ . . . That's just the Russians, but meanwhile I've got the FBI, the FB fucking I – sorry, I'm sorry. I've got the FBI wanting to know who I am and what I've been doing for that vicious fat crook for the last fifteen years, and investigators turning up in my bloody hotel room. I can't stand it, Marina.'

Marina pushed her chair back, stood up and moved round to sit next to him. He looked at her with his head resting on one hand and she put her hand on his forearm.

'Come here,' she said.

Lock turned in his chair so that they were facing each other and close. He put his head on her shoulder, his hands on her back, and for a minute they sat like that, a little awkward, Lock gently jolting with sobs. When he sat up to look at her his eyes were bloodshot and full of tears.

'I'm sorry,' he said. 'I didn't mean to come here and collapse.' He dried his eyes on the sleeve of his jumper. 'It's just . . .'

'Tell me everything,' said Marina, and stood up. She came back to the table with a glass, and poured more vodka for Lock and some for herself. 'I want to know.'

So Lock did. He told her about Paris. He told her what he had learned about Gerstman's death. He told her about the reception waiting for him on his return to Moscow, about his failed attempt to steal himself some insurance, about Cayman, and the FBI, and Webster. And about Webster's card. He talked fluently and forcefully, and in explaining it to Marina some things began to make sense to him. He steadily drank the vodka. Marina listened gravely, sipping at hers, alive to every word.

'I can't go back to Moscow,' he said when he was done. 'You're right. It sucks me dry. There's nothing there any more. Do you know what I feel like? I feel like an informer, and everyone knows, and it's just a matter of time before they come to lynch me. And I haven't said anything.' He gave an abrupt, sarcastic laugh. 'I haven't said anything to anyone.'

'Maybe it's time you did.'

Lock sighed. 'The problem is, I don't have much to tell. That's the hell of it.'

'So what will you do?'

'I don't know. Stay here for ever?' He looked at her steadily. She was still pale. Still beautiful. She didn't respond. 'Can I stay tonight, at least? I'd like to. I miss you.'

Holding his gaze Marina took his hand in hers. 'Richard, no,' she said. 'I hate what you're going through. But we are the same, for now. You and I. That hasn't changed.'

'Even after the letter?'

'That's not what the letter meant. You have to get out. Otherwise nothing can happen.'

Lock nodded, the slightest movement of his head. 'Thank you, though. For writing. I read it sometimes. It's about the only company I have.'

For a second Marina looked at him and in the deep green of her eyes – still clear, still intense – he saw some trace of her love for him, not yet extinguished, communicated to him so sharply in that instant that even he, his instincts withered almost to nothing, could not mistake it.

He broke the silence. 'Can I sleep on the sofa? I've had enough of hotels.' He smiled. 'Not something you've heard me say before.'

'No, Richard. It's not good. Not for Vika. One day, but not now.' This time he didn't nod; he just looked at the flowers on the table. Marina watched him. 'Maybe you should talk to Webster.'

He lifted his head and looked at her.

'Maybe he does mean what he says,' she said.

'For the last three months he's made my life a misery. Now it suits him to finish me off. No.'

Marina thought for a while. 'He's the only person who wants what you want. Something that will hurt Konstantin.'

Lock shook his head. 'No. I don't want to hurt Konstantin.

I just want him to go away. I want to be left alone. I want a new life. I want my family back.' He paused to see her reaction; she took his hand and held it in hers. 'I do. I really do. I can't believe how blind I was to this. To you. You cannot imagine how much I want to wake up here with you next to me tomorrow morning. With Vika in our bed. That's punishment enough. I shouldn't be going through this.'

Marina got up from her chair and stood over him, her hand on his shoulder. 'Richard, I think you should go. Go and sleep. Maybe stay a day or two in London. Come and see us. After school tomorrow.'

Lock sat with his head in his hands and his elbows on the table. That sounded good. But it was just delay. The last freedoms of a dying man.

'How do you get into your garden?' he said at last.

Marina looked puzzled.

'Do you have access to your garden?' he said.

'Yes, it's shared. Why?'

'How do you get to it?'

'There's a door at the back. In the basement. Why? What do you mean?'

'I've had enough. I need a night of freedom. A few days. I can't think with those two thugs in my lap.' He got up to leave.

'That's crazy. Where will you go?'

'I don't know. Anywhere. I am not walking back into that prison of a city. Come on. Show me.'

Slightly wary of him now, Marina told him to follow her. Together they descended the stairs by the light from the street lamps outside; Lock told her not to switch the landing lights on. A minute later they were in the garden, a large open space of lawn lined with narrow planted beds. Marina stood in the doorway and Lock turned to say goodbye.

'Richard, this is crazy. How are you going to get over the wall?'

'Over the shed. It's made for it.' At the far end of the garden, a shed, painted white and looking ghostly in the orange night of the city, sat next to a high brick wall, perhaps twelve feet high, that separated this row of houses from Holland Park beyond. Above the wall spindly branches poked up like twig brooms.

'How will you get down?'

'I'll jump. I'll be fine. It's the first thing I've done for myself in fifteen years.'

He kissed her, and as he turned to walk away she took his hand in hers and held it for a moment; at her touch his bravado faded and he fought the urge to stay.

'I'll be fine,' he said at last.

No one had raked the grass and wet leaves squelched under his feet. In a moment he was on the sloped roof of the shed, and the top of the wall was level with his chest; he pulled himself up and sat, feeling damp seep through the seat of his trousers. Marina was still watching him. He waved to her, let himself down the other side so that he was hanging from his fingertips, and let himself drop.

He landed in a bush, scratching a calf in the process and falling backwards onto his back. He raised himself up on his elbows and lay there for a moment in the muddy earth with rain falling on his face. Sweet London rain. He stood up, brushed himself off and in no great hurry walked towards Kensington High Street. He took inventory. He had the clothes he was in, damp around the backside from his fall but otherwise serviceable; his passport; his wallet, with around four hundred pounds in various currencies; the letter from Marina; and three mobile phones, which he should now turn off. He had read that you could be traced through your phone whether or not it was switched on – even listened to. He stopped and took the batteries out of each, keeping the bits separate in his pockets.

He couldn't remember the last time he had been in an empty park at night. It made him feel like a teenager. His over-coat gave little protection and the trees had now lost nearly all their leaves, but he didn't mind being wet and walked across the huge expanse of grass with his face turned up to the sky. His trousers flapped coldly round his calves in the steady wind. Around the edges of the park lay London like a thin border.

As Holland Park narrowed towards the street he began to wonder how he was going to scale the fence at the end. What if it was huge? He couldn't remember what was there. Through the trees he could see a stretch of wall and a fence behind some thick bushes. It looked high enough to be a struggle, but not worse. As he got closer, though, he saw open arches set into the wall, and in the end he just walked out into Kensington, feeling as light as a cloud.

Newly free, Lock was surprised that he seemed to know what to do. It was half past twelve. No flights, no trains to Paris, probably no trains anywhere. Tonight he would hide in London. He walked up Kensington High Street until he found a bank and drew as much money as he could from its cash-point machine. Then he walked down a side street away from the park, south towards Earls Court. Here he saw no one. There were few lights showing in the mansion blocks that lined the streets; London had gone to bed. Occasionally a car passed and he controlled the urge to turn and look at it. On the Cromwell Road he stood for a minute or two and then hailed a taxi, telling it to take him to Victoria.

He asked the driver to stop by the train station, paid him, tipping him well, and set off in search of a hotel. On the main streets he passed large business hotels, bland and anony-mous enough, but they weren't what he wanted. Eventually he turned down a narrow side road where every house was a guest house: en suite bathrooms as standard, TV in every room. Through their glass doors he could see striped wallpaper and dirty brown carpets, beech veneer furniture and bright strip lights, but no guests or staff, no people at all. Signs hanging in front windows told him which had vacancies. He wondered who stayed in these places, and realized he had no idea. Salesmen? Refugees of one kind or another? Money-launderers on the run?

He walked back down the row and found one that looked neater than the others. The Hotel Carlisle. There were geraniums, a little tatty, growing in pots on the windowsills and its entrance hall was warmly lit by a standard lamp.

At his ring a brisk, unsmiling woman came to the door. It took her under a minute to take his money and tell him where to find room 28. He told her he was Mr Alan Norman, a name that as he said it sounded so strikingly unconvincing that he felt sure that she would question it, but she showed no interest and to his relief didn't ask to see his passport. No one would find him here.

Room 28, at the rear of the house, looked out over the backs of other Georgian houses and a mess of light industrial units and warehouses. It was small: there was enough room for two single beds, a bedside table in between them, and a pine wardrobe so close to a bed that its door only opened a foot. The walls were covered in woodchip paper painted over in a sickly fluorescent green, and in a corner a heavily shaded ceiling light spotlit the navy covers of one of the beds, leaving everything else in gloom. The advertised en suite contained a shower with a worn plastic concertina screen and a tiny basin that overhung the toilet. There was no television after all.

Lock took it all in and was pleased. It was clean enough, and it was his. He took off his coat, hung it on the back of the door and lay down on the bed. He was happy with this newly basic existence but there were things he wanted. He would have liked a bottle of whisky, and some pyjamas. Maybe he would ask the woman downstairs if there was anything to drink. Still, it was just one night. Tomorrow he would catch a train to Newhaven and from there a boat to Dieppe. Then he would hire a car, drive to Switzerland, withdraw all his money and disappear somewhere for a good long time. Go and see Onder in Istanbul and see about a new passport. Onder must know someone; he was the sort of man that would. And then on, somewhere unexpected and a little chaotic. Indonesia, perhaps, one of the remoter islands. Or Vanuatu. The end of the earth.

What would happen then? Malin would look for him. Maybe the FBI would look for him. Perhaps the Swiss. He had forgotten the Swiss. What had Rast said, so unflappably? 'I shouldn't be telling you this, Richard, but maybe you can make use of it. The Swiss prosecutor thinks you have an interesting business, and is becoming very curious.' That was part of it. What if the Swiss detained him at the border? What if they already had enough on him? They could alert the Russians and ship me back home. God. If he had been clever he would have asked Bashaev to find out what the Swiss were doing.

There were other problems with his plan. Could you take that much money out of a Swiss bank? Yes, he was sure you could. He had read stories about people leaving Switzerland with far more than the eight or nine million that he had in there. But what was that money, if they stopped him at the border? Where did it come from? How did he explain it? And how was he planning to carry it around: in a suitcase? To Istanbul? And then, and then: let's say all this worked and he reached Sulawesi, how long would it be before Malin tracked him down? Horkov would know about his disappearance soon – by the morning, he guessed, when Ivan and Arkady finally realized that he wasn't in Marina's flat. Even having

Horkov on your side was terrifying; Horkov and his people tracking you for all time was paralysing.

His head was aching now as the vodka faded. He could feel the muscles in his shoulders tight against his neck and his back hurt. Who was he to escape? In Russia he had grown fat and timid and no longer had instincts he could trust. It was like releasing a pet dog into the wild. And if he made it, what then? A lifetime of the fear he was feeling now.

CHAPTER TWELVE

Webster came home a little after midnight. He undressed in the bathroom and got into bed as quietly as he could, sliding under the duvet and lying on his front. Elsa was already asleep. He lay there for a moment listening to her breathing, slow and deep. She was on her side, facing him, and he could feel her breath on his neck.

'Is it over yet?' she said in a low mumble.

'I thought you were sleeping.'

'I was.'

'Sorry. No. He went to his wife's. Ex-wife's. He's still there.'

'I wonder if they're asleep.'

Webster kissed her on the forehead, turned onto his side and watched the light from the street lamps creep in around the blinds. Lock would be in bed by now, lying awake, no doubt, and considering his choice. He had to be.

The next morning he woke early, before Nancy and Daniel, who were surprised to see him up when they came down for breakfast. He made them French toast with honey and ate two pieces himself. His phone sat on the kitchen table, fully charged and ready for another day of precise little messages from George Black. There had been one this morning, sent at half past six: 'Refreshed team. Subject still at wife's residence. Unknown surveillance in place with same team and car.' Last night the mysterious Ford had followed Lock to

Holland Park, to an address Webster recognized as Marina Lock's, and George had sat discreetly behind it.

Then nothing for hours. Webster walked the children to school across the park. The rain was now falling as a soft drizzle, and their bright coats shone in the grey light. He didn't want to go to the office. There was little point in being there. He could go to Holland Park, to be close to events, but there was no good reason for that, either. In the end, rather aimlessly, he set off walking into the city, wondering whether Lock's reunion with his wife was a good or a bad thing. If he was trying to engage with his old life that was surely good. Webster realized with surprise that he was pleased for him.

It was half past ten and he had reached New Bond Street when his phone rang.

'George, good morning. How is it?'

'We're not sure, Ben. We think we may have had a loss.'

Christ. He checked the urge to shout.

'Go on.'

'Well. You'll appreciate, Ben, there's a lot of activity in the vicinity. There's us watching the Ford and the Volvo and we've had to stay a long way back to make sure we're not detected. Luckily it's a nice wide-ish street with a sweep to it other-wise I'm not sure we'd have caught it at all.' George waited for comment but Webster said nothing. 'So, nothing happened all night. We assumed he'd emerge some time around eight or nine, and we changed the team early to be ready. But there was no movement. Then at 10.13 one of the men from the Volvo, one of the bodyguards, got out and went up the steps to the house. He was stood in the porch for thirty seconds or so and then he went inside. A minute and a half later he ran out of the house and down the stairs, into the Volvo and off onto Holland Park Road, heading west. The Ford followed, and we had the bike on them. But they turned off up Ladbroke Grove, and halfway down they timed the lights beautifully, took a right and there was no way we could make it. In short we lost them. From the way they did it I'd say we'd been compromised.'

'The Ford made you?'

'Yes.'

'So where are you now?'

'I'm outside Claridge's. Our two subjects from the Volvo are in there now.'

'And where the hell is he?'

'I don't know, Ben. There's no way he could've got out the front door. Not with all those eyes on him. Through people's gardens perhaps? Or over the wall into the park.'

'Holland Park?'

'Holland Park.'

Webster thought for a moment. He could be anywhere. He could be on a train to France or seven miles above the Atlantic. 'Keep an eye on the Volvo. Make that your priority. Have someone at the wife's house in case he comes back. What else?'

'Nothing useful.'

'All right. Stay in touch.'

'Sorry, Ben.'

'That's OK. Listen, George, there's one thing you can do. See if you can find out what card Lock's using to pay his bill.'

He hung up. Christ, this was finely balanced – and agonizing with it. If Lock had run, that was good because he needed somewhere to run to. But if they couldn't find him that was useless; and if Malin found him first that would be worse. He dialled the travel agent. Richard Lock hadn't booked himself on any flights that morning. That was something. Then he rang Yuri.

Yuri was a Ukrainian who had once worked for the KGB and then for the SZRU, Ukraine's foreign intelligence agency. He had retired from government service years before, and now ran a small intelligence company in Antwerp specializing in what he called on his website 'technical solutions to information problems'. Much of what he did was bug things: cars, offices, houses, hotel rooms. Today Webster wanted him for something else. Yuri had a means of locating mobile phone signals, to within any particular cell, anywhere in Europe and most of the Middle East. Webster only used it in emergencies, and this qualified. He had no idea how it worked, and didn't particularly want to find out. He gave Yuri Lock's telephone number, a Moscow mobile, told him it was urgent and asked him to see what he could do.

As he hung up his phone immediately rang.

'Hello.'

'Ben, it's George. We've checked at the hotel, discreetly, and he hasn't checked out of his room. One of the bodyguards went off in the car. The other one's still in there. We decided to stay put. I'm working on the credit card.'

'That's fine.'

Webster ended the call and held the phone in his lap. After twenty seconds it rang again. He picked it up without checking the number.

'Hello.'

'Is this Ben Webster?' A voice he didn't recognize.

'Yes, it is.'

'This is Richard Lock.' Webster felt his heart quicken. He didn't say anything. He took the phone from his ear for a moment and looked at the screen: it was a London number, a landline. 'I thought . . . I thought it might be useful to talk through our positions.' Lock's voice was smaller than it had been the night before, but businesslike.

'Yes,' said Webster. 'I'm sure it would.' He paused to let Lock talk.

'I'm concerned that we may be missing opportunities for a settlement.'

'Where are you calling from? You're still in London?'

'Yes. How did you . . . yes, I'm in London today.'

'The number showed up on my phone. Shall we meet?'

Lock hesitated. 'Er, yes. Yes. I have meetings this afternoon but I'm free now for an hour or two. Somewhere neutral, perhaps.'

'Claridge's?'

'Probably better somewhere we won't be seen.' Of course.

'Yes.' Webster thought for a moment. He was slightly unprepared. He needed somewhere entirely out of the way. He should have planned this. 'Let me see. OK, I know. Take a cab to Lisson Grove, and get out where it meets Church Street. There's a cafe on the left about a hundred yards down. I can't remember its name but no businessman has ever been there. I'll be there in twenty minutes.'

'Church Street. I may be a little longer. How will I know you?'

'I'll be wearing a suit. See you shortly.'

Webster turned and with new purpose walked north, looking over his shoulder for taxis. He called George, and Hammer, who was entertained.

'What are you planning to do with him?'

'Get him to see the light.'

Hammer laughed. 'I'd say he's already seen it.'

Church Street was five minutes north of Marylebone but somehow a different London altogether. This was a place where people lived rather than worked. It was lined with stalls selling fish in polystyrene boxes, fruit and vegetables in one-pound plastic bowls, women's coats tightly packed on circular racks, floor polish and washing-up liquid in plastic crates. One stall was given over to gloves in black leather or wool of every colour, another to earrings and bracelets strewn across a table in cellophane packets like squares of ice. It was dry now but a cold wind blew steadily down the street and the market was quiet. Webster ducked between two stalls through to the row of shops behind and found the cafe. Enzo's Market Café. Its window frames were painted pale blue and chipped in places to a dull grey beneath, and in the windows themselves pictures of food, all yellows and oranges and reds, displayed what you could eat if you held your nerve and went in.

Inside, Enzo's was thick with the smell of frying and old oil. Webster ordered himself a mug of tea, took it to a Formica table fixed to the far wall and sat facing the door, busying himself with his BlackBerry so that he would look occupied when Lock arrived. By the window an old man wearing a shapeless brown tweed jacket was closely inspecting a newspaper that he had spread out over the whole table; against the other wall, by the door, two women in thick quilted coats, propped up straight in their chairs, talked about the fortunes of the market. They were the only people there apart from the young man behind the till who looked as if he must be Enzo's son. Lock would make six.

He arrived ten minutes later, self-conscious, his forehead sweating. Webster stood up to greet him. This was Lock, but not the Lock of the magazine pictures he had seen. He was tall, six foot or thereabouts – the pictures had made him look shorter. He was wearing a well-cut overcoat in heavy navy wool but he was anything but smart: he had a day's growth of sandy beard, his shoes looked damp and his grey flannel trousers, badly creased, had light sprays of dried mud around the ankles. He seemed less fleshy than in the photographs, less smooth, and his eyes were tired.

'Mr Webster.' He held out his hand.

'Mr Lock.' Webster took it. It was cold and dry. Lock looked hard at Webster for a moment, as if to establish that they were there as equals and that he shouldn't assume otherwise.

Webster broke the silence. 'What can I get you? I'm afraid this isn't quite what you're used to.'

'No. That's fine. A cup of tea, please.'

Webster ordered and they sat, Lock keeping his coat on.

'Do you have a phone, Mr Webster?' Webster nodded. 'Could I ask you to switch it off and take out the battery? It's probably silly but in Russia you get used to doing it.'

Webster was used to this with Russians; no one else seemed to do it. He told Lock that was fine, and spent a moment trying to slide the back off his BlackBerry. Eventually it gave; he removed its battery, did the same with his regular phone, sat back and let Lock start.

'Thank you for seeing me,' said Lock, scratching at the beard on his chin. His breath was rich and stale, as if he had been eating too much meat. 'I wouldn't have . . . This isn't for pleasure, you understand. I think we may be able to help each other.' He paused. 'You've been busy these last few weeks.'

Webster kept a solemn face and said nothing.

Lock smiled an unconvincing smile. 'I'm beginning to wish that we'd hired you first.' Webster gave a little nod of acknowledgement. 'But what concerns me is that after Paris there's . . . there's no clarity. Too many courts, too many bloody lawyers – charging more than you, I should imagine. I think the best ending for everybody will be agreed outside court. Except the lawyers, perhaps. This thing is hurting my business and costing Aristotle money. A fortune if his fees are as bad as ours. But I'm finding it hard to get through to him. That's where I thought you could help.'

Webster nodded again, slowly. This was good: Lock was talking too much, offering too much. 'And you think Tourna wants a settlement?'

'If it's the right amount, yes. That's how it works.'

'I'm not sure. I think he wants revenge. I'm not sure he

cares about getting his money back. I may be wrong.' Webster took a sip of thick brown tea. 'And Malin? He wants one?'

'Wants what?'

'A settlement.'

'That's irrelevant. It's my business. My dispute.'

'Mr Lock . . .'

'Richard.'

'Richard. With respect, we won't get anywhere with a settlement if you won't be straight with me. I'm not wearing a wire. There's no one else here.' He looked round the room and then back at Lock. 'These are not my people.' A pause. 'Anything you tell me stays with me. You have my word on that. I'm not here to trick you.'

Lock scratched the beard on his cheek again, shaking his head. 'I'm a businessman, Mr Webster. I have a business. When someone attacks that business it's mine to protect. I'm not sure I understand what you mean.'

'Richard, I think you do. You asked for this meeting and I'm happy to be here, but if we can't be open with each other I'll leave. I know a lot about you now. But I knew how you and Malin worked long ago – before I took on this case. I know Russia. I know how it works. Malin is the player, and you're his bagman.' Webster stopped for a moment to let Lock react. Lock had turned his head to one side and was looking down at the floor, his chin cupped in his hand, his elbow on the table. He didn't want to hear this. We're close. 'Richard, I also know that that man outside your hotel room is not a body-guard.' Lock looked back at him. 'Otherwise you wouldn't have had to run away from him last night.'

Lock said nothing for a moment. 'What do you mean?'

'We've been following you. I'm sorry. We saw you go to your wife's house but we never saw you leave. Just now – what, an hour ago? – your two bodyguards or whatever they are had a word with your wife and then tore off. You haven't been back to the hotel. We've checked.'

Lock held Webster's eye. Webster could see resentment in there but resilience too.

'Richard, your time's up. Every relationship like this, every one I've ever seen – you can't break it. Konstantin can't. He needs you as much as you need him. But the outside world can. The FBI can. They're itching to tear you two apart.' Lock had stopped looking at Webster. He was gazing at the table, appearing not to hear, but Webster went on. 'Only, the final act, that tends to be down to the Russians. The guys like you always hang on too long. And when the Russians don't trust them any more, you know what happens. I don't need to tell you this, do I? You know it better than I do.'

Lock pushed his chair back and made to stand up. With defiance he looked Webster in the eye. 'I came here to talk business and you just . . . harangue me. I don't need this. You have no idea how little I need this.'

Webster leaned forward and put his hand flat on the table, a gesture of finality and trust. 'Richard. I'm not here to offend you. But you've got a decision to make. You're here in yesterday's clothes with mud on your shoes for what? Because you thought it would be fun to jump over walls in the middle of the night? You're not the man you were a week ago. Your life has changed.'

Lock stood up. Webster went on.

'Was it part of the plan, to bolt? Or blind panic? Or would your wife not let you stay?'

Without looking at Webster, Lock walked away between tables and out of the door. His mug was still full of tea. Webster saw his face through the window as he turned onto the street. There was no trace of insult there, no anger; only fear, like a man pursued.

Webster drummed his fingers on the tabletop in thought.

Ten more minutes with him was all he needed. He put his phone back together and waited for it to warm up. He needed to call Black and let him know that Lock had left and was heading east on Church Street. His tea was still warm, and he sat with the thick white mug in his hands. He could go after Lock now, catch him up along the street, or he could find him later, let his thoughts do the work. But it had to be today.

His phone chimed awake, and as he picked it up the bell above the door jangled. Lock stood in the doorway with an odd look of contrition on his face. Webster looked up as Lock threaded his way between orange plastic chairs and sat down again. For a moment neither man spoke.

'Can we discuss me?' Lock said at last.

Webster gave a small, understanding nod. 'I think we should.'

'I . . . I went to church this morning. That beautiful one on George Street. Do you know it?' Webster shook his head. 'You should go. Walk through the door and it's like being in Italy. I thought that if I told someone everything then perhaps . . . But I couldn't find a priest. And I wasn't sure what I was there to confess.'

'Sins of omission?'

'Possibly. Yes. I have omitted rather a lot.'

For the next half an hour, Lock talked. He talked about Cayman, and the horrifying spectre of the FBI. He talked about Malin and his growing impatience, about the body-guards and the prison that Moscow had become. He talked about Gerstman, and the terror that still struck him whenever he imagined his death. He left very little out.

It seemed to do him good. Webster listened closely, inter-rupting with the occasional question, and it occurred to him as Lock revived a little that in some respects his own profes-sion was not so different from his wife's. He had felt this before, the beginnings of a strange dependency, a stranger intimacy. Each needed to trust the other, whether that was wise or not.

Then it was his turn. He told Lock what he knew about Malin, and what the FBI would come to know. Lock interjected that the Swiss were also interested, so he thought, and Webster said there would probably be more. He laid out what would happen next: how charges would be drawn up and international arrest warrants issued; how Lock would be forced to remain in Russia; how the newspapers, frankly quiet until now, would feed happily on it for months. He began to remind Lock of the precedents, the helicopter crashes, the drive-by shootings on motorbikes, until Lock cut him short.

And then he described the alternative. Cooperate with law enforcement. Engage independent lawyers. Work against Malin; expose him. Go to prison, perhaps, but claim some small piece of your life as your own.

Throughout, Lock sat and listened, nodding occasionally as if to stay in touch from somewhere far away. He seldom looked at Webster; he stared at the table, out of the window, at the other people in the cafe, which was busier now. He was still in his coat, and underneath its bulk his body looked shrunken and collapsed. When Webster was done he sat nodding steadily for several moments.

'The trouble is,' he said, finally looking at Webster, 'I don't think I know enough to be of use.'

'What do you mean?'

'I don't know enough. Never have. Kesler explained it to me. To hurt Malin you need to show he's a criminal. I don't know he's a criminal. Or I can't prove it. I just know that he's a rich Russian and I own things for him.' He leaned back and tried to find something in his trouser pocket; it sounded full of change. Eventually he pulled out a small plastic rectangle and held it up for Webster to see. 'On here is everything I know. Every document from my files – every transfer, every company, every instruction. I thought I should have it all somewhere safe in case I needed it. But the funny thing – do you know what it is?'

'No.'

'The funny thing, is that it's so clean. Money goes from here to there, it buys things, it grows, but I don't know where it's from. Fifteen years I've been doing this and I don't know – have no idea,' Lock beat out the syllables on the table with the flat of his hand, 'where any of it comes from. I guess, like you guess. But I don't know.'

Webster felt his stomach lift and fall. 'So what did Gerstman know?'

'Did you know him?'

'I saw him before he died.'

Lock frowned a little, as if he was thinking something through for the first time. 'So it was you.'

'I like to think it wasn't. He wouldn't speak to me.'

'Do you know how he died?'

'I have an idea. He didn't strike me as the type to kill himself. Or to do it in that way. So either he knew something, or it was a message.'

'To me.'

'Perhaps.' Webster watched Lock take this in. Either way, he thought, one of us precipitated his death. He didn't say it. 'So what did he know?'

'More than me, I suppose. He was a Russian, for a start. He knew where the money came from. Or some of it.'

'Enough to make him dangerous?'

'Dmitry was much too clever to be a danger to those people. He did everything he could to show Konstantin that. I thought he believed him.'

Webster waited a second or two. His fingers drummed on the table, his foot tapped on the floor. There was a gamble in this next move, since it was still possible that Lock was here on Malin's behalf. Look at him, though, with the livid dark bags under his eyes and the fear in his face; he needs me.

There was something he had to clear first. He looked Lock in the eye. 'Tell me. Do you remember an article about Faringdon? From ten years ago. In English. The only one there's really been. It said that you were buying things for the Russian state.'

Lock frowned, as if rooting through his memory. 'No. There's never been anything. Not until you started.'

'It was by a friend of mine. A Russian woman.'

'No.' Lock shook his head. 'I would have remembered. Is it important?'

Lock was no actor; his face was empty; it meant nothing to him.

'Probably not.' It was strange how a single piece of information could suddenly reveal a person. In that moment Webster understood that Lock was not the sort of man to be told things, but the sort who serves a purpose. A standard component of a more complex mechanism. The realization freed him. 'I went to see Nina Gerstman.'

Lock sat back and crossed his arms. 'Was that decent?'

Webster shrugged. 'I thought I could help her. She thinks it was Malin.'

'Of course it was Malin. How does that help?'

'Perhaps we can show that it was.' Lock waited for Webster to go on. 'I think that Dmitry had some sort of file on Malin. I also think that someone searched his flat a week or so before he died. Prock mentioned it but thought I wouldn't understand. Do you know Prock?'

Lock shook his head. 'No.'

'Dmitry's partner. An unlikely match.' He paused. 'Maybe she'd show it to you.'

'Nina?'

'Yes.'

'Why would she show it to me?'

'Because you're the man who can bring down her husband's killer. Because Dmitry liked you.'

Lock sighed, exhaling through his nose and mouth. 'You're sure there's something there?'

'I think there is. Something that will hurt Malin. It doesn't make sense otherwise.'

'What if there isn't?'

'Then everyone will still want to talk to you, you'll just have less to tell them. You can go back to Russia or talk to the FBI. I'll help you.'

Lock thought for a moment. 'Is she in Berlin?'

'As far as I know.'

'So I go, she gives me this file, this information, whatever it is, and then I come back. What does it do for me?'

'It makes you valuable. Simple as that. Christ, you can take it back to Malin if you like and he'll pat you on the head and love you again. Maybe let you go around on your own. If that's what you want. Otherwise it's the difference between wanting to nail him and actually doing it.'

'It'll never happen. It never happens.'

'It happens. I've seen it. And you're the only one who can do it.'

'And you don't care if I run off?'

'You're not mine to control. But if you do I'll know you got something.'

Lock sighed again, looking round the room at the stallholders coming in for their lunch.

'I'm not very good at this sort of thing.'

'What sort of thing?'

'I'm no spy. I tried it in Moscow and screwed it up. I have no talent for subterfuge.' He laughed a cold laugh. 'Funny. Under the circumstances.'

'I'm quite good at it,' said Webster. 'Let me help.'

There and then Webster made a plan, writing and sketching, angling his notebook on the table so that Lock could make it out. Lock ate a bacon sandwich; Webster left his to go cold as he scribbled and talked.

Lock should leave London straight away. There was no point in delaying. He should take a flight to Amsterdam or Rotterdam. That far he could be traced, but once there he would create a little diversion. Using his credit card he would buy a train ticket to Noordwijk, where his father lived, so that anyone watching would assume he was going home. But he would drive to Berlin in a hire car paid for by Ikertu through an innocent-sounding front company. That way no one would have any idea of his true destination.

From Amsterdam to Berlin was a journey of four hundred miles, probably a seven-hour drive. He could stay overnight in Hannover or push for Berlin in one go. There he would check in to a hotel that Ikertu had again found and paid for. He would be Mr Richard Green, and would be careful not to present his passport when checking in.

'What do I say if they ask?' said Lock.

'Tell them you had your briefcase stolen at the airport and you don't have it. You're going to the embassy in the morning. We'll find you a hotel that won't care.'

Money was important. He should withdraw as much as he could today, in London and Holland, and use cash for everything once he landed in Europe. Phones, too. Lock volunteered that he had dismantled his old ones yesterday.

'Good. Leave them that way. Before you go we'll get you a pay-as-you-go,' said Webster.

And then he should see Nina. Lock should plan his own approach. He knew her, and he could decide what would work best. Webster gave him her address and phone number.

'How do I get back?'

'You arrive at the airport and book yourself on the next

plane back to London. Leave it very late, just before check-in closes. I'll meet you at the other end and take you somewhere safe.'

'What if they find me?'

'They won't. You're not leaving a trace.'

Lock sat for a moment, leaning on the table with his hands clasped together, his thumbs pressed against each other.

'When did you start following me?'

The question surprised Webster but he was happy to answer. 'When you arrived yesterday.'

'No, not this time. I mean, when did you first start following me?'

'Yesterday.' Lock gave Webster an appraising look. 'Really. We had no reason to before.'

'OK. OK.'

'Why?'

'I don't know. The last time I was here I thought someone was following me. Maybe I imagined it.' Lock sat back and rubbed his cheek. 'Why don't you come with me?'

Webster sat back, as if the planning was complete. With Yuri's help he would know exactly where Lock was, but to go with him now was to risk overloading this delicate new trust between them. He needed Lock to think he was in control.

'I could. But this is your mission. I'll be a phone call away. We'll make a spy of you yet.' He smiled, the sort of smile that says everything will turn out fine, no matter how unlikely that might seem.

CHAPTER THIRTEEN

Thirty-five years before, it must have been, Lock had travelled across Germany on roads like this to Altenau, a lake town in the Harz mountains. They had left at night to avoid traffic, his father driving, his mother and sister asleep. Opera played loud on the cassette, the high notes tinny and distorted. Lock stayed awake and watched the car's softly glowing instruments reflected in the window against the dark. On the straight roads his father sat almost perfectly still, his arms locked and steady on the wheel.

That was their second holiday in the mountains. The first they had spent in tents, sometimes in campsites, sometimes in the wilderness, but that year Lock's mother had insisted on a roof and a bath, and Everhart had booked them into a guest house on the edge of town by the lake. They were the only family there, everyone else was there to walk, and Lock and his sister, waking early and playing, were often in trouble for disturbing the other guests. Everhart seemed quietly pleased that they were bringing some life to the place.

For two weeks they walked, and swam, and took day trips to pretty towns. Some time in the second week Everhart declared that he and his son were going for a proper walk, a long one, and early the next day they set off, Everhart leading the way around the edge of the lake through densely planted pines, the needles dry under their feet. Lock's scuffed white tennis shoes slipped on the slopes, and he followed in awe the unerring tread of his father's sturdy leather boots. Even now he could remember every moment of that day. They walked for hours, saying little. Everhart moved quickly, but not so quickly that with the occasional run and skip Lock couldn't keep up. At lunch, the lake by now a long way behind them, they sat in the forest by a stream, ate their sandwiches, and talked about the future: where Lock would go to school, what he might study at university, what he would do to earn a living, where he wanted to live. Everhart shared his tea in the cap of the Thermos flask.

This was the longest Lock had spent alone with his father; it made him nervous and happy. In the afternoon, the sun now over their heads and dropping light down between the trees, they carried on walking, stopping now and then for Everhart to refer to his compass and his map. Above the town of Bad Harzburg the path left the forest for a while, and for the first time they could see sky and hills and woods ahead of them. They stopped for a moment to take it in. Lock's father crouched behind him and pointed across a shallow valley to a dark band of forest encased in a high metal fence.

'You see that fence?' said Everhart. 'That is the Iron Curtain. It cuts Germany in two. You be thankful you're a Dutchman.' Lock imagined vast curtains of gun-coloured metal, swagged apart to reveal some hellish mechanical world beyond.

And what had Lock done? He had gone to live there. Perhaps that's why his father was so appalled. Perhaps Lock had ceased to be a Dutchman in his eyes the moment he had gone east. The thought struck him as he drove past Osnabrück on a stretch of dual carriageway that seemed to go on for ever no matter how fast he went. It was late now, past ten, and he should find a place to spend the night. Stopping seemed luxurious, but he reminded himself that if Webster was right he had time. He might feel pursued, but he was in no hurry.

At Stansted he had bought a suitcase and to put in it a new sweater, shirts, T-shirts to sleep in, socks, underwear, a razor, a toothbrush, a book – *Middlemarch*, of all things; after Cayman he had always meant to read it – a notebook, a guide to Berlin and two bottles of decent malt. These new possessions felt like the starter kit for a new identity that he had not yet defined. In the pockets of his coat he had two pay-as-you-go phones that Webster had arranged. One was for calls to a third, virgin phone, which Webster would keep, the other for any calls Lock might need to make in Berlin. All were for practical purposes untraceable, apparently. And in his wallet he had five thousand euros. He was all set. All set for a raid behind the wall to retrieve his identity.

He had arrived in Rotterdam an hour or so after dark. He had hired a car, a good one, an Audi, since it was less conspicuous in Germany to drive an expensive car than a cheap one, and then set off, the satellite navigation telling him in calm Dutch where to go from time to time. It felt strange to be driving; in Moscow he was driven, and everywhere else he took taxis. He enjoyed the car's solidity, its sureness, the impression it gave that it knew where it was going. He was conscious for the first time in years of the distance between places, between Rotterdam and Utrecht, between Arnhem and Dortmund, and he enjoyed that too.

Maybe in this car the Swiss wouldn't stop him at the border. Maybe he should give it a go. No, he thought. Perhaps after Berlin.

He spent the night in a motel just off the autobahn outside Hannover. The line about his briefcase had worked and he hadn't had to show his passport. It was strange that even now

– he was on the run, for heaven's sake, if you could be on the run from your boss – these little lies unnerved him. He paid cash in advance and wondered whether that would be the thing that finally made the tired-looking Polish clerk suspicious enough to call the authorities. Which authorities he had no idea.

But no one came for him in the night. After a sandwich that he had bought in Rotterdam and a glass or two of the Scotch, he slept a solid, heavy sleep with no dreams, waking just before the dawn with a sore throat and a headache. He hadn't opened a window and the room was hot. He showered and dressed and left in fifteen minutes, discovering as he stepped out into the cold air that it had snowed in the night and was snowing still, fat soft flakes settling on the bonnets and roofs of cars. The road itself was smeared with an ugly grey paste of slush and grit and oil, and the journey took twice as long as it should. But here he was, approaching Berlin from the west, warm and safe.

He didn't know the city. It wasn't a place he had ever needed to visit: Frankfurt, yes, for its banks, but otherwise Germany had never been important in his scheme. He followed the signs to the centre, hoping from there to see signs for Kreuzberg. Through Charlottenburg, through the Tiergarten, past the Reichstag; he eventually found himself on Unter den Linden, driving along the wide boulevard whose name he had heard so often. It was less pretty than he had expected: it looked as if the massive buildings on either side, the hotels and offices and government buildings, had bullied all the leaves off the bare limes and left the trees cowering in the middle of the road.

It was strange to be driving in a city he didn't know. It took him nearly an hour to find the hotel. The Hotel Daniel, in a residential street near the canal. It was small, and dark in a comforting way, and he was shown to his room by a bulky, smiling woman in her seventies who spoke little English but understood him well enough. He gave his name as Mr Green. When he started to explain about his passport she simply waved him away.

The room was papered with red and cream stripes, and fitted out with furniture that didn't match and was a little too good for a hotel of this kind. A double bed with a small mahogany table by its head; a wardrobe, mahogany again and rather grand, with an oval mirror set into its single door; a chest of drawers; a desk and chair. From his window Lock could see through trees the canal and the U-bahn track above it, and beyond that a solid red-brick church and layers of box-like apartment buildings stretching back into Mitte. A train ran past from left to right, its orange carriages the only colour in a world of white and grey.

Lock unpacked his new things, taking his shirts from their plastic packets and hanging them, creased, in the wardrobe. He checked the charge on his phones. Should he call Nina now? Something held him back. He thought for a moment that it was the prospect of seeing his dead friend's wife and being rejected, or not knowing what to say. But that wasn't it. If Nina had nothing, knew nothing, then the last prospect of some sort of dignified escape from all this, however fantastical, was gone. Here in this comfortable room, snow blanking out the world around, that was a moment he could happily delay.

He would write her a note. Or better, a letter of condolence. He was in Berlin, and would very much like to see her. That was natural, after all: they had met, and Dmitry had been his friend.

He took his time with it, writing it out in his notebook first before copying it carefully onto a sheet of the Daniel's headed paper. When he finished he called down to reception and managed to explain in English, Dutch and broken German that he wanted a taxi.

He needed food, and air. Outside the snow was now a grey mud on the pavements. Lock could feel his shoes cold on his feet and knew that icy water was about to leak through the soles and seams. Soft flakes had given way to something between hail and sleet and the easterly wind froze his face. He walked on the main road, leaning into the cold as it came at him, taking in little but the noise of the cars and the people hurrying past him on their way home. He had little idea where he was; he had a map but there was no point in trying to open it.

At Wittenbergplatz he turned left into quieter streets in search of a bar. Thank God for bars. When he found one it was less a bar than a cafe, rather grand and Viennese, but it would do. It was warm, and warmly lit, and he found a booth that seemed the most comfortable thing he had ever seen.

He ordered beer, because this was Germany, and drank the first one in four or five deep swallows. Another came. He looked at the menu and ordered food: gravad lax and Wiener schnitzel.

From his coat he took one of his phones. He looked at it for a while and then put it on the table. It continued to attract him. He wanted to call Marina, to tell her he was all right and that he had a plan, but he wasn't sure he should. Webster had said he could make calls, hadn't he? Halfway through his third beer he surrendered.

'Marina?'

'Richard?'

'Hi. I thought I should call.'

'Richard, where are you?'

'I shouldn't say. I just . . . I wanted to tell you I'm OK.'

'Vika wants to see you. I think she can tell I'm worried.'

Lock rubbed his eyes with his free hand, pinching the bridge of his nose.

'I'll see her soon,' he said. 'Tell her I'll see her soon.'

There was a pause. 'I stood there', said Marina, 'whispering your name over the wall.'

'I'm sorry. I was fine. I should have said.'

They were silent again.

'I did what you suggested,' Lock said.

'What?'

'I got some help. I'm trying to find a way out. It's better already. Being free. I can think more clearly.'

'That's good, Richard, but . . . You're not going to run off? I don't think I could stand it.'

'No. No, I'm not.'

'I thought you had.'

'I'm going to face it. I think I have to.'

Marina was quiet for a moment. 'That's good. That is. We'll help you. I'll help you.'

'I know.'

Another silence, broken by Marina. 'Konstantin called.'

Lock said nothing.

'This morning. He wanted to know where you were.'

'What did you tell him?'

'That I didn't know anything.'

'Was that it?'

'He wanted to know if I had lost trust in him as well.'

'And?'

'I told him I didn't leave Moscow just to get away from you.'

Again, Lock was silent.

'He said . . . he told me that he was trying to save you.'

Lock closed his eyes. 'There's no point in telling me that.'

'I thought you should know.'

'Do you believe him?'

'I think he no longer knows what he is saying.'

Lock nodded slowly to himself. Could Malin really expect him to believe that? There was no point in wondering. He felt tired.

'Listen, darling, I should go. It's going to be a busy few days. I'll . . . I'll call again.'

'OK.'

'Will you kiss Vika for me?'

'Of course. Be careful. Please.'

'I will.'

'If it doesn't work, I've found you a lawyer.'

By twelve the next day Lock was anxious. Nina hadn't called and he had begun to regret the letter; it was time to stop delaying. His first call to her went unanswered, but he left no message. So did his second, two hours later; this time he told the machine who he was, that he was in Berlin and would welcome the chance to see her. He could go to her or she could come to him at the Hotel Daniel.

At three she called; it was a short conversation. She told him that she didn't want to see anyone associated with Dmitry's old world, that he shouldn't take this personally, and that she would be grateful if he left her alone. He tried to tell her that he no longer worked for Malin but it was clear that she had made up her mind. As he put the phone down he wondered what Webster would have done to keep her talking – and what would he do now to force a meeting?

Lock had been in his hotel room all day, reading *Middlemarch* and the guide book and drinking Scotch. He had had breakfast, but no lunch, and his head felt light and tense at the same time. He didn't know what to make of Nina's refusal: was it the end of everything, or merely an obstacle? Part of him, he realized, had never thought that Nina would make any difference; part of him longed to think that she would. Snow had settled thickly overnight and was still falling outside his window.

He decided to walk into town. He couldn't leave today in any case, not in this snow, and he wanted to see people and breathe fresh air. And he needed new shoes. The pavement sludge had frozen in places and in his leather soles he made precarious progress north, across the canal and up Friedrichstrasse, leaning forward slightly for balance and correcting himself with a jerk every time he started to slip. If the snow would only stop he could drive to Switzerland in a day – less, probably. He wondered how far south it was falling. He passed Checkpoint Charlie and stopped for a moment to read the screens that enclosed the construction sites on either side of the road. People had crossed the wall in suitcases, in cars decked out in mourning, suspended from balloons, on death slides, in a hundred ways that defied imagination. Plenty had tried and not crossed at all, shot down by the automatic machine guns trained on every inch of the wall or by the border guards who longed to cross it themselves. Some had been left to die in the death strip between the two walls, the soldiers of neither side prepared or allowed to go to their aid. All in one direction. No one had ever crossed the other way.

He was in a camping shop trying on shoes when Webster rang. The phone gave an irritating chirrupy ring that was strange to him, and it took him a moment to realize it was his to answer. He took the phone out of his pocket and looked at it for some time, hoping that voicemail would pick up, but it simply rang and rang, chirruped and chirruped.

'Hello,' he said at last.

'Richard, it's Ben. How are things?'

'Ben, hi. OK. They're OK.'

'How are you getting on?'

'She won't see me.'

'Why not?'

'She says she won't see anyone from my world. I tried to tell her it wasn't my world any more but I didn't get through.'

'So what are you doing now?'

'Trying on shoes.'

Webster said nothing for a moment. 'What are you going to do?'

'I don't know. It's snowing like crazy here.'

'Richard, do you want to see Nina?'

'I don't know. Yes. Yes, I suppose I do.'

'Why don't you go and see her?'

Lock thought for a moment. Priorities shuffled in his mind. 'Would you see her?'

The line was quiet for a moment. Please. I need help.

'I'll be there tomorrow,' Webster said at last. 'I'll text you my plans.'

'Thank you. She might see you.'

'She might. Are you OK?'

'I'm fine.'

'Hang in there. We'll crack it together.'

Lock left the shoe shop with his old shoes in a plastic bag and his new ones dry and tight on his feet. They had jagged soles and made short work of the ice. He felt newly in control, and set off in search of the cafe where he had eaten the night before. Two nights in the city and already he had worked out a routine. He was too tired to do otherwise.

This part of Berlin was all wide streets and solid apartment blocks. Something about the rhythm of the buildings – the narrowness of the windows, the space between them, the height of the floors – reminded him strongly of Moscow. Their colours, too: creams, dirty yellows, greys. And the streets empty of people in the snow, the pavements a slithery mess, the lamps giving out a harsh blue light. It came to him suddenly and with a panicked chill that this was an eastern city, that he'd been tricked into thinking it was the incorruptible West, that he wasn't safe here. They could get you here, if they wanted to; it wasn't so far away. They probably knew he was here already. He could feel his heart beating fast in his chest and his throat felt swollen, unable to swallow.

He walked quickly now to the cafe, not quite rushing, and when there ordered beer again, and ate soup, and sausages with sauerkraut. He began to calm down, and scolded himself for not having eaten sooner. He wished he'd brought his book. He had his notebook, though, and for a while he sketched in it absent-mindedly. First Webster came out, wearing a mac, a trilby and dark glasses, a flower in his buttonhole and a folded newspaper under his arm. Then Lock himself astride a high wall, one arm and one leg in view. He looked at the images for a second, shook his head as if to clear it and opened a fresh page. He would think this thing through. He drew two lines down the page and gave a title to each of the three columns: *Cooperate, Return* and *Run*. Then he ruled two lines across, and marked the rows *Likely Outcome, Risks, Obstacles*. It took him half an hour to fill up the grid with a neat, close hand and he could feel his mind disentangling as he wrote. This was an odd document, he realized; he wondered what someone would make of it if they came across it. It was odd in part, he understood, because nowhere did it address what he wanted. It hadn't occurred to him to include it, and he wasn't quite sure where it should go.

So on the opposite page he wrote two things. *See Marina*; and *See Vika*. He stopped and looked at the words for a while, and wished that he'd known this so clearly five years before. What they told him now was that he had no choice but to wait for Webster and see this out. He shut the book flat with his hand, as if swearing on it. Then he put it back in his pocket next to Marina's letter, paid the bill and went out into the night.

This was not a lively neighbourhood. Shops were shutting

around him and between them offices were already dark. Berlin felt empty again. He longed for a bar with young people in it; they had to be somewhere. He stood in the porch of the cafe for a moment and looked at his map. Schöneberg was close. The guide book had said something about Schöneberg, he forgot what. He'd try there.

As he walked along Kurfürstenstrasse he passed a man he thought he recognized. He was young, perhaps thirty, and he wore a heavy black cap and a padded raincoat down to his knees. His eyebrows were fair. As he passed he looked at Lock with an air of studied casualness, as if it would be unnatural not to hold a stranger's eye for a half-second. Lock knew the cap. He'd seen it somewhere. Was it in Moscow? No, it was here, he was sure. He walked along staring at the grimy pavement, looking hard for the answer. At Checkpoint Charlie. He had been reading the screens on the other side of the street and when Lock had crossed over he had turned and walked away. Lock was sure it was him. They were half an hour from there now and this was a big city. This wasn't chance.

There's no way they can know that I'm here, he thought. I've been so careful. Webster planned it. Maybe it's one of Webster's people. But why would he follow me now? And there was something about that cap, something eastern, something Muscovite. It was the sort of cap that half the men in Russia wore come winter.

What had Webster said about knowing if you're being followed? Lock turned south down a quiet residential street; he was the only person on it. Two-thirds of the way down he stopped and made a show of patting and exploring his pockets. Then he turned and started walking the way he had come. There was no one there. The street was empty. He turned again, and resisting the strong urge to look over his shoulder, forced himself to walk on. Two streets away he saw a taxi, hailed it, and went back to the hotel, wondering all the while about what he had seen.

Webster's plane was due to land at eleven. He had sent a text saying that he would meet Lock at his hotel at noon or thereabouts.

Lock had not slept. All night his mind turned the same questions round and round. Should he stay in this hotel or move to another? Make a break for Switzerland? Sit and wait for someone to pick him up? He had tried to read but the lines had just slipped past his eyes.

By dawn his skin felt scratchy and greasy and he could smell a sour smell of old whisky and sweat rising from his body. The room was stuffy, its curtains closed. A fug hung in the air. Questions still churned in his head. Malin. What had Malin meant when he called Marina? How was he trying to save him? From destroying his soul by betraying Mother Russia? What else could it be?

And what of Webster, coming to rescue him? Could he trust him?

He realized he couldn't wait in that room any longer. He showered, pulled on a soft new shirt – for a moment felt human – and finished dressing. He pulled the curtains apart an inch and looked out at the street. No movement. No people. He watched for a moment to make sure. Before he left he did something he hadn't done since he was a boy: he plucked two hairs from his head and licking his finger stuck them across the joins of the wardrobe door and a drawer in his chest of drawers. He took a third and balanced it on the lock of his suitcase; a fourth he smoothed onto the door and the door jamb, at ankle height, as he left. Then he hung the Do Not Disturb sign on the handle and went out in search of breakfast.

It had stopped snowing, finally, and Lock walked along the

canal with the low sun in his eyes. Thin ice had formed over the water; in places it looked thick but by the edges geese still paddled. Few people had walked there and the snow on the path, on the black branches of the trees, on the roofs and balconies and fences was still a pure white. Lock's new shoes made a crunching sound as he walked. Occasionally, despite himself, he checked behind him, and saw no one. He passed a woman training a dog, a spaniel puppy, and a man in a huge puffed-up coat walking a whippet. That was it.

He found a cafe serving *Frühstück* and ordered rolls, ham, cheese, coffee and orange juice. He had brought his book, and now he sat and read it, taking it in, ordering more coffee to justify his sitting there. At ten-thirty he paid and set off back to the hotel. This was where he would want to live in Berlin. Quiet. Pretty.

By the time he reached the Daniel he had forgotten about his schoolboy spying ruse. The Do Not Disturb sign reminded him and he checked the door. The hair wasn't there. A shock ran across his shoulders. He knocked on the door and listened carefully for any noise inside. It was quiet. His heart seemed to rise in his chest. He hesitated for a moment, not sure whether to go on or run. Slowly he turned the key in the lock and opened the door. Still no noise. Then he swung the door open in one swift movement and moved back a step. There was no one there. He checked the bathroom, and that was empty. None of the hairs was in place.

Lock turned the key in the door, sat down on the bed and put his head in his hands. Noise filled his head. He would like everyone to leave him alone. For a day. For a day or two.

In his case lay the components of his old Russian phones. He put one of them back together without its SIM card, and copied a number from it into his new phone, asking himself why he was still bothering with this security nonsense. Then he pressed connect and waited. The line rang only twice.

'*Da.*'

'When I came to work for you,' said Lock, talking quickly, standing now and looking out of the window for signs of movement, 'I didn't agree to be followed everywhere by your fucking thugs. Call them off. Call them off, or I will go straight to the Americans, the Swiss, the fucking Caymanese and happily spend the rest of my days in prison. Happily. I don't want to see another goon. I don't want them holding my hand, I don't want them searching my room. I'm fucking serious, Konstantin, don't think that I'm not.'

There was silence for the shortest moment.

'Richard, where are you?'

'What do you mean, where am I? You know exactly where I am. What you don't know is what I want. I thought I'd phone home and tell you. Would you like to hear it?'

'Yes.' Malin's voice was deep and solid, apparently un-moved.

Lock took a breath, let it out through his nose. 'We don't have a future, Konstantin. I definitely don't. The FBI will have my guts. So my choice, it seems, is life at Her Majesty's pleasure or at yours. I don't know which one I prefer. I really don't.'

'Richard. I think you are panicking over a small thing. I was worried that you might and that was why I wanted you to be protected.' He paused. 'Your mistake is to think that the Americans are important. Or powerful. They are not. You work for a Russian business and this is a Russian matter.'

Lock snorted a laugh. 'Ha. A Russian matter. Konstantin, I don't think you understand. This is an American matter, a Dutch matter, an English matter. Anywhere our money goes – your money goes – it's their business.'

'No. That is your mistake.' Malin's voice was even and forceful. 'These people, they can look, they can get excited. They are paid to do this and it makes them happy. But do you think they will find things in Russia? Do you think they will find you there? I am safe in Russia. You can be safe here too. I have paid you well for a long time, Richard. You have been loyal to me but now, when it counts, you run away.' Malin stopped. Lock could hear him breathing, gathering himself, letting him know how grave this really was. 'I can protect you for only so much longer, Richard. I have never wished you any harm. Come to Moscow today – or tomorrow, take your time – and I can guarantee you that in a year, maybe two, there will be nothing left of this. Nothing. And you will look back and think how foolish you were to have doubted me. To have doubted yourself.'

Lock sat down, hung his head and rubbed the back of his neck until a red mark appeared on the skin. He took the phone from his ear, looked at it without expression, and disconnected the call.

'There was never anything to doubt,' he said to the empty room, and lay back on the bed.

CHAPTER FOURTEEN

Webster asked his taxi to stop in the street behind Lock's hotel and walked the final few hundred yards; from habit he never left a taxi right outside his destination. From the air Germany had looked plain and neat, black lines of trees stretching across spotless white fields, the city a jigsaw of red roofs and straight roads, but down here on the ground nothing was immaculate. With one leg still in the car Webster stepped carefully over the frosted puddle in the gutter, struggling not to slip on the icy snow that had been cleared from the other edge of the pavement. He could feel the easterly wind blowing up his flapping suit trousers, and knew that his thin London coat would be no defence against this cold.

He wondered which Lock he would find waiting for him: the plausible lawyer or the frightened escapee. He had sounded distraught on the phone. Not for the first time Webster asked himself whether he was pushing Lock too hard, and again the answer came back: you're his only way out; his other choices are worse; not long now. And a response in turn: I hope you're right.

It felt strange to be making intimate decisions about the life of a man he hardly knew. He had at once a strong sense of him and no sense at all: an idea taken from press articles and company records and court documents and unreasonable assumptions. The Lock he had met in Enzo's had surprised him. He had expected him to have the arrogance of those who gain power without earning it; to have a thicker shell; to be fond of himself in a way that he clearly was not. Sitting in his coat across the table, Lock had seemed already fallen, less bumptious middleman than sinner seeking absolution, as if he knew too well what he had done and how much was at stake. And, after all, wasn't he a victim of the same disorder that had finished Inessa, the same desperation to keep the truth hidden? Webster didn't know whether to be comforted or unnerved by this: it made his own role less significant, but his responsibility to Lock much greater. Responsibility to do what? he asked himself. Find a way out for him; give him a second chance. Keep him alive.

For the first time since Turkey, Webster craved a cigarette.

At the Daniel he explained that he was a friend of Mr Green. Room 205, second floor. He walked up the stairs and found the room at the end of a dark corridor, a single lamp giving out a dim light. He knocked gently on the door, and heard movement inside. The spyhole darkened, and Lock opened the door, only enough at first for him to see down the corridor and know that Webster was alone.

'Come in.'

Webster walked past him. Lock shut the door, and for a moment the two men looked at each other, neither having the right small talk for this very particular occasion. Lock looked harrowed. His hair was greasy and uncombed and he had a small sore, purplish red, at the corner of his mouth. He hadn't shaved since London. Webster scanned the room: the bed unmade, the ashtray half full, the bottles of Scotch on the bedside table, one nearly empty. The window was closed and the air smelled of smoke and sleep and whisky.

'You have the chair,' said Lock. 'I'm afraid we don't stretch to two.'

'How are you doing? Why don't we go and get some lunch? I'm hungry.'

Lock walked to the window and looked out, standing a foot or two from the glass and leaning back. He turned to Webster. 'I'd like to talk here if we can. There's been . . . I'm not feeling very safe.'

'Why not?'

Lock told him about the hairs on the doors and the man with the cap. Webster kept his expression steady but felt a short sting of anxiety: either Lock was beginning to imagine things or this was alarming, and what made this so difficult was that both were credible.

'Perhaps it was housekeeping.'

'The room wasn't made up. I had the Do Not Disturb sign out.'

'Then we shouldn't talk here. If you're right.'

It took Lock a moment to understand. 'Shit. Yes. Of course. God, I hate this business. I don't know how you put up with all this crap.'

Webster smiled but it was clear Lock wasn't joking.

In an Alsatian restaurant in Mitte they sat on wooden chairs at a plain wooden table and ordered food. Lock drank beer, Webster water. They took a table towards the back of the long narrow room, Webster facing the door so that he could reassure Lock that no one threatening had entered. Walking there Webster had looked for a tail and seen nothing.

Lock was uneasy; he didn't eat. Webster quizzed him about his movements since London: had he followed the plan? Had he driven straight from Rotterdam? Where had he stopped along the way? What had he done since he was here? When Lock got to the point where he contacted Nina, Webster thought he understood. Someone was listening to her phone. It was even possible they were monitoring Marina's line. He didn't tell Lock what he was thinking.

'And since Nina?'

'Since the call? I went and bought these shoes. Not far from here. Then I went and had dinner – and noticed the man in the black cap when I was leaving. I did what you said but he didn't follow me, not that I could see. Then I went back to the hotel.'

'And you stayed there till when?'

'Till this morning. I left at about seven-thirty to get break-fast. I didn't sleep well. And when I got back, about eleven, the hairs weren't there. Then I called Malin.'

'You called Malin?' Webster struggled to keep the in-credulity out of his voice.

'Yes.'

'Why on . . . What for? I don't understand.'

'I didn't think about it. I just wanted to tell him to leave me alone.'

'And did you?'

'Yes.'

'What did he say?'

'He tried to persuade me that I'd be safe in Moscow. That . . . that in a year's time all of this would be forgotten.'

'What do you think about that?'

'I don't want to see Moscow again. And I don't believe him. I have a feeling I've crossed the line.' Lock looked detached, almost curious, as if he could picture the line some-where behind him and wondered why he hadn't seen it before.

'What did you call him on?'

'That.' Lock pointed to one of his dismantled phones on the table.

'Well, we can throw that away. And if he wasn't following you he will be now.' Webster sat and chewed for a moment. 'Tell me about Nina.'

'There's not much to say. She told me to sod off. Nicely but firmly.'

'How well do you know her?'

'I've had dinner with her three times. I think it's three. We got on but I wouldn't say we bonded.'

'All before Gerstman left Malin?'

'Yes.'

'So she sees you as Malin's man?'

'She does. For sure.'

Webster took a drink of water and tried to decide how to get Nina to open the door to him. She knew that they wanted the same thing: Malin exposed. He was sure of that. The question was whether she would engage.

'All right. I'll talk to her. If she'll see me. If she thinks you're a wanted man she may soften. Let's go.'

'We can take my car.'

'If you're right they may have seen it. We'll get a cab.'

Webster had the driver pass Nina's flat slowly, Lock lying down across the back seat. He couldn't see anyone. It wouldn't be easy to keep a watch here. The street was one-way and her building halfway down, which meant that you couldn't rely on a car alone. And this was the sort of place where neighbours were observant and vocal. He kept one eye on the cars that lined both sides. They were all empty. It was still possible that Lock was imagining things; he was no longer the most reliable witness.

The driver thought they were mad and said so. He let them out two blocks away in a street parallel to Nina's. Webster paid him and looked at Lock standing by the cab. There was fear and expectation in his eyes. He looked crazed, a mess. Have I done this to him? At best I've accelerated it. When we've seen Nina he can start to recover himself.

'We need to make you presentable. Can you do something about your hair? Smooth it down a bit. Maybe button your coat right up. OK. That's better. Come on, let's go.'

The icy channel worn through the snow on the pavement

wasn't wide enough for both of them and Lock walked slightly ahead, Webster carefully scanning the cars and the houses.

Ahead of them, ten yards from the turning into Nina's street, a man was crouching down on the pavement next to a car. With one gloved hand he was taking the plastic covers off the wheel-nuts; in the other he held an L-shaped cylindrical spanner. As they approached, he stood up, took a step backwards and looked down at his work. He was tall and wore a grey overcoat. Webster put his hand on Lock's shoulder to slow him down. He heard a step behind him, the faintest crunch on the ice, and before he could turn felt his knees buckle under him. As he slumped a dull crack sounded in his head. Pain shot behind his eyes. He fell forward on his knees, the ice and grit stinging his hands. Another crack and then darkness.

He heard voices first. When he opened his eyes he saw grey snow, the wheel of a car beyond. A strip of bright pain ran from the bridge of his nose round to the back of his skull. There was cold against his cheek and in his clothes. He closed his eyes again.

These were German words. Some of them he knew. He raised his head and the pain seemed to flow to a point, like water. A hand touched his shoulder and he turned on his side and looked up, squinting into the light.

'Sind sie verletzt?'

'Was ist passiert?'

An arm reached round him and pulled him up until he was sitting. His trousers were wet against his thighs and there was the taste of iron in his mouth. He reached up and felt his forehead, his temple. Above his ear the hair was warm and clumped. He took his hand away and looked at the blood, frowning.

Lock. Christ. Lock.

He tried to stand but his feet couldn't find purchase on the ice.

I have to find him.

'*Bewegen Sie sich nicht. Wir haben einen Krankenwagen gerufen.*'

There were three people. A man was squatting by him and two women stood close by, their faces full of concern. He put his arm round the man's shoulders and pushed with his legs. The man stood with him.

'*Wirklich. Er kommt gleich.*'

Webster looked down at himself. His body didn't feel like his own. His head reeled and he fought the urge to be sick. I have to move. For a moment he stayed leaning on the man for support and then set off in the direction of Nina's flat, moving each leg with deliberation, his hand outstretched to find the wall.

There were protests behind him.

'*Danke,*' he said, turning. '*Hat jemand gesetwasehen?*' *Did you see this?* The three looked blank and shook their heads. '*Dankeschön,*' he said. '*Danke.*' He walked away and raised a hand, as if to say thank you, please stop.

Nothing was happening in Nina's street. No police cars. No Russians. No Lock. As he shuffled slowly towards her flat one thought filled his head, louder than the nausea, sharper than the pain. This cannot happen again.

By her building he looked back; at the corner of the street his three helpers were watching him. He turned into the doorway, slumped against the wall and pressed the button for her flat. His reflection stared slackly at him from the glass doors; his coat was grimy and his tie pulled down but otherwise there seemed to be little damage. But when he checked his face in the silver intercom panel he saw that one side of his face was red with blood – smeared across his forehead, thick and crimson over his ear and down his neck.

He went to press the button again. Please be in. For his sake be in.

'Hello.'

'Frau Gerstman, it's Ben Webster.' The words were thick in his mouth.

Nina said nothing. He turned from the microphone and spat blood and dirt. He waited for her to speak but she wasn't there. He buzzed again.

'I do not want to see you, Mr Webster. Unless you have news for me.'

He closed his eyes in pain and frustration. 'I have to speak to you.' His voice was earnest now, urgent. 'I was with Richard Lock. He's been taken.'

'Please, Mr Webster. Go. I have had enough.'

'Here, in your street. They knocked me out. The same men who broke into your home.'

Nina was silent.

'The same men who are calling you.'

The door buzzed, just long enough for him to take his weight off the wall and push against it.

Nina met him on the landing again, looking straight at him as he opened the gates to the lift, her arms crossed. She was still in black.

'Jesus.'

'It's OK. It's not that bad.'

She gave him a long, steady look and then without saying anything turned and went into her apartment. Webster wiped his feet on the mat and followed her down the corridor, the damp soles of his shoes still loud on the wooden floor.

Before the sitting room she turned left into a bathroom, more modern than the rest of the flat, all marble and glass. She took a flannel from a rail, wet it under a tap and handed it to him.

'Sit on the bath.'

He pressed the cloth to the side of his head and felt the cold sting against the wound. It came away vivid with blood.

'I let them take him. It's happening again.'

'Wait.' Nina took another cloth from the rail and ran it under the tap. 'Here.' She stood by him and dabbed at the blood on his forehead, wiping it away.

'Thank you.'

'What happened?'

'We were coming to see you.' He shook his head and felt the pain rolling inside it. 'I don't know where they came from. I never saw them. I never saw them.'

'Shouldn't you call the police?'

'They won't find him. I have to find him.' He turned and looked her in the eye. 'I need to bargain with them.'

She said nothing, then broke his gaze and leaned in to him, cleaning blood from the side of his face. He pulled away.

'Nina, I heard what Prock said to you. When did they break in?'

She shook her head, threw the flannel in the bath and walked out of the room.

'Nina.' He followed her down the corridor. The afternoon had clouded, and the light in the sitting room was lowering. She turned on a floor lamp and sat in her chair, staring at the ground. He took a remote control from the coffee table and switched the television on, turning up the sound so that voices and music filled the room.

He crouched by her chair and looked up at her, speaking softly. 'Nina, listen. I'm scared. You know what's happening. I need to know what Dmitry knew. Otherwise Richard is dead.'

'I don't know what he knew.'

'These men have been in your flat. They've been calling

you. They were out there this afternoon, watching. Christ, others may be there now. Until they're convinced, they will go on. Give it up. When they know you don't have it, they'll stop.'

She sighed abruptly, almost a sob.

'I don't want to remember him like this. Being chased for what he knew.'

I have to get on, thought Webster. There isn't time for this.

'Nina, tell me something. Why do you want to hold on to it? What good will it do you?'

'Dmitry didn't want them to have it.'

'Without Dmitry it means nothing.'

Nina was silent. She looked down at her lap.

He went on. 'He'd have done this for Richard. They were friends.'

She sniffed, looked up at him. 'So you trade it for Lock?'

'That's right. If it's not too late.'

'And after that, what good is it? Lock is alive and Malin is what? The same.' She closed her eyes and breathed deeply. She sat like that for a while, and he didn't disturb her. 'It's not mine to give,' she said at last.

'It's the part of him you don't want to remember. Let it go.'

Nina nodded – once, deliberately – and left the room. When she came back she held a small piece of folded paper in her hand. Silently she gave it to Webster, who took it, opened it, folded it again and put it in his pocket.

'Thank you. Call me on this if anything happens.' He left her another card.

She nodded again. He hesitated, as if there was something more to be said. But he knew there was not, and with a single goodbye he left.

From Nina's flat Webster ran east in the direction of the hotel, the cold air rushing against him. He needed a payphone.

How quickly the normal world could fall away and tip you into fear. He offered a brief prayer that Lock was all right; he didn't often pray, but Lock did. In the dark the snow was still falling, heavily now, leaving a thin layer of powder on the ice all around.

He found a phone on Steinplatz. It was open, a steel column with a small sheet of glass above his head by way of shelter. He pulled himself in under the canopy, put his credit card in the slot and called one of the numbers he knew best. As it rang he looked around the square. On this side a mother was wheeling a pushchair towards him; to his left two girls were sliding from long run-ups on the ice. His head pulsed with pain.

'Hello?'

'Ike, it's Ben. Lock's missing.'

'Another midnight flit?'

'No. Worse.'

Hammer listened while Webster explained.

'You OK?'

'I'm fine. Terrified but fine. Furious with myself. I need you to reach Malin.'

'Through Onder?'

'Through Onder. Or Tourna. He may have a number for him. Tell him we have what he wants and if anything happens to Lock we'll send it straight to Hewson at *The Times*. If he lets us know Lock is safe then we'll talk again. And talk to Yuri. One of the phones I bought for Lock has GPS. If he still has it we'll know exactly where he is.'

'All right. What about Gerstman's stuff?'

'Have a look at it. It's in a hotmail account.' He read out the details twice. A user name and a password to unlock the big secret. Please let it be good.

'Got it.' Hammer paused. 'How did they find him?'

'He called Nina. And Marina. Could have been either. It was stupid. I should have thought.' He sighed. 'This is my doing, Ike. I did this.'

Hammer said nothing.

'Would you call the police?' asked Webster.

'I would. Only because if something happens they'll let you know. If something does, that means they'll involve you. But that's OK. You'd probably want them to.'

'OK. Could you call George?'

'To send some people out?'

'Maybe just have them on standby.'

'OK. I take it you're calling me?'

'Until I get a new phone, yes. I'll call later this evening.'

Webster put the phone down. His hand was freezing in the evening air. He put it deep in his coat pocket and ran off in search of a taxi.

He had the cab stop two hundred yards short of the Daniel. Scanning both sides of the road he could see nothing suspicious, just empty cars. He walked past the hotel for some distance and found that clear, too.

He had decided to enlist the manageress; he needed to get into Lock's room and preferred not to risk being caught breaking in. Frau Werfel was not a woman to flap; she looked at his head with curiosity but nothing more. He explained, as best he could in halting German, that he had had an argument with Mr Green and had been knocked over by a moped as he chased after him across a busy road. When he had come to, Green was not there, and this was worrying because he was prone to fits of depression, was depressed at the moment, and may not have taken his medication with him. It was the best he could do. Frau Werfel nodded gravely, as if she didn't believe him but understood these things all too well. Had she seen him? She had not, but she had been busy this afternoon and had frequently been downstairs in the basement. Would she mind letting Webster into the room? She looked carefully at his face, weighing him up. She would not. Webster thanked her and followed her up the two flights of stairs to Lock's floor, watching her thick ankles in their sheepskin-lined boots as they went up step by step. As he walked down the corridor, which was gloomy and hot, he had a violent vision of opening the door to find Lock hanging by his neck, his new shoes twisting in space. He shook his head to clear the thought.

There was no one in Lock's room. Frau Werfel let him in and he made a show of looking in the bathroom for the medication. But the moment the door had opened he had noticed on the desk an envelope he was sure had not been there earlier.

'He seems to have taken it,' he said, coming out of the bathroom, 'which is good. Look, I'd go and try to find him but I have no idea where to look. His phone is turned off. I think I'll wait here for him. I want to be sure to catch him if he comes back.'

'I could tell you when he comes back in.'

'But you're busy, Frau Werfel. I don't want to force you to be at your desk all evening.'

She seemed ready to challenge him. But she merely nodded, wished him a good evening and left, closing the door behind her.

The envelope was unmarked, off-white, small – the kind used for personal correspondence. It looked identical to the hotel stationery in the rack next to it. Webster took a sheet of paper from the rack and used it to flip the envelope over. It was not stuck down; the flap had been tucked inside. Webster tore the sheet of paper in two and using the two pieces to cover his fingers carefully pulled the flap back and out. There was a single sheet of paper inside, folded once. Still covering his fingers Webster removed it from the envelope and spread it out on the desk. It was a piece of Hotel Daniel writing paper.

Its edges were a little bruised, as if it had been in the room a long time before being used.

The paper was covered with an even longhand in royal-blue biro-ink. The script was regular but showed signs of flamboyance: a flourished tail to the 'f', the 'g' looping elegantly up into an 's'. Webster recognized the hand from the signatures on a hundred documents he had recently examined.

> *Since my friend Dmitry Gerstman died I have been unhappy. I have lost a good friend. I lost my family long ago. In the courts and the newspapers I have lost my reputation. I have nothing. I do not want to continue.*

Webster read it again, and a third time, his heart beating heavily against his ribs. He read it once more but it yielded nothing new. He looked around the room to see if anything else had changed. Lock's things were still in place: his old shoes with their water stains by the radiator, yesterday's shirt hanging off the back of the chair by the desk. The bed had been made, and the bedside table tidied: on one side the two books, neatly against the wall; on the other the two bottles of Scotch and an empty bottle of gin, tightly together. The bottle of gin had not been there before, he was sure. Pulling his hand up inside the sleeve of his coat he picked it up by the cap. There was a trickle left in the bottom.

Using a pen to dial, he called reception. Frau Werfel answered.

'Frau Werfel, this is Mr Webster in Mr Green's room. Could I ask when you were not at reception over the last hour? I'm sorry but it might be important.'

Frau Werfel gave a small harrumph to let Webster know that she had been very helpful but was beginning to tire of all this irregularity. 'I can't say. Before you arrived I had been there for half an hour, I suppose, because some guests arrived at about half past four.'

'And did anyone else come in in that half-hour?'

'No one, Herr Webster. Is that all?'

'That's all. Thank you very much, Frau Werfel.' He longed to be able to do something. He did the one thing that was of any practical use and called Berlin's central police station. He explained to them that his friend had gone missing and that he had just found what looked like a suicide note in his hotel room. The police asked him whether he had tried to call his friend. Yes, of course. Did he have any idea where his friend might have gone? No, none; he understood that there was little the police could do, but they could find photographs of Richard Lock on the Internet and perhaps circulate them to their patrol cars. The German policeman snorted and said yes, they could do that.

He hung up and looked out of the window. The street below looked the same as before. He could tell from the snow on their bonnets that all the cars he could see were cold and hadn't recently moved. There was no movement; only the snow falling thickly, round flakes dropping like rain, sometimes flurrying in a gust of wind. He drew the curtains and stood for a moment with his hands together, gripping the material, his eyes closed. This cannot be happening again.

He had to speak to Hammer but didn't want to leave the room in case by some miracle Lock returned. He took a risk and used the hotel phone on the desk. Even Malin's people weren't agile enough to have tapped these lines by now. In any case, it didn't really matter. Let them hear it.

'Ike, it's Ben.'

'Well?'

'I'm at the hotel. This isn't a secure line. There's a bogus suicide note and an empty bottle of gin that wasn't here when we left four or five hours ago.'

'So there's a pattern.'

'There's a pattern.'

'Do the police know?'

'They know he's missing and depressed.'

'OK. I just left a voicemail message for our fat Russian friend. Our favourite Etonian had a number for him. I didn't want to involve the client yet. I don't know which of his mobiles it is. I could try the client but I figured that he wouldn't have any number we didn't already have.'

Webster grunted in agreement. 'What about Lock's phone?'

'The signal's dead.'

'Christ.' Webster pinched his eyes closed with his free hand. 'The files?'

'They're next.' Hammer paused. 'I don't know what else we can do.'

'There's nothing else.'

'You OK?'

'No. I'm tired of making mistakes.'

'I've been thinking about that,' said Hammer. 'When did Lock call Nina?'

'Yesterday morning. Marina the night before.'

'And by the afternoon there's someone tailing him? That's quick work.'

'I think they were PIs. Locals.'

'Locals don't fake suicides. Not the ones I know anyway.'

'The Russians could have got here late yesterday.'

'That's true.'

Webster thought for a moment. 'Might be worth checking.'

'That's not easy.'

'Have our travel-agent friend check for last-minute bookings.'

'What about private flights?'

'Yuri should be able to help.'

'OK.' Hammer paused. 'What are you doing now?'

'I'm going to stay here and go quietly nuts. He may come back. If you need me call the Hotel Daniel and ask for Mr Green in room 205.'

'OK. Don't do anything stupid.'

'OK.'

There was nothing else to do.

He sat on the bed and picked up Lock's copy of *Middlemarch*. The spine was broken about a hundred pages in and the book fell open naturally. Six hundred pages left. He wondered whether Lock would have the chance to finish it.

Where was he now? In a dark basement somewhere; in a van barrelling out of Berlin; in the river, deep under the squares of ice that flowed on its surface like cold fat. How would they do it this time? Throw him under a train; off a bridge; from a window? He saw Lock, stupid and terrified, pulled along by two slab-like faceless men, his eyes wide and red, knowing and not knowing what was next; Lock in a bright cell, his clothes filthy, a crowd around him, the only colour in the scene the red line across his throat.

And for what? A vain quest for some distant, flickering justice that Webster knew he would never grasp.

He jerked his head back and beat it against the wall. Fresh pain stabbed at his wound. He did it again, his eyes looking up to the heavens, imploring them, filling with angry tears. And again, harder.

CHAPTER FIFTEEN

Even before he opened his eyes Lock was conscious of motion. He was lying down, he knew that, and shaking gently, unevenly, sharply jolting every now and then. A rumbling sound went through him. His knees were up and his feet pressed against something solid. He tried to move his hand to his head but his arm felt weighed down, as if no amount of effort would release it. He was hot and wanted air; he wanted to take air deep into his lungs but something was stopping him and each breath was short, tight, painful as he inhaled. Everywhere – in his head, in his stomach, rising into his throat – he felt nausea: surging, ebbing, always there.

Against his instincts, he opened his eyes a crack. It was dark, but orange light was pulsing across his vision. He opened them wider and with pain lifted his head an inch or two. He was in a tight space. One arm he couldn't move at all, the other only a few inches. He could see his knees, and beyond them things were racing, lights were flashing past, white lights and yellow lights. They were spinning round him. He forced himself to watch for a while and slowly the space grew sharper. He made out a tree between the lights, and windows, and a wall. That was the world. Then where was he? He looked to his right. A man's head, and the man was sitting down. He was in a car. He was being driven, at night, like a small child who has been told he can sleep on the back seat.

His body wanted him to be sick. He shut his eyes and

resisted it, but he couldn't control the urge. He rolled on his side and felt all his muscles lock in a violent spasm. Then he collapsed onto his back once more.

'Fucker.' In Russian. The voice came from the front of the car. The head of the man in the seat turned round to look at him. More words in Russian followed. Lock couldn't make them out. The smell of vomit reached him and made him gag, but he felt a little clearer, a little more like Richard Lock. In the stink he could smell gin. He raised himself up on his elbows and looked down at his body. He recognized his coat, his new shoes. This was him, all right. The same him.

Outside the window a city was flowing past. He tried to catch some of it, a shop name, a street sign, but the car was too fast and his eyes too slow; they slipped from point to point. It was definitely a city: the buildings were tall and the streets so wide that sometimes the buildings disappeared from sight. When they slowed he could hear other cars, tyres rolling on wet tarmac, engines sawing through the gears.

The whole of his head hurt, from his forehead to the nape of his neck. He could sense the shape of his skull enclosing the pain. He tried to think through it. He remembered being in the taxi, with Webster, and walking ahead of him on the ice and seeing Webster fall. Then nothing, just emptiness. An impression of a bare bulb hanging from a cord, but nothing more.

He needed to know where he was. He forced himself to sit up a little further, his head now resting against the car door, closed his eyes for a moment, and passed out.

People flitted through his dreams in a feverish, messy procession. No one stayed for long. He could hear their chatter but not grasp what they were saying, even when they were talking to him. Some images stuck: Marina, her back to him, typing on a clanking typewriter a message that he couldn't read; Oksana in the sea, beckoning; a huge, inflated Malin comical behind a tiny desk; Vika on a beach, pouring water from a plastic watering can onto the sand. Whenever he reached out the scene quickly switched: that lawyer, Beresford, steering him in a panic against a tide of people on some nameless Moscow street; Webster holding up a thick black hair like a piece of wool for him to inspect.

When he came to, he barely knew that time had passed, let alone how much. He was still; the car was still. The door behind him opened and his head flopped back into space. Then he felt hands on the collar of his coat pull him backwards and up, and he was on his feet, standing on unruly legs. The icy night air braced him, and when he lifted his head he found he was with two men, one short and one tall, both wearing long coats and black caps. Behind him the car locked with a faint beep. The taller man put his arm round his shoulders and together they walked up a frozen pavement. The man was surefooted; Lock knew he wouldn't slip.

For the first time Lock looked around him. The street was wide, dark, empty. He felt snow landing softly on his nose, on his cheek. A single car passed. Up ahead a brighter street crossed this one, and he could see traffic and trees lit yellow by the street lamps. The smaller man said something softly in Russian: keep him upright. If they're happy talking Russian in front of me, Lock thought through the dense fug in his head, I'm not meant to survive.

He twisted away from the man holding him, trying to free his shoulders and run, but his feet could find no purchase on the ice and the man merely held him up, his powerful arm keeping him from falling. The smaller one, walking slightly ahead, turned and gave the other a taut look.

Twenty yards from the car the smaller man stopped by a large metal double door set back slightly from the road in a shallow recess. Lock looked up in time to see a massive building above him, several storeys high and as wide as the whole block. Then he felt the strong arm around him pull him in. The smaller man pressed four numbers on a keypad with a gloved hand and the door opened.

Lock squinted at the sudden, stark light stretching ahead of him down a low, wide corridor. Its white walls were streaked with black marks, and plaster showed in places through flaking paint; the floor was tiled with large linoleum tiles, like a hospital. The men walked Lock, staggering, into the building, his feet skipping clumsily along, trying to keep up. They passed two dark-grey doors with small frosted windows and stopped by a pair of lifts on either side of the corridor. The smaller man pressed the button and called one. By the lifts were two large metal bins on wheels and in them Lock saw a white tangle of sheets like screwed-up paper. There was a smell in the air of soap powder and steam that made him want to lie down in a clean bed in a warm home. He could feel his head lolling on his neck as if he were coming in and out of sleep.

The lift door opened with a low creak. Lock was shuffled in and propped against a metal wall, the tall man finally taking his arm away. He felt the lift jerk a little under him and presumed that it was going up. The smaller man pulled a tissue from his pocket and looking up at Lock dabbed flecks of vomit from his chin and lapels as a mother might clean up a child. Lock watched him with a puzzled, helpless frown. The man was pallid, brittle-looking, his almost translucent skin showing clearly the shape of the skull beneath. His irises were light grey against milky whites. Straw-coloured hair showed under his cap. He looked vicious but less powerful than his friend.

The lift trundled up. Sixth floor, seventh. Eventually it stopped on the eighth floor, the last. The small man pulled Lock away from the wall by the arm and the door slid slowly open. From the lift opposite a maid in a pink housecoat, a white maid's cap on her head, was pulling a trolley laden high with toilet paper and bath caps and slippers in transparent plastic bags. Her back was to Lock and the two Russians and they were forced to wait. As she reversed out onto the landing she turned, saw the three men, and began to smile before she realized that something about them was not right. The small man had his arm linked through Lock's, and the taller of the two was right behind them, ready to push Lock out of the lift. The maid looked at Lock as if for explanation. In that moment he shrugged himself free of the smaller man's grip and half lunged, half fell towards the trolley, now blocking the corridor. His shoulder smashed into it, wheeling it round and knocking pens and tiny bottles of shampoo onto the floor. Pushing the trolley end on into the small man, who tottered backwards, off balance, Lock backed into the other lift, clawing at the closing door for support and pressing madly at the bank of buttons. He watched the tall man try to push past the maid; as she crouched to pick up her things he stumbled over her back. The last thing Lock saw through the narrowing crack was the man's outstretched hand, failing to find a grip.

It was quiet in the lift. With a gentle jolt it began to descend. Lock leaned against the wall, the metal cold against his temple. His nausea had subsided, but his head throbbed with grim intensity. So this is what had happened to Dmitry. It was possible that he wasn't even conscious when he died. He may not have known.

The lift stopped. The fifth floor: in his panic Lock had pressed the wrong button. As the door opened he hit frantically at the ground-floor button, then at the button that closed the doors. It appeared to do nothing; in its own time the door inched back. Above him Lock thought he could hear the metallic clatter of steps being taken three at a time. When the door shut the noise stopped.

He pinched his eyes with his hand. He had to work out

what to do. He felt in his pocket for his phones, but found only the smashed remains of one. Christ. The numbers over the door counted slowly down. No ideas came to him and he struggled to stand. He took deep breaths to steady himself. Two. One. Ground. The corridor was still empty. He set off away from the street door, lurching against the walls. At the end of the corridor he turned right, on instinct, shouldering into a maid carrying an armful of towels. Ahead of him was a pair of wooden swing doors, in each one a small glass pane at head height. He heard a door open behind him and quick steps coming his way; over his shoulder he saw the small man running towards him, his rubber shoes squeaking on the linoleum, his coat open and swinging at his sides. Lock forced his legs to work faster but he couldn't control them. They gave, as if the tendons had gone, and he crashed through the doors in a running fall, rolling into the room beyond.

He was on his back. His hands felt carpet under him, and he could hear piano music playing. Lumbering over onto his knees he looked sluggishly around. People were looking at him: people in deep chairs having drinks, people standing at reception checking in. In the centre of the room, setting off the sober marble and the deep dark wood, was a vase full of tall flowers: lilies, delphiniums. He was in the lobby of a hotel. Still on his knees, Lock glanced behind him. Through the glass in the door he could see the black cap and ghost eyes of the small man, watching him. Lock stood up, painfully, and steadied himself. The concierge and a receptionist were having an urgent, whispered conversation; then the concierge gestured to a doorman, who was walking purposefully towards Lock. Lock held his hand up, and started walking shakily past the flowers towards the revolving glass door that led into the street, feeling everyone's eyes on his back. The piano music played on.

Out on the street the cold hit him again, making his eyes

water. This was the bright street that he had seen earlier. He scanned it from left to right. To the right, at the corner of the hotel, stood the tall man, his arms crossed. Just standing, watching Lock. Lock stepped back onto the steps of the hotel and turned to go back in. Through the glass he could see the small man standing by the flowers in the middle of the room. For a moment his mind was blank. No useful thought was there. He had got this far on luck and what remained of his instinct.

It seemed he had a tiny scrap left. Going back up the steps he walked through a door to the left of the revolving doors, wrong-footing the doorman who was now on the other side. He walked towards the small man, who looked briefly taken aback. But instead of tackling him or challenging him, Lock climbed clumsily onto the table and with the sole of his shoe kicked the vase over, shouting as it fell, in his head or out loud he didn't know, the words mangled and slow: would you *just* leave me the *fuck* alone.

Guests sitting nearby with their drinks recoiled but the heavy glass vase remained intact, landing on the carpet with a thud and spilling flowers and water onto the floor. Lock looked down at the strange scene he had made. He felt high above it. The small man had stepped well away from him, and was now by the exit. The doorman, joined by a colleague, was at the table, trying to work out how to get Lock down with the minimum of fuss. The only noise was the Chopin still piping from the speakers in the ceiling.

'English,' said Lock to the doorman. 'Very drunk.' He sat down to slide himself off the table. The doorman took Lock firmly by the arm and walked him across the lobby to a door behind reception. His colleague followed.

Everything Lock looked at slipped away. The more effort he made the more it slipped. He tried to focus on a single point but there were no points. He felt himself being guided to a chair and pushed gently into it. There was a desk, and a computer, and beyond them a man with a moustache like a brush and above it a red, bulbous nose.

This man introduced himself in broken English as Herr Gerber. He was the head of security at the hotel and he was going to call the police. He said some other things in German, but Lock didn't understand them. 'Police' he understood, though, and '*Polizei*', and he explained in broken phrases, stumbling through the words, that he was an important English businessman and that someone was trying to kill him. Gerber looked at him for a moment and then reached for his phone. Lock, holding up an unsteady hand, told him to wait and reached into his back pocket, expecting his wallet to be gone. To his surprise it was still there, and still full of money. He took two notes out, looked at them carefully as if making sure they were real, and put them deliberately on Gerber's desk side by side.

'I need to call. One call.'

Gerber left the notes where they were and angled the phone towards Lock.

'Ikertu,' said Lock. 'I don't have the number. London.'

Gerber looked at him, shook his head and sighed. He tore a piece of paper from a pad in front of him and passed it across to Lock with a pen. Lock wrote on it feebly and passed it back. Gerber turned to his computer and after a minute took the phone and dialled a number. He passed the receiver to Lock.

The person who answered the phone refused to put him through to Webster, and Lock didn't have the energy to argue. He left a number that Gerber gave him, and for two minutes the three men just sat in the office, not talking. Gerber busied himself at his desk; the doorman manned the door. Lock felt like his head was full of metal, and his gut ached. He could feel the nausea steadily returning and hoped it would wait until he was clear of the hotel. He wasn't sure his money would stretch that far.

The phone rang. Gerber answered and passed the phone to Lock. Lock talked laboriously and then passed the phone back to Gerber who, after a minute or two and a few grunted words of German, put the receiver down and said to Lock, 'Give me another five hundred.'

Lock frowned. 'Why?'

'I'm going to drive you.'

'Where?'

'Out of town. To meet your friend.'

CHAPTER SIXTEEN

When the call came through Webster was asleep on Lock's bed, his head uncomfortably against the headboard, his chin pressing down onto his collarbone. As the phone rang, a loud old-fashioned ring, he opened his eyes and felt familiar pain along the side of his head. Lock and Inessa had been in his dreams. How could he have slept?

He had expected Hammer, and at first didn't recognize the slow, stretched voice on the other end of the line. Then, with beautiful clarity, it made sense. It was Lock. He was alive. Hammer had got through to Malin. The deal was starting.

Lock sounded ill. Webster couldn't make out what he was saying. When Lock passed the phone to Gerber, Webster had assumed that this was part of the ploy: he would now negotiate Lock's release and the handover of the dossier. As he listened though, confused, it slowly became clear that something else was happening. Gerber was German, without any doubt, and incensed, in a rather bureaucratic way. He didn't sound tense. He didn't sound like he wanted anything. All he wanted was for Webster to come to the hotel now to pick up his friend. Only at that point did he realize that Lock was free. He looked up and said a silent thank you to the heavens.

Webster told Gerber that Lock was in danger and would pay to be taken from the hotel safely. Gerber grunted and said he would drive him to the north side of Gartenplatz; his car was in the car park under the hotel and Lock could lie down

292

on the back seat. They would be there in fifteen minutes and would not be seen.

Instantly awake, relief and excitement coursing through him, his head forgotten, Webster washed his glass in the bathroom sink, put the books back on the bedside table, plumped up the pillows, smoothed out the covers on the bed and pulled the curtains open.

He looked at the note: what an innocent-looking document. He took two sheets of paper from the rack and three pens from his pocket. One was a blue biro. He clicked the point into place and began to write on one of the sheets of paper, carefully copying Lock's hand from the note. *Since my friend. Since my friend.* It needed to be rounder, steadier. He began to find some rhythm. *Since my friend Dmitry Gerstman died I have been unhappy.* The tails weren't quite right but that didn't matter. Taking the clean sheet he worked quickly through a fair copy. He sat back and looked at it. Not bad. It wouldn't persuade a specialist for a moment but it might fool a glance, which was all he wanted. He folded it as the note had been folded, put it in an envelope and left it on the desk where the note had been. The original he put carefully back into its envelope and into the pocket of his coat. He tidied up, putting the scraps of paper in his pocket as well.

Checking that the room looked exactly as it had done he turned out the light and left. He picked up his bag and went out, telling Frau Werfel that he had found Mr Green and would be bringing him back shortly.

He needed a payphone and a taxi. More snow was falling, gently now. The hotel steps were newly icy and he came down them carefully, holding on to the railing. At the bottom he looked up and saw a car approaching from the west, going faster than was sensible on these roads: a grey Mercedes saloon, only the driver inside. It stopped across the entrance to a garage ten yards short of the Daniel and a small man wearing an overcoat and cap got out. He walked quickly towards Webster, half sliding on the ice, twisting in mid-stride to lock his car. As he turned back the two men came face to face and in that moment knew each other. Webster could see Lock's torment in his unsurprised, colourless eyes.

Neither man wanted to be detained. Each had his own purpose: to clean up Lock's room; to rescue Lock. For a second they stood, a yard apart, in an unlikely impasse. The man shifted to the side to let him by. As Webster moved past him, their eyes still locked, the man tripped him, sweeping his foot across and catching him on the ankle.

Webster lost his balance on the ice and fell heavily on his side with a leaden thud, the compacted snow hitting him like iron, his cheek pressing against the frozen sludge on the pavement. By instinct, like a boy, he reached out an arm, caught the bottom of the man's trousers and pulled hard towards him. The man's feet went from under him and as he fell on the small of his back Webster scrambled with skating feet to get up. But he was barged from the side and the man was on top of him, hands grasping for his throat, Webster's reach just long enough to keep him off. For a second they were joined in each other's grip, raging eyes staring. Webster took a hand from the man's shoulder and as he fell, off balance, jabbed him with two fingers in the eye; trying to get to his feet, his leather soles slipped hopelessly and he found himself on his knees, like a choirboy, reaching towards the car's door to pull himself up. The man pulled at Webster's coat, using it to get upright, until he too was on his knees, up close, searching for grip with his feet, reaching inside his coat pocket. His eyes were bright with fury. Webster grabbed the man's lapels, arched backwards, and snapped his head down with all its weight on his brow. He felt bone crack. The man's body slumped in its clothes and Webster let it fall.

His breathing was short, his heart beating wildly. He

looked up and down the street. He could see no one. He opened the man's overcoat and went through his pockets. Euros, cigarettes, the car key. A knife. From his belt hung a holster and a matt-black pistol. No papers of any kind. Webster took the gun and the knife and pulled himself up against the car, panting, his trousers stiff with cold and ice. He picked up his bag and set off towards the canal, as quickly as he could, stopping only to slash two of the Mercedes' tyres and take a note of its number plate on his phone. The street was clear.

As he walked, quickly, almost a run, checking over his shoulder to make sure the man hadn't revived, he looked at the gun. It was a Makarov, a Russian make. That was no surprise. What was puzzling was why the man had attacked him: it made no sense. Crossing the canal he threw the gun far out into the water where the ice had yet to form. I'm the only link they have to Lock, he thought. Why not simply follow me? Because I knew who he was, and I wouldn't have let him.

He found a phone. He was still out of breath, and exhilaration was giving way to cold. Pulling his collar up, he leaned against it and dialled Hammer's number. It rang only once.

'Lock's safe. I don't know how. I think they slipped him something. I'm picking him up now. Look, I need you to find us a bolt-hole. Somewhere not too far from Berlin where no one would think of looking.'

'Why don't you just come home?'

'Because I think we can end this here. I'll explain later. I'll call in half an hour.'

It took him five minutes to find a cab. Inside the heater was blowing and it was hot and dry. He gave the address and opened his window an inch. The driver – middle-aged, Turkish – drew his scarf around his neck and asked him if he was crazy, letting the cold in on a night like this. Did he want to kill him? Webster shut the window and looked out at Berlin. Mitte was busy. Just after nine on a Friday night. Everyone seemed young here. Frau Werfel aside, Webster couldn't remember seeing a single old person in the city.

The cab drove north, past the Adlon, past the Hauptbahnhof. Eventually it pulled in to the side of the road. '*Wir sind hier,*' said the driver. 'Gartenplatz.' Webster asked him to wait and got out. An immense gothic church rose up in black over the square. In the darkness he couldn't see Lock and he could feel his breath quickening again, but then he spotted him at the other end of the road, propped against a lamp post.

'Richard,' said Webster, walking up to him. Lock's eyes were closed. 'Richard.' Lock didn't respond. What had they done to him? Webster touched his arm. 'Richard, are you OK?'

Lazily, Lock opened his eyes. He blinked twice and pulled his head back a little as if unable to focus.

'Richard, it's Ben. Come on. You must be freezing. I've got a cab. Come on.' He put his arm round Lock and guided him carefully to the car, Lock struggling to keep his head upright. 'Jesus, what have they given you?' Lock didn't reply. Webster opened the door and eased him inside, his hand protecting his head.

'Is he drunk?' said the driver.

'He's not well.'

'Is he going to be sick?'

'He'll be fine. Can I borrow your phone?'

The driver turned to look at Webster.

'You don't have a phone?'

'No. I need to borrow yours. It's a short call. I'll give you a big tip.' The driver shrugged his shoulders and passed his phone back behind him.

Hammer had found a guest house in Wandlitz, twenty miles north of Berlin. Lock slept, leaning against the door of the car.

With his head hanging on his chest he looked like a wooden posing doll slumped on a shelf. Webster watched him, chastened. This wasn't the man he'd been pursuing. That man was a cipher: a name on documents, a picture in magazines, a series of assumptions about his kind. This man breathed. He had weight and form. His face showed that he had loved and feared. On this cold night Webster felt finally awake.

The place wasn't easy to find, and the driver missed it twice before Webster spotted the tiny sign pointing between two large villas. They drove down a narrow drive overarched with bare lime trees and pulled up in front of a large white house lit by two floodlights.

Webster got out of the car. It was no longer snowing, the wind had dropped and the air was pure and heady, alpine. The moon was a day or two short of full but by its light he could make out beyond the floodlights a sailing boat and a jetty held firm by sparkling grey ice. For a second he was thrown; this couldn't be the sea. No, of course; this was one of the lakes. Wandlitzsee. He had heard of it. From somewhere in the dark he could hear the steady cracking of water freezing at the furthest edge of the ice. To his right, white ice in layers on the shore reflected the moon in clusters of pinprick lights.

Hammer had called ahead. Heaven knows what he had said but the proprietor of the Villa Wandlitz could not have been more obliging. He introduced himself as Herr Maurer, took the bag and, while Webster paid the driver, helped walk Lock into the house. When Webster began to explain that his friend was ill, that he had a migraine, Herr Maurer said that he knew, that this was a shame and he hoped Herr Webster's friend would be feeling better come the morning. He didn't want to know about credit cards or passports or anything else. Instead he took two keys from behind the reception desk, showed Webster and Lock into the lift and took them to adjoining rooms on the first floor. Breakfast was from seven until nine, but if they wanted to sleep late he would be very happy to make something specially for them. He didn't even seem to notice Webster's filthy clothes or the blood dried on his temple. Webster thanked him and said goodnight.

He took Lock's coat off and draped it over a chair. It gave off a faint smell of vomit that he hadn't noticed before. He shuffled him over to the side of the double bed, turning him round and letting him collapse onto it, took off his shoes and folded the duvet over him.

'Do you want some water?'

With his eyes shut Lock frowned tightly and shook his head. Webster filled a glass from the bathroom tap and set it down on the bedside table. He left the bathroom light on and the door open between their two rooms.

For some time he sat in his room in the dark, looking out of the window at the moon and the lake. He should go downstairs and borrow Herr Maurer's computer to look at Gerstman's files. He should call Hammer. He should call Elsa. More than anything else he should work out how to make this end well. There was a way, he was sure, slowly forming in his mind.

He looked at Lock. What was going through his head at the moment? Nonsense, with any luck. Or nothing. He went to the bathroom and inspected his wound. A patch of brown hair stuck down gave it away; otherwise you wouldn't notice. It would wait till tomorrow, and so would everything else.

Elsa woke him. Through his dreams he slowly made out the buzz of his phone as it skittered across the bedside table. He answered it full of sleep.

'Hello.' There was pain behind his eyes. He remembered his head.

'You're there. Why didn't you call last night?'

He sat up a little against the pillows. There was a small patch of dried blood on the sheets.

'I'm sorry, baby. I didn't get in till late. I thought you'd be asleep.' Through the curtains he could see sunshine. It must be late.

'Then send me a text.' A pause. 'I called but it went straight to voicemail.'

'That's strange.'

'I was worried.'

'I know. I'm an idiot. Sorry.'

Neither said anything. Webster could hear voices in the background, the radio. *I should have called; that was stupid.*

Elsa spoke first. 'When are you coming back?'

'I wish I knew. Could be today. Could be as late as Tuesday. I think I'll know today.'

'Are you OK?'

'Everything's fine. How is everyone?'

'Playing upstairs. Nicely for the time being.' Elsa was quiet for a moment. 'You've had a strange letter. It's addressed to Saint Benedict Webster, care of the Websters. It's sitting staring at me.'

'How big is it?'

'A4, a normal envelope.'

'Where's it from?'

'Oslo. Sent yesterday.'

'Odd. I don't know what that is. I'll deal with it when I get back.'

'I don't like it. It's like an unexploded bomb.'

'Unless it's big and fat it's not a bomb. You're going nuts.' He paused. 'Send it to Ike.'

'I'd rather open it.'

'OK, that's fine – open it.'

He heard her put the phone down. He began to think

about the day; he had to look through Gerstman's documents, talk to Hammer, talk to George. He should get up. The line was still quiet.

'What is it?'

'Jesus, Ben. Oh, Jesus.' Her voice caught as she said it.

'What is it? Tell me.'

'I knew there'd be more of this shit. Why are they sending this here? Who the fuck is doing this?'

'What? You have to tell me.'

'It's . . .' Elsa took a breath, collected herself. 'It's a photograph of a body. A woman's body. On a table. Her throat has been cut.'

Webster felt sick. His mouth was dry. He wanted to scream with rage.

'The bastards. The fucking bastards.' He got out of bed, went into the bathroom and smacked the wall hard with the flat of his hand. He looked down at the sink, his forehead against the mirror.

'I'll have Ike come and pick it up. You shouldn't have seen that. I'm sorry, baby. I'm sorry.'

'It's Inessa.'

He couldn't say the word at first. 'Yes. It's her.' It was as if they had dug her up. For more abuse. He took a deep breath, and another.

'Are you OK?' said Elsa.

'I'm fine. I'm fine.' More breaths. Don't let them affect you. Don't let them in. 'It's you I'm worried about.'

'I've had enough of this. I don't want these people in our lives.'

Webster said nothing. His head was full of noise. For a moment neither said anything.

'There's something else,' said Elsa.

'What do you mean?'

'In the envelope.'

'What is it?'

'A cutting. From the *FT*. "Russian metals group lists in London".'

GMK. Generalny Metalligurchesky Kombinat. Which still owned the aluminium plant in Kazakhstan, and a dozen like it across Russia and beyond. What was it doing there? What obscure message did it hold?

'You've got to come home.'

Not now. Especially not now. He sighed and closed his eyes tight. 'I can't.'

'You're not serious?'

'I can't. You know what that says? That poison? It says we know you so well, piece by piece, that we can do what we want with you. It's meant to make me scared. To lose it. Well, it won't work. It won't fucking work.'

'It scares me.'

'I know, baby, I know. But believe me they are not going to do anything. This is easy for them. They just send a letter. There's no comeback. Nothing is going to happen.'

'They sent it to our home.'

'So that you'll persuade me to give up. Same with the email. I'll have someone sit outside the house.'

'I just want it to stop.'

'I'm going to make it stop.'

'Come home.'

'I can't. Not now. This has to end.'

It was noon and the sun had some warmth in it by the time Lock woke. Webster was outside sitting on a bench by the lake with his eyes closed, his face to the light, his thoughts scattered. He had never seen those pictures. He assumed they were from the morgue in Oskemen; there had never been a post-mortem. The package had unsettled him, not because it had scared Elsa, though that was the worst thing about it, but because he didn't know what it meant. The email had been a simple warning; this was not only darker but less clear. Did it mean that Malin knew what had happened to Inessa? That Webster never would? Perhaps it was merely a display of knowledge and power. Perhaps all it said was: I understand you; I know the pain you have known; I can create more at will.

But it didn't scare him. Nor did the man who had sent it, or the ease with which he could picture his dead eyes and his dark will, his unnatural world narrowed to a single point of malice. For ten years he had challenged himself to imagine that mind, and now that he was confronted by it, now that he thought he recognized it again, its horror had been robbed of all its force. No. What scared him was his own power to corrupt, to imperil. If it weren't for his silent obsession, Gerstman would be alive and Lock would be where he once was, compromised but safe. And what scared him more was that even now he couldn't stop. He still had work in Germany: one last idea.

He heard footsteps on the gravel and looked up. A haggard Lock was making his way slowly towards him.

'Good morning,' said Webster, his hand shielding his eyes from the sun.

'It is, isn't it?' said Lock, squinting around him. His eyes were grey shot through with red. 'Where are we?'

'Wandlitzsee. I brought you here last night.'

'After the hotel?'

'After the hotel.'

Neither said anything.

'How are you feeling?'

'Awful. My head feels like it's been minced.'

'Are you hungry?'

'Not in the least. I want air. And water.' He sat down on the bench and with effort crossed his legs. He groaned. 'What happened?'

'I got hit on the head. You disappeared. Four hours later I get a call from you and you're in the Adlon with their head of security.' Webster waited for Lock to supply the rest but he said nothing. 'I'm sorry. I failed you. I should have realized how serious they were.'

Lock gave a small nod. His skin was grey, dark under the eyes. He said nothing.

'You told me that someone had tried to poison you.'

Lock looked past Webster at the lake and shook his head slowly. 'Christ. I hardly remember anything. That guy changing his tyre, then nothing. I can remember a man with a moustache, and me telling him that I was very drunk. And being in a hotel. Jesus.' He rubbed his forehead with the heel of his hand. 'Was it Malin?'

'I assume so. An hour and a half after you called Nina two men booked themselves on that night's Aeroflot flight to Berlin. Both Russians. One was thirty-one, the other thirty-five. Does that sound like them?'

'They were Russian.'

'Hammer's working on them.'

Lock nodded faintly. 'Did you rescue me?'

'I wish I had. You did it yourself.'

Lock laughed, a pained chuckle. 'Really? That's a first.'

Webster smiled and glanced down at his hands. 'I got you some things, from town. I didn't bring your stuff from the Daniel.'

Lock scratched the back of his head. 'I am feeling a little vagrant.' He took a deep, deliberate breath. 'It's nice here.'

'We're safe I think. The only way they'll find us is if they find the taxi driver, and it would take an army to do that.'

'What about the hotel?'

Webster smiled. 'My boss arranged the hotel. We're honoured guests. Herr Maurer has been told that you are an important English businessman suffering from a rare nervous complaint and a nasty scandal back home. You were staying in some fancy place just outside Berlin but the English press found you and now you're hiding here. He's happy because we're paying him four times what everyone else here is paying. If anyone calls he'll let us know.'

'Shouldn't we just go? Back to London? Isn't it over?'

Webster turned and looked at the lake. It was frozen to about forty yards out now, and where the ice met the water ducks played. Nothing else was moving.

'Nina gave us what we wanted,' he said, turning back to Lock, still shielding his eyes.

'The files?'

'He kept them in a hotmail account. From the looks of it he'd save a new batch of documents there once a month.'

'You've seen them.'

Webster nodded.

'Well? What are they?' Lock's eyes, tired before, came alive.

Webster looked down before meeting Lock's stare. 'They're not what we thought they were.'

'Jesus.' Lock pushed his hand back through his hair. 'Not what *you* thought they were. Fuck. I knew I shouldn't . . .' He closed his eyes and sighed, a long, sad sigh. 'What are they?'

'I looked at them this morning. They're all the purchase agreements between Langland and the companies that sell it their oil. Every one, all the time he was there. They're conclusive proof that Langland makes a turn on every trade, and that the Russian producers suffer.'

'I don't understand. That sounds good.'

'It's not bad. Journalists would love to see it. But it's never going to convict Malin of fraud. Companies can sell to Langland at any price they like. You'd have to prove collusion. Which means finding a Russian executive prepared to say it's going on. Which isn't going to happen.'

Lock turned away from Webster and folded his arms. 'I'm freezing.'

'Let's go inside.'

'And go on with this? To what purpose? To earn you a fee?' Lock stood up and looked down at Webster, blocking out the sun. 'You should ask yourself why you're in this game, Ben. Are you helping me? Screwing Malin? Or just enjoying yourself? Which is it?' Webster didn't respond. 'I think we should go. I'd go and pack my case but I don't have any fucking things.' Lock turned and walked slowly towards the hotel.

'Richard.' Webster got up and followed him. 'Richard, wait.' Lock carried on walking, his feet now crunching on the gravel. 'That was the bad news.'

Lock stopped and turned, his face dark. 'If there was any good news you'd have told me by now. What is it?'

'Malin tried to kill you. In Germany.'

'That's good?'

Webster looked around him, hesitating, then back at Lock. 'I have an idea. It could finish him.'

'You're serious?'

'It's a serious idea. But you need to decide whether it's good. I'm not pushing it.'

'No, you're not. Christ. What sort of a world do you live in? Is every day like this?' He stared at Webster. 'Running around, dreaming up plans? Let me ask you something. When do you start to play? Or do you just move the pieces around?' Webster didn't reply. With a will he held Lock's gaze. 'Tell me. If I'd have died, what would you have done? Found another me? Sent someone else off to the front line? Fuck, Ben, if it wasn't for you I'd still be in Moscow and none of this would be happening. Would that be so bad? So Malin's bent. So what? So the fuck what? Everyone's bent. Tourna's bent, Jesus. He's worse. And all those blue-chip companies, you think they haven't got someone like me to hide things, help them avoid tax? They've got legions of them. I'm just one man. And I'm not fucking dispensable, all right?'

'This was always going to happen.'

'What?'

'This was always going to happen. You can't keep stuff like this hidden. It comes out.'

'And you just help it along? Is that it?'

'Something like that.'

Lock laughed, a hard, sharp laugh. 'That's great. That's noble of you. Ben, we both work for crooks. We play our parts, and that's it. And if we didn't, someone else would. That's the world.'

Webster put his hands in his pockets and looked down at the ground. He didn't feel like defending himself; didn't feel that he could. Lock was right. It was time he stopped dressing this up.

He sighed and looked Lock in the eye. 'Look. I'm sorry. I underestimated Malin. That was my mistake. Perhaps you . . . you could take Dmitry's files to Malin. To show your loyalty. You'd be back in the fold.'

Lock shook his head. 'No. No. That's not what I want. Christ, Ben, you can't lead me this far and then send me back. I'm not the same man. I can't do it any more.'

Webster was quiet.

'Is that the idea?' said Lock.

'No.'

'How risky is it?'

'I told you. That's for you to decide.'

'No. You're in this too. Let's go inside. Christ knows I'm in no hurry to get in a car. We decide together.'

Webster sat down in an armchair in the corner of his room and reached into his briefcase. He took out his phone, a straightforward Nokia, and pressed a combination of keys.

Lock sat on the bed and watched. Webster put the phone down on the coffee table in front of him. A voice started playing over its speaker.

'*Thank you for seeing me . . . I wouldn't have . . . This isn't for pleasure, you understand. I think we may be able to help each other.*' A pause. Lock looked at Webster. '*You've been busy these last few weeks . . . I'm beginning to wish that we'd hired you first.*' Another pause. '*But what concerns me is that after Paris there's . . . there's no clarity.*'

As the words continued to play Lock said, 'What is this? Is that me?'

Webster nodded.

'*. . . I think the best ending for everybody will be agreed outside court. Except the lawyers, perhaps.*'

'How did you do that?'

'*. . . hurting my business and costing Aristotle money. A fortune if his fees are as bad as ours.*'

Webster leaned forward and picked up the phone. He pressed a button and the voice stopped.

'When people find out what I do they want to know if I have any gadgets. I always say no. This is the only one. A man in Belgium made it for me. Gave it to me, actually. He was rather pleased with it.'

'I should have frisked you.'

'You wouldn't have found anything. This was on the table.'

Lock shook his head. 'Can I see?'

Webster handed the phone over. 'When you take the battery out, it starts recording. When you put it back in, it stops. It's a brilliant idea. Mossad had it first, apparently.'

Lock held the phone in his hand and inspected it closely. 'What I could have done with this.'

'Exactly. That's my idea.'

Lock looked up. 'This?'

'Part of it.' Lock waited, still toying with the phone. Webster went on. 'What's the worst thing Malin has done?'

'We don't know. That's the point. Unless you count destroying my life.'

'Quite. He tried to kill you. And we're fairly sure he killed Gerstman. But the only evidence we've got is you, and the note that they left.'

'What note?'

'A suicide note. They left it in your hotel room.'

'Jesus. What did it say?'

'That you'd lost your family and your reputation, and that Dmitry's death had sent you over the edge.'

'Do you have it?'

'Yes, I took it from the room and left a dummy in its place. It may have fooled them.'

Lock nodded.

'Do you want to see it?' Webster said, leaning forward as if to get up.

'Like seeing your own obituary,' said Lock, as if to himself. He shook his head.

Webster sat back. 'But it won't be enough. We can probably prove it's not your handwriting, but there won't be fingerprints and even if there were they wouldn't help.'

'So?'

Webster collected himself. 'Malin wants the dossier. He also wants you. If you go back to Russia we'll never see you again. So we bring him here, control it very carefully, and you talk to him. You ask him why he tried to have you killed.'

'He'll never say anything.'

'You'd be surprised what people will say when they know no one's listening.'

Lock thought for a moment.

'He'll never come.'

'He will. He'll come for you.'

Lock looked down and smoothed the hair on the side of his head – twice, three times. 'And what do I want?'

'What do you tell him?'

'Yes.'

'That doesn't really matter. The one thing that isn't going to happen is that you hand over the dossier and he meets your demands.'

'It might.'

Webster considered this. He looked at Lock; his face was puffy, the skin on his cheeks still a sickly pale. 'OK. We could play it like that. You can try for both. Or either. In any event it needs to sound convincing, I suppose. What would you ask for?'

'A separation. I'd sell up. Or I'd look like I was selling up. He'd find a buyer and I'd sell to them. In return I'd want some money and a guarantee that he leave me alone.'

'A guarantee?'

Lock shrugged his shoulders. 'I know. But if I'm gone and the story's OK why draw attention to it by finishing me off?'

Webster nodded slowly. He gave Lock a candid look. 'We don't have to do this. We can go back to London. Get you somewhere safe.'

'I'm not really up to thinking.' Lock stood up, one hand on the bed for balance. 'I'm going to lie down.'

'But if we do it, we should do it soon. You should call Malin today.'

CHAPTER SEVENTEEN

Lock said yes. After an hour in his room he knew what his answer had to be.

He had sat and watched the lake, like steel now under cloud that had moved steadily in from the west. It was overhung by black trees that looked sketched in charcoal; its furthest shore he couldn't see.

He had never been close to death before, and now that he had, he couldn't remember it. Malin had robbed him even of that. But he knew that things had changed. His life – this sickly thing he had been living – had come to a point. In Berlin they had rendered him senseless, but in truth he had been senseless for years: serene, peaceful, a fool amongst knaves. To stumble to his death, unseeing and unthinking – that was the right way for that life to end. And it had. It was over. It wasn't just that he could no longer bring himself to protect Malin; he could no longer stand to protect his old self. The FBI, the Swiss, Tourna, the journalists, the joke-makers in Moscow: they could have him. They had been right all along and if they had to prove it, crow about it, then let them.

Malin, though; Malin was his. Lock wanted that inflated, bullying life reduced, its power drained away, its crookedness laid bare. He wanted Malin to understand what it was to be nothing; to be a beggar; to be undone.

He found Webster in the restaurant, the only person in the neat, bright dining room. The place smelled faintly of toast and fried bacon. Webster was stirring a cup of coffee, the spoon chinking against the side; only his table had a table-cloth.

'You alone?'

'They don't serve lunch. Herr Maurer's wife made me an omelette. I'm sure she'd do another.'

Lock shook his head. 'Just the smell in here is enough. Thank you.'

'Coffee?'

'Water.'

'Sit down.' Webster got up and went into the kitchen; he seemed to be making himself at home. Lock looked out of the window, which gave onto neat brick outbuildings by the side of the hotel. Herr Maurer was wheeling a tall white fridge on a trolley towards a white van whose doors were open at the back.

Webster came back with a bottle of still water, a bottle of fizzy, a glass and a bowl of ice.

'I didn't know which you wanted.'

'What do you think they gave me?'

'They gave Dmitry something called GHB. It's made of floor cleaner.' Lock didn't say anything. 'But there was a bottle of gin in your room that I don't remember seeing. Was that yours?'

'No. No gin.'

'Then they probably gave you quite a lot of that as well. If not from that particular bottle.'

'That makes sense. I can taste it on my breath.'

Webster held up the bottle of still water to Lock, who nodded.

'We should do it.'

Webster finished pouring and passed Lock the glass.

'Are you sure?'

'Utterly. I owe it to Nina. Not to mention Marina and Vika.

Christ, and everybody else.' He took a drink. He could feel it cool and mineral in his throat.

Webster watched him, as if expecting more. Lock drank again.

'You're certain?'

'Certain.'

'Then we have a lot to do.'

Lock called Malin that night. Webster had written a script for him, and told him to keep his tone professional. This was a deal, like any other.

Webster had bought new phones from town that afternoon. Six more; they were getting through them. He had also spent hours talking to people in London about the operation. Security people were flying out, and would be there that evening. Nina was going to stay with her sister in Graz. Lock marvelled at how precisely each move had to be plotted. He was coming to rely on Webster, he realized: swapping one controller for another.

It was late in Moscow when he called. Malin would still be up, though. He slept little.

The line rang five times before he answered.

'Richard.'

'Konstantin.'

'Where are you?'

'Somewhere you can't find me for once.' They spoke Russian.

'I wish you would come home.'

'It isn't home any more, Konstantin. Let's be honest, it never was.' Webster, standing over Lock, tapped his finger on the script on the desk. Get on with it.

'Richard, I am perhaps the one man anywhere who can protect you. Don't listen to anyone else who says he can.'

Lock glanced up at Webster, who nodded. 'Konstantin,

I have a proposal. I have something you want, and you have something I want. I have Dmitry's file. I know you've been looking for it.'

The script paused here to give Malin time to respond, but he said nothing.

Lock went on. 'I can promise you that you won't find it unless I help you. I'm prepared to give it to you in return for my liberty and a sum of money to compensate me for the trouble you have caused me. I will also ensure a smooth handover of my ownership interests to a party of your choice. I would recommend a Russian entity of some kind.'

'How much?'

'Wait. I'm not finished. I will also undertake to talk to any law enforcement agency only about matters within my competence. I will not speculate about anything else. As Kesler will tell you, that won't be enough to do you any harm. Not in Russia. I may not be so lucky but I'm happy to take that risk. Finally, you will undertake to leave me alone and let me live my life. The same goes for Nina Gerstman.'

Malin was silent for perhaps ten seconds. Lock glanced up at Webster and shrugged. Then Malin spoke. 'Is that it?'

'In essence, yes. When we meet we can discuss details.'

'How much?'

'Ten million dollars.'

Malin grunted. 'Where do you want to meet?'

'Be ready to fly to Europe on Monday morning. I will call you again at midnight tomorrow night and let you know which airport. The flight will not be longer than four hours from Moscow. When you land I will call you again and give you a time and a place to meet.'

'That's not enough time to file a flight plan.'

'It's Russia. You'll manage.'

The line was quiet. Eventually Malin said, 'Let me call you back in an hour. I need to think.'

'No you don't. If you don't say yes to a meeting now I will call the FBI immediately and give them the files. They'll enjoy them.'

'If you have the files you can tell me what's in them.'

'You can find out when I see you on Monday. This isn't a trick.'

Silence again. Lock imagined Malin, that blunt face processing what it had heard.

'Call me tomorrow night,' said Malin and hung up.

Lock felt Webster's hand on his shoulder and looked up.

'What did he say?' said Webster.

'That we should call tomorrow.'

'That's good. Very good. Did he say he was coming?'

'No. But I think he is.'

'How was he?'

'Same as ever. He doesn't give much away.'

'You were good. Confident.'

Lock smiled. His head was clearing and for the first time that day he thought that he could eat.

Later they ate together in the restaurant. There were three other guests: a party of Americans, a husband and wife and their friend, all retired, they said, and travelling round Germany and the Netherlands for a month. For ten minutes before dinner Lock and Webster swapped small talk with them in the bar, Webster engaging with them while Lock, still feeling delicate, sat back. The friend had been in Wandlitz ten years before when the hotel had just opened; she had come in the summer and swum in the lake. Webster moved the conversation on to their trip. Yes, they had been to Berlin. What an extraordinary city – an historical monument in itself; but such violence it had known. Webster was good at this, Lock thought. Eventually, to Lock's relief, he said that they must go and eat, and they took their table.

'Nice people,' said Webster.

'Nice people. Very nice. They've had a good life.'

'No self-pity, please. You told me you were feeling positive.'

'No, I mean it. They've had a good life. That's good. It's nice to meet some normal people. I can't remember the last time I did.' Lock took a sip of water. He pulled his napkin off the table and shook it open on his lap. 'Do you know what I was going to do before I called you in London?'

Webster shook his head. 'No.'

'I was going to run away. I had it in my head that if I could get to Switzerland I could withdraw all my money and disappear. I know someone in Istanbul who I thought could get me a passport.'

'Where would you have gone?'

'I don't know. Vanuatu. Some Indonesian island. Somewhere with sunshine and no government to speak of.' He smiled. 'In Switzerland I've got nearly nine million dollars. If I live another thirty years that's three hundred grand a year. That's enough.'

A waitress came and asked if they were ready to order.

'What can you manage?' asked Webster.

'Very little.'

'Boiled rice and carrots is what you want. And a glass of red wine.'

'Why on earth would I want that?'

'Good for upset stomachs. Trust me. I wouldn't have anything else.'

'OK. But no wine.'

Webster ordered in German. 'So what happened? Why didn't you go?'

'I remembered that the Swiss had been asking questions. They'd had one of my people in to talk to them in Zurich. Did you know that?'

Webster shook his head.

'So it wasn't you?'

'Not us.'

'I don't suppose it matters. I thought they'd stop me at the border and that would be that.' Lock took some bread and broke a piece off. He took a small, tentative bite and chewed gently. The bread felt strange in his mouth. 'But I shouldn't think they would have.'

'They might. But not yet, probably.'

'Exactly. I think I was scared. Or I just didn't want to go.'

'Paradise not all it seems?'

'I don't think I could lie in the sun every day any more.'

'So what do you want?'

'I have no idea. No idea.' I do, thought Lock. I want to live in London and see my wife and child. To say it out loud would be to jinx it.

Lock and Webster barely saw each other on Sunday: Webster went to Berlin to meet a man called George and find a location for the meeting, and Lock spent the day in his room drawing up a plan for the handover of Faringdon.

In the afternoon he walked around the lake on a path of compacted snow, watching the ducks, the metal rigging on the masts of boats pinging softly in the wind like cowbells, black branches laden with frosted white sagging above his head. There was a light mist on the water and everything was silver-grey. Twenty yards behind him one of George's people followed.

He wanted to speak to Marina. She would be worried. Webster had explained that if he did Malin would hear the call, learn the number of Lock's phone and attempt to trace it. Even if that phone was then dismantled and thrown on the growing heap of defunct mobile carcasses, Malin might still be able to work out from which cell the call had been made, and though time was now running short and his chances of doing so quickly on a Sunday slim, they couldn't risk his discovering their whereabouts. But Lock had insisted, and so Webster had suggested a simple solution, good enough to last the half a day or so they needed: they would phone the switchboard of a friendly company in London, which would phone the switchboard of a friendly company in New York, which would then forward the call to Marina's number, so that all Malin would see, in the first instance and without a good day or two of work, was a pair of apparently unconnected numbers that had nothing whatever to do with Lock. That, Webster had said, ought to be enough, provided that Lock made sure he didn't mention precisely where he was, what he was planning, or with whom he was planning it. To Lock, who really only wanted to tell his wife that he loved her, it all seemed absurdly cautious.

He made the call. A minute later he heard Marina's voice on the line, somehow unexpectedly close.

'Hi. It's me.'

'Richard. Thank God. Where have you been?'

'I'm sorry. It's been difficult to call.'

Marina was quiet. 'You should have let me know.'

'I'm sorry. Really.' A pause. 'How are you?'

'Scared. Where are you?'

'I'm sorry, sweetheart. I'm fine. I didn't mean to worry you.' Despite himself he felt a thrill of reassurance that she had been thinking of him. 'I think I've found a way out.' He waited for her to respond. 'I can't really talk about it but I'm seeing Konstantin. I think I can make a deal.'

'I spoke to him.'

'He called again?'

'I called him.'

Lock felt a small leap of fear – not of Malin, but of plans

unravelling. He stopped walking and looked across the lake; his bodyguard stopped a few feet behind him.

'You called him? Why?'

'To see how much of him was left.'

'What do you mean?'

'I told him that my father was watching what he did. That if he hurt you he would finally be lost.'

'What did he say?'

'That his conscience was clear. That I had no reason to fear him.'

'You believe him?'

'He said one day I would know he did everything he could for you.'

Lock snorted. 'Everything is right.'

'I think he believes it.'

A dozen sarcasms occurred to him. Justified, possibly: she had encouraged him to turn, and now she seemed to be suggesting that he turn back. He saw them clearly, but he didn't feel them. She was merely as scared as he had once been.

'Don't believe him,' he said, feeling a rush of energy at the thought that this whole business was now his to end. He would dictate terms to Konstantin; he would free himself; he would end this fear that had slowly etched away his life, and hers.

'I just . . .'

'Don't. He's got nothing left. He wants you to persuade me.'

'Will you talk to him?'

'I am talking to him. Tomorrow.'

'Not in Moscow?'

'I can't say.'

The line was quiet. He could see her eyes, creased in a frown, full of sadness.

'I could be back in London tomorrow,' he said. 'Or the next day.'

Still silence.

'Marina?' He knew that she was crying. 'Sweetheart, it's OK. I have something he wants.'

'OK.'

'It's changed. Already.'

'That's good.'

He could hear a catch in the rhythm of her breath; the lake was silent but for the rigging gently clinking. He looked for ducks but couldn't see any. 'Where's Vika?'

'Next door. We just finished lunch. She'll be in in a second.'

'Will you kiss her for me?'

'Yes.'

They were quiet again, and Lock knew that Marina was crying not from fear alone but from hope: she was proud of him again, and as it made her weep it filled him with lightness, almost jubilation. This was going to work. Not everything was jinxed.

'I should go,' he said.

'You should.'

'It's going to be OK.' He hesitated. 'I love you. I'm sorry I ever forgot that.'

'I know.'

'I'll call you tomorrow. When it's done.'

By Monday morning Lock was calm. Strangely so: all the alarm, all the anxiety of the last month had left him, and he knew they wouldn't return. Malin was coming. Lock had called him the night before and told him, in few words, rather enjoying himself, that he was to fly to Berlin. Malin was coming – not as his master but as his petitioner. And no matter how today ended, he would be his master no more.

Lock woke early, a little after six. He could see from the light under the door that Webster was awake. He sat in the dark and imagined the day. Malin would land some time this morning. In a few hours they would phone him and tell him to come to the Staatsbibliothek No. 2 on Potsdamer Strasse at noon. The Berlin state library. Webster had explained that it was open without being unmanageable, busy without being hectic. It was a sober, quiet building where the meeting could be controlled.

Outside the sky had turned from black to deepest blue.

They drove into the city in George Black's car. Lock liked Black. He wasn't a big man but there was a certainty about his manner, about the way he held himself, that made Lock feel safe. There were four of them in the car: Black, Webster, Lock and a well-spoken young man called James, who drove. George and James were at once exactly like their Russian counterparts and nothing like them at all. For one thing they were much more polite.

Twisting round in his seat Black explained that there were four more men already in Berlin. They were stationed in and around the library and would make sure that Lock was safe. 'Not', said Black, 'that he's likely to try anything out in the open.' When they got to Berlin two of Black's men would be inside, two outside. Lock would wait in the car a few hundred yards away with James. When Malin arrived, and only then, James would drive Lock round and he would be escorted into the building. During the meeting itself three men would be watching from a short distance and three would patrol the area. When the meeting had concluded, Lock would be escorted quickly and easily to his car and driven to a rendezvous just north of Berlin. The second car would conduct counter-surveillance on the first to make sure it wasn't followed. Throughout, Webster and the team would sit back. It was important that Lock appear to be alone, even if Malin would assume he was not.

Webster had instructions for him too. They discussed the phone.

'You've got your two phones. When you sit down, take them out of your pocket and take the batteries out of each. Ask Malin to do the same. Try and look a little anxious. Make him think you're the one worried about being overheard.'

'He won't recognize either of them.'

'That's OK. He knows you've got new phones. Now the recorder starts as soon as the battery comes out. Leave it face down. There's another battery in there that'll give an hour of recording time, maybe a little more. It records straight onto a hard drive. There's no noise, and no signal. You don't have to worry about it at all. Don't look at it. Forget it's there.'

Lock nodded. He rested his hand on the briefcase next to him. It contained all Gerstman's documents, printed out on Herr Maurer's computer.

'Chances are he'll have people with him,' Webster went on. 'That's OK. You'll have your people everywhere. We'll hang back unless something happens. But he's not going to want anything to happen to you while he's around. So all you have to think about is talking to him.'

'How should I start?'

'Any way you like. Don't think too hard about it. Let it come out. He's expecting you to be angry and upset. So be upset. Challenge him.'

The roads were fast now and lined with ten-foot metal screens; Lock felt that he was being channelled along them to his destiny.

As they came off the motorway the screens fell away. They were on the industrial edge of the city. Lock saw chimneys like towers erupting white smoke into the sky, scrappy patches of land undeveloped, water towers like inverted rockets tarred jet-black. There were no footprints in the snow here, no people walking. Then a McDonald's, and a furniture warehouse, and beyond that the suburbs; close by the car, pinched apartment buildings in concrete and pebble-dash ran the length of each block, and the pavements were filthy with old snow. After a while the streets opened out and the houses relaxed and people began to appear in the shops, in the parks, at the bus stops. Lock had never seen all this, not before. It was new to him to see things. A row of poplars the shape of peacock feathers. A red leather bag against a woman's tan shawl.

'You OK?' Webster broke his reverie.

Lock turned to him. 'I'm fine.'

'Not nervous?'

'Not at all.'

The car turned into Tiergarten and Lock watched the silver birches tick past him. Beyond the park's gates they emerged into a large open space, a mess of road and street lamps and traffic lights and slushy channels cut through the snow. The channels led from one huge modernist building to another, each somehow in its own world, like rivals. Lock looked to his left and saw fin-like orange panels on a jumble of cubes and curves; to his right a sleek concrete structure in grey; ahead of him a low, massive box of black steel and glass. Watching over them stood a church with a green copper roof, its ugly square tower ringed in yellow and red brick. The sky was huge and grey above it all.

'This is Potsdamer Platz,' said Black.

'It looks like an architecture competition,' said Lock.

'That's the library,' said Black, pointing past James to a building on the corner of the space. It was squat, jagged, irregular, made of grey and yellow concrete blocks and sloping glass in black frames. Screens like washboards masked the windows along one wall. It was set back from the road; next to the others it was reticent, erudite, scholarly.

'Was this east or west?' said Lock.

'Both,' said Webster.

They carried on past the library and crossed a bridge over the canal. Fifty yards further on James pulled over to the side and Black and Webster got out.

'I'll call you when he shows,' said Webster and gave Lock a calm, encouraging smile as he shut the door.

James pulled out again and took the next left into a quiet street. Halfway down it he did a three-point turn and parked.

'This is it,' he said.

'This is it,' said Lock.

It was James's phone that rang. He answered it without saying a word, put the car into gear and moved off. Lock checked his palms; they were dry.

James parked just out of sight of the library. A man that Lock didn't recognize came to his door and opened it.

'Good afternoon, sir. You need to go to the cafeteria area. As you go in, turn to your right and you'll see it. The subject is sitting at a table facing the door. His bodyguard is standing a little way behind him.'

'Thank you.'

'Good luck, sir.'

Lock checked his pockets for the two phones. They were there. He set off.

His chest felt light, the briefcase heavy in his hand. He smoothed his hair with his free hand as he walked along. Please let this work. Let him say it. Let him say the words. I want to tell the world that I brought him down. I want everyone to know. I want the journalists to know. I want Kesler to know. And Chekhanov. I want Andrew sodding Beresford to know, and all his superior English friends.

I want my father to know. And Marina. How I want Marina to know. And Vika. One day, Vika.

And Malin. In there now with his blank gaze and his impenetrable will. I want him to know that it was me.

The library was busy and hushed. An old lady with snow chains on her boots clanked across the stone floor. Lock moved towards the cafeteria. There he was. Sitting by one of the plate-glass windows that lined that side of the building, alone at a yellow table, his bulk absurd on a spindly metal chair. On the table in front of him was a cup of tea and an envelope. Stood with his back against a pillar a few yards away was Ivan the bodyguard. I knew he was special, thought Lock. Ivan watched him as he neared the table.

Lock could feel his heart beating in his throat. Four tables away he saw Webster studiously reading a German news-paper. The cafe was quiet but some of the tables along the window wall were occupied: a bearded man with a laptop; two girls eating sandwiches; a young man in a cap and thick black glasses leaning over papers he had spread out across his table.

'You came,' Lock said, in Russian.

Malin turned his head an inch towards Ivan and nodded. Ivan stepped up to Lock and asked him to spread his arms and legs. Lock, uncertain, did as he was asked, looking around him in quiet disbelief that this could happen so blatantly in such a place. Ivan ran his hands quickly down Lock's sides, his legs, the small of his back, and then patted his stomach and chest. Reaching inside Lock's jacket he pulled out the two phones, inspected each briefly and handed them back, before open-ing the briefcase and glancing inside. He nodded to Malin and stepped back again. Lock took off his coat and sat down, putting the briefcase on the floor by his chair.

'Phones please,' said Malin.

Lock looked at him, holding his eye for a second.

'OK. And yours.'

He reached into his pockets and pulled out the two

phones. He slid the back off each, eased the batteries out and left the parts on the table. Malin did the same with a single phone.

The two men looked at each other. Malin's eyes bored into Lock's. Lock tried to understand them, to see something in there that he had not seen before. But they were the same: matt, dead, reflecting nothing. In his black coat and grey suit, the white shirt and the red tie, he looked exactly as he always had.

'You look bad,' Malin said.

Lock returned the gaze. 'Thanks for your concern. I'm fine.'

'You looked better in Moscow.'

'I feel better here.'

Malin made a faint shrugging gesture, as if to say that he wasn't going to argue the point.

'Did you make the transfer?' said Lock.

With the palm of his hand Malin slid the envelope towards him an inch. Lock reached for it and opened it.

'It's in escrow,' said Malin. 'Someone we both know. He'll release it when he hears from you.'

Lock looked at the single sheet of paper. It was confirmation of a wire transfer made to an account in Singapore. He put it back on the table and, reaching below his chair, opened the briefcase. He took out a sheaf of A4 paper and set it down in front of Malin, who picked up the sheaf and began to work his way through, putting each page down on the table as he inspected it. Lock watched him steadily deal the pages, licking his thumb occasionally as he went.

When he had put down the last sheet from the batch he breathed in and let it out noisily through his nose.

'This is it?'

Lock didn't reply.

'This is everything?'

'Yes.'

'Bullshit.'

'That is everything. Downloaded from Dmitry's hidden email account. I can give you the details.'

Malin shook his head. 'You think this is worth ten million?'

'Yes.'

'Ten million, for invoices?'

'It's what you wanted.'

Malin laughed, once, his big frame shifting up and down. 'No, no, no. This is not what I wanted. This is not what I needed.'

'What does it matter?' said Lock. 'You have what you've been looking for. It's over. So it doesn't say very much. That's good, isn't it?'

Malin raised his eyebrows but said nothing.

'It means you killed Dmitry for nothing. That's not so good. But why should that bother you?'

Malin rubbed his chin, the folds of flesh pressed together between his fingers. He shook his head.

'I cannot go back to Moscow with this.'

Lock frowned. 'What do you mean?'

'They will think I have lost my mind.'

'Who will? Who's they?' Lock could feel a pain in his throat.

Malin sat back in his chair, adjusting his weight. He took his time. 'Richard, who do you think I am?'

Lock shook his head. 'I don't know what you mean.'

'I have been trying to protect you, Richard. All the time. Because I understand your position. Better than you think. But you have caused me problems. You and Dmitry. It would have been better if he had stayed.'

Lock leaned in to Malin, his voice low but urgent. 'Protect me? What, by having your goons fill me with Christ knows what and throw me off a roof? Was that how you protected Dmitry too?'

Malin leaned forward too, his hands clasped on the table. He lowered his voice. 'None of that was me.'

Lock tried to swallow but his mouth was dry. He longed for water. He could see the small moles on Malin's cheek.

'You or your people,' he said. 'I don't care.'

Malin shook his head gently. 'Richard, I told you when we last spoke. I could not protect you for ever. If you had come back to Moscow you would have ceased to be a risk.'

'I'm not a risk to you. I don't want to be a risk to you. I don't want anything to do with you. That's what all this is about.' Lock's voice was louder now. 'We can leave each other. For good. Separate. Divorce. I'll disappear. I will cause you no trouble. You know that.'

'Richard, it's not for me to decide.'

There was a roaring noise in Lock's head. He couldn't think.

'What?'

'You and I are the same, Richard. An agent of convenience for someone else.' He paused. 'Those were not my men trying to kill you. They were government men.'

Lock looked away from Malin and out of the window. He saw bicycles lined up neatly in their racks. Evergreens like Christmas trees laden with snow.

'I came here for two things, Richard. This,' he put his hand on the pile of paper, 'and you. If this had been valuable, I could have gone back and said that you were still loyal. Maybe you could have stayed here. Maybe. But now you have to come with me. I cannot go back with this alone.'

'I'm not going back.'

'Richard, understand this.' Malin leaned further forward. He spoke in a half whisper. 'You have worried some very important people. Kremlin people. They see the interests of

Russia at risk. They see their own interests exposed. They have made it clear to me that I must clean up this mess. If you come back to Russia, with me, you will be safe. Outside Russia they will not let you exist.'

'I can't go back.'

Malin said nothing for a moment, his eyes steadily on Lock. 'Richard, you know what happens to people like us when we are not useful any more. I am on the verge of not being useful. Your only hope is to come with me and let everyone forget about this episode. In two years we will both be where we were.'

Lock shook his head. His jaw was set, his head full of sound and rage.

'And Dmitry? Where will he be?'

'It was too late for Dmitry.'

'Then it's too late for me.'

Malin sat back. 'I'm sorry, Richard. I can't let you choose.' He turned to Ivan, just an inch again, and nodded.

Lock saw Ivan walk towards him and his hand reach into his coat pocket. Lock pushed his chair back and began to stand. He shouted – 'Help! Stop!' – and as he stood brought his hands up to push Ivan away. Webster was shouting, as were other English voices. He saw Ivan's hand come out of his pocket and in it a syringe; felt his powerful hand on his upper arm. Then the grip released and Lock, off balance, stumbled backwards and fell down against the window. When he looked up he saw Ivan being held by two of Black's men. The syringe was on the floor. Malin was still sitting at the table, his expression unchanged; Webster was by him.

Malin stood up. He looked at Webster. 'We are leaving,' he said, in English. He sorted the papers on the table into one pile, picked it up and walked past Ivan and Black's men. Ivan shrugged himself free and followed.

One of Black's men reached down to pick up the syringe. There was a clear liquid inside; it was still full. He handed it to Webster, who was collecting the phones and the envelope from the table.

'Come on,' Webster said to Lock. 'Let's go.'

Lock stood up straight. Faces stared up at him from the tables around. Two library security guards were here now and one of Black's men was calming them down. *'Wir verlassen. We're leaving.'* Webster guided Lock through the tables, out into the main hall and towards the door.

'You OK?'

'I'm fine.'

'What did you get?'

'I think we're both finished.'

As they reached the entrance Black joined them.

'I'll go first.'

Lock followed Black through the revolving doors, Webster right behind him.

He squinted as he came out into the air; the sky was still heavy with cloud but the snow was bright. He could see Malin and Ivan walking up the path towards Potsdamer Strasse, Malin walking slowly with heavy, rolling steps. He saw Black five yards ahead, scanning from side to side. Lock waited for a moment, turned to see Webster emerging from the door. From far away he heard a dull crack, like a stone falling on dry wood. His shoulder was thrown back, his arms flailed in space. He fell backwards and his head hit the icy ground. Webster's voice came to him.

'Richard. Fuck. Richard! George!'

He looked up. Flat grey sky. Webster's hair. There was heat in his chest, and cold.

'Richard. You're OK. Richard. Can you hear me?'

He felt his lips move as he tried to speak. They were dry;

his mouth was dry. 'I want Vika to know.' Each word separate, on its own.

Webster's voice. 'Know what, Richard? Know what?'

'It was me.' He closed his eyes.

EPILOGUE

It took eight days for Webster to get back to London. He wanted to accompany Lock's body but the police hadn't finished with it, so he came back alone.

He flew into a sunny Heathrow on a half-full plane, all tourists and families. As it taxied to its stand the stewardess wished everyone a pleasant stay in London and hoped they would enjoy their Christmas shopping.

In the cab he sat back and looked down at himself. He had been wearing the same suit for two weeks; his trousers were concertinaed round the crotch and his shoes were stained with Berlin snow. His fingernails were bitten and ragged, his lips chapped from the cold, the skin on the back of his hands so dry that it had begun to peel. His feet were fat from the flight and his neck ached. He wanted to go home and see his children.

At least it was warmer here: there was no slush on the roads and the pavements were dry. The shop windows were draped with tinsel, and coloured lights zigzagged across the streets. In Shepherd's Bush he watched a man in collapsed evening dress sitting asleep at a bus stop, his bow tie hanging limply round his neck, his head by turns slumping onto his chest and jerking him awake. It was eleven, and in another hour or so oddly constituted groups of men and women would start making their way to their Christmas lunches. Usually he liked this time of year, when London steadily relaxed to a slightly drunken stop.

On Holland Park he stood for a long time looking up at Marina's flat. He had bought flowers round the corner; the florist had suggested lilies. Behind the house ran the high brick wall that Lock had climbed to escape into the park just a week before. Webster imagined the congestion in this quiet street that night: Lock's bodyguards, Black's men, the third car, all lined up to keep one poor lawyer in check. The third car should have told him. He shook his head, disgusted with himself.

Had Lock known how much he was fleeing from that night, perhaps he wouldn't have looked back. If Webster had shown him the unseemly queue of people waiting on his every move, perhaps he would have braved Switzerland, changed his name, made it to some untraceable speck in the Pacific. Got away.

But this is where they would have found him. Eventually. Lock was too weak to endure his exile alone for ever. As I would be, thought Webster. As any decent man would be. Any sane man. They would have found him through Marina, and the ending would have been the same.

He sighed, and tried to smooth the hair on the top of his head. If I am sane. If I am decent. He checked his tie and walked up the path to Marina's door.

She buzzed him in without saying anything. As he climbed the stairs he was conscious of how sticky he felt, how grimy from airports and planes and taxis.

Marina was waiting for him on the second landing. She was wearing a plain dress in dark grey and a black shawl. Against the black her skin was the palest white. She wore no make-up and her hair was tied back, so that nothing distracted attention from her eyes: dry, tired, a strange light shining through the green. She held out her hand and he put his suitcase down to take it.

'Mr Webster.'

'Mrs Lock.'

'Please.'

He followed her into a living room that overlooked the street. Light-grey sofas, a cream carpet, a console table to the right with photographs in simple silver frames; one of Lock, tanned and smiling, younger, his pale-blue shirt unbuttoned, behind him grass-green trees out of focus; one in black and white of him looking down at a baby bundled in his arms.

'Please, sit down.'

Webster sat in an armchair with his back to the window, Marina on a sofa to his left, her hands clasped in her lap, her eyes calmly on his. He put the flowers down on a coffee table in front of him.

'Thank you for seeing me,' said Webster. 'I . . . I wanted to let you know how very sorry I am.' He looked down, rubbed his hands together. 'Really. I wanted . . .' He could find no more words.

'Mr Webster, thank you. Please understand, I know little about you. I know that you helped my husband. He talked about you when he called. He said he had some help, and I assume that was you. I am grateful to you for that. But before that you hounded him. I do not know you, and I do not need to. I have no interest in judging you. I told him he should call you, so perhaps I played my part.'

Her voice was even and precise, with a steady rhythm. Webster felt faintly shamed by her composure.

'I wanted to see you, Mr Webster, because . . . I want you to tell me how he died. I want to know what happened since I last saw him here. He called, but he said nothing. I would like to know.'

'I can do that. I can tell you.'

Webster told her what he knew. He left out nothing: not his mistakes, not his culpability. And he told her what he thought: that Lock had been killed to safeguard a secret; that the secret was indeed safe; that they would never know who was responsible.

'What about Konstantin?' said Marina.

'He's back in Moscow. The Germans didn't press charges. They arrested his bodyguard for attempted kidnapping.' He paused. 'My guess is that he'll be quietly retired. If he's not too dangerous.'

'When . . . When Richard was shot, what did he do? Konstantin.'

'He walked away. When I looked up he was gone. I saw him again after they'd picked him up at the airfield. They brought him in as I was sitting in the police station. He told me he was sorry about Richard. In Russian, as if he knew I'd understand.'

Marina nodded, her eyes clouding.

'For what it's worth,' said Webster, 'I think he meant it.'

'But he walked away.' Her voice was quiet and for a moment afterwards they were silent. 'And how was he that morning? Richard. How did he seem?'

'Like his mind was made up. The man I met in London was scared. He wasn't scared that day.'

Neither said anything for a moment. Marina rubbed her eyes and looked down.

'He said something to me as he was dying,' he said.

Marina didn't respond. She sat with her hand across her eyes.

'He said, "I want Vika to know. It was me."'

Marina took her hand away from her face and looked at him. Her eyes were wet with tears and she wiped them away.

'What does that mean?'

'That Malin was finished. That Richard had done what he wanted to do.'

Marina said nothing.

'I don't know what else it can mean.'

She nodded. 'Mr Webster, I . . .'

Webster shifted forward in his seat.

'I think I should go. I should go.' He met her eye. 'I'm sorry for my part in this.'

'You thought you could rescue him. There are worse things. I never stopped thinking it.' She looked down. 'I think you may have done more than me.'

Webster watched her for a moment and then stood up. 'If you ever want to talk again . . .' He reached into his pocket for a card.

Marina shook her head. 'It's all right, Mr Webster.' She stood. 'I'll see you out.'

Outside, in the cold again, Webster stopped on the porch and took off his tie. He had bought it at the airport that morning: dark-blue, soberly patterned. He rolled it loosely and put it in one of the building's dustbins.

At the end of the short path to the street he looked back at the house and for a moment could see Lock on the other side of the wall, with mud on his city shoes and soft rain in his hair, alone in the vast darkness of the park. The image stayed with him as he walked to the main road. His hand was sweating around the handle of his case; he felt an urge to throw the thing away, and with it the work shirts and the exhausted razor blades and the chargers for his phones.

He found a taxi in moments. 'Hampstead please. Well Walk.'

Hammer answered the door just a moment after Webster's double knock, as if he had been passing, or waiting.

'Ben. It's good to have you back.'

'Thank you.'

'Come in. Let me take that.'

Webster gave Hammer his case and walked past him into the hall, dark despite the sun.

'No Mary?'

'I have no idea what she does with her days. I'm never usually here.'

'I'm sorry. I couldn't face the office.'

Hammer guided him towards the study. 'Let's go in here.' He moved over to his chair, sat and smiled. 'You'd have met with ranks of concerned faces. They're all worried about you.'

The room was cold and the fire, as before, was laid but unlit. A spotlight on the desk by the window picked out a mess of files and papers. Outside the sun shone starkly on the brown-grey bricks of the houses across the street.

'That's sweet of them.'

'Yes and no. They know it could have been them. But for the grace of God.'

'I doubt that.'

Hammer said nothing but raised his eyebrows just enough to indicate that there was more to say. For a moment the two men sat, Hammer drumming silently on the arm of the chair with the pads of his fingers, Webster looking around the room – at the fire, the books on the walls, the piles of newspapers on the floor – and occasionally catching the steady eye opposite him.

Hammer broke the silence. 'I was expecting a call from the Germans.'

'I managed to persuade them to leave you alone.'

He nodded. 'They want you back?'

'If there's a trial.'

'Which there won't be.'

Webster said nothing. No trial; barely any investigation.

'Malin?' said Hammer.

'He went home yesterday. I'll be amazed if they see him again.'

'Maybe no one will.'

'Quite.'

More drumming. 'And how are you?'

'I'm OK.'

'Really?'

Webster sighed. 'Yes and no.' He took a phone out of his pocket. 'These are his last words. Well, nearly his last. I can't stop listening to them. Can't get them out of my head. If I'd heard this I would have understood. I could have saved him.'

'It worked?'

'It worked. I didn't want to tell you over the phone.'

'The police don't know?'

Webster shook his head. 'I gave them the suicide note and they ignored it. And the syringe. The whole thing was hopeless.'

'So what was said?'

'Do you want to hear it?'

'Yes, I do.'

'It's in Russian.'

'Talk me through it.'

Webster pressed a sequence of buttons and put the phone on an upholstered stool between them.

'That's Lock's voice. That's Malin.'

'What are they saying?'

Webster described the scene – the bodyguard, Malin at the table, Lock calm, Black's men positioned around – and went through the conversation, as he had in his head a hundred times. The whole thing lasted less than three minutes. The exchange of papers; Malin's disappointment; his insistence that all along he had been protecting Lock. As they listened and he talked Webster took off his watch, cleaned its face on his shirt and stared absently at the slow, strict progress of the second hand.

'Do you believe him?'

'I think Lock did.'

'And you?'

'I do. There's no way he'd have had Lock die next to him. Look at the mess he's in. Look at the papers.'

Hammer nodded. He had stopped tapping but now he started again.

'So who did it?' he said.

Webster sighed. 'The next man up. Someone in the Kremlin. A faction in the Kremlin. It's Russia. We'll never know.'

Hammer grunted. 'They were there already.'

'The Russians?'

He nodded. 'Those two guys on the plane? They had nothing to do with it.'

'How do you know?'

'They spent a night in the Holiday Inn at the airport. Then I couldn't see them anywhere. They vanished. In the end I found a hotel in Hannover. They were there for two nights, then Dortmund for two nights. They're salesmen. They sell fertilizer.'

'How far is Hannover from Berlin?'

'They couldn't have done it. You said it. This wasn't Malin.'

Webster nodded. 'The Germans weren't interested either way.' He looked down at his hands. 'I should have listened to Alan Knight. He tried to tell me this was different. I thought he was being paranoid. I think he had reason to be.'

'Never underestimate the power of your opponent,' said Hammer, as if repeating a familiar refrain. Webster nodded, still looking down. 'If you know who your opponent is.'

'No news of Alan?'

Hammer shook his head. They were silent for a while.

'Sorry about the press,' said Webster.

Hammer snorted. 'God, don't worry about that. I'm afraid that will do us no harm. Especially once Tourna starts blabbing about it.'

'Christ. How is the client?' He had all but forgotten Tourna.

'Happy as a clam. He thinks you're wonderful.'

'You're not serious?'

'I am. He wants to hire you.'

'He didn't mind the cost?'

'He told me he'd have paid it twice.'

'He's grotesque.'

'Oh yes. I called him on Monday evening to tell him what had happened and warn him there'd be some press. On Tuesday he called me to congratulate me. He knows there's no way Malin will survive this.'

'I wish I felt better about that.'

Hammer said nothing.

'Did he mention Lock?' said Webster.

'Not a word.'

Webster shook his head and gave a silent sigh.

Hammer watched him for a moment. 'You should go home.'

'Nothing happened at my house?'

'Nothing.'

'Thanks.' Webster made to stand up, then stopped himself, as if he had something to say. They looked at each other for a moment. 'I'm not sure when I'll be back.'

'Take your time.'

'I'm not sure I will be back.'

Hammer simply watched him with mild eyes. His hand pulled at his chin, his fingers closed over his mouth.

'I just came from Marina Lock. I had to pass on his last words.'

Still Hammer said nothing.

'I should have given them to his daughter, because they were for her. But she wasn't there. All week I've been imagining meeting that little girl – Christ, I don't even know how old she is.' He shook his head. The words were fast, his tone harsh. 'All week I've been imagining telling her and dreading her asking me who I was. Terrified. Who am I? I'm the man who finished off your father. The man who made him pay for his frankly banal mistakes. But that's OK, because this other man you may have met but probably don't remember, he's finished too.' He stopped, collected himself. 'I was relieved. I didn't even ask where she was. Better for her that I didn't.'

Hammer held Webster's eye and nodded gently, bringing his hand away from his mouth.

'How do you feel now about Gerstman?'

'What do you mean?'

'Do you still feel responsible?'

'Yes. I think I set things off. Primed the mechanism.'

'But you went on with the case.'

Webster frowned slightly, looking closely at Hammer for a hint of his meaning.

'I did.'

'I'm not criticizing you. But we go on. It's who we are. We weren't made to leave things alone.'

'That's just it. I want to leave things alone. I want to leave them exactly as they are. It doesn't matter whether that's me or not.'

Hammer nodded. 'I'm not saying that in time you'll feel better. You won't. I had a source hang himself once. Years ago, before Ikertu. To this day I don't know why he did it and to this day it makes me feel sick. You won't feel better. But you will see better.'

'See what?'

'What we do. Why we do it. That on balance we do some good.'

Not for Gerstman. Not for poor Lock. And for Inessa, he would never know.

He looked away. From the light on the bare trees outside he could tell that the day would be gone in an hour or so.

'Take some time,' said Hammer. 'Come back in a month. Two. But come back.'

Webster looked down at the floor and nodded once, the merest inclination of his head.

'Thanks, Ike. We'll see.'

Webster walked east across the Heath. The sun shone low through an avenue of bare limes and picked out in crazed patterns the dead leaves on the ground. It was half past two, and Nancy and Daniel would be out of school in an hour. The park was quiet: some runners running, some mothers pushing prams. At the top of a hill he came into the light and there was London beneath him in a bright, cold haze. He walked along a wall of deep green holly and then down the shaded passageway to the pond. Two old men were drying themselves with white towels on the wooden deck. In the changing room he took off his coat, his shoes, his suit, his shirt and his socks, and stepped outside in his shorts. The air pinched his skin. At the end of the diving board he stopped, looked up at the sky above him, a perfect ultramarine, looked down at the green-black water below, and dived, the cold embracing his hands, his head, his tired body, shocking him awake.